T0025751

THRONE OF LIGHT

A DAWN OF FIRE NOVEL

THRONE OF LIGHT
A DAWN OF FIRE NOVEL

GUY HALEY

BLACK LIBRARY

A BLACK LIBRARY PUBLICATION

First published in 2022.
This edition published in Great Britain in 2022 by
Black Library, Games Workshop Ltd., Willow Road,
Nottingham, NG7 2WS, UK.

Represented by: Games Workshop Limited – Irish branch,
Unit 3, Lower Liffey Street, Dublin 1,
D01 K199, Ireland.

10 9 8 7 6 5 4 3 2 1

Produced by Games Workshop in Nottingham.
Cover illustration by Johan Grenier.

A CIP record for this book is available from the British Library.

ISBN 13: 978-1-80026-017-7

See Black Library on the internet at

blacklibrary.com

Find out more about Games Workshop
and the world of Warhammer 40,000 at

games-workshop.com

Printed and bound by CPI Group (UK) Ltd, Croydon, CR0 4YY

It is the 41st millennium.

Ten thousand years have passed since the Primarch Horus turned
to Chaos and betrayed his father, the Emperor of Mankind,
plunging the galaxy into ruinous civil war.

For one hundred centuries the Imperium has endured xenos invasion,
internal dissent, and the perfidious attentions of the dark gods of the
warp. The Emperor sits immobile upon the Golden Throne of Terra,
a psychic bastion against infernal powers. It is His will alone that
lights the Astronomican, binding together the Imperium, yet not one
word has He uttered in all that time. Without His guidance, mankind
has strayed far from the path of enlightenment.

The bright ideals of the Age of Wonder have withered and died.
To be alive in this time is a terrible fate, where an existence of
grinding servitude is the best that can be hoped for, and a quick
death is seen as the kindest mercy.

As the Imperium continues its inevitable decline, Abaddon, last
true son of the Primarch Horus, and now Warmaster in his stead,
has reached the climax of a plan millennia in the making, tearing
reality open across the width of the galaxy and unleashing forces
unheard of. At last it seems, after centuries of valiant struggle,
mankind's doom is at hand.

Into this darkness a pale shaft of light penetrates. The Primarch
Roboute Guilliman has been wakened from deathly slumber
by alien sorcery and arcane science. Returning to Terra, he has
resolved to set right this dire imbalance, to defeat Chaos once and
for all, and to restart the Emperor's grand plan for humanity.

But first, the Imperium must be saved. The galaxy is split in twain.
On one side, Imperium Sanctus, beleaguered but defiant. On
the other, Imperium Nihilus, thought lost to the night. A mighty
crusade has been called to take back the Imperium and restore its
glory. All mankind stands ready for the greatest conflict of the age.
Failure means extinction, and the path to victory leads only to war.

This is the era Indomitus.

DRAMATIS PERSONAE

FLEET PRIMUS

Roboute Guilliman	The Imperial Regent, the Avenging Son, the Last Loyal Son, the Returned and Sainted Primarch
Sergeant Beryn Hetidor	21st Catachan Light Infantry, seconded

TORCHBEARER 308TH EXPEDITION, ANGEVIN CRUSADE RELIEF

Racej Lucerne	Sergeant, Unnumbered Sons of Dorn
Avias	Techmarine, Unnumbered Sons of Dorn
Lycopaeus	Apothecary, Unnumbered Sons of Dorn

BLACK TEMPLARS, ANGEVIN CRUSADE

Beorhtnoth	Castellan
Alanus	Sword Brother
Mortian	Chaplain
Botho	Neophyte
Hengist	Neophyte
Alcuin	Warrior-serf

LOGOS HISTORICA VERITA

'The Founding Four'

Fabian Guelphrain	Historitor Majoris
Solana of Mars	Historitor Majoris
Deven Mudire	Historitor Majoris
Theodore Viablo	Historitor Majoris

Yassilli Sulymanya	Historitor Elevate
Serisa Vallia	Historitor Designate
Guilin	Historitor
Resilisu	Archivist

FLEET TERTIUS, BATTLE GROUP IOLUS, SECOND ITERATION

Vitrian Messinius	Captain, 10th Company, White Consuls/ lord lieutenant Fleet Tertius
Eloise Athagey	Commodore and groupmistress
Finnula Diomed	First lieutenant and shipmistress
Semain	Second lieutenant, first watch
Basu	Third lieutenant, first watch
Ashmar	Fourth lieutenant, first watch
Gonang	Seventh lieutenant, first watch, vox-master

FLEET TERTIUS, BATTLE GROUP IOLUS, UNNUMBERED SONS OF GUILLIMAN

Ferren Areios	Captain, First Company, First Battalion, First Division
Vanus	Sergeant, First Company, First Battalion, First Division
Isupi	Techmarine, First Company, First Battalion, First Division
Covarn	Sergeant, First Company, First Battalion, First Division, 22nd Squad
Meketo	First Company, First Battalion, First Division, 22nd Squad
Sobelius	First Company, First Battalion, First Division, 22nd Squad

ADEPTUS ASTRA TELEPATHICA

Black Ships Fleet

Phyllia Torunda	Knight-Excubitor, Chamber Astra of the null maidens
Essene	Adept-Captain
Silensiori MacPherson	Navigator, House MacPherson

Srinagar Astropathic Relay

Rumagoi	First transliterator
Colus	Assistant transliterator
Yolosta Sov	Astropath Exultatia
Wesu Sveen	High-Telepathicus

INQUISITION, ORDO XENOS

Leonid Rostov	Inquisitor
Hayden Lacrante	Investigatus
Benidei Antoniato	Interrogator
Cheelche	Xenos gunslinger

XVII TRAITOR LEGIONES ASTARTES, WORD BEARERS

Kor Phaeron	Dark Cardinal, Bearer of the Word, Lord of the First Host
Pridor Vrakon	Dark Apostle, Lord of the Third Host
Xhokol Hruvak	Captain, Master of Hounds
Tenebrus	Sorcerer, the Hand of Abaddon
Tharador Yheng	Sorceress, acolyte of Tenebrus

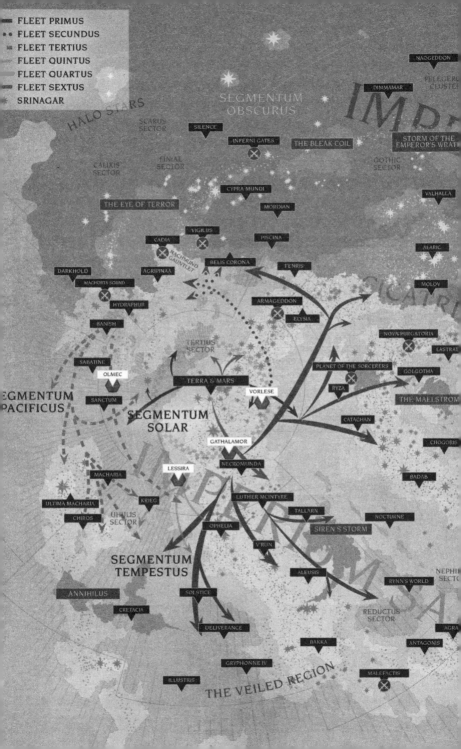

Chapter One

CHOZTECULPO

STOP, IN THE NAME OF THE EMPEROR

THE HAND OF ABADDON

'It's bloody freezing up here,' said Cheelche. The alien's words were harsh in Lacrante's vox-bead, an extension of the cold wind burning his face. She was right. It was freezing. *'Rostov better not be much longer. I'm going to die in this drekking climate. I'll be a lump of ice, I tell you I will.'*

Lacrante looked up at the tower jutting from the crag behind him. There, Cheelche waited, sighting down her rifle from somewhere in the geometric frontage. The stonework provided a mass of ledges overlooking the town. A sniper's dream, if it weren't for the weather. Wind hit the mountain and rushed upwards into town, hard as fists. It snapped through the narrow streets clinging to the rock with teeth of snow that bit at Lacrante's exposed skin. He could stand only a few moments watching the saloon before he was forced into the shelter of the doorway opposite, where he'd steal a moment to recover, then go back out again, in case he was needed.

'For the sake of my unlaid spawn, can this take any longer?' Cheelche grumbled.

'They'll be out soon,' said Lacrante quietly. 'It was a good contact. A transaction, that's all. Money for information. In and out, that's what Antoniato said.'

'Yeah, *what do you know about it, new boy? It's never that simple,*' she grumbled. *'Freezing.'*

'I've been investigatus for two years now,' said Lacrante. He got annoyed when Cheelche patronised him, and it happened often.

'*Investigatus? Still new,*' said Cheelche. '*New* and *naive. This is going to go wrong, just you wait and see. It always bloody does.*'

Antoniato would have calmed her. He had a way with Cheelche that Lacrante did not. His time on Rostov's crew hadn't taught Lacrante the knack of jollying the sour little xenos along. Sometimes, she got on his nerves, and that wasn't just because he'd been brought up to find all alien life despicable.

Lacrante rubbed his face, leaned out of the doorway again and peered up the steep street. He saw no one. It was unlit, narrow, grim with refuse, little more than an alleyway made of steps. All the streets were like that. The buildings were squat, made of blocky stone to a severe xenos pattern, adapted by the monks who made Azazen their home. Light spilled in tightly defined stripes from slit windows, cutting the cobbled steps into neat sections of shadow divided by the shining performances of snowflakes. A little noise emanated from the taverna Lacrante watched, but each roar of laughter and stray phrase of music was shredded by the wind, and all sense of warmth it conveyed was snatched away.

He ducked back into the door, his skin needling. Steam gushed out with every breath, carrying off his precious body heat.

Chozteculpo was a nowhere town clinging to a nowhere mountain that clung to a nowhere planet. Though in the Segmentum Solar, Azazen had been off the main warp conduits for millennia, hard to get to, right on the edge of wilderness space. In Imperial terms it hardly mattered, and by virtue of its isolation had been untouched by galactic events.

Things were changing. The upheaval of the Rift had forced the warp routes deeper into virgin territory, enough to open up the frontier, and the monks found themselves living in uneasy coexistence with criminals and adventurers using the world as a layover before heading out into the uncharted sectors. Though the war seemed a long way from Chozteculpo, it had become a dangerous place, especially after dark, and few people were abroad.

Lacrante looked out again, shivered, clamped his teeth tight to stop them chattering. One of the local gangly xenos stumbled past, bundled up so heavily against the wind it could have been human, if it were not so tall and misproportioned. Its head was bent against the weather, the reek of drink coming off it strong as promethium fumes. That sort was common hereabouts; you'd not find aliens on a more important Imperial world. He had no idea what the species was called. Lacrante pulled himself back into the doorway, and the being paid him no heed as it stumbled by.

The minutes dragged. His joints ached.

'Any sign yet?' said Cheelche.

'You can see from up there just as well as I,' he grumbled. His fingers were numb.

'My left eyeball's frozen solid. I'm sure of it. I daren't take it off the scope. It'll come out.'

'Take it up with Rostov,' Lacrante said, and switched off his vox-link, sick of Cheelche's moaning. 'If he ever comes out of there,' he muttered to himself.

The saloon was hot with many bodies crammed together. A fire of dried dung burned fiercely in the centre under a conical flue of moulded clay, the smoke sucked up so hard by the wind the chimney hooted.

Rostov was playing tarot. He looked steadily into the eyes of his opponent, hand of cards curved in his gloved fingers. The man stared back, face studiously blank. Geometric tattoos in black covered the man's face, and his hair was greased into two horns dyed green. He was dirty, skin patterned with ground-in dirt between the tattoos. The lines in his face suggested a tendency to shout and scowl. He was scum, probably a murderer, certainly a thief. Weapons were prominent on a leather vest so stiff with filth it sat up on his fat gut as he hunched over his cards. He was the sort of man it pays to be wary of, but Inquisitor Rostov did not think him so dangerous.

Rostov glanced at the cards. Playing with the tarot was a mildly blasphemous use of the Emperor's oracle, and forbidden in most civilised places, but though Rostov found it distasteful he knew the game well enough. He had a good hand. He took a stack of gold coins, and let them drop one after another onto the stake between them.

'Confident,' said the man. He grinned, showing filed teeth full of decay.

Rostov let the last coin fall. It slithered down the pile. 'Maybe I have reason to be, Ser Tapind.'

Tapind's grin widened further and he theatrically looked away, pointing his nose into the air. 'Ser, is it? Nice manners. We don't have much call for those out here.'

'Do not take my politeness for weakness,' said Rostov. 'Perhaps you could tell me what I came here to learn, and I will make it worth your while.'

Tapind hunched lower. 'Not yet. I like to play. Finish the game, and I will tell you what you want.'

'I don't understand why we can't just pay you,' said the Imperial Guard veteran accompanying Rostov. He was not young, but yet not old. No grey in his brown hair, though his face carried a network of fine lines. He was well muscled. When he moved,

the patched uniform he wore under his heavy fur coat strained.
Behind his chair a plasma gun was propped against the wall.
A heavy gun with a tendency to catastrophically overheat, it
needed strength and nerve to wield.

'Because I like to play,' said Tapind, and gave him a dismissive
look. 'You can learn a lot about a man's character by the way
he lays a tarot hand, and I can read you, sonny. You look like a
deserter, and this fellow, your boss... I ain't never seen skin so
red like that. He's got a touch of the xenos on him, this one.'

To the people in the bar, Rostov did look strange. His hair
and beard were fair, and that contrasted strikingly with the reddish cast of his skin. He looked like a man with sunburn, in a
town where the sun rarely shone.

'I fit well within the accepted categories of sanctioned human
form,' said Rostov. 'The organisation I represent would not have
it any other way.'

'Is that so? I don't sell information to just anybody. Gotta be
careful. Game's a good way of gauging what kind of man you
are, so – play.'

Rostov shrugged. 'As you wish, but I assure you, we will learn
what we came to learn.' He looked to his companion. 'Take
your turn, Antoniato.'

Unlike Rostov and Tapind, Antoniato had no skill in hiding
his thoughts. He jingled his coins in his hand, hesitating before
laying his stake. He drew another card from the deck. He
frowned and dithered over which to put into play, biting at the
stubbled skin beneath his lip. His fingers hovered over one card,
then another, before he finally settled on a third, plucking it
from the fan clenched in his fingers and laying it on the table
with a soft curse.

'The blind seer,' said Tapind, cocking his eyebrow. 'Interesting
choice.' By that he meant bad, and he made sure Antoniato
knew it with another black-toothed grin.

'I'm no good at this, alright?' said Antoniato.

'I noticed.' Tapind took his turn quickly, his move already formulated. He put down a large bet. 'Are you going to match me or not?' He spoke only to Rostov, Antoniato already discounted.

'How the Throne should I know?' Antoniato grumbled.

Rostov stared at Tapind. 'I'll invoke my pass, see what you've got.'

'Suit yourself,' said Tapind. He laid down his card, a golden-armed warrior brandishing a burning sword. Everyone in the faith knew that image. 'Emperor Among Us. Ain't no higher spread than that,' Tapind said, as he completed the layout on the table. 'I win. Nice to meet you, boys. Now pay up, and get out. I ain't selling no words today. I don't like the look of you. Cards don't lie.'

Tapind reached for the money. Rostov gripped his wrist.

'Let's say I raise the stake.'

Tapind scowled. 'With what?'

'Prudent agreement.'

'Never heard of it, and there is no higher card for this spread than the Emperor Among Us.' He jerked his head at Antoniato. 'Don't think to shake me down. Your muscle doesn't scare me. I've got powerful friends in these parts, so back off. You lost fair and square.'

Rostov released Tapind's wrist, and dropped something from his sleeve into his hand. He held it over the table, hidden by his fingers. Curious, Tapind paused raking in his winnings.

'I'm not talking about cards,' said Rostov. 'I'm talking about you making a sensible choice. Prudent agreement.'

He laid a small ivory amulet down on the wood with a click. It bore an Imperial barred 'I' overset with a skull, in the forehead of which a small ruby flashed. Tapind blinked at it in shock.

'You recognise this seal, yes? Now will you talk to me?' said Rostov calmly.

Tapind's expression turned scared. 'You're an inquisitor. Holy Throne of Terra! What the hell do you want with me?'

The dreadful word cut through the hubbub of the taverna. Suddenly, a dozen pair of eyes were on the gaming table. Antoniato tensed, flipped aside his furs, one hand going to his holstered laspistol, the other resting on the bulbous nose of the plasma gun.

'What are you doing all the way out here?' Tapind asked his question, but stood rapidly, ready to leave without an answer. 'I'm not talking to you. It's a death sentence on me. I knew there was something off about you.'

'It's a death sentence if you don't,' said Antoniato, taking his turn to grin.

Tapind shoved away from the table, money forgotten. 'Stay away from me.'

'If you speak to me, the rewards will be great,' said Rostov.

'Not great enough. All the wealth of Terra is useless to a dead man.'

'Then you have a dilemma, because leaving will not prevent your death.'

Rostov's words proved prophetic. There was the wheezing bark of an energy weapon by the door. A yellow flash lit up the saloon. Half of Tapind's face disintegrated and splashed over the wall. Blood soaked into plaster.

There were two attackers: a squat human in a filthy heatsuit, and a rangy, humanoid xenos with a tall cap and flat face on its thin, cylindrical head. They didn't have time for a second shot. Antoniato had his pistol in his hand and was firing before Rostov had turned in his seat. The crack of the lasgun beam in the air was loud in the confined space. The xenos assailant was flung against the wall, leaving a stripe of copper-green blood as he slid to the floor. The human loosed off four poorly aimed energy blasts as he fumbled for the door handle. Antoniato threw himself under the table and returned fire. Throughout, Rostov stayed seated, calm with the coherent light of death flicking around him.

The man fired again, got his fingers on the latch, then fled into the night. A blast of freezing air pushed the fire in the taverna hearth flat before the door slammed and the flames jerked up to attention.

Antoniato surged up off the floor, sending the table crashing down. Coins bounced everywhere. He fired again. His laspistol left a guttering hole in the taverna door, but the man was away.

'Lacrante!' Antoniato shouted into a handheld vox-caster. 'Contact's down! One assassin, human, xenos-weapon armed, heading your way.'

'In pursuit,' Lacrante responded.

Antoniato switched his aim from patron to patron. Hands were raised. A man shifted in his seat. 'Nobody move!' he shouted.

Rostov remained serene. With deliberate movements he collected his seal from the floor and stood from his chair as if he had just finished a meal in a fine restaurant. 'Cheelche, keep your eyes on the target, but you are not to shoot,' said Rostov into the vox-thief at his neck. 'I want this one alive.'

Rostov stopped by the body of the alien assassin, searched it briefly, lifted up a talisman hung about its neck. An eight-pointed compass wheel etched into a spread-fingered hand: the mark of the thrice-damned Warmaster Abaddon's chief servant.

'Damn it. Now we're back to square one,' said Antoniato.

'The killer knows something,' Rostov said, and got to his feet. He pointed to the money lying on the floor. 'Keep it, for your trouble,' he told the bartender.

With Antoniato covering him, the inquisitor opened the door and stepped out into the night.

* * *

'*Lacrante! Contact's down!*'

The saloon door burst open and a human male staggered out, nearly lost his footing on the thin snow coating the steps, stumbled into the far wall, then ran into the dark, the charge lights on the weapon in his hand glowing bright in the gloom.

'*One assassin, human, xenos-weapon armed, heading your way.*'

'In pursuit,' said Lacrante, and set off at a sprint up the alley steps. He keyed his vox back on.

'*What are you mammals up to down there?*' Cheelche voxed.

'Didn't you see him go out? Single target!'

'*You try seeing anything when your eye is literally frozen and your scope's hazy with frost.*'

'Just cover the door,' Lacrante said. 'Don't let anybody follow me.'

She said something he didn't hear. Lacrante raced around a corner into the full force of the winter. Freezing air tore the heat from his body. He was a fit man, Lacrante, but a combination of his heavy clothes, the altitude, the steepness of the streets and the cold had him puffing like a lho addict in the last days of life.

Fortunately for him, the fugitive was no better acclimatised to the environment. The man skidded on the snow compacting on the stone, and Lacrante gained ground unseen. He wasn't noticed until a couple huddled against the cold stepped out in front of Lacrante from a side alley.

'Get out of the damned way!' he shouted, almost crashing into them. One of the two fell, and Lacrante was forced to hop over their legs to avoid being entangled. They shouted after him as he slipped and bounced off the wall. He was lucky not to get a bullet between the shoulder blades in that place. He trusted to the Emperor to shield him.

When the shouts cut through the wind, the man looked behind. Spotting Lacrante, he ran faster.

'Throne,' Lacrante cursed. He pulled his laspistol and let

off a shot, but the slippery cobbles made his aim lousy. Tiles exploded on the low eaves overhanging the street.

His quarry ran like Horus and his devils were on his heels.

They were getting higher, following the twisting alleys towards the town's centre. Lacrante kicked over piles of frozen refuse as he caromed off the wall, and he half-fell, half-ran on. The man took another corner. Lacrante followed, and he burst out onto Chozteculpo's via principia, Merchant's Row. It was hardly worthy of the name, being only a little wider than the rest and not very long, but it was lit by barrels of burning animal oils, and vendors stood by stalls of wares and food stands where coals roasted skewered examples of the smaller local wildlife. There were more people there, enough to make a crowd, and that slowed his target down.

The man shoved his way through the throng. He glanced back. Lacrante had a glimpse of a pale face behind goggles. Sweat-steam puffed up around his heatsuit seals at his throat.

'Stop him!' shouted Lacrante. 'Stop, in the name of the Emperor!'

Heads swung round to look. Lacrante's call to action had the opposite of the desired effect. Not wishing to get involved, the crowd parted, and the man went free. He let off a shot behind him. Some sort of low-yield plasma weapon. Lacrante ducked. A fizzing yellow ball sliced the air over his head and scattered the crowd. His target man was now racing down a long corridor of people, but clear enough to run meant clear enough for a shot.

Lacrante dropped to his knee, ripped off his glove, steadied his gun on his forearm and aimed at the receding fugitive, his finger resting on the trigger. Cold metal burned him.

'Emperor guide my hand,' he whispered, and squeezed.

A flash of red chased the man, connected with his leg, and sent him crashing down into a portable grill. Embers and meat skewers skittered across the road. He tried to push himself up and screamed as he put his hand on a hot coal. He was still trying to rise when Lacrante came up behind him and rested his gun against the man's head.

'Don't move,' Lacrante said. The man moaned, his injured leg ramrod straight, his burned hand cradled against his chest. The crowd looked uneasily on. Hostile eyes peered out from behind heated goggles and the gaps between scarves and hats.

Planets like Azazen were hostile in the extreme to all but the lightest touch of Imperial authority. There were a lot of people giving him ugly looks, and several of the local xenos in evidence. They in particular had good reason to hate men like Lacrante. Hands moved towards weapons.

'This is an Imperial matter,' he said as firmly as he could. He was so cold he could barely speak. 'Get back. Be about your business.'

The assassin spoke through gritted teeth. 'That's not going to work. You've made a mistake. There's no governor here. No law. Not even yours.'

Lacrante switched his gun from face to face, jerking it by way of emphasis. Most of the bystanders moved off, shooting looks varying from fearful to aggressive. Three of them did not.

'Shit,' Lacrante said.

The assassin hissed, a reptilian noise of commingled amusement and pain. 'You could take one for sure, maybe two if you're good enough, but not three. You're dead.'

'Shut up,' said Lacrante. The snow was coming thicker and stung his eyes. He raised his voice. 'You three, withdraw. I have no quarrel with you.'

'Maybe we have one with you,' said one man. He wore an oiled poncho over a heatsuit, and moved it aside, revealing a long-barrelled slug pistol at his belt. The others showed their own weapons. One drew a laspistol. The other unslung a rifle of non-human make from his back.

'Let's see how good you are, outlander,' said the leader. He spat, an obvious distraction to cover his draw, but his hand barely brushed his gun before Lacrante had drilled a hole through his chest. It was a good shot, and fast, Lacrante swung his gun around to take the second, expecting to die at the hands of the third.

He did not. Lacrante's shot passed over the second man when he was dropped by a high-angle las-fusil beam. The third was warned of his own demise by the whooping roar of a plasma gun discharging, not that it did him any good. The stream hit him as he turned, and he lit up from within like a lantern, sunfire burning in his mouth and eyes. He opened his mouth to scream but released only his own vaporised lungs. In a second he was reduced to a carbonised mess in the snow.

The prisoner made to crawl off. Lacrante pinned him to the ice with his boot.

'Don't even think about it,' he said. 'You're done. I'm not alone.'

His vox-bead crackled. *'Miss me?'* said Cheelche.

'Yes,' said Lacrante. 'Nice shot. Thank you.'

'Maybe you won't be such a dumb Terran ape and run off on your own in future, eh?'

Rostov and Antoniato were coming down the street. Rostov spooked people, and Lacrante thought him being a witch was only the half of it. There was something that hung over him, a presentiment of doom, or the sense the Emperor Himself was watching you through his eyes. His presence cleared the street; even the vendors withdrew, leaving their grills to gutter in the wind. Antoniato was laughing, his sun gun spewing steam into the frigid night.

'"Stop in the name of the Emperor?" Is that the best you've got, Lacrante?'

'It seemed appropriate,' said Lacrante, and holstered his gun.

'You have him,' Rostov said. His boots crunched to a stop

on the snow, and he looked down at their captured prey. 'I am pleased.'

'This is an inquisitor,' said Antoniato to the man. 'You know what one of those is, right?' He shouldered his plasma rifle and together he and Lacrante hauled the prisoner up. He jabbered in an impenetrable dialect.

'He was speaking Gothic just fine a moment ago,' said Lacrante.

'Remind him how to communicate,' Rostov said.

Antoniato punched the man in the face. He swore. Rostov fixed the prisoner with his uncompromising gaze.

'Who are you working for?'

The man spat blood. 'I don't know what you are talking about.'

'Don't play stupid,' said Antoniato.

Rostov ran a finger around the man's neck, until he snagged a cord and hooked it out, pulling up a bronze amulet. Like the xenos in the bar, he too wore the eight-pointed wheel of Chaos stamped into an open hand. Rostov looked at it with intense disdain.

'Where is the Hand of Abaddon? You wear his sigil. Tapind knew something, you silenced him. Who gave you the kill order? That will do for a start.'

The prisoner hissed some local curse. Antoniato pressed his knee into the man's wounded leg. The prisoner grunted.

'Show my master respect,' Antoniato said.

The man bared his teeth. 'Why? I am a servant of the Warmaster, the true lord of mankind. I have no care for your evil god. You will never break me.'

'The power of the false gods is as nothing compared to the power of the Emperor.' Rostov yanked the amulet, snapping the cord, and tossed the symbol into the snow. 'They will not help you. The eye of the Emperor is upon you, and He sees all. You will tell me everything and die painlessly, or you will beg for mercy before I am done, and I will still know every thought you have ever had.'

The man stared defiantly back. Rostov regarded him a moment, then looked from Antoniato to Lacrante.

'Take him to the ship. We are finished with Chozteculpo. Cheelche, time to go.'

'Got you, Leonid. I'm coming down.'

Antoniato and Lacrante dragged the assassin away. Rostov remained a moment, surveying the untidy pile of streets leading up the mountain, like a man who feels another's stare upon his neck and searches for the watcher.

Seeing nothing, he turned and left.

In moments, the snow had covered their tracks.

Chapter Two

A SORCERER INTRIGUED

DARK CARDINAL

MASTER OF HOUNDS

'Do not look upon him directly. Do not address him. Ask no questions of him, my acolyte.' Tenebrus' whisper cut the darkness with the hiss of a knife slicing silk.

'Yes, my master,' said Tharador Yheng.

Retinas flashed silver as Tenebrus looked upon her. 'I am growing fond of you, Yheng. If anyone is going to kill you, it will be me.' A hint of sharply curved teeth came and went in the shadows. 'Do not give Kor Phaeron any cause to dislike you. It will end badly.'

'Yes, my master,' Yheng said.

'It is important you say nothing. My plans have reached a delicate point. Remember why we are here. We have many responsibilities, many goals. There are higher powers than Kor Phaeron in this world. It is to them we pay obeisance, not him.'

Yheng was on edge. Her powers had grown, her sense of communion with the gods was deep. She could be the warlord of any great host of mortals, of that Tenebrus had assured her, and yet there, deep in the dark of Kor Phaeron's cathedral ship, the *Dominant Will*, she felt weak, at the mercy of the universe's caprice. No longer illuminated, but blind. The darkness around her was intentional, mocking her for her ignorance; she was aware of the Word Bearers' fondness for metaphor. She should not have been scared by mere lack of light, she had spent her life in Gathalamor's catacombs, but neither knowledge nor experience of the dark was a comfort to her in that long, black hall. In that place she was the mistress of nothing. As much as she despised him, she was grateful for Tenebrus' company.

There was a hint of light in the hall, no more; enough to glance from edges of cruel obsidian, and suggest forbidding faces crowding out of sight. She had the sense of a high ceiling, and of walls no more than ten yards apart. She walked down the middle for fear of what might lean out of the darkness to grab her. She was close enough to Tenebrus that he could have reached behind and throttled her with his long, repellent fingers, if he wished. Still she stayed close, hating the comfort that he provided her.

Tenebrus' feet shuffled on the stone. The tapping of his staff accompanied the jingle of Yheng's body jewellery. They were tiny noises, rodent noises, as nothing to the dark and the quiet and the sense of foreboding, yet loud and obvious for want of other sound. Silence followed them closely, affronted by their presence.

She clutched her staff tighter across her body, tempted to call the cold fires of the Powers into being about its head to light the way, though she had been forbidden from using her magic. She did not know when. She did not know by whom. She had no recollection of entering this long, oppressive corridor, and only the haziest apprehension that they were on Kor Phaeron's ship. They might well not be. They might be anywhere. She could have been there forever.

Her thoughts strayed again to her spells. As he did too often, Tenebrus read her mind.

'Do not think of using sorcery,' said Tenebrus. 'Use your power in this place, and you will attract the kind of attention neither of us desire at this moment. The walls of reality are thin here. We are not in control.'

They reached a flight of stairs. Only her childhood underground saved Yheng from a tumble, her sharp eyes catching the gleam of glass or polished stone. They laboured up them for a long time. Yheng's lungs and thighs burned with effort, for the steps were as steep as they were slick.

'Master?'

'Yes, Yheng?' Tenebrus was not unduly taxed by the climb, and answered with an indulgent air.

'Could you not exert your will, and push back the darkness?'

'I could,' said Tenebrus. 'I could withstand the scrutiny of whatever beings the Dark Cardinal has trapped in this place.' He made a strange sound. Laugh or sigh, Yheng could not tell. 'You can feel them, can't you? Looking at us? They hunger very much.' He sounded wistful, as if remembering some pleasant time in the past. 'But I won't use my skills here, for diplomacy's sake. Kor Phaeron regards himself highly. It is important for these... priests.' He said the word with a certain dismissiveness. 'They must show themselves to be masters, the intercessors between we puny mortals and the gods. I have no wish to antagonise him. They do not like sorcerers, Yheng. They don't like me and they will not like you, for all your devotion to dear, departed Kar-Gatharr.'

Again the twinkle of silver eyes, the glitter of cruel teeth.

'You are thinking that I am Tenebrus, that I am Hand of Abaddon, that I should not approach one even as mighty as Kor Phaeron as a supplicant, but as a master in my own right.' He let his voice rise into an indignant shout, then laughed again, a liquid sound, halfway between beautiful and abhorrent. Yheng found it pulling her towards him, alluring as the biolights displayed by predatory animals. 'Between you and I, I agree,' he said, whispering theatrically once more. 'These pompous prelates should acknowledge my superiority, but they will not, so I must swallow my pride. The Warmaster has plans of his own, and demands I treat well with the Word Bearers. Abaddon is, for the moment, my master, and he is Kor Phaeron's master, though the Dark Cardinal does not like to admit that. We shall reach an accord.'

They reached the top of the flight. A dull boom sounded somewhere within the architecture of the ship. Chains rattled on hollow drums. Doors creaked open ahead of them, and firelight spilled outwards. For a moment, it blinded Yheng, so bright after the dark, before her eyes adjusted to the leaping flicker illuminating the walls, ceiling and floor of the corridor, all made of the same black, glassy material. Figures crowded every inch of the wall in deep reliefs so lifelike it appeared they had been writhing freely in forbidden acts until the light smote them, and turned them instantly to stone.

Flames danced on real pain, real pleasure. These were not statues, she was sure. She kept her eyes ahead for fear they might tempt her to join them.

The doors swung outwards with increasing speed, coming to a sudden halt with a noise like cannon fire.

A great cathedrum was beyond.

A welcoming party stood behind the gates, three of the Word Bearers' Dark Apostles armoured in heavy Terminator battle-plate, guarded by a further full score of Terminator-armoured warriors. While under Kar-Gatharr's tutelage, Yheng had learned much of his parent Legion. The giant bodyguard were the Anointed, the greatest warriors of the True Creed, and some of them were as old as the Imperium itself. Tenebrus did not care for their holiness, but she did, and bowed deeply before them.

The central warrior priest came forward. He went bareheaded, showing a face full of malice. Verses from the Book of Lorgar were branded into his flesh with exquisite skill. For all his might, he was obviously a man, enhanced by ancient arts, grown huge, but unmarred by mutation. Tenebrus, on the other hand, was so heavily touched by the gods' favours his humanity had become debatable. There was something of the deep sea to Tenebrus, an echo of ancient pelagic predators. His eyes were completely black, his lips non-existent, his mouth a simple slice in his pallid, grey skin. The mouth had a grin that was far too wide, and showed a myriad of hooked, needled teeth. His fingers were long, multiply jointed, crustaceous, like dead crab legs stirring in polluted currents. He was too thin, and from the curve forming at the top of his spine, too weak to support his own weight properly. His ears were receding, his nose becoming vestigial.

From the way the priest sneered, it appeared Tenebrus was correct, the Word Bearers disapproved of the sorcerer, yet when the priest spoke, it was with all due ceremony.

'Tenebrus the Sorcerer comes to our halls at this, the height of our glory. We bid you welcome, Hand of Abaddon.' He bowed his head. The giant suit of armour he wore did not move. 'I am Pridor Vrakon, Dark Apostle of the Third Host. Our lord, the most mighty and blessed Dark Cardinal, Kor Phaeron, Lord of the First Host and Master of the Word, awaits you.'

Vrakon moved aside. The two other priests parted. Each of the Anointed took a heavy step backwards, their armour rumbling, opening a path for the Hand and his acolyte that was sufficiently wide for them to pass, but leaving so little room that the crimson warriors loomed close enough to touch. Yheng forced herself to remain erect as she followed Tenebrus, and kept her fear hidden.

The Anointed were frightening. Tusks jutted from their helms' breathing grilles. Trophy racks added to their imposing height with grisly displays of skulls. Their breath growled out of masks like the snorting of bulls. Their armour smelled of hot metal and perfumed oils, of daemon-trace and strange spices. She swallowed a sigh of relief as she passed the last of their number. She could not appear weak, but she struggled not to turn about and flee. Their hateful stares were on her back all the way down the grand aisle of the cathedrum.

Huge columns soared overhead, so high Yheng was not even sure that there was a ceiling behind the darkness and the fog of incense, where half-glimpsed, winged things cut through the smoke. Torches and firebowls lit the way, firelight flickering on inscriptions curling round and round the pillars. In gibbets swinging from endless chains, mortals moaned in holy ecstasy, their bodies mortified to aid their communion with the gods in ways Yheng found hard to stomach.

There were a few other mortals about, skulking in the shadows, all of them bearing slave marks alongside their cult tattoos. There was not one standard human there as free as Yheng.

Members of Phaeron's First War Host stood sentry by each pillar. There were hundreds of them, so many that Yheng wondered why so few Word Bearers had been present on Gathalamor. Were the divisions Kar-Gatharr had hinted at between Abaddon's servants so great that one Legion would allow another to fail? Once, she had thought her upbringing among the beggar-lords adequate preparation for any intrigue, but this was a new level of treachery. This was the playing field of kings.

Kor Phaeron sat fully armoured upon a throne of purple iron. Silent champions, each a lord in his own right, stood around his dais with their weapons ready.

The place was heavy with power. She felt the overwhelming

pressure of eternal beings peering in from their hells at the doings of mortals. A moment of great import was upon them.

Yheng could not resist looking up at Kor Phaeron before the warning of Tenebrus returned and she snatched her gaze to the floor. But already the majesty of the Keeper of the Faith had burned itself into her mind, and though she looked away from him, his image remained in her sight. She fell to her knees, and bowed her head until her forehead pressed against the warm stone, eyes screwed up tight, yet still it was as if she looked full upon him, as if his power demanded he be seen, even by the blind. She watched everything play out while she grovelled, seeing without seeing.

Incredibly ancient, the Dark Cardinal was as dry and desiccated as a mummy laid to rest for a thousand years or more, awakened at the appointed time to serve his unearthly masters. His face was long, with a nose like a desert ridge, sunken eyes peering either side from cavernous sockets circled violet. His head was unusually large, and looked so even within the yawning cowl of his Terminator battleplate. A dome of a skull swept up, completely hairless, cables plugged into scalp ports, and utterly still. If his eyes had not darted with impatience from Yheng to Tenebrus and back, she could well have believed him dead. She was familiar with the warriors of the great Legions, their strength, intelligence and fortitude bestowed upon them by ancient science, but it was to the gods Kor Phaeron owed his might, Tenebrus had said, alluding to some difference between Phaeron and other Space Marines that he had refused to elaborate upon, and that had seemed to amuse him. Now Yheng saw it for herself. For all his age, he was an imposing man, infused with the graces of the Powers. A dark aura flickered around him. Kor Phaeron was powerful, mighty, gloried by the divine, but he was not one of the Legiones Astartes; it was obvious so close to him.

She attempted to contain the thought lest it get free and anger the cardinal.

Much to her relief, Tenebrus spoke before her thoughts betrayed her.

'My Lord Kor Phaeron, I bid you greetings and amity in the sight of the Four in the warp. Let our meeting further the goals of the true faith, and free mankind from miserable ignorance.'

Kor Phaeron curled his lip. His sunken eyes did not blink once as he and Tenebrus matched stares. He shook his head slowly, and held up an admonishing finger. There were empty mounting points on the backs of his gauntlets. The claws they were designed to hold rested on a pair of stands either side of his throne. The mounts clicked and whined as he spoke.

'You say the words of the faithful, but you do not believe,' Kor Phaeron said. He stood with sudden violence, an eruption of metal. His armour rumbled.

'I am as faithful to the gods as you, my lord,' said Tenebrus. 'Why otherwise would the Warmaster have chosen me as his trusted advisor? I only worship differently to you. I respect your fervour. Can you not respect my own manner of faith?'

'There is only one faith, sorcerer – the true faith,' Kor Phaeron said. He came down the steps from his throne, each step shaking the world. 'I see your lack of respect in your twisted body. You take the gifts of the Powers, and they exact their price from you. If your worship were purer, then so would your form be.'

Tenebrus wrapped his long fingers around his staff. 'Others see the changes wrought on me as blessings from the Four.'

Kor Phaeron smiled. It was the cruellest, most unpleasant smile Yheng had ever seen.

'They can be blessings, but all I see on you are warnings. You take too much and worship too little. You make the mistake countless other sorcerers have, that the gods serve you.

The truly faithful serve, completely. The Powers remind you,
and remind you, and still you do not listen.'

'Yet I serve,' said Tenebrus.

'You take,' said Kor Phaeron. 'To be a servant of the gods is
to give them all, not to expect power in return.'

'You have power,' said Tenebrus mildly.

'I have been given power so that I may serve. I seek no aggran-
disement for myself. I only wish that the true faith be spread
through the galaxy. The salvation of mankind is my mission.'

'What an interesting theological difference,' said Tenebrus.
'Despite it, we must cooperate, the Warmaster demands it.
Your reputation is great, Dark Cardinal. You could preach to
me for a week without once repeating yourself, or so I have
heard your many admirers say. But time is short. Shall we, dare
I suggest, cut to the heart of the matter? Our masters have an
eternity. We do not.'

A look of the most chilling fury settled on Kor Phaeron's face,
then passed, fast as a cloud driven over the sun by the wind.

'Before we speak of those matters, I wish to see this dagger
you would thrust into the heart of our greatest enemy. I must
know what is said is true. Show me the ring.' Kor Phaeron held
out his hand.

'If that is what it will take to buy your trust, I must disap-
point you. I do not have it. The Ring of Bucharis is safe. You
will see it in action soon enough. High Magos Xyrax of the True
Mechanicum labours even now to recreate what we achieved
upon Gathalamor. When the weapon is ready, and in position,
then you shall witness its power, not before.'

'I take it Xyrax does not have the ring either,' said Kor Phaeron.

'Of course he does not!' scoffed the sorcerer. 'Do you think I
would be so foolish? The Gift of Bucharis is a great weapon, a
decisive weapon. The key to it cannot be in any hand that the
Warmaster does not trust completely. It is safe.'

Kor Phaeron snorted dismissively. 'Abaddon is playing with fire allowing you to guard something so powerful. It should come to us, that we might safeguard it until the appointed time.'

'Oh, come now,' Tenebrus said. 'Abaddon is the anointed champion of Chaos. He has been chosen by your gods, our gods. Surely by my finding and wielding of the ring, you must see that there is not only one manner of devotion?'

Kar-Gatharr's last words came back to Yheng while the two lords of Chaos spoke. *'What kind of victory Abaddon wins is more important than the victory itself.'* What did that mean? What contest had she pushed herself into?

'We follow as the gods dictate,' said Kor Phaeron, though the words were hard said.

'We have more pressing problems, do we not?'

'You have witnessed what I have witnessed.'

Tenebrus became grave. 'I have seen something, yes. Portents, omens. I was considering coming to you when the Warmaster's order reached me, then he and fate demanded we meet.'

'What have you seen?' Kor Phaeron asked. 'Tell me exactly, so we may know we are in accordance.'

Tenebrus sighed. Spittle dripped from his wide mouth and pattered on the floor.

'I have seen a golden figure bound to a throne. I have seen his chains break. I have heard the cry of a child. I have seen the crusade of Abaddon scattered, and the armies of believers destroyed. I have heard the death screams of gods.' He shifted his stance. His staff clicked on the floor. 'I have seen the end of everything we believe in, if we behave without wisdom,' he said. 'What do your own auguries say?'

'They show many things, but all foretell disaster,' said Kor Phaeron. The mounting points for his claws twitched. 'Saints, visions, a rising tide of psykers, an indomitability of spirit within the Imperium where all hope should have died. The false faith of the corpse-worshippers is strong. The Anathema stirs. He no longer sleeps, but works through His servants. And there is something else.' The cardinal's expression darkened. 'The Powers have granted me vision of a child. A most terrible child.' For the briefest moment, his air of assurance departed him. 'Its coming betokens doom for us all.'

'The return of our most implacable foe.'

'Perhaps.' Kor Phaeron's arrogance came back with redoubled force. He leaned forward, his sunken eyes ripe with hatred. 'You will find this child for me. Abaddon commands it. I command it. You will find it now, or you will suffer the consequences. That is my command, and you will obey.'

'I see,' said Tenebrus. He thought a moment. 'It is clear that I cannot answer this question myself. Higher authorities must be consulted. To involve the one I would question, I will require something. Or rather, a someone. You must provide this to me.'

'Your condition has been anticipated,' said Kor Phaeron.

'Has it?' said Tenebrus. 'This is not a simple request, easily fulfilled. Our vessel must be a worthy sacrifice. One who represents the perfect mixture of hopelessness and faith, powerful in the warp themselves, one who has known the highest honours and the lowest despair.'

'Such a being could be made easily enough,' said Kor Phaeron.

'Naturally,' said Tenebrus. 'With time, any powerful follower of the corpse-lord could be broken, but do we not have time.'

'The child must be found,' agreed Kor Phaeron. 'Soon. The gods have let it be known to me. Disaster awaits us if we do not act.'

'If we do not have time to mould an individual to suit our purpose, then one must be located to serve as sacrifice. The Black Ships. You have means of finding them.'

'We hunt them as we turn the worlds of the corpse-lord against Him,' said Kor Phaeron. 'We have means.'

'They would be a good place to look for the perfect vessel.'

Kor Phaeron nodded. 'There are many such ships, many such individuals. Give me exactly what you require, and it shall be found.'

'Of course,' said Tenebrus. 'I must ask my whispering daemons, but the information will be easy to come by.'

'Then that is how we shall begin, with a hunt.' Kor Phaeron turned to one of his champions. 'Send for Xhokol Hruvak. Send for my Master of Hounds.'

Chapter Three

DROP ASSAULT

A DISHONOURABLE TASK

WILD TALENTS

The Overlord's void shields collapsed within minutes of the craft breaching the atmosphere. A few minutes more, and the shrapnel of airbursts was ringing from the hull. The ship was strong, forged of adamantium and ceramite, but a direct hit from the anti-air cannons would break it, and then they would be dead. Strictly speaking, it wasn't the ordnance that would do the damage, but the rigours of re-entry. The smallest crack in the hull and the air mix would vent. Blowtorch atmosphere would rush in, heated by compression, its stacked shockwaves would batter even the internal organs of the Adeptus Astartes. The craft would be torn apart by its own speed, and tumble ruined to the planetary surface far below. There was a chance Captain Ferren Areios could survive that, but it was minimal, strong as he was.

Areios was a Space Marine. He felt no fear. He felt nothing at all.

He felt nothing as the ship bounced down through the turbulent, laminar flows of the atmosphere. Nothing as a lascannon shot punctured the outer hull, and turned a spot of the deck right in front of him into molten slag, through which a spout of wind roared. He watched the breach cool without emotion, realising that, seeing as he wasn't dead, they'd passed the danger point of speed and pressure and were now into the true flight layers of the atmospheric envelope. He stared at the hole, his enhanced mind idly linking its rate of solidification with the numbers racing down to zero in his retinal display as the ship came in to land.

He looked up a few seconds before impact, primed his weapon, and datapulsed ready orders to his command cadre.

'Company, ready!' he shouted, his voice having to compete with the roar of the drop, even when broadcast directly into the ears of his men.

Three full squads of veteran Intercessors accompanied him, along with his personal squad, the Company Ancient, Techmarine, a Chaplain and an Apothecary, all garbed in the livery of the Ultramarines, though they did not have the honour of belonging to that brotherhood; grey chevrons crossed over the ultima badges on their left pauldrons, marking them as Unnumbered Sons of Guilliman. Yet they possessed other honours of their own: they were First Company, First Battalion, of the First Division, already renowned among their kind.

'Ready!' his men replied with one voice.

The Overlord hit the ground with a shell's violence, throwing the mag-locked Space Marines forward. Areios felt muscle fibres tear in his calves, and the ligaments of his ankles stretch too far. He had time to think that they would ache for a while in the morning, again without feeling, before the twin assault ramps slammed down and tocsins clamoured all down the transit bays' lengths. Battle's light poured into the ship. The world outside was aflame. The airframe shook with the pounding of the Overlord's weapons: heavy bolters, Ironhail autocannons, and lascannons clearing the way for the warriors of the Indomitus Crusade. He saw enemy troops waiting for them in slit trenches in a broad killing field, a glimpse only, for they were torn to sprays of mud and rags of flesh by the gunship's arsenal.

Areios was out first. His was a high rank and he had the pick of the company armoury, but he favoured his bolt rifle still, the one he had carried since his awakening. He came out with it firing. His power sword he kept sheathed.

The attack force was still coming down all around their target. His company's four Overlords were already on the ground, three of them disgorging infantry, the fourth deploying a pair of Repulsors, dropping them from its loading clamps without landing. Five hundred yards ahead, over smoking fields of death tilled by boltgun and las-fire, an artillery battery was dug in and surrounded by a network of trenches and razor wire. A ferocious storm of anti-aircraft fire kept the Overlords back. Steep embankments faced with plasteel sheet demarcated the site. The fortifications followed the patterns of star forts millennia old, projecting limbs tipped with strongpoints that allowed fire down every line. Perfect for holding mass infantry or armoured assaults at bay, but little obstacle for Areios' men.

The Space Marines fanned out, roaring battle cries praising Guilliman and the Emperor. Power armour grunted. Over a hundred warriors were propelled by ancient technologies into an unstoppable charge. Gunfire whipped out to greet them from bunkers in the ramparts, slamming into armoured bodies. A few of his men fell, but the majority of the enemy's fury was measured in chips of ceramite, not blood.

Four hundred yards.

Areios leapt over a steaming crater where a slit trench had been only seconds ago. Blood oozed from the torn earth, and his boots splashed in it. He brought his cartograph front and centre in his retinal display, his objectives lined in red, the members of his company in green. Hazards flashed.

'Minefield, front. Forward fast!' he shouted. They did not have time to stop.

One of his men was thrown into the air when he stepped on a mine. He cartwheeled head over heels and landed in the mud, his half-ton weight imprinting his shape into the ground, but the mine had not compromised his armour, and he got up, and though limping, continued his charge towards the ramparts, leaving behind a perfect mould of himself.

In the centre of the defences, the big guns jerked on their firing platforms, pneumatic legs absorbing enough recoil to stop them shaking themselves apart, but still enough energy was released to make the ground shudder. The crews were aware death was coming for them, but fired on with admirable discipline, vying to win the favour of their wicked gods by loosing the most shells towards Tiantin City's castle-cathedra. More mines went off as Areios' men ran through the field. Their bolt rifles kept the artillery guard pinned in their trenches, but the bunkers were a problem. Autocannons trained on his men hammered at them until they fell. Each targeted Primaris absorbed a punishing barrage, but fall they did, toppling into the sucking mud of the trench complex, armour broken. His company Apothecaries peeled off to save those they could, salvage the gene-seed of those they could not. He heard the terrible, ceramite-cracking bang of an absolver bolt pistol; the mercy killing of a warrior too injured to survive.

Areios ducked a sprayed fan of autocannon shells. Tracer shot streaked the air. Hollow, ringing bangs sounded behind him as they found one of his men.

'Repulsor zero four, target priority bunker left. Repulsor zero five, target priority bunker right,' Areios commanded. He would have preferred to have come down further out, and cut across on a more oblique line to take the access road into the defences, whittling down the defenders as they came. Messinius had over-ruled the strategy. He had demanded more speed. The lifespan of the Tiantin complexes' void shields was measured in minutes.

The Repulsors' motive jets roared, lifting their tails up and pushing their noses down. Contra-grav fields pounded the earth, setting off the mines all around them, so that they were followed by plumes of earth as they went in. Turrets swiv-elled, bringing compact artillery to bear on the bunkers. Each fired off a fusillade, their turrets tracking and still firing as they flew past. Pulverised rockcrete lofted up in floury bursts, and the bunker guns fell silent. The tanks rode up as they passed the ramparts of the trenchwork, then were off, hunting out more targets. Warriors rose up to chase them off. Ineffectual las-fire lashed ceramite hulls, but one trooper within the first line hefted a rocket launcher. Flame spiked backwards from the launch tube. Repulsor zero five took the hit, losing half its engines, and it coasted to a halt.

Areios sighted down his gun. Still sprinting, he held it per-fectly level, and excised the heavy trooper's head from his shoulders with a single shot.

The traitors had no choice now but to rise up to meet the Space Marines, and they lined their trenches and let fly. Who-ever led these men was talented, reserving his warriors until they were close enough that their lasguns might prove effective, and ordering groups of ten to target individual Space Marines. Several of his men were surrounded by storms of coherent light. A handful were brought low, ceramite vaporised by dozens of hits until the outer layers of battleplate were breached, and the warriors beneath slain.

Two hundred yards.

More of his warriors were taken out of the fight, though most of these were only injured, and only seven mortis runes showed in his tactical displays. Areios pulled a frag grenade from his belt and depressed the detonator. The trench rampart rose up five feet, the earth backed by stamped plasteel revetments to match the angled outer facing. Areios ran up it, taking the laser fire fully on his front, and cast the grenade in front of himself. It detonated as he slid down into the trench behind, and he briefly saw a crowd of fanatical faces before they vanished in fire. Shrapnel pinged from his ceramite. He arrived covered in the blood of the traitors, his boots stamping the ruin of their bodies flat.

More blood followed, and swiftly.

His men poured into the trench, slaughtering the unaugmented humans with ease. The traitors had been promised the world as their own to rule for their gods, and held that to be an undeniable truth. They died still thinking it would be theirs, believing in victory even as they were crushed under the fists of the Emperor's avenging angels.

Though a large deployment of Space Marines, the Unnumbered Sons assaulting Suladen were objectively few; only hundreds against hundreds of thousands of foes. Areios' group split once they were in the trenches, each treading their own path towards victory. Individuals in blue ceramite took on dozens of enemies each. It was dirty work. Had the old Areios been there to think about what he did in the mud and the blood, about how many lives he ended, he might have been appalled, but the old Areios was dead. The man he had become had not been programmed to think, only to obey. He moved smoothly, bolt rifle held ready, each twist and corner of the trench covered and, where the enemy waited for him, cleansed. So true was his aim that every time the gun barked it heralded the death of another of the traitors. He took their return fire on his armoured front, unflinchingly, always facing his enemy. A lucky round from an autogun broke one of his eye-lenses, another penetrated the soft seal in the crook of his elbow, and lodged in his flesh, but though it pained him, and the loss of the retinal display in his left eye was inconvenient, he felt the tears in his muscles from the Overlord's landing to be the worse injury he suffered.

The trench muted the sounds of battle. Rockets screamed overhead, and shell impacts shook the walls, but the soft pattering of soil falling from the sides seemed louder. He heard shouts and the brutal bark of bolt weapons, all deadened by the earth, but of the enemy he saw or heard little until he was on top of them, and when they saw him they came at him with their weapons raised and hatred in their eyes. His battleplate cogitator switched all his tactical feeds into his right eye, and tagged his foes with indicators of threat. They were all insignificantly low. By and large, he was content to follow his battleplate's lead, switching his gun from target to target with robotic efficiency, one bolt sufficient for each soft human body. The explosions of the mass-reactives painted the walls with gore. Where he passed, the trench bottom was muddy with blood.

Reports came in from his officers. He kept half an eye on his warriors' locations, but imposed no formation on them. He allowed them to hunt alone. Breaking out of close-squad tactics was useful experience for them. Cawl's hypno-training had embedded in the Primaris Marines a reflexive affinity for cooperative warfare, a tendency strong in Guilliman's geneseed already, but the Primaris lacked the flexibility of the Firstborn. The older Space Marines switched from mutually supportive actions to sole heroics far more fluidly than the Primaris newcomers, even now. It was not a skill he needed his men to learn – they had the skill, it was more an attitude they needed to embrace. They would not always fight in such overwhelming numbers as those that had landed on Suladen. Legends told of groups of Space Marines five or ten strong holding worlds against incredible odds. His warriors were not ready for such deeds yet.

Over nine hundred Unnumbered Sons were making planet-fall, each group assigned critical, first-strike objectives, and they were but the spear tip of Fleet Tertius' forces in that warzone. Twenty thousand Astra Militarum were scheduled to begin landing within the hour, five thousand Mechanicus troops to follow, accompanied by a cohort of the Legio Cybernetica. There would be hundreds of fighting vehicles, similar numbers of aircraft, and units from other organisations ranging from a few operatives to thousands of personnel. The sky shook with voidship engines as these other elements were brought into play. Each part of the war machine was tasked with its own goals, each inextricable from the others, all vital if Suladen was to be taken out of the traitor's hands with its infrastructure and population intact. And so, if it wounded Areios' pride a little to be given so lowly a target as this artillery battery, he knew in his hearts that his mission was as vital as any other, and he would perform it to the best of his ability.

He reached a juncture of the trenches where the enemy were already dead. Five of his Space Marines waited there, their livery obscured by mud and gore.

Their leader snapped a quick salute.

'Captain.'

'Sergeant Vanus,' Areios acknowledged him.

He brought his tactical feeds to the fore. His squads were converging on the central point. The red dots showing suspected and confirmed clusters of enemies were blinking out, leaving the trench complex swarming with blue.

'Return to squad formation. Begin assault on the guns on my mark,' said Areios, each word clipped and free of emotion. His ammunition count was low, so he spent a valuable moment exchanging the clip. As he did so, he noticed part of a traitor's scalp wrapped around the back of his left hand. He flicked it off without a second thought.

The magazine clicked home. His men were in position. Minimal casualties. His command squad rejoined him. He nodded to the Ancient. The standard bearer twisted the grip in his banner pole, deploying the crosspiece. From this, the company colours unfurled, brilliantly dyed hyper-silk. It bunched up limply under the battlefield's breeze, before the fibres swelled and gave it volume, and the flag showed itself fully.

Ahead, the heavy guns of the enemy continued to fire, now targeting the primary landing zones outside the city. The commanders of the Traitor Guard had reorganised their siege lines quickly. It would do them no good. There was a killing ground between the trench line and Areios' target. A final defence of prefabricated walls enclosed the innermost precinct. In gun pits, the tops of the anti-aircraft weapons could be seen, searching the sky. It looked formidable but was not. Bombs would have done the job. An orbital strike would have achieved the same, but Messinius had been clear: Suladen must be taken with minimal damage.

Areios cared little for the populace. He would have slaughtered them without compunction if ordered to do so, but he saw the strategic wisdom in the lord lieutenant's plan.

Bolt rifles clicked around him. The line of his troops was one man deep, encircling the enemy artillery park like a noose around the neck of a condemned man.

'Company,' he commanded. 'Attack.'

They clambered out of the trenches and walked across the dead ground. They did not charge. Gunfire coming towards them was met with ruthless efficiency. Twenty bolt rifles fired through the slit of a bunker eradicated whatever was within. The heavy weapons stationed inside got off no more than three shots each. The Space Marines on the far side reached the final defences first. The last defenders died quickly. Ceramite boots thumped onto metal duckboards. Shouting followed.

The artillery crews continued to fire, exhorted to continue in the face of certain death by a pair of mortal priests. These were targeted and killed immediately when clear lines of sight were established. Loaders were blown to pieces while moving shells, setting them off. A few las-beams flicked out at the First Company, shows of defiance with no potential to harm. Victory was in sight.

And then, with the passing of a heartbeat, it was not.

The first indication was a dulling of the light, and a drop in temperature so precipitous Areios' battleplate systems peeped out a query. He recognised the signs too late, and had no time to shout a warning before the ground erupted in a shower of earth as a spire of rock twisted up from beneath.

Boulders fountained up around the spire, raining down all around. They were big, and propelled back to the ground by more than simple gravity, crashing into Areios' men with force enough to crush their power armour. A tumbling rock the size of Areios' torso slammed into his pauldron, staggering him, and causing him to fire off his weapon involuntarily. The rain of stones did not stop, but grew worse, and the nature of the projectiles changed, becoming sharpened darts of rock that sped with unerring accuracy at the Primaris Marines.

Areios recovered, stumbled back to his feet, his pauldron grinding about on broken mounts. He drew in his breath, and roared out over his company vox.

'Rogue psyker,' he said. 'Defence pattern sigma.'

Areios saw him then, coming at them from behind the guns, rising up within a vortex of whirling stones and earth. The tax-onomy of psykers was complex beyond Areios' learning, but he knew this sort as a geokine: a wild, telekinetic talent con-nected to the earth somehow. How it could be so, or why, made

no sense to him. It was entirely illogical, a matter of esoteric
spirituality. It was a nonsense to any sane mind, but the Long
War had moved beyond the boundaries of sanity millennia ago.

All that mattered to Areios was if he could kill it.

As the psyker swept across the ground towards the Space
Marines, power crackled around his indistinct form, leaping out
to touch random bits of stone or soil in his protective vortex.
A sort of crude, rocky armour further shielded him, re-formed
stone wrapped about his wrists and his chest. He held both
wrists up, like a savage displaying his muscles, his eyes bla-
zing. Beyond that, Areios could see nothing, the majority of
the geokine's features hidden by the perpetual rockfall cocoon-
ing him.

The vortex moved across the ground. A squad of Areios'
warriors ran at it, firing everything they had, but their bolts
exploded in the whirling shrouds of pebbles and grit.

The psyker's response was swift and deadly. A convulsion,
like a rope buried in sand suddenly whipped into sight, tore
across the ground. The wave cast off debris in every direction
before hitting them and throwing them off their feet, scattering
their cohesion. Areios roared out orders, telling his men to
fall back, to get away from the witch and concentrate fire as
the squad died. A flash from the geokine's eyes turned a boulder into molten lava that slammed into one warrior. Another
was dragged beneath ground turned suddenly liquid by rough
hands of living stone. A third was transfixed by a rain of min-
eral daggers.

'Get back!' Areios shouted. 'Engage at safe range. Cover me.
Attempting solutio extremis.'

Areios ran forward, his hand flipping open a pouch at his belt
where a single grenade was nestled. Covering fire flew by from
all quarters, none of it effectual. Bolts shattered against rock,
their explosions swallowed by clouds of sand. He refrained from

firing himself, trying to draw as near as he could before he was noticed. A trio of plasma streams succeeded where bolts failed, hitting the vortex, turning it to glass and steam. The spinning rocks absorbed the energy, but molten material spilled inwards, splashing on the psyker's skin, and he screamed.

The vortex wobbled, stones thumped down from the sky. Areios thought that he might not have to deploy the weapon, but the psyker recovered, and sent a tsunami of rock towards the trench line the Hellblasters occupied. It exploded into a spined fan of stone when it hit, garlanded with the impaled bodies of Space Marines.

His men had spent their lives well. He had his distraction.

Areios dropped his gun and ran up the side of a mound churned up by the psyker. He pulled the grenade free from his belt as he reached the top. He had only one. It was cylindrical, black with a grey band around the middle. A skull adorned the top seal. Upping his supplementary musculature's power boost to maximum, he jumped, primed the grenade and flung it hard to get it through the protective vortex.

The psyker turned towards him, showing a face wracked with pain and hatred. Beneath the witch marks and corruption inflicted upon the wretch by his connection to the warp, Areios was surprised by how young he was.

The grenade clanged into the vortex, almost deflected before it went off despite the force of Areios' throw.

A sphere of leaden energy burst out. Not of the mortal plane, it was unimpeded by the stones, and although it barely touched the psyker, that was sufficient. He screamed. The vortex dropped to the ground.

Psyk-out overspill washed over Areios. He was no psyker, but even so gentle an encounter with the weapon made him sick to his core. He felt his soul gutter like a candle in a breeze, his battleplate's machine-spirit shut down, and he too fell.

He lay dazed, his armour systems offline, until the earth began to rumble, and his vox crackled back on. Gunfire picked up. The psyk-out grenade, so rare and potent, had bought him only seconds.

Fighting the weight of his dead armour, he crawled on hands and knees to where the youth had fallen. Pebbles rose quiveringly into the air. The earth thrummed to a constant tremor. The psyker was ahead, listlessly rolling, not quite conscious. Bolts zipped overhead, but his position protected him. It was down to Areios to finish him. He called on his armour again, and got no response, so crawled on. The psyker was getting to his feet, his shielding gyre of stone rising with him.

On the third attempt, Areios called his machine-spirit back. His displays came on. Power surged through the warplate. Areios launched himself forward, putting all his considerable strength and that of his armour into the leap, and hit the youth. His underfed, young frame crumpled under the impact, and they both went down. Areios landed on top of him, breaking every bone in his body.

The psychic phenomena ceased. Areios got up, drew his pistol, pointed it at the psyker's head, but did not fire. The youth was dead. He looked even younger now, barely out of childhood, Areios thought.

'Company, advance,' he commanded. He marked the positions of his fallen men on the company noosphere, directing the Apothecaries to retrieve their gene-seed, and went to get his gun.

A few moments later and it was all over. The cannons stopped. Grenades saw to a couple of the anti-air guns too defiled to guarantee the purity of their machine-spirits. The rest were deemed salvageable by Areios' Techmarine. Efforts were already beginning to collect useful war materiel.

A flight of Astra Militarum landers roared overhead, bound

for the landing zones. The cessation of the bombardment had already been noted, yet Areios reported his success formally anyway, as his training dictated he should.

'Captain Areios, First Company, First Battalion, First Division. Confirm primary target eliminated.'

The void shields of Tiantin City glimmered in the distance, strengthening again now they no longer weathered incoming fire. Though churned up by the siege and the counter-attack, the lands around the city were not too badly affected, at least beyond the traitor lines. Farms, forests and exurbs were still recognisable as such. The trenches would be bulldozed. Agricolae servitors would till land fertilised with corpses. Suladen would return to its dull but useful existence.

The Imperium would persist. That was worth the lives of a few of his brothers.

'*Fleet command receiving,*' an anonymous voice responded, '*mission objectives updated.*'

The chime of incoming data announced his new orders. He was about to read them when one of his sergeants voxed him from the far side of the compound.

'*Brother-captain, I have a group of twenty traitor Astra Militarum who have surrendered. Their leader is offering intelligence in exchange for their lives. What shall I do with them?*'

A leader reacts according to his own temperament. The merciful might spare them. The zealous burned them. The cunning interrogated them. Areios was none of those things. For him, actions of war were dictated purely by immediate tactical consideration.

'They will have nothing to tell us. They made their choice. They will serve only as a drain on resources as we advance. Execute them all.'

A brief rattle of boltgun fire drifted towards him as he read his orders, and then it was done.

'Techmarine Isupi, stay here and catalogue this weaponry for delivery to the fleet logisters. Choose three men to help you. The rest of you, we leave now.'

A fresh faceguard was found for Areios, and he exchanged it with the damaged part of his helmet. Ammunition was brought up.

Re-equipped, he gave the order.

'Forward! For Guilliman! For the Emperor!'

He passed the corpses of the executed men on his way out of the artillery park. He did not even register them, for the next killing ground was already shining in the runes of his display.

Chapter Four

TIANTIN CITY

A DRINK

AN UNFORTUNATE DEATH

The bells of Tiantin City rang without stopping. Priests led processions dressed in the black and white of mourning, their faces smeared with ash. Woeful versicles called out from laud hailers drew responses of murmurous thunder from the crowds.

'This is a fine display of contrition,' said Vitrian Messinius. He turned from the open window, his half-cape swishing about his armour's power generator, like a flag displaying his impatience. 'Yet they should not have turned in the first place.'

'Close the window, Vitrian,' said Eloise Athagey. She sprawled upon the couch, a large glass goblet in one hand, with an insouciance he suspected was deliberately calculated to goad him. For a groupmaster, Athagey had an antagonistic relationship towards authority, provided it was not her own being challenged, of course. 'Sit down, have a drink. It's another planet taken with minimal bloodshed and precious little material damage. Lord Guilliman will be pleased.'

'Will he?' said Messinius. He stalked over to the centre of the room where Athagey sat. 'The Segmentum Solar was supposed to be secure. Now rebellion flares within striking distance of the Throneworld in every direction we look.'

'You're being overly dramatic.'

'I am not one for theatrics.' The parquet flooring squeaked under his weight as he came to a halt and stared down at her. 'Would Fleetmistress VanLeskus be pleased, that we dally here putting down these insurrections when our schedule demands we be away into the Segmentum Pacificus?'

'She sent us here. She knew what we would face.' Athagey's good humour cracked.

Messinius felt a little guilty bringing up the fleetmistress, but as much as he liked Athagey, she could be insufferably arrogant, a tendency that needed curbing from time to time.

'That is why we are soon to be reinforced by two battle groups from Fleet Sextus,' she went on, explaining a strategy he already knew. 'Together with the elements from Quartus and Quintus, we number seven battle groups across four sectors.' She scowled and cradled her drink. 'VanLeskus is jealous of my success, otherwise I wouldn't be here holding the back line.'

'I am sure she has other reasons to assign you this duty,' Messinius said. 'Good reasons.'

'Yes? Then why are you here? You're supposed to be the commander of all Space Marines in Fleet Tertius. You should be with Tertius Alpharis One, not out here with me.'

'She has her reasons for that as well,' Messinius said again.

'Not sharing glory. That's reason enough for her. She won't want her perfect record of victories put down to the help of a Space Marine, especially one so high in the primarch's favour. While she's off gallivanting, we have to hold the line. Still, it is for the best, because we are doing a good job of removing these fallen brethren of yours from these worlds.' Her gaze went distant. 'That will be borne in mind when talk of advancement comes around.'

'You are being needlessly self-centred. There are larger things at stake than your status. Think of your duty, not of your honour roll.'

She looked stung. 'Do you really think all I care for is my own career? I jest. Mostly.'

Messinius answered with a hard stare.

'I am wounded. We do good work here.'

'Wounded or not, jesting or not, you underestimate the sons of Lorgar at our peril. We are here because they present a genuine threat to the security of Imperium Sanctus that is as great as those found further out from Terra. Put away your ego. There is some plan at play here.'

'Beyond destroying the Imperium?'

'Are you deliberately being provocative today, Eloise? Forces of the Warmaster have always wanted that. It is the how that we must be wary of. We should be thankful you are here to stop them.'

'Was that an attempt at flattery?' She smiled sweetly up at him. 'Do stop being such a bore. Have a drink.' Messinius ignored her gesture at the table, well stocked with beverages by nervous planetary officials, close by the couch. 'Relax, if that's even possible. And step away – it's like looking up a bloody mountain when you're standing over me like that.' Her smile deepened. 'An impressive, awe-inspiring and even beautiful sight, but one does get a crick in the neck.'

Messinius grunted and stepped back.

'And now a smile, Vitrian?'

'One hundred years have I served. These last years with you have seemed particularly long,' he said.

'A veritable touch with the point. I shall take that as a compliment. Now, have a drink, I insist. It's an order, in fact.'

Messinius raised an eyebrow at Athagey's goblet. Large in her hand, it would barely provide a mouthful to him.

'I'll get it for you.' She stood up, and went to the table.

'It worries me that the Word Bearers spend so much time and effort to rile up the populations,' Messinius said. 'They are demagogues and false prophets, and doubtless they seek to destroy morale and delay us. Yet I cannot see the immediate strategic worth in turning these systems. They offer no appreciable gain other than distraction. Their nature as holy worlds is a provocation, provocation is distraction. That begs the question, what are they distracting us from?'

'How can you be certain distraction is their aim?' said Athagey. 'You forget that these men follow the whims of mad gods. They undermine the faith of the people. For a Legion of zealots, surely that is a goal in itself?'

She poked about the table, looking for a vessel big enough for the Space Marine. She settled on a tall bronze goblet in the Ascanian style. She filled it with wine. The half-bottle open was insufficient, so she opened a second.

'They forget that the Emperor is their god, lord lieutenant. They feel He has abandoned them. The enemy offer an alternative, as blasphemous as it is to say so. There are many more psykers emerging on these worlds. The people are presented with terror daily. They seek protection.'

'Is that so?' said Messinius. 'Then let the barking of boltguns remind them of who their true protector is, not only their master, but He who vouchsafes the very continuance of their lives.'

'That is more or less what I was going to say, though not so belligerently as you.' She handed him the goblet. In Messinius' gauntleted hand it seemed ridiculously dainty, though it had been crafted to heroic proportions. 'You are in poor spirits.'

'This is a miserable form of war,' Messinius said. 'We slaughter those who would be loyal were it not for the privations they must endure, spreading greater suffering as we do, the slaughter we commit ensuring others will fall under the spell of diabolical priests who use our successes against us.'

'It is not quite so simple,' said Athagey. She raised her glass. 'Your health.'

'Yours also,' said Messinius. He drank. The wine was pleasingly sharp on his tongue, conjuring up a great thirst in him. It had been hours since he had refreshed himself properly, he realised, so many duties he had, and he had the unseemly urge to drink it all down. He refrained.

'You see, I find all this encouraging.'

'Explain,' said Messinius.

'The Word Bearers are embarked on some sort of holy crusade, that much is obvious to me. Their targeting of the Black Ships is a worry, I admit, but on the whole their primary goal appears to be to subvert as much of the Emperor's faithful as possible – that's why I believe they are targeting these cardinal and shrine worlds. It is almost...' She searched for the word.

'Vindictive,' said Messinius.

'That's the word,' she said, and tilted her glass at him. 'But vindictiveness never won a war. They are too bound up in their faith. They miss larger prizes.'

'I fail to see how that is encouraging.'

'Because it means they are working on their own,' she said. 'If they are working alone, they are working towards their own agenda.' She smiled. 'And that means that the Warmaster has no control over them. Don't you see? The enemy are divided. We have been fighting this war for nearly half a decade. We were reeling from the opening of the Great Rift. The Imperium was divided. But as our efforts progress I see it is they who suffer from division, not us. By all rights, they should have moved on Terra by now.'

'What about Fleet Secundus?'

'Fleet Secundus is the stopper in hell's gate, that is all.'

'An interesting theoretical,' said Messinius, who had picked the term up from his time with Guilliman. 'But you make a fundamental error. You assume they will follow a logical path. Do you think the Rift was opened by logic? Do you think their daemonic allies respond to reasoned argument? Captain Areios was forced to deploy a psyk-out grenade today against one of their witches. The enemy are weaponising our own citizens against us. It is bad enough when they take up arms, but when they wield the powers of the warp, how are we, in our mundane armour with our mundane guns, supposed to fight these wild talents? If the primarch taught me one thing, it is that we fight a war against foes who do not think as we do, whose goals are inexplicable. When their efforts were restricted to planetary conquest and raiding parties, their greater strategy did not matter. Each threat was met and dealt with on its own. We did not see the strategy beneath. We do not see the strategy now. Abaddon has had ten thousand years to formulate the manner of his revenge. I, therefore, take no comfort in the knowledge that the Warmaster has not yet advanced on the Throneworld, or that the old Legions appear divided. When it comes, their attack will be from an unexpected direction.'

'So then, you must agree that simple distraction is probably not their game.'

'Maybe,' he said. 'If you are correct then I fear we may soon feel the touch of their sorcery on a much grander scale, and I fear we may be helping facilitate it.'

'How?'

'Death. Blood. Suffering. All these things are useful to them.' He dipped his head in thought. 'Every move we make is fraught with danger.'

'But we must make them, and there is no primarch here to tell us what to do. We – you and I, and all the rest of the commanders of these fleets – must choose. Why do you think I like drinking?' she said. 'Listen, the priests will begin cleansing the populace. There will be an inquisition. There will be burnings and horrors just as bad as those inflicted by the enemy. We can do nothing to prevent that. It is necessary. So let us not dwell on the suffering to come. Let us drink together and celebrate this victory, which was won quickly and well. Let us drink to all the people who have been saved from the dominion of Dark Gods, and all those who will now not turn from the light of the Emperor, and whose souls will be saved by the Adeptus Ministorum. Let us remember, also, those who were tempted from the light into the darkness, and mourn their failure. And finally, let us drink, Vitrian Messinius, to you and I and a task well accomplished, because tomorrow we will have to do it again, and then again, until the stars are free of evil, and the peoples of mankind might sleep safely in their beds and no longer fear the night.'

'You and I will not see out that war,' said Messinius. 'It has lasted for ten thousand years, and will exceed our span by ten thousand more.'

Athagey smiled again, sadly this time. 'Then that is another reason to drink,' she said.

There was a knock at the door.

'Enter!' Athagey shouted.

A harried-looking official of the Departmento Munitorum came inside.

'My lady, we have had a communiqué from Fleet Tertius high command. You must attend with a response immediately.'

'VanLeskus, eh?' she said, letting her annoyance show.

The official held out a lead cylinder dangling seals. Athagey took it, opened it, took out and unfurled the flimsy within, and read it with a frown.

'Bad news?' asked Messinius.

She nodded, still frowning. 'From Xeriphis. The assault there has failed.' She crumpled up the flimsy. 'That damn fool Dionis has let Battle Group Iolus be practically wiped out by the Word Bearers. He's dead.' She looked up at Messinius. 'They're going to merge the groups.'

Messinius could not read Athagey's expression.

'Is that good news or bad news, as you would see it?'

'Honestly?' she said, and took a long drink of wine. 'I have no damn idea. But my ambition aside, it's not good news is it?'

She set down the goblet and scooped up her coat.

'If the planetary governor wants to speak to anyone, you can speak to her, lord lieutenant,' she said as she went for the door. 'I'm busy. VanLeskus wants a report immediately.'

Chapter Five

SRINAGAR

THE PEARL

MISTRESS SOV

Lumens flickered, causing First Transliterator Rumagoi to look up from his work. The whole room trembled. Dust sifted from the vaulted ceiling. Unlit chandeliers swayed on their chains.

Rumagoi waited for the tremors to subside, shook debris off the scroll he'd been writing, then finished off his transliteration, clucking his tongue all the while at the bits of plaster getting stuck in his nib.

'Saves on pounce, I suppose,' he muttered. He sanded the ink, tightly rolled it, applied the prescribed seals of purity, and pushed it into a scroll case.

A knock came at his door, loud, but restrained, and quick enough to betray his visitor's nerves.

'Just come in, Colus!' he shouted, shaking his head. 'Stupid man.'

The door swung open. In that part of the astrotelepathic relay, all the doors were wood, with iron hinges and latches. Srinagar was a moderately prosperous world, but a mix of the stars' behaviour and the collective psychic powers of the choir wrought havoc on machine-spirits, forcing the servants of the Adeptus Astra Telepathica to rely on simple mechanisms.

'She's at it again,' the younger man said. 'Another incident.' He wore a green felt skullcap with the Adepta mark, and long green robes like Rumagoi's, if far less ornately embroidered.

Another tremor shook the mountain.

'I can see that, Colus,' said Rumagoi, when it passed. 'Calm yourself. It will be fine. It is better not to let your passions run too high. Unbalanced humours in so empyrically charged an environment are a danger to us all.' He got up from the desk and went to the door. Colus nodded. His eyes kept flicking up to the chandeliers, expecting them to start swinging again.

'Yes, first transliterator.'

'You must be able at all times to keep a level head and a calm heart.'

'Yes, first transliterator.'

'We are the custodians of some of our Imperium's most precious assets. It does not do to upset them, especially now, in these difficult times.'

'Yes, master.'

Rumagoi tapped Colus in the centre of the chest with the sacred scroll case. 'So you keep your head, my boy. Got that?'

'Yes, yes, I am sorry.'

'And get out of my way?'

Colus stepped back. Rumagoi went to the pneumatic message tube, and sent the scroll on its way.

'To the Pearl, then,' he said. 'Come on.'

Rumagoi and Colus left the office and emerged into the upper circuit of the wheel. The choir itself was housed in a sphere of seamless duratanium at the heart of the mountain. The administrative offices were in a circle of lesser metals and artfully fitted stone that circled the choir like the rings of Saturn in the holy system of Sol. The wheel was psy-baffled, but budgetary restraints were such that the offices had more protection than the corridors, and as soon as he was out of his quarters, Rumagoi could feel the storm pressure of hundreds of powerful minds casting thoughts across the cosmos.

Other robed figures hurried past them. The whole relay was in a state of uproar, Rumagoi noted disapprovingly.

'How long before the first tremor did she begin her recital?'

'Merely seconds before I alerted you, first transliterator,' said Colus. They moved quickly along the ring, sandals slapping. A further tremor shook the building. Worried gasps echoed.

'And is she receiving a message, or is it visions again?'

'A vision, I think. It escalated quickly this time. I set off as soon as it started.' He sounded hurt at Rumagoi's insinuations that he'd tarried.

'Which suggests the epicentre of the event is moving closer to Srinagar,' said Rumagoi, partly to himself. 'Have you evacuated the Pearl? I don't want another incident.'

'The duty transliterators have been moved out. All locks and access rites are in effect. We've increased psy-drain between the astropathic cells and around the mountain, in the Spherus Claustrum, and the sphere itself. The machines are running at eighty per cent. We'd better hope she doesn't get more insistent.'

'Good, good,' said Rumagoi distractedly. 'You informed Sveen?'

'Immediately.'

Lesser adepts moved aside to allow Rumagoi's grand personage to pass, and they made the third-spoke crosswalk access quickly. They descended from there to the lofty Hall of Utterances, which led all the way back to the First Portal. From the Second Portal a long corridor of armaglass reached out – a walkway bridging the Spherus Claustrum, the gap between mountain and choir sphere. After interruption by the Final

Portal, the corridor turned into an open bridge crossing the radius of the sphere to the focusing pearl at its centre.

Rumagoi and Colus gave their credentials to the Second Portal gatekeeper, went into the preparation room and donned the psy-suppressive headdresses all who would approach the choir must wear. They took this ritual seriously, not simply because of the holiness of the rite, but because death was the inevitable consequence of poor observance when exposed to such psychic might.

When they were properly garbed, then blessed by a priest, the three doors barring the way opened with violent motion, and they went through onto the armaglass walkway.

The astropathic relay on Srinagar was one of the largest in the Segmentum Solar, part of the grand, oblate sphere of dozens that surrounded Sol. Through these conduits, messages were sent out from Terra across its galaxy-spanning empire. To say the relays had a vital role to play was only the half of it, as Rumagoi was fond of saying.

Srinagar was particularly important. The violent dance of its binary stars created a vortex in the warp, a plus-non-ultra astropathic conduit, as they marked it in the Adepta. Being sited so close to such stellar brutality was a risk, however. To protect the relay, it was buried deep within a mountain, and the city that served it was housed in the caverns to the west for the same reason. It was a great and holy thing that their facility mimicked the Astronomican itself, which was another phrase Rumagoi liked to overuse, although the similarity was slight, and in fact, being within an artificial cavern in a mountain was the whole of it.

The Spherus Claustrum was nonetheless impressive. Through the armaglass of the bridge they had a fine view of the cavern, carved out of the living rock at the height of the Imperium's might, and the relay at its heart. Giant resonators covered most of the Spherus Claustrum's interior, and the bright lights arranged around their conical spikes hid what they did not cover, reducing the rock behind to black uncertainty.

The choir sphere itself was made with an incalculable treasure of duratanium, and was held aloft by adjustable pistons as tall as the towers in Srinagar's underground cities. The focusing array atop the sphere was incredibly delicate, and it was easier just to move the whole structure than disturb the ancient technology. With the mountain shaking as it was, Rumagoi looked to the array nervously.

The aperture superior was open. A hole bored through the place where the mountain peak had been. It faced a focusing hole in the top of the sphere, and was matched by the aperture inferior below the relay. The lower gap let in the cables and conduits that fed the complex; the upper, through a range of adjustable silver panels, helped focus the teleprayers, extending the range of the relay even further, though only when it was safe to do so. Just then the weather was calm, so the superior showed the night sky, where stars burned brightly; there were naturally no orbitals directly over the relay. The sense of unreality coming off the sphere made the stars seem false, as if they were painted onto a canvas screen.

All of Rumagoi's and Colus' senses suffered. As they walked across the bridge, they could not trust what they felt, heard or tasted, and on the worst days they experienced hallucinations, reality interference from the Imperium's esoteric communications network. That was *with* the blocking helms they wore. Without them they'd be dead.

On numbed feet they reached the Final Portal. Lines of astropaths changing shifts waited to be admitted – just his luck that the incident take place over shift-change, thought Rumagoi. Those leaving were grey with exhaustion, and needed to be helped along by their serfs, and all there were prematurely aged either with the efforts of their role, in the case of the psykers, or by exposure to their abilities in the case of their servants. Rumagoi went to the front of the lines, where shielded machine-spirits read his aura.

Colus wrung his hands. 'This isn't good,' he said.

The mountain shook again. The great pistons holding the sphere in place moaned and hissed, their efforts to dampen the tremors coming after too great a delay.

A panel in the wall opened, revealing the sphere-side gate-keeper sitting within a gilded cage. The bars were hung with crystals, and festooned with warding amulets to keep him sane. His head was fully encased in a sphere of zinc and copper, fine wires earthing it to rods buried in the walls. Thick eye-lenses showed nothing of his face, but instead reflected light in silver ovals, like the eyes of deep-sea fish. He was voiceless, and so gestured at the pair to step into a booth, where they underwent yet more security checks and a further round of spiritual pur-gation, this time performed by auto-bless.

Rumagoi addressed a bronze skull set over the apex of the door-keep's cage. 'No one to come in or to go out until we are done.'

The eyes flashed and a clunk and a grinding came out by way of reply.

The outer door opened. The sphere was double-skinned, with a labyrinth of passages winding through machinery in the interstice by which means the astropaths reached their places. Through the outer door they passed into an antechamber where lesser doors led into the skin of the sphere. They ignored these doors. Their route lay ahead, through a round, quartered portal.

Their auras were read again. A circle of psy-wards lit and extinguished. Mind locks buzzed along with the sound of bars retracting. A sense of imminent power built, then the quar-tered doors opened soundlessly, and the full measure of the relay's might rushed out as an immaterial wind, buffeting their essences. Rumagoi steeled himself and walked briskly through: even in a situation like this, appearances had to be maintained. His amulets grew warm, almost uncomfortably hot. Colus huddled behind him, seeking shelter from the psychic pressure in the lee of his being, and finding none.

The door closed behind them, sealing them into a sea of competing energies of both the material and immaterial sort. An oppressive silence choked them. The insides of their skulls were mapped by foreign minds. They were still aware of the tremors shaking the relay, but these seemed now to pass through the substrate of reality, bypassing earth and steel to tremble instead the bedrock of their souls.

'Come,' said Rumagoi, unable to utter more than that one word.

A thousand thrones lined the inside of the sphere. Half of them contained astropaths, their mouths agape in silent screams as they shouted their thoughts into the warp. Many walkways wound around the sides of the orb to exit via small doors, and a few tower-piers jutted out, to allow access to various machines, but only the bridge went to the centre of the sphere, where a pearlescent orb five yards in diameter nestled. They moved towards it with the laborious pace of men fighting a powerful current. Contra-grav engines set all of the inner surface of the sphere to a nominal down, and so competing tides of gravity tugged at the transliterator and his aide along with the psychic swell.

They arrived at the Pearl spiritually and physically discomfited, barely able to open the door set into the orb. The trunk of cables emerging from the bowels of the world via the aperture inferior held the Pearl aloft. All Imperial attention from beyond Srinagar bore down on this single point. There were very few men who had the mental strength to enter this holiest of holies. They were privileged, and they were cursed. Rumagoi could feel his life force draining from him. How many years of his life would he lose because of this crisis? Three? Four?

Rumagoi put his fears aside. He had his duty.

The door slid aside. They stepped within. When the door closed behind them, the pressure dropped, because in there everything was funnelled into the focus, leaving the interior relatively unaffected. They both let out breaths of relief.

'Service to Him is everything,' Rumagoi said, and mopped at his brow with his sleeve.

The inside of the Pearl was of modest volume. Much of it was taken up by a clear cylinder. Within, supported and sustained by thick amnion, dwelled Mistress Astropath Exultatia Yolosta Sov, the focal point of the relay.

'Good day, mistress,' said Rumagoi to her with a little bow. Then, to Colus, he said, 'To work.'

He and Colus split. Rumagoi headed counterclockwise around the astropath exultatia. Colus went clockwise. Sov stirred in the fluid. Light suffused the tank with shifting amber glows, picking out her limbs and the tubes that fed her.

'Check the vox-thieves and the auto-scribers, Colus,' said Rumagoi. 'Let's see if we can't figure out what she is trying to tell us, and give me timings of all her utterances correlated with the tremors. I have a feeling we will finally be able to offer convincing proof that these seismic disturbances are caused by Mistress Sov.'

'It is not the weather? The astrameteomancer's officio says Gar is going through a period of heightened activity.'

'This is a psychic, not a material phenomenon, Colus. A disturbance of her mind transmits itself as a disturbance to our soil. If only that imbecile Sveen would look at the data.'

'Yes, master.'

'In the meantime, I shall listen to her,' said Rumagoi, more to himself than to Colus. He went to a metal desk built into the curve of the Pearl. It was mismatched to the organic sheen of the containment unit; the heavy wooden chair, its carvings worn smooth by generations of hands, matched the desk about as well. He sat down at the station, where he picked out switches from a tall bank and flicked them.

A yellowed skull nestled in the middle of the toggles. Tiny lumens set into the optic foramen of the sockets flashed. Coiled copper wires ran over the dome of frontal bone, giving it a mocking coiffure, when viewed a certain way. Spools of polarised diamond tape clattered in a fretted box bolted to the wall, recording every thought the astropath received.

'Ident,' the skull grated.

Rumagoi fought back his irritation at providing his credentials. It was all part of the procedure, but he had the sense of time escaping him, and that if he were not quick, he would miss something vitally important. He needed to speak to Sov now.

He announced himself, presented his eye to a cup to be scanned, and finally pushed his sacred punchcard into a slot at knee height below the desk.

'All the equipment is working, master,' said Colus while Rumagoi waited.

'Then get the readings!' Rumagoi snapped. 'Must I tell you how to do everything?'

'Ident confirmed,' the machine-spirit grated.

A sounding horn swivelled down to ear level. A speaking tube unlocked and went slack in its clip. Rumagoi tugged it out, barely able to contain his impatience. He pulled a notepad and a graphite stick from his breast pocket. He cleared his throat, and began to speak slowly and clearly.

'Mistress Sov, can you hear me?'

The sounding horn crackled with soft static, then there came an electronic hiccup, and the noise of a human sigh blended with the hiss.

'Darkness rises from beneath. Lost sons rampage. Sustenance denied, a stolen fruit corrupt. Twin heads, twinned eyes, forward and back, an aquila of the foe.'

'I said it wasn't a teleprayer,' said Colus. 'There's no originating code stamp or nodal passage data. It is a vision.' He paused. 'Like I said,' he added quickly.

'It is much too literal for a prayer,' agreed Rumagoi, with deft shorthand taking down the mistress' words. He sucked air through his teeth. 'It's happening again.'

To underline his observation, the entire structure shook.

'He comes unpromised, unlooked for, a herald bears the torch. An empty throne, a throne of skulls, a throne of lies, a throne of pain...'

Rumagoi wrote quickly. Her words had the weight of prophecy.

'What does it mean?' asked Colus.

'How should I know?' said Rumagoi. 'It's a vision, isn't it? Do you expect me to interpret it immediately? Do something useful! Have you checked the equipment?'

'Yes, I said it is working fine, master. And I have exloaded the data you require.'

'Fine,' said Rumagoi distractedly. His hand had been trained since youth in automatic writing and was moving of its own accord now, responding to words his ears did not hear.

Sov's rambling faded to nothing, then returned as a loud shriek. The Pearl shook. Mistress Sov's speech came quicker.

'The father of deception strides the stars in search. Twisted paths betoken chaos within chaos. The word is shouted loudly, loudly!'

The tremors became more insistent. Small objects skipped over the tables around the edge of the room and bounced off the floor. A pipe broke free of its connector and hissed bromide. The psychic pressure in the room became unbearable. Rumagoi's hand slithered about the page like a serpent, far beyond his control. Colus crouched into a ball upon the floor, close to tears. Warning lights flickered on the machines.

'*Cardinal points in all directions. Bearers of the word bring violence to those who speak afar. The maiden will be undone. From out of fury comes light. A lord unlooked for returns without power. Crossing, he is crossed!*'

The shuddering subsided.

'*Crossing, he is crossed,*' the woman said. Her voice dwindled to a sigh. '*They seek what is all around them.*'

'*He is coming.*'

The shaking ceased. There was one final, hard aftershock that set the Pearl asway. Rumagoi looked around. Colus got cautiously up.

'What happened?'

Rumagoi shook out his hand. It was cramped from the writing, and stained with pencil black. 'Whatever it was, it's over now.' He got up. Mistress Sov floated serenely in her tank. The lights in the room suggested the relay was working normally, although outside he could hear screaming. Every time Sov suffered a vision of that strength, it cost them a few of the weaker astropaths.

'Should we think about replacing her?' asked Colus.

Rumagoi ran his finger across his spidery writing, scowling at its illegibility.

'Not yet,' he said. 'She's still too useful.' He tapped the page. 'Is there something you have divined?'

Rumagoi nodded, disturbed. He stood up, closed the book, and tucked it back into its pouch. 'Inform relay command we are coming out. Have them contact High-Telepathicus Sveen. I will not be denied this time. I need a petition to see the planetary governor, priority vermilion excelsior, and it will not wait. I need Sveen's seal. I need his approval. He will give them to me. Once he's looked at this, he'll understand.' He sighed. 'Finally. He may even agree to send out for aid.'

'What is it?'

Rumagoi frowned at his notes.

'I haven't got it all, but it's the enemy, among other things,' he said. 'According to this, they're coming here, and soon.'

Chapter Six

VOID SABRES

ULTIMA FOUNDING

FAREWELL TO THE FOUR

On a breezy, chill afternoon, the Void Sabres Chapter of the Adeptus Astartes was born.

A little over a thousand Space Marines stood in ranks arranged according to company, specialisation and office. Behind them were arrayed a hundred war machines of varying types, gifted them by the primarch to ease their task. Their Ancients stood with standard poles held aloft, though no flags did they yet display. In the distance, behind them, the towers of the city of Olda were blackened and broken. The Space Marines' efficiency in making it so brought this reward.

A new brotherhood was to be founded.

The lines of the Space Marines rose and fell, following the brutalised ground in perfect formation no matter the weapon-scars or shattered boulders they stood upon. Although the land they occupied was marked by war, their livery was perfect, newly painted, deep umber and bronze colours glinting with the light of afternoon skies. They had the uniformity that new Chapters had, before the tales of their deeds were wrought into their armour, but even then, at the beginning, with all of them having fought since the start of the crusade, there was a smattering of badges of one kind or another, and honour markings scattered on greaves and pauldrons throughout.

'So their story is begun,' murmured Deven Mudire, prompting a wry glance from Viablo.

'That's rather a whimsical sentiment for you, isn't it?' the void-born said, and returned to his work. His pen scratched over parchment held in place against the wind by glass paperweights.

Mudire shrugged, too melancholy to offer a retort to his comrade. 'Poetry is a gift of mine.'

'Like modesty,' said Fabian Guelphrain, prompting Solana to smile.

The Founding Four historitors of the Logos Historica Verita watched the foundation of the new Chapter from the rise of a hill to the west. They had the benefit of rank, and their little camp was richly provided. A tassled canopy shaded the long table that they worked at. Servants stood in attendance with refreshments, carrying trays of glasses covered with paper caps against the ash and dust. Nearby, a second table waited with dishes of food under cloches warmed by burners. That was for later, for a celebration none of them really wanted. Before their feast they performed their role as chroniclers of the crusade, except Mudire, who had vacated his place and stood on the lip of the slope, letting sun and breeze caress him.

'Are you not just a little moved?' Mudire demanded of them, a good way towards anger.

Fabian had another jest ready on his tongue, but he let it die when he caught the look in his colleague's eyes.

'Yes,' he said. 'Yes, of course I am. This is a sad day.'

Mudire would not be mollified. Ire and sorrow mixed explosively in him. 'We have worked together for years. We have all risked our lives. We have built a new Adepta under the primarch's hand, and now it's over, and all you can offer are insults?'

'It's not like that,' said Fabian. 'It's not over.'

'This is a beginning,' said Solana. 'Deven, Fabian was only teasing you before.'

'Then he's got no sense of occasion,' Mudire muttered.

A lesser member of the order came and laid out fresh parchments for Solana. She gave him quiet thanks.

'I'm sad, but times change,' she said. 'Things move on, according to the plan of the Machine-God. It is His will, the Emperor's will.'

Mudire turned back to look over the new Chapter. 'Oh, to be spared the will of gods.'

'How many Ultima Founding Chapters is this now?' Viablo asked aloud. 'I have it marked here as one hundred and three, but does that cover all those made during the crusade as well as those founded at the Primaris Revelation?' He looked to his notes again. 'Does anyone have a different number? I would hate to have to amend this.'

'Clean first draft, every time,' said Fabian. 'That's you, Viablo.'

'I find it efficient, Fabian,' said Viablo. 'There is a little point agonising over words when there is so much to do.'

'My dear Theodore,' Mudire protested. 'Can you not stop working just for a moment? We are to be parted after today. Does that not mean anything to you either?'

Viablo did not stop writing. 'Of course it does, Deven, but we do have a job to do first, recording the founding of this Chapter with all due respect.' He smiled. Viablo had an insolent grin he used rarely, and that surprised all who saw it. 'After that we can get drunk and weep as much as you like.'

Fabian sighed and set down his stylus, shunted his words into storage, then wiped away his work from his tabula cera with a wave of his hand. Wax rippled and re-formed under the gesture.

'I am almost in accord with Deven,' said Fabian. 'What does it matter if all the details of the founding of the Void Sabres, the one hundred and fourth Chapter of the Ultima Founding...'

'Aha!' said Viablo. 'Thank you.'

'...are not recorded? There is more to history than simply writing it down. One must live it.'

Viablo continued to write. 'Are you serious, Fabian? Our role is as recorders and investigators. We are the witnesses of history, not its agents. We should remember our place.'

'Well, I have never been entirely comfortable doing what I'm told.'

'Why do you not tell that to him?' said Viablo, and gestured upwards with the barbs of his quill. A flash of light in the sky was followed by the rumble of atmospheric penetration, a low drumroll that beat upon the hills about the brutalised city. 'The primarch's on his way.'

'I will,' said Fabian, and slapped the table with both hands, pushing himself up. 'It's why he gave us all this job in the first place, no? I don't see a single one of you taking orders completely on the straight, so I say why don't we have a drink now? Let's see these bold warriors on their way with proper ceremony, with a toast!'

Looks passed between the four.

'I agree,' said Mudire, eventually.

'I thought you would, Deven, but what about you two? Theodore? Solana?' Fabian asked. Solana's smile was permission enough. Viablo made a show of being upset, but he habitually drank more than the rest of them put together, and needed little convincing.

'Oh, very well,' he said, with false reluctance.

Guilliman's ship was roaring down, growing larger in the sky, burning with the rigours of re-entry, so that it appeared like a god coming down from heaven to pass his judgement on the earth.

'Resilisu, if you would do the honours, please?'

Fabian's ancestral servant stood by the drinks trolley. The ground was so rough they had opted for a tracked servitor module, whose part-dissected head was on display rather off-puttingly beneath a scratched dome of plastek in front of the bottles. Resilisu bowed. He had never managed to shake his impertinent air, and even dressed in the uniform of the Logos serfs, he managed to look scruffy, but he was brisk enough in bringing refreshments to the historitors, and deft as he handed out and filled glasses that rattled as the primarch's craft came in to land: the monstrous, glorious, double-headed eagle gunship *Aquila Resplendum*.

'Now, Deven, come and sit,' shouted Fabian over the scream of landing jets, taking a sip of Orlwood-infused bitter rum to soothe his dusty throat. 'Theodore is right, we really should be writing this down.'

The servo-skulls of the historitors rose up from their roost-rack, vid-eyes flashing, flew out over the newly forged brotherhood, and began to record.

Aquila Resplendum set down amid a thunder of jets and swirl of dust. Great motivators whined. Its wings and twin heads moved into landing configuration. It had not finished settling into its claws before the feathers upon its breast unlocked, and the debarkation ramp folded down and out from the hull.

Monstrous in the Armour of Fate, Roboute Guilliman marched out with a modest entourage comprising two dozen mortals of various sorts. His Space Marine equerry, Hurak, was the sole transhuman in the group, pale skin striking even at that distance. There was the usual collection of priests. Notaries from four Adepta were on hand to record the founding in the appropriate tomes, the largest and most important of which was Guilliman's own yard-high copy of the Index Astartes, bound in leather and metal and so heavy it had to be carried by two men at either end of a pole hooked into the book's spine.

The ruined city, the thousand Space Marines and their arma-ments, the primarch, and his ship – hunched over him like the living embodiment of the Emperor's will – created a charged, martial scene. In the display, the might of the Imperium was on show for all to see. It would make a very fine painting, thought Fabian, and he made a note to pass his vid-capt on to the fleet artists.

Yet this was a lesser event than those that had come before. At the start of the crusade, each new Chapter's birth was accom-panied by great fanfare. No longer. When Fabian had enquired why ceremonies were stripped back so, the representatives of the Adeptus Administratum and Departmento Munitorum insisted that Guilliman was pressed for time, with a great many duties, and that the difficulties of war made ceremony difficult. Fabian had sympathy with these reasons, holding them to be more than simple excuses, for he believed it was a mark of the primarch's dedication to his roles that he found a moment to give his blessing to the Void Sabres' brotherhood. But it was not the whole story. Fabian could not help but think the frequent nature of these events had had an effect on their grandeur. What had once been momentous was now merely notable, no matter what the official line was or what his own writings averred.

The historitors recorded by script and vid all that occurred. Fabian knew they all had similar thoughts on the matter, and tried as much as they could within the limits of the dry, formal stylings of their chronicles to forgive the Lord Commander.

Even so, even diminished, the birth of a new Chapter was a sight to behold.

Guilliman's entourage spread out, flanking the last loyal son of the Emperor with banners that flapped noisily in the breeze. A stand was brought out for the Index Astartes, then a high chair set behind it. The Recorder of the Rolls, an aged scribe, sat in it, and a small table was set up next to him, with bottles of ink and numerous pens. The scribe cast a critical eye over his supplies, gestured to the index bearers, who reverently opened the book to its first blank page. Only when the Recorder of the Rolls was happy did he give a slight nod to the primarch, and Roboute Guilliman began.

As was his habit, Guilliman swept his gaze across the assembled men before he spoke, letting every one know that he was seen.

'Warriors of the Indomitus Crusade,' he said, and his voice, clear and powerful, carried across the landscape with no need of amplification. 'You were taken from your homes with no explanation, put to sleep for thousands of years, changed beyond recognition, a fate none of you anticipated and few of you were given the opportunity to agree to. And yet, you have submitted yourself to the will of the Emperor. You gave yourself to our Imperium. You allowed blades to be forged of your bodies, weapons to be made of your minds. Woken from your slumbers, you were cast into battle. Many of you died. After losing your families, you have lost men you regarded as brothers, and not only to war. You have forborne your units being reorganised, and your postings changed. You have shown great and unsurpassable loyalty!' He paused. Flags snapped in the breeze. 'Now, I must ask that you give up your fraternities once again, for the last time. You have served me faithfully in the Unnumbered Sons. You will be unnumbered no longer. You were Sons of Corax. You are now the Void Sabres. Each of you has shown the greatest bravery, the greatest obedience. This world is yours in recognition of your steadfastness. It is a responsibility. It, and the sectors around this system, will be yours to aid. Obligation is your reward. Service is your wage. These are the blackest of times, and there is little more that I can give to you than my trust. Honour it, and die as heroes of the Imperium.'

Fabian and his colleagues watched in silence. There were parallels between the Void Sabres and the Founding Four. Fabian could easily imagine that Guilliman's words were intended as much for the Logos Historica Verita as for the Adeptus Astartes.

'Come forward, Adrin Phas, First Chapter Master of the Void Sabres.'

A warrior in heavy Gravis battleplate advanced and knelt at Guilliman's feet. The exchange of oaths began, and these Fabian had heard many times before. Phas swore he and his warriors would uphold the rule of the Emperor, turn aside all threats. He swore to defy the xenos, the witch and the traitor. That was the crux of it, though the oaths were much longer. For five minutes Phas recited them without notes, without pause, and without faltering. Fabian could have done the same but the minds of the Adeptus Astartes were superior in many ways. Master Phas would have had no need to memorise the oaths laboriously. He would have read them once. That would have been enough.

Fabian sometimes wondered if that facility lessened the sincerity of such promises. Had Fabian had to commit such a long declaration to memory, he would have read and reread and rehearsed the words many times. Each iteration forced confrontation with the promise, and therefore consideration, which, though perhaps seeming cursory at each pass, was made genuine by repetition. When an unmodified man made an oath like that, he did so in full understanding of what he pledged. Did a Space Marine? They were made to be obedient, and trained to give all to the Emperor without question. Was the promise of a warrior who had little choice the same as freely given fealty, and hard-thought promises? What use was an oath from such a man?

Once, Fabian had thought Space Marines angels, and when that faded, for a long time he had been under the impression they were more than human. That, too, was wrong. He had met Space Marines who were little better than automata. He had known others with poet's souls. Both extremes were rare, but he had decided on the balance of it, their lack of self-determination, their engineered loyalties, and the absence of the gentler emotions made most of them lesser than natural men.

Fabian glanced down at his tabula. The wax bore his thoughts in full, unconsciously transmitted via his stylus. He could erase them, but instead, after a brief hesitation, he pressed the button at the side of the device, transferring the information to his data-slate via a plasteel-skinned cable before he cleared the surface. Let his musings be recorded, he thought. The historitors' purpose was the truth. Too often now, the members of the Logos censored themselves.

His oaths given, the Chapter Master rose. His heraldry was recorded by the Recorder of the Rolls into the Index Astartes, the second illumination after the Chapter badge in the entry detailing the Void Sabres. The particulars of the Chapter would be disseminated by astrotelepathy throughout the Imperium, as far as was possible, and added to other copies of the index.

And so error will creep in as the visions are misinterpreted, and thereafter dissension, and in some distant, future time there will be conflict over misremembered detail, Fabian thought.

Phas read aloud the entry that told of him, an insufficient paragraph to describe even a few short years of heroism, and signed. He went back to his brotherhood.

After the Chapter Master came the ruling officers of the Chapter's subdivisions: the Master of Sanctity, the Chief Librarian, the Master of the Apothecaries, and the Master of the Forge. They had their own oaths to give, and their own marks to make in the great book. Ten captains then, with shorter oaths, though their duties would be hardly less burdensome. The afternoon wore on. The day was long there, but the nights had an edge, and as the sun crawled towards the horizon, the temperature fell with it, until the historitors shivered. Furs and hot wine were brought to them, and their glasses of spirits recharged often, so that by the time the battle-line brothers of the Chapter recited their own oaths en masse, their basso profundo voices shaking the landscape, Fabian was getting quietly drunk.

Colours were presented. The first was the Chapter banner, given to the Chapter Ancient. Then standards to each of the companies. In reverent silence, they attached the flags to the crossbars and let them unfurl in the breeze. Simple designs rippled, to be added to with honours in the years to come.

Guilliman gave them another proud look. 'You are now the Void Sabres Chapter of the Adeptus Astartes, and will be until you die. Cherish your brothers. Serve your Emperor. Protect your assigned territories. You fly no longer with the crusade fleets, but I rely on you just the same. Your Emperor values your courage. Go to your duties. Your deeds will be remembered. Your sacrifices celebrated.'

Fabian felt the words personally. Would he be remembered? To how many loyal servants of the Emperor had those promises been made, only for their names to crumble into dust with their bones? Too many, he thought.

'Ave Imperator.' Guilliman saluted the Space Marines, fist to chest. The returned gesture was a thousand gunshots of ceramite on ceramite.

'Ave Imperator!' the Void Sabres shouted back.

Guilliman went back into his ship without further word. His servants followed him. The Index Astartes was reverently hoisted back upon its pole. The ramp closed. The *Aquila Resplendum*'s twin heads looked skywards, and with screaming rockets rose ponderously back into the sky, where it accelerated into the evening, and vanished into the stars.

Viablo laid his pen down first.

'Well then,' he said. 'Dramatic as always.'

'I listened to his words,' said Mudire softly, 'and they were spoken to me, to us all. I am sure of it.'

The Void Sabres were departing, boarding their transports and gunships, and going away to their camp at the site of their future fortress-monastery, yet to raise its spires and guns over the plains of their home world.

'I felt them too,' said Fabian. 'He was speaking to us.' He sighed, experiencing a penetrating, emotional numbness that robbed him of feeling. He flexed stiff fingers. 'This is it, then.'

Viablo nodded solemnly. The joints in the brace supporting his slender, void-born frame whined quietly.

'Do you know where you are going?' said Viablo.

'No,' said Fabian. 'Do you?'

'I am to remain with Fleet Primus, that's all I've heard.'

Fabian felt a stab of envy, but tried not to let it show. Viablo was the obvious choice as Guilliman's personal chronicler; he was far more even-tempered, and more diligent, than Fabian.

'I'm joining Fleet Octus,' said Mudire. 'Solana is to travel to the forge worlds to act as herald for our little organisation.'

'You all know where you're going?' Fabian said.

'It appears so,' said Mudire.

'Then why have I no idea what my orders are to be?' said Fabian.

'A special role, no doubt,' said Mudire, and his envy of Fabian was the equal of Fabian's for Viablo. *Only a few years in, and already we are a nest of vipers,* thought Fabian, *vying for position, bad as a High Lord's court.*

'Let's not be sad,' said Solana. 'Let's have this feast we've waited for all day.' She was trying to be cheerful, but her voice was strained.

Servants were moving, lighting fire bowls, activating heaters. Lesser members of the Logos came and took away their work for archiving. Fabian glanced at them, wondering which, if any, would one day take his place at Guilliman's side.

'It's best not to see this as the end,' Solana went on. She stood up unsteadily, for she was unused to drink, and yet like them all seemed to have the need for it then. 'The Logos will live on forever, thanks to us.' She raised her glass. 'To the Founding Four, may our fraternity never die.'

Mudire looked like he might cry.

'The Founding Four!' Fabian shouted, competing with the noise of gunships taking off.

The historitors lingered long into the night, and drank much.

It was many years before any of them saw each other again.

Chapter Seven

THE SEER

PROUD SISTERS

KHYMERAE

The bells ceased their clangour, and the strobing lights went out. The tithed moaned in relief at the temporary reprieve. Gavimor tried to unclench his muscles. His head still rang, his eyes were blurred. The headache that was his constant companion was at its absolute worst at the times of the suppression. The aftermath of the noise and light had him struggle to form simple thoughts, though he had figured out soon after being brought aboard that that was rather the point.

Gavimor decided to sleep. There was nothing else to do, and the psy-wards drained his strength so much that a leaden exhaustion had hold of him all the time. When he woke, he was unrefreshed. The few hours he was awake, he slipped often into drowsing, when the lights and the bells were not in play. The vitality that was his before the ships had come was gone. Being aboard was like being ill, but worse, and never-ending, with no respite from weakness, no hope of recovery. At first he wondered if they drugged the food and water as well, to enhance the effect of the warded chains and the suppressor machines, but they gave them so little to eat that it didn't matter if it was drugged or not. A man could not live on such rations. He was starving. He thought he might be dying.

The discomfort of lying on the decking grille was considerable, worse now he had lost so much weight. The feel of the hard, witch-hating iron digging into his flesh edged into genuine pain. He was bruised all over. They had no ablution facilities; their waste was collected in foetid slops beneath the deck, infrequently emptied, even less frequently cleansed, and the smell rose up unconquerably from beneath. And he was one of the lucky ones. The tithed had been taken aboard in whatever clothes they had been wearing. He had been outside when they had come for him, enforcers from the witchfinder's office with one of those terrifying off-world warrior women who guarded the ship. Consequently, he had his coat and a decent suit of clothes. It was too hot to wear the coat in the hold, but he at least could use it as a pillow. He guarded it jealously, and vigilantly. There had been murders over possessions. His coat was filthy now, and stank, but it was better that than laying his head directly on the deck grille, and it blocked out some of the smell of the slops.

If he slept, it would all go away.

He tried to settle. The ship was troubled by warp storms again, lumbering from side to side in a way that made the tithed moan in fear.

He cursed the others for their wailing, and rolled over, jamming his robe under his neck. His chains dragged at his wrists and ankles, catching on the ulcers they had rubbed into his skin. The lamentations of the other tithed rasped at his psyche. The smell of so many bodies, their excreta gathering beneath the deck grille, their sweat, their despair, took their toll on his sanity. It was unbearably stuffy. He screwed up his eyes and tried to ignore them. Once, he could have drawn on the deep wells of his soul to replenish himself; that was his gift, or curse, he supposed. Whether gift or curse, it had been stolen. Now, when he tried, all he experienced was a harsh, nerve-jangling tingling, and the alacrity of thought he once enjoyed was replaced by a grey fog that filled his throat, pressed at the backs of his eyes, and lured every musing from its rightful path.

'Don't sleep,' whispered Evee.

'Leave me be,' said Gavimor, managing to conjure a little of his old superiority from his misery. 'You are not to bother me. I command it.'

'You're no one to tell me what to do now, my lord,' she said mockingly. She'd had a pretty voice when they had been herded into the hold. It was cracked now, and ugly. 'We're both the same in here. No airs and graces for either of us.'

'I am a man of rank. You are a manufactory drudge. Leave me alone!' he snarled.

'You are nothing. I am nothing. We will be lucky if either of us survive this voyage.'

Gavimor curled himself into a tighter ball and ground his teeth together. 'Just be quiet. There is nothing to do but sleep.'

She was quiet for only a second.

'I wonder where we are?' she asked.

'We are in the warp,' Gavimor said.

'How can you know that?' she said. 'How do you know we are not in realspace? I mean, I can feel when we change from one to the other, but which is which?'

'I know because I have travelled, and you are a manufactory drudge,' he repeated the insult, spitefully this time.

'This drudge says wake up,' said Evee. 'It's happening.' Chains clanked as she moved closer. She was too close already. Each tithed had a space twenty inches wide to call their own. Her breath washed over him, sour with dehydration. 'He's doing it again.'

'He always does when the noises stop. He's mad. We're all going mad. I'm going to go mad if you don't let me sleep.'

'He might say something important this time.' There was a note of hope in her voice, and that was the cruellest trick of all.

Gavimor sighed. He pulled in his limbs, fighting the bone-deep ache afflicting him, and sat up.

The hold was dark. The few dim lumens shining from cages out of reach up on the walls gave just enough light to see by. Heavy ribs reinforced the ceilings. They were thirty feet high, a criminal waste of volume, Gavimor thought, when they were all so tightly packed. Hundreds of the tithed were laid out on the hard deck, arranged head to foot in fanned patterns and tight rows that were designed only with the maximum utilisation of hold space in mind, and no consideration for human comfort.

The tithed lived in their individual worlds of misery, isolated from one another by gulfs of pain, though their bodies touched every time they moved. The psy-dampers had unique effects on each, depending on their curses and relative psychic strengths. Whatever the result, none were spared. Many sat or squatted listlessly, hair grown lank over the course of their voyage, staring at the space between their feet. Others wept constantly, or tore at their flesh so ferociously they were disfigured by their own hand. There were those who tried to sleep, like Gavimor, smothering the nightmare their lives had become with blessed unconsciousness. Many of them had ship lice. Sickness was rife. Insanity more so. Deaths were common. The dead sometimes lay in their chains for days before they were collected.

A blankness pushed down on them from the ribbed ceiling. It could not be seen, but it was most assuredly felt, a weight like water falling onto the candles of their souls, snuffing them out. The ship vibrated constantly with the work of arcane machines. Strange lights shone sometimes from between the joins in the ceiling ribs. Gavimor had never considered himself a witch. He had had no idea, believing himself to be simply luckier than those around him, using his Emperor-ordained gifts to rise up from the lower orders of nobility to the higher, and taking his family with him, all in service of the Imperium. His arrest had been as unexpected as it had been terrifying. Telepath, they had said; seer, they had said, each label condemning him a little more. And it was true: when asked to explain how he knew the things he knew, he could not say. What he had taken for intuition was in fact the same evil he had been taught to abhor his entire life. The revelation had destroyed him.

How little he had known. Now he was going to serve for real, they had been told. He was going to Terra to bow before the Golden Throne.

Though cut off from the flashes of presentiment and insight his gifts had given him, Gavimor was an intelligent man. Nobody knew what happened to the witches once they were taken up in the tithe. He had not given it a second thought before he had been accused, tested, and found deviant himself. Now he thought about nothing else. The conclusions he drew were not heartening. Every time the ship punched its way into the warp, he prayed they would not reach their final destination. Every egress into realspace eventually brought far-off cries, as others of their kind were brought aboard. Five stops they had undergone. He thought the ship must be full. He thought their voyage would soon be done.

Only one person in all that cavernous prison seemed to retain his abilities. Nobody knew his name. He had not said a single lucid word in the months since they had been brought down there and clapped in irons, but he spoke much: wild, nonsensical words that had about them the feel of prophecy. For that, they called him the Seer.

'He's going to do it right now,' said Evee. When Gavimor was slow in looking, she kicked his ankle.

'Ow, don't do that.'

'Then look. See.'

The Seer was three spaces over from Gavimor. Between them was a woman who stared without blinking at a spot on the wall. She had not eaten for a week and was wasting away. After her was a naked, sullen man who spat at anyone who spoke to him.

The Seer was a slight, younger man who had not changed like the rest of them had. He was dirtier, thinner, and his hair was longer, but his demeanour was the same. His eyes were as wild as when he had been brought into the hold, no more, no less, darting back and forth as if he followed some exciting drama visible only to him. Unlike the others, he showed no fear, and no despair.

'He's going to speak.'

'He's mad. He's always been mad,' said Gavimor. His own voice was a croak. He'd been given nothing to drink for two days. He wondered how many of the tithed witches would make it to Terra. He wondered if anyone cared.

'He's not. He's the only one. None of this affects him.' She raised a filthy hand and gestured at the ribbed ceiling.

'I doubt that's possible.'

'And what would you know about it, oh trader in refined sugars? Did we have a sideline in witchfinding?' She giggled at her joke. When they had been brought aboard, Gavimor had spoken much of his family and accomplishments in a bid to preserve his dignity and separate himself from the riff-raff he shared the hold with. He regretted it now.

The Seer drew in a sharp breath.

'See, it's starting,' Evee said. 'He is going to say something!'

The ship juddered with a tearing noise of metal, like something had caught on its hull, and it took a stomach-churning drop. Distant generators whooped. The tithed moaned, but

Evee remained fixed on the Seer. The sullen man caught her eye and shrank out of the line of her gaze.

'He's coming!' the Seer shouted suddenly, so loud Gavimor jumped.

'Goldengoldengolden. Moving through and in... He is there! But he comes. He comes and he will save. Rejoice!'

Another impact, a hollow boom. A sense of dread rushed over them like the wind.

'It's the Emperor, I tell you. He's talking about the Emperor,' said Evee.

'He's talking madness. How can he see anything except what's right in front of him? I can barely even think with these things on.' Gavimor raised his clenched fists, displaying his bonds.

'He can, because it's the Emperor he sees. He's watching over us.'

'I am almost certain He is not.'

'He is!' Evee said sharply, and slapped him.

'So you are an expert on the warp now? Fine,' said Gavimor. The ship was shaking. The storm was bad. The empyrean had been plagued by tempests ever since the Rift opened. The chartists his family used had wanted their fees doubled, those that would agree to sail. Most of them wouldn't. 'I'm going to sleep.'

'Gloryglorygloryglory,' shrieked the Seer. 'I see him! Golden and perfect! I see him!'

Gavimor lay down. He was determined to sleep. The ship's lurching progress could not stop him, nor could the devout wailings of the Seer, or the moans of the other tithed at every bump and skip the vessel made. Lulled by the despair of others, he finally drifted off.

Silence ruled the decks of a Black Ship. Upon the bridge of the *Sacrificium Ultimum*, Knight-Excubitor Phyllia Torunda sat in her black throne. She wore black power armour of a severe style, all sharp edges and points, the high mouthpiece signifying her oath of tranquillity coming up to just below her eyes. The armour was void sealed, as befitted the mistress of a ship's warriors. It was partly made of iron, that metal, properly treated, being proof against the warp, and inlaid with complex hexagrammatic wards of silver wire. The throne amplified her own qualities, and around her space was dead, all but cut from the warp. Thus intensified, her nature impinged upon reality, making it flicker like a bad vid-feed if she was looked upon directly.

The crew did not look directly upon her. Nor Adept-Captain Essene, who looked steadfastly away from her if he could, staring over her head from his own command dais. Even he, specifically chosen for his own near-inert psychic nature, could not stand a blank soul of such dead intensity.

Torunda and her troops were only one part of the ship's defences. Intricate machineries trapped the minds of the cargo. Owing to the dangerous spiritual nature of said cargo, carefully tuned Geller fields, more powerful than anything found on other ships, kept out the daemons of the warp. The power draw taxed the ship's reactor and the number of lives spent to maintain them was high, but for the safety of the Black Ships, no cost was too great.

There were three Black Ships in that flotilla, who with their escorts were cutting their way through the warp towards Terra. They rolled and bounced over perturbations in the soul-stuff, yawing and diving. A lesser commander would have ordered them out of the warp, and gone off at sub-light speeds to seek a safer path. But such diversions could take years, centuries, and Torunda's duty was among the most important in all the Imperium. It was the Black Ships that provided the personnel for the Astronomican. The fleets found men and women suitable for the soul binding. They hunted out children who might one day make inquisitors, or sanctioned psykers, or other stranger and more powerful agents of He on Terra.

The ships brought the people who kept the Imperium together. The witches they gathered provided service, where they would otherwise bring only danger.

But this was not the ships' most important purpose.

The Black Ships were victuallers, providers of the Emperor's meat. Without a constant delivery of psykers to the machineries of the Golden Throne, the Astronomican would go out, warp travel would become next to impossible. It was even whispered in certain, highly placed circles that should that happen, the Emperor would cease to be.

Knight-Excubitor Phyllia Torunda and Adept-Captain Essene were well aware how vital their roles were. As Essene guided his ship through the warp, Torunda kept watch over everything and everyone on the command deck.

The crew worked without speaking, their faces covered with black hoods, only the tips of their fingers poking from their sleeves. With the exceptions of the astropaths, the Navigator, and certain other members of the Adepta charged with evaluating the cargo en route to Terra, everyone aboard was carefully chosen from the least psychic examples of humanity, right down to the lowest menial. None were above the Sigma grade on the Imperial Assignment, though those of Tau and below were preferred. Even the human components of the ships' servitors were thoroughly tested for residual talent before being brought on board.

Then there were the Sisters themselves, members of the proudest order of the null maidens. When the Chambers of Oblivion and Judgement had faded into history, become scattered bands and whispered myth until so recently resurrected, the Chamber Astra had never gone away, but continued its grim role of leading the Great Tithe. It was they, the Sisters in Black, who led the hunts for rogue psykers, investigated lapses in the levy and protected the Black Ships from the precious prizes they carried and the monsters that would devour them. It was they who ruined lives and purged worlds in the name of protecting mankind.

She was proud, Phyllia Torunda, and she knew her vocation well.

A red lumen blinked, catching her eye. She raised her left hand, the fingers flickering through a series of rapid gestures. A locutor-servo-skull rose from a niche in the wall, spinal tail disconnecting with a hiss. It rotated in the air, and bowed down, its laser-guided gaze resting on her hand.

'Psy-augury command,' it said, reading Torunda's gestures and broadcasting them. The crew understood null maiden thoughtmark, but as they had to stop their labours to look at her, she used machine-friendly Orsköde to speak through the translexer skull. 'Warning lights on proximity boards. Explain their meaning.'

Essene looked down. His face was grey and solemn. The mental rigours of commanding such a ship were great. No one performed this service with their soul intact, and no one did it for very long.

'Quadrant three, upper left board,' he said. 'Psy-augury, investigate.'

A crew member – they could have been male or female, their identity was lost under the folds of their robes – went over their instruments. When they spoke their voice was artificial, sexless, hard.

'Perturbations detected. Gravitic disturbance to empyrical wave-patterns suggestive of true-matter mass within the warp. Indicators rising.'

Another five lights flickered hesitantly into being on the board, then burned steady and true.

Again, Torunda's hand fluttered. 'Describe the nature of the mass,' the skull translated.

'Four, possibly five or six separate objects, moving true in relative spatial dimensions. They are gaining on us.'

Torunda stood and turned to face Essene. Both hands moved quickly, now with the more complicated thoughtmark.

Ships. Is it them? she said.

Essene gave her a long, sorrowful look. 'Mayhap,' he said, then he gestured to his vox-commander. 'Inform Navigator MacPherson to shield his eye, then open a link to the navigatorium.'

There was a murmur of conversation, robed figures worked. A hololith buzzed and crackled, struggling to initiate. Finally, an image wavered on showing a Navigator of mildly aberrant form in the costume of House MacPherson. He and Torunda could never be in the same room. Her soullessness would blind his warp sight. It might kill him. As for him, he was bathed in the light of the warp from his open oculus, a lucent poison that chilled the standard crew to look upon, even in the false form of the holo.

Silensiori MacPherson was sitting in his chair, head bolted into place. His warp eye was covered with a mirrored shield.

'Adept-captain,' he said, through misshapen teeth that ground audibly on each other, *'the currents are strong and we have a major emotional wavefront bearing down from the third house of the fourth sign. I would ask you to keep this brief.'*

'Are we being followed?' Essene asked.

'Yes. There are six capital ships, several escorts. I can see them if I look behind us. They are daemon-friends, borne up on the wings of lesser gods. The chief vessels are Traitor Astartes strike cruisers, ancient vintage. I cannot see their colours, but I would guess they are of the Word Bearers Legion.'

'It is them,' said Essene. 'Those who have been targeting the League.'

Then we are being hunted, said Torunda.

'We will fare better in the void. Can you find us a smooth exit from the empyrean?' asked the adept-captain.

'No,' grunted Silensiori MacPherson, with obvious effort.

'Then find us any way,' Essene commanded. He got to his feet. 'Begin preparations for emergency warp egress. Prepare void shields for activation. Start realspace engine initiation sequence. All hands ready for battle.'

The lumens went out, replaced by the bloody red of combat lighting. Alarms began to pulse through the crewed sections of the ship.

There are too many of them to triumph over. We should stay in the warp, signed Torunda. *They will not expect us to fight here, and my Sisters will wreak havoc on their diabolical slaves.*

'You would, but the warp is their domain, knight-excubitor. They will catch us, and we shall die. You cannot banish an infinity of Neverborn and repel Traitor Astartes. You suggest a desperate tactic. Nobody ever fights in the warp if they have a choice. Outside the empyrean, they will not be able to summon their daemons onto the ship. The psy-baffles will see to that.'

A bad translation will leave us helpless.

Essene's head moved within his cowl, considering her suggestion. 'Noted, but it is my judgement that if we leave the empyrean, we may evade them. If they follow, we may outrun them. We may not have to fight. We will make them pay in the warp, but we shall certainly perish.'

'They are gaining on us,' MacPherson said. *'I need to see with my truesight – close down the hololith or suffer my gaze. I will find us a way out.'* The Navigator's phantom shrank to a single ribbon of light that vanished from existence with an audible crackle.

'Have the astropaths contact the other ships. Have all follow our lead. Inform me the minute they have responded. Helm, you are to follow Silensiori's guidance exactly,' said Essene.

He sat back down. Crew members worked quickly. More lights on the board came on, shifting in patterns. They were scrutinised, and interpreted.

'They are closing,' a member of the psy-augury staff reported. 'Real-term distance transliteration four thousand miles and narrowing.'

'They are moving into boarding range,' Essene said.

They would not dare, said Torunda. *They would be torn to pieces before they pierced our Geller fields.*

'They are daemon friends,' Essene said. 'The creatures of the warp will help them, and they will flood aboard in unity with the Neverborn. Astropathic command, any response from the others?'

'*Sanctioned Suffering* has replied,' an operative responded. 'They are prepared to drop warp. No response from the *Striga Venor.*'

Essene fell into a thoughtful silence.

'Take us out. With the Emperor's guidance, they will see our actions and respond appropriately. Transfer total directional control to Navigator Silensiori MacPherson, by the order of the Adeptus Astra Telepathica. He has command now. Knight-Excubitor, go to your warriors.'

I have anticipated this. Many ships have been targeted in this sector. We are ready for combat, signed Torunda.

'Then I pray to the almighty Emperor that your skill at arms will be enough to preserve us,' said Essene dully.

Torunda strode from the command deck, her locutor-skull buzzing dutifully after. Klaxons sang, and the ship bucked like a frightened animal as it fled out of the warp.

The distant screams of the damned burning in the soul forges underlay the chanting of priests. The ship vibrated to the thrum of warp engines. Bells tolled to mark off the passing of the hour.

'They are fleeing the warp, they run before us. Us, us, us,' the Navigator moaned, and his appendages shivered.

'Do you hear that, my brothers? The prey is started. The chase begins in earnest.'

Xhokol Hruvak grinned, and leaned forward. He reached out an absent-minded hand to pet the beasts by his throne. They snapped at him, but could not bite, their skinless jaws bound tight by steel traps, and they quietened soon enough under his attentions, as he worked his fingers along their heads and backs, massaging exposed muscles.

His command deck was a spotless place of worship, staffed by priests and lords of liturgy. Stone, brass, bone and steel worked in perfect combination to evoke the majesty of the Powers. To this order, there was one notable exception. The ship's Navigator was a calcified horror of hair and flesh hanging by quivering ropes of sinew from the command deck ceiling. Somewhere in that squirming mass was a man's soul, perhaps even his original form, buried by accreted mutation. He had long ago outgrown the Navigator's blister, and been installed directly into the bridge. Now the sole remaining indication that this being was born of woman was the single human eye that rolled, yellowed and veined and large as a game ball, beneath his staring warp eye. This was uncovered. The warriors of Xhokol Hruvak's host moved about before it freely. They had long passed the point of madness. A Navigator's witch-sight held no terror for the masters of daemons.

'Then they are doomed,' said the Word Bearer. He patted the head of one of his beasts indulgently. 'Once more you lead us to our prey – good, good, Atraxiabus.'

The other two warp beasts whined and growled to see their pack-mate receiving this praise. The chains holding them in place chinked. Xhokol was their master, and they followed him well, but they could turn at any moment, and then they would tear him to pieces for his favouritism if they could.

'I see... I see them leaving now,' said the Navigator. His corpulence shook, showering vile fluids into the shallow pool beneath him. Thralls moved forward instantly to clean away the splatters of the liquid that escaped. They were hard-worked. Their job was never done.

'I told you, Pridor Vrakon. I told you, brother, that we would find this psyker the sorcerer requires.'

Dark Apostle Pridor Vrakon's Third War Host travelled as guests on Xhokol's ships. Vrakon rode the command deck with its master, standing close to Hruvak's throne, though not so close an idle lunge from the huntsman's khymerae might take him unawares.

'I am impressed you have tracked the Black Ships through the warp, and it is clear to me that rumours of your prowess are well earned,' said the Dark Apostle from the depths of his Terminator armour. 'But are you sure this is the correct fleet? These vessels are heavily warded. Are your... creatures' – he curled a tattooed lip – 'not affected?'

Xhokol Hruvak continued to pet his warp beasts, dividing his attention between them more equally. Their jealous growls subsided.

'The khymerae are half-rooted in the materium, brother. They are not affected by conditions in either realm, but hunt true, and Atraxiabus has the finest of senses. Is that not so, my glorious hound?'

Atraxiabus bowed its head, as if in modesty at the praise.

'They are impure things,' said Pridor. 'Not of the Four.'

'Are you trying to upset me?' said Hruvak. 'I do not care what you think. You say they are impure because they are not the creatures of the Four. But I say that they are more refined than any lesser daemon of the Powers. They are expressions of the warp in its purest form, the children of interactions between mind and matter. They are living nightmares, beholden to no law of either realm. Perfect.'

'They are animals,' said Pridor.

'Then try to command them, and do what I do with them, and experience failure,' said Hruvak. 'I am the Master of Hounds, the huntsman of Kor Phaeron. What are you? Another mumbling sage regurgitating the same old wisdom, while I sacrifice the bloodied hearts of my quarry to the Four!' He stood, and raised his right arm. A single claw blade slid from a housing on the back of his forearm, sharp as a serpent's tooth. A power field crackled upon its sword length, and with it he saluted to his gods. 'To warrior Khorne, sage Tzeentch,' he said, turning to huge effigies of the Great Powers. They dominated the walls they were set into, each within a huge alcove decorated with skulls, armour, weapons and other offerings pleasing to their eyes. 'To perfect Slaanesh and generous Nurgle. I exalt them, and they reward me.' He bowed his head, flourished the claw sword; it rasped back into its sheath. 'If my beasts are impure, I am impure, and then I would not enjoy their favour, would I? But I do, Pridor Vrakon. I enjoy their favour very much.'

'They leave, they leave,' gurgled the Navigator from his single, drooling orifice. His giant human eye rolled around its socket. A faint nimbus of dark power played around the other. 'First one, now another, the third will be close behind.'

They felt the last Imperial ship's exit soon after, as a ripple under the keel.

'Follow them, now,' Hruvak ordered.

'Following, following, following,' said the Navigator.

Ancient mechanisms trembled throughout the vessel. A faint keening sounded. A judder ran down the ship's spine, and a certain, indefinable feeling of change. They were out into realspace.

'Feel that,' crowed Pridor Vrakon. 'How smooth. How perfect. How must the servants of the false corpse-god envy the ease with which we traverse the sea of souls? That was

a particularly fine egress. Maybe you are right, Hruvak. How
many Neverborn do you have imprisoned on board this ship?'

'I have many, from the highest bought by hard bargain, to
the least and most pathetic slave. My hounds hunt beings of
pure spirit as well as those of flesh, after all. It is not hard for
me to find what I want.'

'Impressive,' said Vrakon. 'But will they stand against the null
maidens aboard those vessels?'

'They will not,' said Hruvak, 'but the khymerae will. They
are half-real. Superior, like I said.'

'Open the oculus,' a voice went up. 'Open the oculus!' The
crew were largely made up of uniformed thralls who differed in
appearance from their Imperial counterparts only in the mode
of their dress and their devotional tattoos. But there were a
great many god-speakers among them, chanting out the num-
berless names of the Four, and it was from one of these the
command came.

The oculus shutter was a double-skinned iris affair, with a
cover both sides of the giant rose window. Each of the leaves
of the iris was a bright silver, engraved on every surface with
Lorgar's mysteries, and inset with copper. They slid open with
the rasp of blades running along each other, revealing equally
heavily decorated mullions in the form of the octed, supporting
massive armaglass panes. Through it, the Word Bearers could
look right down the ship to its arrowhead prow, from where
long banners of corposant streamed, gathering in teasing fingers
around the daemon sculptures festooning the hull. Screaming
faces in impossible colours bled away into the black of interstellar
realspace. Unreal suns faded as the warp rip behind them closed,
plunging the fleet into the hard diamond light of faraway stars.

Ahead were the Black Ships. The khymerae shifted, and the
tentacles upon their backs, all safely bound in canvas sheaths,
quivered.

'Their disposition rather proves my point,' Pridor Vrakon said. 'Easy pickings. Unless that one contains our prize? It will be hard to catch.'

The Imperials had come out of the warp in disarray. The Black Ship Vrakon indicated had emerged far ahead of the other two, and was making good its escape, its engine stacks burning bright. A few of the fleet escorts had gathered themselves around it, and were maintaining good formation.

But the others were far less fortunate. One of them was limping away at what must have been less than half-motive. The Black Ships had a very modest support group compared to the fleets of old that once accompanied them, an indication of the pressures on the Imperium. Those escorts that weren't with the fleeing vessel wallowed. Two of them were afire, broken by bad egress. The third Black Ship was tumbling slowly end over end, its engines out.

'Great Tzeentch lays an easy path for us today,' said Xhokol. He swept his hand extravagantly at his hounds. Their faces and their upper limbs pointed at the stricken vessel. 'Therein is the one we seek. Neither it nor its sister shall escape.'

'The third will.'

'Two from three is a good score,' Xhokol retorted, 'and a far better one than you have so far made. These will be the fifth and sixth of the Emperor's black vessels I have taken. How many have you brought in tribute to the Four?' Xhokol Hruvak took up his helm from its rest upon the back of his throne and secured it in place. 'Truly, today we shall be blessed by the gods.'

Chapter Eight

SACRIFICIUM ULTIMUM

WARP SPAWN

GAVIMOR'S FATE

The *Sacrificium Ultimum* shook with incoming fire, and Torunda wished with all her heart that Essene had heeded her suggestion to fight the traitors in the warp. They would have had little chance, but some chance was better than none.

She thought this as she charged into a junction and her executioner greatblade cut through the breastplate of a crimson-armoured traitor. Gas burst from severed supply lines, and he went down with a vox-amplified moan. Another moved in to take her from the side, but she struck upwards with her elbow, her Vratine power armour accelerating the blow, caving in the faceplate of the warrior, and his head snapped back. Guns barked behind her. A Prosecutor squad was arriving from deeper in-ship, their bolts sparking off the Word Bearer in fiery sprays. Shrapnel rattled off her helm. The warrior swung around, firing his massive boltgun to the rear, and Torunda ran on, her locutor-skull trailing her, trusting her Sisters to deal with him. This pair were isolated pathfinders, far ahead of their fellows. Her skills would be better used elsewhere.

Lex-grid text scrolling before her eyes warned that the foe were coming aboard in number: thirty, maybe forty of them from three assault boats latched onto the ship's hull like parasites. The Word Bearers were enslavers of daemons, but there were no Neverborn as yet, and she suspected they would see none. There were many perils to the things of the warp on board a Black Ship. But even unsupported by their supernatural allies, the Word Bearers were still Space Marines, with Space Marines' strengths, armour and weapons.

The outer layers of a Black Ship housed as many ordnance batteries as one would find on a ship of the line, but the deep interior was different: a mass of cavernous holds linked by long, sombre corridors that seemed to go on forever, and led to nowhere but despair. The hull was heavily armoured, but the ships were primarily prisons, designed to keep their cargo in. If an enemy penetrated the defences and made their way into the centre, they were difficult to contain. Intruders multiplied the problems presented by the cargo.

Somehow, their attackers had known exactly where to strike the ship, had bypassed the outer levels, and were running amok in its vulnerable innards.

Torunda ran up a short flight of stairs into one of the wide principal corridors, and nearly lost her head to a fusillade of bolt shots. She threw herself into cover behind a stanchion with a demi-squad of Telepathica armsmen, and found herself looking at a massacre. A score of the *Sacrificium Ultimum*'s soldiery were taking on a squad of five Word Bearers, and being destroyed for their impudence. The Space Marines paced slowly shoulder to shoulder up the corridor towards the stairs, boltguns barking, each micro-missile they fired punching through cover and armour and obliterating their mortal targets. The chill air steamed with blood heat, and fyceline smoke added to it, making a hellish fog.

A Black Ship had far more armed crew than a warship of comparable size, but that didn't matter when facing the wrath of fallen angels. Shotgun pellets clattered from power armour. Lasgun beams marked the contorted writing covering the plates with black, but the Word Bearers strode on unharmed, guns switched from target to target with murderous efficiency.

She rapidly clicked her tongue into the vox-pickup, a staccato dash-dot code version of battlemark, ordering her warriors to reinforce her location. Tactical overlays showed up the other intrusions into the ship. The enemy were split into half-squads, it seemed; that was the only reason they could be in so many places at once, but they were clearly converging, all of them making their way towards the holds. The battle would be decided there.

Lex-grid messages filled her helm. Two squads of Sisters were coming up from the stern with armsmen in support.

She readied herself, releasing the hilt of her sword with her left hand. Her fingers flickered. The skull's translexer spoke for her.

'Remain here. Support coming. Keep in cov–'

One of the traitors pivoted, and put a bolt right through the locutor-skull. The reactive core blew as it passed through the machinery at the servo-skull's back. Bone and metal burst like a grenade, peppering the armsmen. A combat visor shattered and one man cried out, blood streaming from a ruined eye.

I can wait no longer, she signed in battlemark, directly at the remaining men. *Provide cover.*

The men intensified their fire, and she ran down a tunnel of laser light. By the grace of the Emperor, bolts skidded off her armour, none penetrating, to explode on the ceiling and walls. She couched her greatsword at waist height, like a lance.

More gunfire sounded as Torunda's Sisters attacked the enemy from the rear. Two of the Word Bearers turned about to face the new foe. The bolters the null maidens carried were of a much smaller calibre than those of the Space Marines, and struggled to penetrate Astartes battleplate, but one of the giants went down under concentrated fire from the squad, only wounded, but out of the fight.

The warrior she charged fired. She saw it happen in the crawl-time of combat, the crack and the flash in the barrel as the primary charge ignited, an explosion of flames from the muzzle vents as the bolt exited the weapon, the hiss of the short-burn rocket motor as it accelerated towards its target, towards her. Something that happened in fractions of a second seen in clear stages. But though she saw, her percipience granted her no extra speed, and when she leaned to the side, it was not far enough. The bolt cracked Torunda's rerebrace, the explosion bruising the flesh beneath. It hurt, yet spoiled her charge but little, and she crashed into the warrior.

Her opponent was huge. The size of Space Marines never failed to leave an impression on her.

Her greatsword scraped along his torso with frantic explosions of disruption lightning as the field gouged a line in the ceramite. The Space Marine backhanded her with his left hand, sending her crashing back, her neck whipped round so hard muscles tore and her vision danced. He levelled his gun, but never fired, as the tip of another sword emerged from his breastplate, ancient black blood cooking off in its power field. The warrior toppled, his hearts destroyed, showing one of her Vigilator Sisters, who stood for a second in triumph before bolts hammered into her from her shoulder to her hip, pushing her sideways, folding her in half, then blasting her to pieces. Torunda staggered up. The corridor was a confusion of groups; friend and foe meeting and overlapping.

Something swift moved through the smoke. Skinless hunting cats, they appeared to be, nightmares in sinew and bone. Ordinarily, such things would shy from the Silent Sisterhood, but these were fearless, pouncing on them, and sinking long, ivory fangs into their necks. They barged through men and women, knocking them over, disembowelling them. She recognised them as khymerae, lesser warp spawn born in the storms of daemon worlds, or so the grimoires in the libraries of the Somnus Citadel told. They were literal nightmares, bad dreams given flesh, and half-real, more resistant to the null fields of her Sisters than other sorts. They flickered in and out of being. Bolts passed through them without harm, as if they were phantoms, though their return attacks were deadly enough.

One saw her, coiled, and sprang.

Torunda braced herself to meet its attack. Her sword was knocked wide, so she released it and grabbed for the creature's neck, her fingers burying themselves in the slippery meat of its exposed muscles. It was heavy, and her elbow buckled, and she was pressed back, its naked skull snapping at her.

Torunda drew upon her nature as a soulless pariah, and the creature's savage growls turned to whimpers. They were resistant, but not immune. It wrenched back, trying to flee, but Torunda had it fast, her fingers pushed between its muscles, clamped about the workings of its throat. She dug her fingers deeper, and drew out the poison of the warp.

The thing's flickering increased; it thrashed around. Black vapour boiled from it as she obliterated its hateful essence. It gave out one last mewl, and went limp. It had become insubstantial, light as foam, and she heaved it off herself to the ground, its warp-made flesh dissolving before inimical reality.

Her triumph was short-lived. The last of her Sisters died before her, one choked to death in the fist of a Word Bearer, another two shot down from beside.

A whip cracked out of the smoke, licking through the fumes and sending them into agonised curls. It was twenty feet long, a beast-tamer's tool. To use it in that confined space required skill. The tip wrapped around Torunda's wrist, the wielder yanked her off her feet, and she was dragged through the gore and the bodies, as hand over hand the treacherous giant hauled her in.

The newcomer bent down, grabbed her about the throat and hoisted her into the air.

'You killed my pet,' he said, though he seemed more curious than angry.

Torunda gripped his fingers, trying to take some of the pressure off her neck. He turned her a little, and examined her.

'You are a strong one, soulless maiden,' he said. 'But not strong enough. Do you know how many of your kind I have slain?' He gave a strange bark that might have been laughter. 'I thought your days were done. Curious what ancient wrongs the thirteenth primarch stirs back to the surface.' He made another noise, of distaste, choppy and aggressive through his voxmitter. 'By the gods you are abhorrent things. Your presence is like acid on my spirit.' But he did not let her go.

More of the Word Bearers gathered in the corridor. One of them spoke impatiently: a champion in ornate Terminator armour covered with dark blessings.

'Have you finished playing, Hruvak? Is this the place?'

Hruvak looked at his surviving beasts, now prowling around and around, lidless eyes fixed on the corridor wall.

'This is the place, Pridor Vrakon. He is within.'

'Then make me a breach.' The leader waved at his men. 'Quickly. Bring this wall down.'

Melta flasks were brought up and clamped into place. Their triggers were primed, and a rapid beeping emanated from them. The others withdrew to a safe distance, but the one called Hruvak stayed in place.

'Are you going to speak before I crush your neck, little maiden?' Hruvak asked. 'It is your last chance. A final prayer to your pathetic god? Maybe you wish to beg for mercy? Perhaps you might turn. I daresay the Powers could find a use for you.'

The melta bombs detonated, initiating a fusion reaction in the wall that flash-heated the plasteel white and blasted metal vapour down the corridor. The smoke thickened. All Torunda could see were Hruvak's glowing eye-lenses.

She shook her head.

'Suit yourself,' Hruvak said, and squeezed.

The last thing she heard was her neck breaking.

Gavimor was awoken by a tremendous impact and a cacophony of screams. Something had hold of the ship, lifting its stern up with such violence that it overwhelmed the vessel's artificial gravity. It turned over, and the tithed were flung down in their chains to dangle over the sudden drop. Shrieks followed as bones broke in unforgiving manacles. Gavimor swung out. A wave of effluvia sloshed from the slop tanks, drenching him in shit. The ship wallowed. The tithed screamed again. There was a deafening roar from somewhere, then the unmistakeable, horrible sensation of transition from the warp. Even through the psy-wards that blunted their abilities, the tithed felt it, like claws raked through the stuff of their souls. Lumens burst. The ship yawed violently, then either whatever had hold of it let go, or the gravity plates reasserted their influence, and the world returned to its usual orientation. Gavimor hit the deck hard, his head leading the way to new and painful sensations.

He rolled over, and got into a crouch. His scalp was bleeding into the filth caking his hair, and he struggled to wipe the stinging mix of blood and waste from his eyes. The injured cried in the dark.

Alarms blared from every quarter, dull through the hold walls but urgent nonetheless. There was a sensation of undirected movement in his innards that lasted for ten minutes or so. The ship shook again, this time from multiple small impacts. He helped Evee up and checked her over. She didn't seem to be hurt.

'What's that?' she said. She was terrified.

'Someone is firing at the ship,' he said. Something large hit the hull; their captors wouldn't have had time to raise their void shields. He suspected they were dead in space. There was another explosion. The ship trembled. The surviving lumens blinked off then on again.

Another series of impacts, lighter this time, then a series of three closely spaced booms of metal on metal. Strange noises clunked through the ship's structure. Then there was quiet. The tithed waited in tense silence. After a little while weapons fire came, and grew louder.

'That's inside. They're inside,' he said.

'Has someone come to rescue you?' Evee asked, wide-eyed.

Gavimor almost laughed. 'I'm not that important. Nobody's that important.'

Through the thick hold walls, they heard the banging of guns and unholy shrieks. More explosions sounded, closer now, and closer. He waited for the crushing weight of the psy-dampers to be lifted, but the attackers were too wise to unleash the abilities of the ship's cargo. The gunfire reached a climax, then died back. Gavimor waited; everyone held their breath, letting it out in a shriek when the wall glowed with white heat and burst inwards, flinging gobbets of molten metal into the hold. Dozens were killed by the detonation. Dozens more suffered horrific injuries. The catatonic woman died, her skin peppered with burns glinting silver. The sullen man's face was smashed in by a gobbet of metal that lodged in his skull, where it cooked his brains as it cooled.

One of the ship's unspeaking wardens was flung through the smoking hole. She hit the wall hard, her black armour crumpled,

and she fell dead to the deck. With eyes streaming from the
metal vapour and the spilled effluvia, Gavimor glimpsed other
armoured figures moving in the corridor outside, huge and
imposing, the silhouettes of their battle gear unmistakeable.

'The Adeptus Astartes!' he said. 'The Angels of Death!'

But what came through the breach was no loyal servant of
the Emperor.

A Space Marine in crimson armour entered, careless of where
he stepped, crushing the dead and living alike. Ribcages burst,
skulls were pulped. Blood and fluids poured into the cesspool
beneath the deck.

He resembled the holy warriors of the Emperor only superfi-
cially. A pair of horns curved up from his helmet. The edgings
of his armour plates were chased with bronze and fashioned
into small spikes and half-wheels of arrows. The massive, blocky
boltgun he bore was decorated with a row of spikes upon the
back, and a screaming daemon's face framed the muzzle. Part of
a tattooed human hide flapped between his legs as a tabard, the
leather from the arms left intact and dangling. The words upon
the skin were mirrored on his armour plates, an angular form
of writing that appeared to writhe when looked upon directly.

The warrior crushed a bloody road through the hold, until he
reached the narrow aisle between the captives that gave their
gaolers access to the cargo. As he moved away from Gavimor,
he drew a long, serrated blade and looked from side to side,
stopping every few paces to lean down and end some unfortunate's life with a flash of steel. The tithed drew back from him
as far as they could, eyes downcast, desperate not to attract
his attention.

Another followed, and went to the other end of the hold. He
too killed a few as he went, seemingly for no reason other than
sport, and the coppery, abattoir reek of human blood mingled
with the scent of sewage and burned plasteel.

When the Space Marines were at opposite ends of the hold, covering the human contents with their guns, something else entered.

Gavimor felt its approach through the dulling effect of the psy-baffles as a sense of dread. Then a thing that looked alive, but which Gavimor instinctively knew was not, paused on the lip of the breach and huffed deep breaths. It was a huge beast, like a great cat, but wet, skinless, its musculature exposed. A pair of tentacles danced over its back. Multiple eyes stared out from the bare red bone of its skull. There was a silver ring drilled through the back of the skull, and another Space Marine bent to this to clip a leash of chain in place, then wrapped the other end of the leash about his hand. His armour was heavily decorated, several plates covered in brazen reliefs depicting hunting scenes. He looked up and down the cowering cargo a moment, then reached up, and with one hand removed his helmet, revealing a bronzed face covered with script.

He handed his helm to another warrior.

'Down, Atraxiabus,' he said to the beast. 'Seek.'

Gavimor's dread grew. The beast growled before it came down into the hold's reek, padding over bodies and broken metal. Where it encountered the hex-chains, it paused, sniffed with caution. When it stood upon them, it skittered back, causing its handler to yank on its leash.

'Steady, Atraxiabus,' he said. The warrior kicked aside the chains to clear the way for his pet. 'By the Powers, the stench in here,' he said. He looked around him, the dimness of the hold seemingly no barrier to his sight. 'Seek!' he said again, yanking once more upon the beast's chain to reinforce his command.

The feline-thing snuffled its way along the rows of the tithed. It stopped occasionally to investigate more closely. Bloodied drool leaked from its mouth to drip on whimpering captives. It nuzzled and scratched at weeping people, then abandoned them, padding closer and closer to Gavimor, heading unerr-ingly towards the Seer, he was sure. Gavimor's heart pounded. His body screamed at him to flee, but there was nowhere to go, and he was bound fast by the hex-chains.

'He is coming, he is coming, he is coming, he is coming,' the Seer chanted quietly. He'd probably been chanting it the whole time. Gavimor wished he would be silent. He quailed, but could not stop watching. Evee put her hands on his shoulders, look-ing for comfort. For once, he did not scold her.

The beast reached the Seer. It growled, long teeth flashing in its lipless mouth.

'Is this of interest to you, Atraxiabus?' asked the warrior. 'It is certainly noisy enough.'

The beast shuddered at the speaking of its name, and mewled.

'He is coming, he is coming, he is coming, he is coming,' the Seer muttered, oblivious to the nightmare creature staring at him.

The beast went stock-still.

'He is coming, he is coming, he is coming, he is coming...'

In a blur of movement, the monster struck, opening its mouth wide enough to engulf the Seer's head, and clamped sabred teeth around his neck. The Seer's hands went up, spread wide, a polite gesture of surprise. The monster shook its head. Bones cracked. Its teeth sawed at the man's flesh, tearing it to ribbons. Blood sprayed. With the wet pop of parting vertebrae, the crea-ture took the Seer's head off. The raised hands twitched. Blood pumped in a red fountain from his ruined neck. The beast thrashed about, working its jaws around the head, until with a single, powerful bite it clamped them shut, cracking the skull. It devoured it there and then. The noise alone made Gavimor want to vomit.

The body fell.

'Not that much interest. Was that it, Atraxiabus? You sought only a meal, did you?' He tutted disappointedly. 'Come now, concentrate. Seek the spoor. I command you.'

The monster gave its handler a look full of animal hatred, but crouched low. Bits of grey-pink matter ran in its slobber.

'Seek!'

Slowly, slowly, it turned, and looked Gavimor straight in the eye. The tentacles sprouting from its shoulders ceased waving and pointed directly at him.

'That one?' the Space Marine said.

Atraxiabus growled.

Evee let go, and moved back as far as her chains would allow her.

The Space Marine adjusted his grip on the beast's leash, taking the slack out of its chain, though the creature moved not a single one of its exposed muscles, but stared at Gavimor with an intensity that hurt his soul.

The beast's eternal glare was broken by the arrival of another lord, this one even bigger. He stepped through the breach in the hold wall, his armoured suit so large that he towered over the beast handler and the two sentries.

'Hruvak, has your creature found Lord Phaeron's prize?'

Hruvak snorted. 'If you call this a prize, then yes, found it we have, Apostle Vrakon. This is what the sorcerer wanted. Atraxiabus is never wrong. She always finds her prey.' He stepped back to allow Vrakon to approach Gavimor. The skinless creature growled, and slunk back a few steps, though its alien eyes remained fixed on Gavimor.

The tithed witches around Gavimor moved away, leaving him exposed. Vrakon bent down, gripped Gavimor's face and turned it side to side.

'He does not seem like much,' said Vrakon. 'To your feet.' His voice was parchment dry, yet commanding. Somehow, Gavimor found enough courage to respond.

'I cannot,' he said. He held up his chains to show them.

'I see. Hold them higher,' Vrakon said.

Trembling, Gavimor did as he was bidden, lifting up the lengths of chain binding his wrists together until they were over his head, and his back ached, and the connecting chain pulled painfully at his ankles. Vrakon drew a sword almost as long as Gavimor was tall, and thumbed a switch near the hilt. Lightning flickered down its length, and ozone bit at Gavimor's nostrils.

'Higher!'

Gavimor lifted up the chains. The muscles in his wasted back screamed, but he held them taut, and turned his head aside.

Vrakon hooked the blade under the chains. Even before he looped the chain tight and cut backwards, the metal was beginning to fritter away. The chains parted. Loose links bounced free. Gavimor pulled the chains through the staples on the manacles, freeing his ankles, and dropped them on the floor.

'Now rise,' said the Apostle.

Legs trembling, Gavimor stood for the first time in months. Muscles unused to movement burned with effort. His back popped, he had been sat hunched for so long.

'This beast,' Vrakon said. 'Do you know what it is?' He gestured at the creature. It growled again.

Gavimor shook his head.

'Speak. You have a voice. Use it,' said Hruvak. 'You stand before the servants of the gods. The one who addresses you is no less than a Dark Apostle.'

'So,' said Vrakon. 'Do you know what it is? I will not ask again.'

'No, my lord,' said Gavimor.

Once, years before, he had encountered high, off-world officials of the Adeptus Administratum who were conducting a tour of the sector. When his world had been visited, his father's processing plants had been chosen as model examples of local industry. The whole family had turned out, on pain of disinheritance. He had been very young, and the men and women and their bodyguards had filled him with terror. They were the embodiment of power. They could have ended his life with a word, they could have destroyed his family, burned his town, extinguished all life on his world. These things had been impressed on him by his aunts and grandmother before the meeting, and he knew in his child's heart they had been as frightened as him. Memories of the adepts had given him sleepless nights for years afterwards.

The Space Marines were far more terrible.

'It is a khymera, a creature of the empyrean,' Vrakon said. 'Formed from the nightmares of the living. They occur only in the most holy of places, upon worlds where daemons walk freely. To see one and live is a great privilege.' He looked back at the huntsman. 'Is that not so, Hruvak?'

'It is so, Apostle,' said the huntsman.

'You look upon a creature who has run at the feet of the lords of the warp,' Vrakon said. 'Do you not feel blessed?'

Gavimor stared mutely back. His mind was blank of anything but terror.

'They are used by ignorant xenos as beasts of war, to tear apart the bodies of their foes, whereafter, like a nightmare, they will fade from view,' Hruvak said. 'We are not ignorant xenos. We are the exalted of mankind, the most perfect of all creatures to have been made in this galaxy. We are the chosen of the gods, and so these things can be induced to serve us. They make peerless trackers, if properly bound. This one has found you. Do you know why?'

Realising that his life depended on the whim of these beings, Gavimor once again managed to speak.

'No, my lord, I do not.'

'We are looking for something,' Vrakon said. 'Our master

is troubled by visions. He would have an answer. We need
someone who can see them better than I. Tell me, have you
witnessed a burning figure, the temples of the Word cast down?'

Gavimor shook his head.

Vrakon raised a hand, one finger outstretched, and pointed
at Gavimor. 'Then it is not him,' said the Apostle.

'It is him,' said Hruvak. 'My khymerae are infallible. Atraxiabus led us to him. This is the one. Atraxiabus does not see the way
we see. Unless the sorcerer was wrong, and provided the wrong
spoor,' he added. 'But the beast is not. If he is not the one, then
Tenebrus can explain why to Kor Phaeron. It is no business of ours.
We have done as required. Now what of the rest?' the huntsman
asked. 'They would make worthy sacrifices to the pantheon.'

'Once, perhaps. Before the Rift, this hold of woe would have
been a prize. Bright morsels to offer to the gods.' Vrakon shook
his head. 'No longer. The galaxy of late is full of their kind.
Souls like theirs are common currency. I care not for their fate,
Hruvak. Feed them to your beasts, if you will.'

'They will thank you for the feast,' said Hruvak.

Motors grinding, Vrakon turned abruptly around, his tread
shaking the deck as he made his way back out.

One of the sentries came to Gavimor and grabbed his arm,
dragging him painfully through the hold to the breach. He
managed a final glance at Evee's terrified face, before he was
hauled out into the corridor. Dead Imperial servants lay about,
dismembered by boltgun shots, their weapons in lifeless hands.
The dark armour of null maidens shone with blood. There
was another of the khymerae in the corridor. A sharp whistle
summoned it into the hold.

There was a roar, and the screaming started.

'Thank you, my lord,' Gavimor called at the Apostle, certain he should say something. Vrakon either did not hear or
did not care.

'You are right to thank him, though you will suffer more than the wretches you leave behind,' his guard said. 'But be thankful. Your pain will be gratefully received. You serve the pantheon now. There is no greater honour than that.'

Chapter Nine

HETIDOR

STRATEGIUM

GUILLIMAN'S COMMAND

'You look like shit,' said Sergeant Hetidor.

The Catachan leaned on the doorway to Fabian's quarters, his bulk filling it. He was a striking-looking man to Fabian, who was used to grey, prematurely aged people. Hetidor was the exact opposite: dark-skinned, so vital he seemed to vibrate with life. His biceps were as big as Fabian's head. Fabian had heard that other Militarum regiments sometimes referred to the death-worlders as 'baby ogryns', to explosive results if the Catachans heard. They weren't mutants, exactly – their over-muscled bulk was the result of the human form adapting to the high gravity of their home – but they did look different, and in a polity like the Imperium, difference led all too often to mistrust, and to scorn.

Fabian thought people were stupid. You would have to be insane to pick a fight with the likes of Hetidor, orthodoxy be damned.

'Too much bitter rum. And kazeq. And beer. I think there

was some hot wine as well.' Fabian pushed a neatly folded suit of clothes into his holdall, but it wouldn't fit, so he forced it until it did, and winced at the effect on his head.

'That's my boy,' said Hetidor. 'You're finally a man then. I won't say it was a pleasure teaching you, but I have a sense of achievement at what we did together.'

'Thanks,' said Fabian feebly.

'When you came to me,' Hetidor continued, 'you were a pasty-faced, overweight, overprivileged Terran hive weakling. Now you've got at least a twenty per cent chance of surviving a fair fight. I'm impressed.'

'I've been meaning to ask. Are they all as charming as you on Catachan or did you get some sort of special schooling?'

Hetidor's eyes glinted with wicked humour. 'The jungle's the best education you'll get, Terran. It's a shame you didn't experience it. On the other hand, maybe it's best you didn't. You'd've been carnosaur feed back home. But at least you can shoot straight now.'

Fabian nodded, which did little for his hangover. 'I suppose I have you to thank for that.' He finished stuffing his bag, and did up the clasps.

'It's not just me. I'll admit there's some talent in you. Grudgingly admit.'

Fabian reached out his hand. 'I'd be dead if it weren't for you.'

'And the primarch, and that Space Marine that's always stepping on your shadow.'

'Are you ever serious?' asked Fabian.

'Life's too damn short.' Hetidor did not take Fabian's hand, but instead unclipped the cover of a canteen hanging off his belt and drew it out. 'Have a slug of this. Catachan tradition, before we part.' He slapped it into Fabian's hand.

'Really?' said Fabian, suspecting another prank. Hetidor was a complex man, driven, dedicated to perfection, but prone to actions that were often juvenile. This was a characteristic of Hetidor's people, Fabian gathered, and he put it down to surviving a world that was bent on killing them from the moment they were born. Every moment alive was greeted with cynical joy.

'Really. Sort of. Just drink it.'

Not taking his eyes from Hetidor's studiously neutral face, Fabian pulled off the cap and took a mouthful of the liquid inside. He pulled a face to cover the burn in his gullet. It didn't work, and he began to cough.

'What is this?' he gasped. 'I thought you said I'd feel better.'

Hetidor laughed. 'Maybe I was exaggerating a bit. Don't you feel better?'

His head buzzed. 'I feel like I'm getting drunk again.'

'Then you feel better,' said Hetidor. He clasped Fabian's shoulder in his enormous, meaty hand. 'Stay safe, historitor.'

'You too, sergeant.'

Heavy, armoured footsteps approached. Brother-Sergeant Lucerne of the Unnumbered Sons of Dorn was coming.

'Well met, Fabian, Sergeant Hetidor,' boomed Lucerne.

'Here already, Racej?' said Fabian wearily.

'The chronograph on your quarters' walls speaks the truth, all the time, you have only to look at it,' said Lucerne.

Fabian squinted blearily at the clock.

'I find time getting away from me today, my friend.'

Hetidor could not match Fabian's familiarity with Lucerne. At the Space Marine's arrival Hetidor went instantly rigid and threw a perfect salute. Fabian's two mentors had encountered each other many times, but their conversation rarely progressed beyond formal greetings, which puzzled Fabian. Lucerne and Hetidor were similar in many respects. Both pursued their duty with utter dedication, and both also made light to better endure the horrors of what they must face. Fabian thought that they should get on famously, if only Hetidor would look past his awe and see Racej Lucerne for a man, and not as an Angel. But he could not. Hetidor was superstitious, a jarring character trait in one so bluff.

Lucerne's scent was strange. His bulk, especially when armoured, was overwhelming. Even after all this time, Lucerne frightened him on some level, but he overcame it. When he was with Lucerne, Fabian did not think himself in the Emperor's presence. Hetidor did.

'Are you not ready then, Fabian?'

Fabian shook his head. 'I am. I have packed all I need.'

'You do not look ready. You look... ill.'

'Overconsumption,' said Fabian tiredly.

Hetidor spoke. 'Permission to be at ease, my lord.'

'Granted,' said Lucerne.

Hetidor took something else from his belt and pressed it into Fabian's hand, serious of a sudden. 'Take these before you see the primarch. You don't want to embarrass yourself.'

'Antitox? You take these? You don't suck the juice out of a snake or something?'

'We're not savages, historitor.' Hetidor saluted Lucerne, gave Fabian a nod and left.

'A curious man,' said Lucerne.

'You frighten him,' said Fabian.

'I mean him no harm,' said Lucerne.

'I didn't mean like that. He's in awe of you.'

'I see,' said Lucerne. 'There are certain misconceptions about we Space Marines and our relationship with the Emperor.' Lucerne paused. 'I am glad you see past these things and are not scared by me.'

'I'm not scared of you, but I am scared of everything else. He's not scared of anything but you, so he's got that over me.' Fabian examined the antitox Hetidor had given him, a small metal tin with a pharmacological marker.

'Are you going to take those?'

'I am,' said Fabian. He popped off the lid, tipped out a couple of tablets and crunched them between his teeth. He pulled a face. 'I'm sure they make these taste like dung just to punish you.'

'Are you ready? Lord Guilliman should not be kept waiting.'

Fabian grimaced. The bitter taste of the antitox coated his mouth back to front. 'If I can keep these down, I will be. Let's go.'

'What about your bag?'

Fabian looked down at his baggage, a single holdall. 'I've summoned Resilisu to take it.'

'You should take it now. It will save time.'

'I know, but he should be there, when we go. This is our last chance to say goodbye.'

'You have not made your farewells?'

'No,' said Fabian.

'Well, you should. And do it properly.'

'Why do you think I want him to take the bag down to the ship?' said Fabian, a little exasperated.

The historitor took one last look around his cramped quarters, the little cot set into the wall, the sink with its tin-flavoured water, the inadequate wardrobe. Without realising it, he had somehow managed to spend four years of his life in there.

He stepped away without a backward glance, and sealed the door. Doubtless there'd be a similar cell awaiting him where he went next.

'Where are we meeting him? His scriptorium?'

Lucerne smiled apologetically. 'The strategium.'

'Typical,' said Fabian. He rubbed his sore head. 'I really would have preferred the quiet of the primarch's library today.'

It could have been Fabian's hangover, but he was sure the strategium was noisier than usual. There were men and women from all over Fleet Primus. He saw multiple battle group badges, and uniforms from other crusade fleets scattered throughout the crowd. This was besides the usual coterie of fleet-unaffiliated officers from every branch of the Imperium's military forces.

The strategium was a huge space hollowed out of the super-structure behind the *Dawn of Fire*'s command deck. The ship's original strategic facilities had been insufficient to run an under-taking the size of the Indomitus Crusade, and a large part of its command spires had been given over to the purpose when it was refitted to be the flagship. There were whole decks full of cogitation systems, and the craft's astropathic choir was second to none. Despite all the resources at the primarch's fingertips, it mystified Fabian how Guilliman managed to coordinate the war. It was too big for him to fully comprehend, and sometimes he had a fear, and he thought it a rational one, that the whole thing was a headless monster, blundering across the stars with only the appearance of direction.

Guilliman conferred with four of his groupmasters on a grav-stage above the gargantuan hololithic display pit. Fabian felt the familiar thrill of terror at their coming meeting.

'Emperor alive,' Fabian blasphemed quietly. Lucerne presented their credentials to a Custodian. In front of the Emperor's guard, Fabian had more sympathy for Hetidor's reaction to Lucerne. He managed to control his animal fear of the Astartes, but the Custodians were another matter.

'Wait here, the lord regent is busy,' said the Custodian. Dozens of names coiled around a scroll worked into the decoration of his armour. Fabian dared not pick one to address him by. He invariably chose badly.

'Thank you, my lord,' he said.

Fabian and Lucerne stepped off out of the way into an alcove at the side of the pit. The immense three-storey display domi-nated the strategium. Currently, it was occupied by a view of

the galaxy in full three-dimensional representation. Billions
of stars turned the air milky. Fleet Primus' position at Elysia
was marked by red arrows that faded into pale ghosts as they
stretched back towards Terra, describing the route it had come.
The other fleets were similarly depicted, as far as was possible,
their various battle groups splitting and recombining as the
effort to stabilise Imperium Sanctus continued. Enemy movements were depicted in their own hues. All manner of threats
were shown. A giant cloud of bright green where orks flooded
the cosmos. Dark green where necrons rose, most concentrated
at the fiercely contested borders of the Pariah Nexus. Dark gold
arrows showed the advances of Chaos hordes; purple tendrils
where tyranid hive fleets hunted for prey. Cutting it all neatly
in two was the shifting wall of the Great Rift, displayed in mot-
tled reds, its shoals reaching out to other rips in reality that
had proliferated and expanded since the day that Cadia died.
Thousands upon thousands of icons marking active warzones
overlaid all this, too many for Fabian to take in. It was completely overwhelming.

'You could follow the whole crusade from here,' said Lucerne,
inspecting it with a strategos' eye.

'I really couldn't,' said Fabian. His hangover had been reduced
to a faint ache by Hetidor's pills, but now his head swam for
reasons of sensory overload. 'You might be able to.'

'Only with great difficulty,' admitted Lucerne. 'It is beyond
any one mind to process well, except Lord Guilliman's.'

Lucerne spoke the truth. There were hundreds of adepts
whose only role was to update the immense amounts of data
constantly coming in to the *Dawn of Fire*. They occupied cel-
lular booths higher up the walls like bees in a hive, their efforts
multiplied by choirs of brain-butchered servitors and the decks
of machines that worked away, night and day, beneath the strategium. Every three minutes, the display was updated, rippling

with data-inload, the galaxy taking on a new form that differed from the preceding image only in tiny but crucial details. The noise was great. Although every person in that room did their work quietly, there were so many of them their whispers built one upon the other until the strategium hissed and shushed like a sea.

Fabian looked at that gargantuan light weave of the galaxy, and tried to guess where he might be sent. He could not. There were a great many unappealing choices.

Guilliman finished his consultation with the groupmasters. They trooped off. When the grav-stage was empty, Guilliman went to the controls and disengaged it from its docking bay, and piloted it down through the holo of the galaxy to the level where Fabian and Lucerne were waiting. Stars played over him as he approached. They went forward to the docking bay, and there Lucerne got down on one knee and bowed his head. Fabian opted for a salute.

'My apologies for the delay, historitor majoris, Brother-Sergeant Lucerne,' said the primarch. 'As you can see, I am a little occupied at the moment.'

'You have my apologies, my lord,' said Fabian. 'I am taking you from your work for reasons that are not very important. If you would give me my orders, I'll be on my way.'

'Nonsense, Fabian,' said Guilliman. 'Your work will always be meaningful, and so I have made a little time for you. Besides, I wanted to say goodbye. Come aboard. Let us go somewhere quieter.'

Fabian and Lucerne got onto the grav-stage. Guilliman, huge over the controls, guided it back up through the holo-lith, passing the clamp where it was originally docked, and up to the top of the circular chamber. Guilliman piloted the machine to a halt by a jetty backed by a door. Mechanical arms reached out to guide the stage in. Once the stage was locked in place, Guilliman stepped off. Fabian and Lucerne followed. The door opened before them, keyed open by Guilliman's armour signum, and they went into a small conference room.

'My little refuge from the tumult below,' Guilliman said. The room had a table and chairs suited to varying human statures. Guilliman's was obvious as the largest, reinforced to take the weight of the Armour of Fate. 'Though I can spare you my attention, I am afraid I must be brief,' he said, taking his throne and gesturing to others where Fabian and Lucerne might sit. He began their business immediately. 'Fabian, you have been a fine servant, and I am grateful for the work you have done for me. It sorrows me that you are to depart Battle Group Alpharis, but the Logos Historica Verita is well established here, and you and the other members of the Founding Four have a great deal of experience I would see applied elsewhere. Some of the other crusade fleets are not so well provided. Other Adepta have co-opted the functions I intended the Logos to fulfil, and they are not always so amenable to my wishes.'

Though he did not openly name them, the primarch was speaking of the Inquisition, and various sub-departmento of the huge Adeptus Administratum, both of which had proven resistant to the Logos' activities.

'So,' Guilliman went on. 'Wherever you go, I wish you to assess the status of Logos operations. Where they are inade-quate they are to be reorganised, where they are non-existent, they are to be established. You will continue your other duties of chronicling the present war, unearthing the past, and pro-viding me with all other forms of intelligence.'

'Then you are not sending me to the Pariah Nexus?' he asked, for that was the place that he feared the most to go.

Guilliman gave him a curious look. 'No. I am not. Did you think so? Why would you say that?'

When asked, Fabian realised he didn't know. The thought

had just occurred to him, so he stammered out the first thing that came into his mind.

'I wondered. I expected some dangerous assignment of sensitive nature, or else you would have told me what I was to do earlier.' He was also afraid he had failed somehow, and was to be quietly sidelined with a distant or perilous posting. He did not say so. He was sure Guilliman could read it on his face.

'The Pariah Nexus is well covered by members of the Logos, as Battle Group Kallides is of Fleet Primus, and took a full complement. You trained Appointed Historitor Smigh well. Reports come in regularly, when they can reach unstilled space to use their astropaths.' Guilliman was still looking at him strangely.

'Smigh is a little florid, but thorough,' said Fabian grudgingly. 'Could I ask where are you sending me then, my lord? And why haven't you told me yet? I'm just curious, you understand, because you did tell the others.'

Guilliman spoke without pausing to think. The primarch's mind ran at far higher speed and capacity than a standard human's, but there was something to his words, the tone, perhaps, that Fabian thought sounded considered; as if he had formulated them carefully beforehand. Another man might not have seen this, but he had spent more time in the primarch's company than most.

'I had not decided, that is why,' said Guilliman. 'You are a troublesome man, Fabian, in many ways. But you are also that little sharper than the rest. I do not place such useful servants of the Emperor hastily. It took me some time to decide where you might be of best use.'

'Which is where, my lord?' prompted Fabian.

'You are impatient today, historitor. Very well, I too am pressed for time. First, you are to be sent into the Segmentum Solar. A conflagration has begun there, rebellions, motivated by the false prophets of the enemy and facilitated, I am sorry to say, by the dire situation many worlds even so close to Terra find themselves in. You are to accompany a torchbearer mission to reinforce a crusade of Black Templars who have recently come to our attention. Lucerne is to convey Cawl's Gift to them, and you will be accompanied by fifty of the Unnumbered Sons of Dorn to provide immediate reinforcements.' Guilliman looked to Lucerne.

'They have been chosen, my lord,' said Lucerne. 'All the most devout, the greatest believers.'

'I do not agree with this veneration of the Emperor by the Adeptus Astartes,' said Guilliman, 'but it is important that the Black Templars are fully integrated with the Primaris programme, so I trust that you have taken the most suitable for the Chapter's temperament.'

'Wait, you knew where we were going?' Fabian asked Lucerne.

'I did,' said Lucerne.

'Then why didn't you tell me?'

'It was not my place to do so,' said the Son of Dorn.

'Oh,' said Fabian, nonplussed.

'At this moment, battle groups of Fleet Tertius, Fleet Quartus, Fleet Quintus and Fleet Sextus are embroiled with forces of the Word Bearers Traitor Legion throughout an arc of space from the galactic north-east of the Segmentum Solar to the galactic south-west, with further warzones extending beneath the median galactic plane,' Guilliman went on. 'While there, Fabian, you are to ensure that the historitors have adequate representation within these fleets. You will find small numbers of your order present in all, but I wish you to assess their efforts, restructure them as necessary, and apportion the historitors I am sending with you to each battle group as you see fit. Their mission is especially important because they may find themselves used alongside members of the Adeptus Administratum's Officio Verus. The line between useful propaganda and outright lies is a treacherous one. Members of the Historical Revision Unit are also at play in that part of the galaxy. Whoever you station in these fleets will have their work cut out for them.'

'Will my departure be delayed to give me time to choose them, or have you already chosen them?'

'They have been chosen,' said Guilliman. 'Fifteen, in total. I trust you will approve of my selection.'

'Of course.'

'Yassilli Sulymanya is to be your second.'

'An excellent choice,' said Fabian, pleasantly surprised.

'You will encounter resistance at expanding the Logos mission on some worlds there. You may find it in the fleets as well. I trust that you will overcome it.'

'It's become rather a habit,' said Fabian. 'What are my orders after this little adventure?'

'To the galactic north. You will make a few further stops, with the same objectives, it's all in your briefing.' He pushed a data-slate on the table towards Fabian. The historitor took it, but left it unactivated. 'Thereafter you are to head for the Nach-mund Gauntlet, and pass through to Vigilus.'

'Imperium Nihilus?' said Fabian incredulously.

'You are to work with the Lord Defender of Ultramar, Marneus Calgar, who I have sent to stabilise the situation there. You are to assemble as much information about Imperium Nihilus as possible. This is your primary mission.'

'Not gather histories?'

'You are to give the full appearance of doing so, but your efforts are to be in compiling data on the state of the Impe-rium beyond the Rift.'

'Then I am to be a spy,' said Fabian flatly.

'You are to gather intelligence, Fabian, which has always been part of your role.' Guilliman paused, and gave the historitor a long, earnest look. 'You know full well that my return has not been universally welcomed. At least in Imperium Sanctus we have a reasonable idea of who opposes us. In Nihilus, we do not. As an adept of the Logos, you will not attract attention gathering this information, but that does not mean it will be easy, or without risk. I do not send you lightly into danger, Fabian. Believe me when I say that I thought long and hard about where to station you.'

Guilliman paused. Fabian's expectation of compliments was dashed.

'You are disobedient, headstrong, insolent, and selective when it comes to obeying orders.'

'My lord!'

Guilliman spoke over him. 'All of which are qualities I require in a man who must work on his own,' he said calmly. 'You will be the first historitor to pass into Nihilus, Fabian. This is a vital role. There are full orders on the slate, but I am expecting you to operate on your initiative. You may be supplied with other historitors in time. I have provided my seal so that you may sequester personnel from other Adepta. You may also, at your discretion, establish your own Logos cell. Do as you see fit. Chapter Master Calgar will grant you other resources as required. But for the coming years, you must be prepared to work on your own.'

'Years? On my own?' said Fabian, looking at the dead screen of the slate.

Lucerne looked to Guilliman. The primarch gave a nod.

'Not alone, Fabian. I am to accompany you all the way to safeguard your life.'

'No other of the Logos has been granted the honour of a Space Marine bodyguard,' said Guilliman.

'And I thought you thought I was expendable.' Fabian's joke fell flat.

'Far from it,' said Guilliman. 'Though, sadly, your journey will be unusually perilous.'

'Marvellous.' He took in a deep breath. 'How long will I be there?'

'That I do not know,' said Guilliman. 'At some point, we will have to take the fight to Nihilus. When, I have yet to determine. There is too much to do still in Imperium Sanctus...' He stopped himself. 'That is for another time. You have your orders, historitor. I cannot tell you when we will meet again, but we shall, of that I am certain. I expect to call you to me before I cross the Rift. But make no mistake, that could be years away.'

Fabian stood, clicked his heels together and bowed. Then he hesitated, and held out his hand. Though he remained seated, Guilliman did not hesitate to reciprocate. He extended his own hand, enormous beyond compare in the gauntlet of the Armour of Fate. Fabian could only take the finger, like a newborn grasping at its father. It was the first time he had touched the primarch, and with a thrill of awe and adulation, he realised that he gripped the hand that held the Emperor's Sword, that had touched the Emperor, that had written the books that had laid the foundations for the Imperium. He would never be any closer to his god than that. And although Fabian was lax in his observance, the sentiment was powerful enough to make him stammer.

'I-I... I wanted to say thank you, my lord, for everything. If it was not for you, my life would have been very different. And though I have been in peril, discomfort, terror and often close to death since I entered your service, I would not have it any other way.' He smiled awkwardly. 'You have my sincere apologies if it sometimes appears otherwise.'

'Fabian,' said Guilliman, 'among the many gifts the Emperor gave me was the ability to read men, and I know a good one when I see him.' The lord of the Imperium withdrew his hand. 'Now, if you would excuse us, I must have a brief word with your guardian here.'

Fabian glanced at Lucerne, and back at the primarch. Two colossal, gene-engineered faces stared down at him, and he suddenly felt small and powerless.

'Of course, my lord,' he said, and bowed again. 'I shall await Brother-Sergeant Lucerne outside.'

Chapter Ten

A PRIMARCH'S BURDEN
LOOK AFTER HIM
OTHER ORDERS

When Fabian had gone, Guilliman turned his full attention upon Lucerne. It was difficult to bear the primarch's scrutiny. Lucerne was one of the small proportion of Primaris Space Marines who had emerged from Cawl's hypno-indoctrination with their faith intact. To remain calm in the primarch's presence was thus doubly hard for him. He held Guilliman's gaze as best he could, trying not to think that he was looking into the face of the son of the Emperor, and a man the Adeptus Ministorum had declared divine in his own right.

'Brother-sergeant,' said Guilliman. 'I must discuss the Black Templars with you. You wish to join them, I understand.'

Lucerne nodded. 'It seems appropriate. They are among the few Adeptus Astartes Chapters who worship the Emperor openly.'

'You believe in His divinity, do you not?' Guilliman asked, although he would have known what Lucerne believed.

'Yes, my lord, with all my heart.' Lucerne felt awkward saying this to the regent. Guilliman paid lip service to the Adeptus Ministorum, but he did not believe. To Guilliman, as to most Space Marines, the Emperor was a man, not a god. 'I was training to be a priest when I was taken,' he said, feeling the sudden need to excuse his beliefs. As soon as the words left him, he was as suddenly ashamed; both for his faith, and for needing to justify it.

Guilliman nodded sympathetically. 'I choose you because of your faith, but yours is a task of a temporal nature. You must be careful with the Angevin Crusade. The Black Templars are fanatics, but they are great defenders of the Imperium and form a valuable bridge between the Chapters of the Adeptus Astartes and the Adeptus Ministorum. It is vital that these reinforcements are accepted by them. I cannot have dissenters within the Space Marine Chapters. If they reject the Primaris, it will become known.'

'Why do you have reason to fear they will reject the technology?' said Lucerne. 'I understand your concern, but the Black Templars' marshals have already accepted the Primaris. I understand word has come down from High Marshal Helbrecht, that he has commanded they be inducted into the Chapter, and that the Diet of the Marshals ratified his desires.'

'As our own announcements said. The glorious news was promoted throughout the fleets, and the Primaris presented as a gift from the Emperor. But the truth is not so straightforward,' said Guilliman. 'Not all the marshals are in agreement. The Black Templars are entirely non-compliant with the Codex Astartes. Their numbers are unknown. Their marshals and Chaplains are fiercely independent.'

'What can you tell me of this particular crusade, my lord?'

'Their Marshal Angevin sent oaths of fealty to me personally, but he is dead, and I am suspicious of his successor. They were already sent the Primaris technology, with a torchbearer fleet of the first wave. Their arrival in the same warzone as the Black Templars was logged, contact was made, Angevin acknowledged their presence himself, and he gave his oath. Then they came under attack, and nothing more was heard.'

'Surely it could have been the circumstances of war?'

'All theoreticals are possible,' said Guilliman grimly.

'Then you believe they rejected Cawl's Gift?'

'I believe it could be worse than that.'

'Impossible,' breathed Lucerne.

'Nothing is impossible. The crusade vanished, but reappeared recently. There are several active crusades fighting in the Segmentum Solar at the moment, drawn there by their oaths with the Adeptus Ministorum to protect the cardinal worlds. They were instrumental to the recent victory at Talledus, for example. I received intelligence on the Angevin Crusade from the Logisticarum of Fleet Quintus that says they are much depleted, but the detail that caused me concern was that they have not one Primaris brother among their ranks. Twenty were sent, along with the associated technology and templates for their creation and the forging of their arms, and yet the crusade shows none of this, despite the two groups meeting. Now, it could be accident, as you say, but I ask myself, is it really likely that twenty of your brothers, shepherded as they were by a member of the Adeptus Custodes, would leave no trace in this manner? I want you to take your brothers to reinforce this crusade. Then I want you to find out what happened to the torchbearers sent to them. Here are details.' Lucerne's helm chimed with an inload notification.

'I understand,' said Lucerne gravely. He marvelled that Guilliman could be so involved in this matter, so small in the grand scheme of the war raging from one end of the galaxy to the other, concerning as it did handfuls of warriors when billions fought, or that he had even noticed it.

'That is not all, and I am sorry that I must further add to your burdens.' Guilliman's tone was grave indeed. 'The other matter concerns the nature of the warning we received about the Pariah Nexus. Specifically, how it relates to Fabian, and why you must go with him on his assignment to Nihilus.'

Lucerne frowned. 'It involves him, how?'

'You are not to tell Fabian any of this, do you understand?' said Guilliman. 'Not a word. I know you and he are close. You must swear this to me.'

'Then I swear that I shall say nothing. By the Emperor, I swear.'

Guilliman nodded. 'Then listen. When the Great Rift opened, messages were sent from all over the Imperium pleading for aid. The usual channels on Terra, which I gather were inadequate to cope with the normal level of traffic already, were completely overwhelmed. The Pariah Nexus is one of the greatest warzones in the galaxy, but it took some time for news of it to reach me. It is in fact something of a miracle that it did. That is the crux of this matter.'

'A miracle, you say, but you do not believe in such things.'

'I use the word deliberately,' said Guilliman. 'Thousands of reports arrived, all bearing different information, sent from hundreds of worlds via multiple channels and arriving with different dates, all warning of the rising threat in the Nephilim Sector. There were so many they should have been unmissable, but owing to the poor structures of communication employed within the Adeptus Administratum they could have been lost in the background noise of the war. Indeed, they almost were.'

'But it was not so.'

'It was not so,' agreed Guilliman. 'You will recall that I received a delegation from the Adeptus Administratum some time ago, and that shortly after that Battle Group Kallides was diverted into the Nexus from this fleet, with others sent after.'

'Yes, my lord,' said Lucerne.

'The delegation presented me with messages from several sectors, many hundreds of them, and those only a representative example, that spoke of the same thing – of necrons awakening on scores of worlds, of great xenos fleets emerging from nowhere, of whole systems going dark. They spoke of a stilling of the warp, where no messages could be sent and no fleet might sail, and a strange lethargy that afflicted the populations caught in those zones.'

'Is that surprising?' said Lucerne. 'It is my understanding the necrons have been stirring in that part of the galaxy for some time. The scale of their activities there is impossible to hide. News would have reached you eventually, my lord, and it did.'

'The messages were not surprising, no,' said Guilliman. 'And you are correct in assuming that the threat would have been relayed to me in time. But it got to me earlier than the bureaucracy would otherwise allow, and if it were not for one decision I made, I would have found out about it even sooner, before we left Terra, even.' Guilliman paused. 'Would you find it surprising if you were to learn that virtually all of these messages somehow contrived to be referred to Fabian's desk, and that I did not receive them only because he had been removed to help found the Logos?'

'All of them?' said Lucerne.

'Nearly all of them,' said Guilliman.

'That's uncharacteristically...' Lucerne searched for a tactful word. 'Efficient for the Adeptus Administratum.'

'The odds of it happening all but guarantee impossibility. I have a testimonial from one of Fabian's ex-colleagues about the affair. It was he who delivered them to me, and if it were not for him I perhaps would not have known until it was too late. This man had a long, hard fight to convince his superiors that the delegation be sent. It was against protocol and therefore against great resistance that he came to me. It almost cost him his position, and his life. The Imperial bureaucracy is...' Guilliman's eyes narrowed. He stopped himself going further. 'And now this. Fabian comes in here, and asks if he is to be sent to the Nexus. I find that... curious, and therefore what I must ask of you is all the more important.'

'What is the significance of this?' asked Lucerne, though his voice trembled at the possibilities coursing through his mind.

Guilliman looked at Lucerne earnestly. 'There is a radical theoretical held by some parties that the Emperor is stirring. Psychic incidence is up all across the Imperium. There are saints, multiple reports of the Legion of the Damned, warning visions that save worlds, and many other things of that nature. If it is so, and we take this matter of the Pariah Nexus into account, it could appear that the Emperor has some special purpose for Fabian, otherwise why did all these messages find their way to his desk? And we must ask ourselves, is it only coincidence that Logister Gunthe found and recommended Fabian to me at the very moment these messages were heading to him?'

'The Emperor's plans are not for men to understand, not even His sons,' said Lucerne, bewildered.

'You are more right there than you can possibly know,' said Guilliman. 'I cannot rule out the possibility that Fabian is important somehow. Although once I would have found all of this entirely incredible, I am now too exposed to the bizarre to dismiss this chain of events as coincidence. If there is some current of fate carrying Fabian along, it may be unwise to ignore it, and if it is the Emperor Himself manipulating events...'

Guilliman searched Lucerne's face, and the Space Marine realised that Guilliman was telling him this because he did not have an answer to these strange occurrences, and Lucerne, who had faith, might offer him some insight.

Guilliman, firmly again.

'My lord, I apologise for my ignorance, but if you are even
contemplating that this might be a sign from the Emperor, why
not send us to the Pariah Nexus?'

'Because there are more so-called gods exerting their will upon
the mortal plane than the Emperor, and they are all opposed to
our victory. I myself was targeted by each of the four powers
whilst in Ultramar and on the Terran crusade. Some of their
tricks were subtle enough that I nearly succumbed.' Guilliman
took in a deep and weary breath. 'The Emperor has not spoken,
nor has He moved, for ten thousand years. I saw Him, Lucerne,
and what I can remember of the experience is contradictory and
painful, and although from a certain point of view He and I did
communicate, I do not believe He is capable of acting directly
in this way. The only practical is that these seeming miracles are
nothing of the sort.'

Guilliman left no doubt in Lucerne's mind what he was conveying.

'This is a warning about my faith, my lord.'

'If you choose to see it that way,' said Guilliman, 'then you
are wise. We hope for intervention from greater powers. When
that apparently occurs, we accept it blindly. That is a risk. Hope
is a weakness the Dark Gods are eager to exploit. Fabian represents this.'

'But what if it is your father?' said Lucerne, struggling to keep
his voice level. He had been told of a miracle. Wonder threatened to overcome his discipline.

'Then what do I know?' A little bitterness crept into Guilliman's tone. 'By doing this, I could well be enacting His will,
don't you think? He manipulated us all, my brothers and I, in
the time before. But what if this isn't the Emperor? What if,
and I judge this more likely, Fabian is a pawn in some incom-
prehensible game? Our need for hope blinds us to manipulation

from without. Remember, it is not in the enemy's best interests that the necrons rise, either, especially if what Cawl believes is true about the Nexus. By setting us against the necrons, Abaddon or his masters could remove two threats at once. Therefore, I believe that it is more likely that the warning was the work of the enemy.'

'I understand,' said Lucerne. His face set. 'I also understand what you are not telling me.'

Guilliman paused meaningfully. 'Then you can do it?'

'I would have no choice,' said Lucerne, 'if it were necessary, though it would be done with a heavy heart.'

Guilliman appeared relieved. 'Let us hope it never comes to that. I meant what I said. Fabian is a good man. If this is the work of our foe, he is being used unwittingly. He would never turn on me knowingly. I would rather that you looked after Fabian, sergeant, for I have grown fond of him.'

'I swear I shall do so, as long as there is breath in my body. He is my friend.' Lucerne got up from the chair, and knelt again at the feet of his lord. 'But I also swear, should it transpire that he is a tool of the enemy, that I will kill Fabian Guelphrain without hesitation.'

'I don't like it,' said Fabian. 'This is all very suspicious.' They were heading from the primarch's quarters to the Palatine Hangar that served the spires. They passed hundreds of people all moving with purpose through the corridors, threading in and out of each other's paths like a particularly determined flock of birds.

Lucerne caused these messengers and middling officers to swerve. He was deep in thought, but as Fabian was a naturally garrulous man, always impatient for his turn to speak, he did not notice Lucerne's silence.

'He told the others weeks ago where they were going. Why

aren't I staying with Fleet Primus? Am I expendable, is that it? Or has that damned aeldari witch told him something about me? He's getting rid of me, isn't he?' Fabian looked up at his hulking companion. 'Lucerne, are you listening to a word I'm saying?'

'I hear everything, my friend,' said Lucerne. He plodded like a patient teacher not wishing to outpace his young charge. 'Believe me, the primarch holds you in nothing but the highest regard. He is fond of you. He told me so himself.'

'Right,' said Fabian. 'Then why all this subterfuge? What is it we're really going to do?'

'Is being the first historitor to cross the Great Rift and deliver reports for the primarch's personal attention not enough for you?'

They waited for a large personnel lifter, standing firm in the flood of people that flowed out when the doors opened.

'It should be, shouldn't it?' said Fabian.

'It should,' agreed Lucerne.

'Aren't you going to tell me what a great honour it is? That's what you usually say.'

'No,' said Lucerne. 'You know that already.'

They got into the lifter. It raced down several dozen floors. They were silent while surrounded by so many other ears, only recommencing their conversation when the car came to a spine-compressing halt, and they continued down larger corridors towards the hangar.

'I'm still perplexed.'

'Be grateful with the plans so far revealed, for the–'

'Emperor has a plan for every man, yes yes, I know that one,' said Fabian. He pulled a dissatisfied expression. 'What were you talking about in there, with him?'

'If I could tell you, I would have already,' said Lucerne, and he gave Fabian a smile, though his eyes were sad. 'The Emperor has His plan for me as well.'

Machines trundled by, dragging cargo containers. Huge blast doors opened and shut to a secret rhythm, each whooshing compression of their giant pistons heralded by spinning yellow beacon lights and the angry honks of klaxons. There were Space Marines on patrol in that area, and they saluted Lucerne when they passed him.

They went into the main landing deck of the Palatine Hangar via an armoured postern. It bustled with vigorous activity. Five battle groups of Fleet Primus were moored above Elysia, a world famed for its drop regiments. Thanks to its elite armies, the system had weathered the post-Rift period well, and was fanatically loyal. Supplies flooded into the fleet, while damaged ships were undergoing repairs at the system's orbital complexes. There was a mood of optimism. The Space Wolves had been recontacted and reinforced, shouldering the burden of dealing with the ork threat in that part of the galaxy. After months of shared, brutal warfare against the xenos, it seemed that the orks were sufficiently contained that Guilliman could move on.

Their shuttle was undergoing final flight checks before their departure. It was a small lighter, the kind of thing that Fabian hated flying in. They were slow, unarmoured and unarmed; helpless in every way, but in a system like Elysia where no enemy was in sight, he could tolerate it.

Beside the lighter, clad in a uniform of blue-grey, Fabian's holdall straps clutched in his hands, was Resilisu. He was making a strange attempt to stand to attention, his hips thrust too far forward and shoulders too far back. He hadn't seen them. Fabian placed his hand on the moulded wings of Lucerne's plastron aquila, slowing the giant.

'Would you mind waiting here for a few moments?' asked Fabian. He looked from Resilisu to Lucerne.

'Of course.' The Space Marine stopped, a new obstacle for the deck crews to avoid. 'But we must depart soon. We can spare only a minute or two.'

Resilisu saw them both and his face brightened. Fabian's team of historitors were already aboard the ships that would take them on their voyage, but a couple of aides were loading the lighter with the last of the equipment they would need, and Fabian stepped to the side to get out of their way.

'Master, your bag,' said Resilisu. He held out Fabian's holdall. Fabian almost laughed. He had known Resilisu all his life, and not once had the older man showed the level of deference he did now. But the mirth died in his throat when he noticed the tears brimming in Resilisu's eyes. 'I wish,' he said, stopped, cleared his throat and continued in a stronger voice, 'I wish I was coming with you.'

Fabian took the strap and slung the bag over his shoulder. Resilisu's hand remained out; he didn't know what to do with it, now his last service was discharged.

'You know it's better that you don't,' said Fabian. 'This is going to be a long, dangerous trip.'

'I don't care about that.'

Fabian looked his servant up and down. His uniform had been laundered and pressed, but he still managed to make it scruffy somehow. He had new rank markings on his chest and shoulders, and they were fresh enough to shine, nary a scratch as yet. Fabian smiled. That wouldn't last.

'Well, you shouldn't have made yourself so indispensable to the Logos' tabulae annales, should you? They made you an archivist, I see.'

Resilisu stiffened, but he was proud. 'I'm sorry, master...'

'You don't have to call me master any more.' Fabian put his hand on the old man's shoulder. 'You're a person of consequence in your own right. You've done enough. Your family has served mine for longer than either of us know, but times change.

Let us agree that it is good that they change. The primarch is here. There is a new beginning for all of the Imperium. It is only right that you should experience some benefit yourself.'

Resilisu returned his smile, but his voice wavered. 'What would our forebears say, to see it end like this?'

'There were some wise people among them,' Fabian said. 'I am sure they would say that nothing lasts forever.'

'I am sorry. I promised your father that... I promised that...' Tears spilled freely down Resilisu's face.

Fabian surprised them both by embracing him hard.

'You promised you would serve me as faithfully as you had him, and you also told him you would be as a father to me, and you have. Thank you for everything, my dear friend.'

Unsure at first, Resilisu relaxed, and returned the hug.

'He would have been proud of you,' said Resilisu. 'I am proud of you.'

A klaxon bleated. The aides finished loading the equipment crates. Heavy footsteps approached. A transhuman throat being cleared is a fearsome noise, but Lucerne did it as gently as he could.

'Time to go,' said Lucerne. 'The *Solemnity* and *Interlocutor* are ready to sail. We have to leave now.'

Fabian released Resilisu.

'Goodbye, old man,' he said.

'Do not do anything rash,' said Resilisu.

Fabian laughed through his sorrow. 'It's much too late for that,' he said.

Lucerne guided Fabian into the lighter. He could not look out as the craft prepared to leave, nor as they lifted off, and passed through the atmospheric field and into the crowded anchorages over Elysia.

He looked away to wipe his eyes, and hoped Lucerne did not notice.

'Where are we going first, anyway?' Fabian asked, ten minutes into the flight.

Lucerne was wise to the ways of humanity despite having left his behind. He was checking his armour seals very thoroughly, and was politely paying no attention to Fabian's sadness. 'We're going to the warp nexus at Lessira,' he said, tightening an armouring bolt in his vambrace. 'That's where the suppression fleet is gathering.'

Chapter Eleven

A SMALL SETBACK

LORD TENEBRUS' IRE

THE ARGENT ROD OF CAIUS

'This is a most unwelcome development.'

Tenebrus hunched over a font holding oily black liquid. The font was an exact replica of the one he had possessed on Gathalamor, and while the room that contained it differed from his cathedrum lair on that planet in shape, in essence it was the same: a kingdom of rustling shadows. Dim light illuminated nothing. His skin was a pallid smear. His eyes dangerous glints. The roof seethed with movement where his attendant daemon-servitors crawled about their roosts.

Xyrax had presented Tenebrus with both the quarters and the shades when they had fled before Fleet Primus to the *Paracyte*. Though Xyrax's ship throbbed with all manner of industry, and every wavelength was busy with the work of its extensive augury arrays, in the darksome home of Tenebrus the noise was completely absent. Thanks to sorcery, or perhaps the intervention of the gods themselves, Tenebrus existed in a place apart.

He dabbled at the surface of the liquid with his long fingers.

He scowled at what he saw, though at that moment the liquid appeared as nothing but a glossy black to Tharador Yheng. No one could see into its depths, unless the sorcerer allowed it.

'My lord, if I may, what troubles you?' said Yheng softly. She had learned to be wary of Tenebrus' affable manner. A cruel temper waited beneath.

'It is unfortunate that the Dark Cardinal is aware of the child's existence. My daemons suggested we would have more time to find it ourselves...' He frowned. 'Now we will not catch the prize without others knowing. A shame. Still...' He became thoughtful. 'I will be able to perform a ritual of divination of the appropriate strength. If I am doing it at Kor Phaeron's behest, he will not become suspicious, so every setback has within it the seeds of success, do you not think, Yheng?'

Yheng didn't answer.

'Hmmm?' prompted Tenebrus. Silvered eyes and shining teeth glinted at her. Overhead, the shades whispered.

'Yes, my lord.'

'Do you understand what I am saying, Yheng? Kor Phaeron has strong warpcraft of his own. Any attempt at a ritual of the scale needed to find the truth of these visions would have attracted his attention, and that might have caused problems.' He paused. 'Yes, yes, maybe it is for the best. A situation we can exploit. There will be other interested parties, dangerous interested parties. Perhaps we should let Lord Kor Phaeron, prophet, Dark Cardinal, the Keeper of the Faith, defend us from the attentions of his gods?' He raised a hand up in mock worship. His voice lowered. He sneered. 'I have rarely met anyone who is as pompous as a priest, and Kor Phaeron is the most pompous of them all. He has no power but what the gods bestow. He is a leech, stealing from the achievements of others. Let him enjoy the intrusions of daemon, mortal and god alike on our behalf once the invocation is done. The news will be out, but eyes will be on him, not us. I will perform my duty to him, and in doing so to the Warmaster, and thus serve myself.'

'You are strong and powerful, my lord,' said Yheng. 'You need not bend the knee, master.'

'A flatterer!' scolded Tenebrus, but enjoyed her blandishments just the same. 'You will learn. None of these results are exclusive. Anyone who serves more than one master must learn to aid them all with every action, where they can, while at the same time serving themselves. Is that not so, my acolyte?'

Tenebrus' smile sent a jolt of terror through Yheng. By now she was certain he had guessed that her first master, the Word Bearer Kar-Gatharr, had sent her into Tenebrus' service purposefully, that her original role was one of spy. She could see it in his black eyes.

She had become conflicted. Her loyalty had been to the Word Bearers, at least so far as Kar-Gatharr represented them, but she had not yet revealed herself to Kor Phaeron. She was sure Tenebrus saw all this. In fact, she was increasingly sure it was the only reason she was still alive.

'We must prepare, you and I,' Tenebrus said abruptly. 'You have become potent. You have more than enough skill to aid me in this invocation.'

Yheng stood tall. She did not deny it. Modesty was not a virtue any true follower of the gods should suffer.

'Tell me what I must do, and it shall be done,' she said. 'What sacrifice will we offer?'

'Nine devout slaves, all followers of the Changer. They must be witches.'

'They will be found among your followers.'

'Nine more must be holy men loyal to the corpse-lord of Terra.'

'Those also can be provided from Kor Phaeron's prisoners. And the rest? We will need nine more.'

'Your learning continues apace,' said Tenebrus. 'They should be a mixture. The innocent, and the damned. The mad, and the sane, the deluded, the wise, the willing, the unwilling. Tzeentch is a fickle god. He is apt to find design where none exists. The composition of the final sacrifice is not of great concern, only that it be done, for he will see purpose in whatever we decide, and he will approve. Blood and souls will not be enough. You must bring me...' He thought a moment. 'Fetch the Argent Rod of Caius too, from my treasury. We shall break it, to show the sincerity of our devotion.'

Her eyes widened. The rod was an ancient relic, a marvel of lost technologies, and daemon-haunted besides.

'The value of the rod is incalculable,' she said.

'It is, but poor coin buys bad service. We invoke a great lord of Chaos, not some whimpering, unnamed Neverborn. Royal guests must have royal gifts.'

'Who are we to invoke, my lord?'

Tenebrus grinned slyly.

'We shall speak with one who sees all, and knows all, treacherous though his words may be. After all your studies, you must know of whom I speak.'

'The Fateweaver,' said Yheng quietly.

'Just so,' said Tenebrus with a self-satisfied nod. 'Are you frightened?'

'Yes,' said Yheng, for although she had conjured minor daemons on her own, and had assisted Tenebrus in seeking the aid of greater powers, Kairos Fateweaver was almost a god in his own right, Tzeentch's favoured, a king among daemonkind.

'That is well. Such beings are to be feared, even by the likes of us.'

He turned from the font, flicked the oil from his fingers, then licked them clean. The sight always disgusted Yheng, such sensuous relish he took. She stopped herself looking away.

'We begin preparations immediately. Kor Phaeron cannot be kept waiting, and nor is it in our best interests to delay.'

'No, my lord.'

'He has found us a suitable vessel.' He waved his hand, and Yheng felt a pain in her temple. When it dulled, she found new knowledge there: of a prisoner, a noble, locked deep in the ship, taken as part of the corpse-lord's witch-tithe. His name was Gavimor.

'He is on this ship?'

'Go to him,' said Tenebrus. 'Prepare him for the ritual. He must be purified to receive the Lord of Change. It will be easier for us if he accepts his role. Convince him if you can.'

'I will begin immediately.'

'Good, and fetch me someone to eat on your way out. I am hungry.'

Tenebrus walked over to her, and caressed her cheek with long, vermicular fingers. Yheng shuddered under his touch. His eyes held more than one kind of need, and it revolted her.

'I would rather not consume you, my acolyte,' he purred, 'but I will if you are slow in feeding me. I have a powerful hunger on me, so best be quick about it.'

Chapter Twelve

BLOODY HANDS

THE CHAIN OF CONSPIRACY

THE ROAD TO SRINAGAR

Inquisitor Rostov hunched over on his chair, fingers clawed before his face. He forced them to relax so he could tug on his gloves. After doing so, he clenched his fists, taking solace in the creak of leather, knowing he was somewhat protected from his clairvoyance while his skin was covered. He always wore his gloves when he was not alone. The only time they came off was when he interrogated a subject.

Rostov's witch-curse was of a kind that encouraged caution. Pain opened the doors of another's perception wide to him, but the doors were never closed, not fully. A careless touch, a brush of skin on skin, sometimes that was all that was required for him to see within a person's soul, and seeing always brought pain of one kind or another. A flash of joy taunted him with what he could never have. Another's love highlighted his solitary life. Another's sorrow only added to his own tally. Misery was omnipresent, most of it caused by the Imperium he served, and so much was inflicted by himself. He had to protect himself.

It was better not to know what others kept locked in their skulls, unless the Emperor demanded it. Then the gloves came off, and the knives came out.

He was the Emperor's torturer, red of hand and deed. It was his privilege and his burden.

The questioning was done. His hair was still damp from the pulse-shower. Though he had cleansed himself thoroughly, he could still smell the guts of the subject in his nostrils. He had not dried himself properly, and the clean shirt he had put on was damp, but he had needed to be clothed. He could not bear another moment of the running water. It was too warm, too liquid. Like blood.

The man from Chozteculpo had led them to another world and another man. No doubt the Hand thought his servants shielded from prying eyes. Single-person message chains were hard to unravel. Where many people knew an organisation's secrets, uncovering them was easy. In a need-to-know chain, if one link had the mental strength to resist interrogation, whatever cult or conspiracy they served was safe.

That was the assumption. In truth, a chain was by necessity joined. Each part had to know something, and some parts had to know more than others, and sometimes it did not matter how strong someone was. No one could resist Rostov. The old saw about chains being as strong as their weakest links was a fallacy – every link could be broken, if the right forces were applied.

That last session had been hard. The man – Rostov preferred not to think of his name, piles of screaming meat did not have names – was hardened against physical and psychic assault. He had held out almost to the point of death before agony had forced the locks on his mind and let Rostov in. It amazed him that these traitors would endure so much for the monsters they served. Now he was exhausted. The dead man's pain was now his pain. His nerves tingled unpleasantly with aftershocks of the torture. His own faith and loyalty were polluted by the subject's treachery. After the sessions, Rostov did not know where he began and the subject ended.

There must be a limit to how many times he could do this.

Antoniato was still cleaning the interrogation chamber. The stream of a high-pressure hose drummed faintly against the thick walls. Rostov was in the antechamber alone with his thoughts. His retinue let him be. They were open to him, even now, in his hour of meditation. He had found that familiarity opened the doors almost as well as touch. He could see their thoughts as flashes if they came too close. Cheelche and Lacrante assumed he was digesting the intelligence he had learned and planning his next move. Only Antoniato knew that was not the case, that he brooded on the atrocities he must perform in order to serve the God-Emperor. Only Antoniato knew that the pain haunted him, whether inflicted on innocent or traitor. Only Antoniato knew that these brief periods of respite were necessary not so that he could succeed, but so that he would remain sane.

Antoniato understood, but Rostov was forced to keep him at arm's length. The irony being that Rostov knew Antoniato best, so his mind was most open to him.

Rostov closed his eyes, trying to push out the images of the tormented subject. He shut his conscience to his pleas, to his remembered screams. He took out the little effigy of the Emperor upon the Golden Throne that he wore around his neck, and clasped it in prayer.

'Oh Emperor, who dwells in pain so that I might live, aid me in your service. Make me strong as you are strong, let me endure as you endure, make me righteous as you are righteous.' Under the power of his devotions, the images faded, came back into revolting clarity, faded again, like sand pictures gently inundated by the rising tide, each lap of water revealing the picture as it receded, but blurring the edges with successive advances, until only a swirl of grains, the components of the image, of the horror, were suspended in the liquid.

The only way to leave them behind was to leave himself. He felt his spirit rise a little; not far, just enough that the concerns of life seemed petty and unimportant.

'Oh Emperor, most mighty, most just, oh Emperor who guards the souls of all, who guides with His everlasting light, guard me, guide me. Aid me in my service, so that I may serve you well, and bring low your enemies.'

Rostov could almost see the Emperor when he prayed, upon the Throne of Terra, His golden face perfect in its suffering. He did not know if it was a true vision, or his imagination. Either way, it made the blood worthwhile.

The faint drumming of the hose on the metal walls died away. The door opened. The smell of blood and suffering followed Antoniato out, still strong under the chemical reek of counterseptics.

'My lord,' said Antoniato.

Images of the God-Emperor and of blood vanished. Rostov had a flash, sudden and brilliant, of a warm day, a beach, the ocean sighing pleasantly upon the sand. A child's voice, out of sight.

Another vision, or more imagined comforts?

The vision fled. Blackness followed. He was back fully in the chamber, soul rooted to flesh. The prayer died on Rostov's lips. He could feel Antoniato waiting patiently.

'Yes?' he responded eventually. He did not yet open his eyes.

'I have disposed of the corpse. The room is cleansed.'

'You do your duty well and without complaint,' said Rostov. The statement came out more harshly than he intended. 'Thank you,' he said.

'The shipmaster is requesting orders,' said Antoniato. 'Navigator Throol reports that conditions in the warp are calming.

He suggests we leave soon. There are more storms on the way, and they will delay our passage.'

'Then we must go,' said Rostov. He opened his eyes and his hands. He regarded his talisman a moment, then put it back inside his shirt. He could still smell the ocean, and the scent was stronger than the blood. Most curious.

'It was a successful interrogation, my lord,' said Antoniato. 'He knew a lot, and told you everything in the end, but I must ask, which way first? We have a dozen names. Four systems. The agents of the Hand of Abaddon are widely spread. What are they doing?'

'They are looking for something,' said Rostov.

'What?'

The beach, the waves, the crying child.

'What are they looking for, my lord?'

'Srinagar,' he said suddenly. He made no conscious decision. The name sprang to his lips. 'We will go there,' said Rostov. He put aside his suffering, locking it away behind the iron bars of his will. The beach went with it. He stood.

'May I ask why then, Leonid? There were three other systems named.'

Rostov looked at him. His blue eyes were cold. Antoniato took an involuntary step back.

'I do not know, but the Emperor guides us, and He wishes us to go to Srinagar. Inform Shipmaster DiFerrius and Navigator Throol to make immediate preparations for departure. Rouse our astropaths. I will call in favours from others of the ordos. They will investigate the remaining systems. But we are bound for Srinagar ourselves.'

Antoniato was not convinced. 'It's a little impulsive for you,' he said.

'It is, I suppose,' said Rostov. And it was. He frowned.

'Then how do you know that is where the Emperor wants us to go?'

The weight of the talisman around his neck seemed more present than usual, as if it were a living thing, and listening.

'Faith,' he said. He had no other answer than that.

Chapter Thirteen

A NEW PRISON

RESPITE

SHADOW PEOPLE

They hooded Gavimor and took him out on a small craft. He remained unable to see for a long time. Eventually they landed, and he was marched down corridors full of terrifying scents and sounds, until he was deposited in a room, and the hood was wrenched away by a standard human who Gavimor only saw from the back as he departed. He was alone for the first time in months.

By the light of a single lumen he examined his new surroundings. He was in a small cell made entirely from featureless black metal. A cot occupied one corner, with a mattress pad on it, upon which he sat. The door was set at the top of three steps. There was a suction ablutorial jutting from one wall. He knew little of the great foe of the Imperium beyond rumour and horror stories passed on by word of mouth, but from what he did know, he was surprised at how clean the room was. It seemed... ordinary.

He was on another ship. He recognised the throbbing of

engines and the constant machine noises a void craft makes. These sounds were also produced in ground or orbital facilities, but changes in acceleration and shifts in direction that could be felt in the humours of the body told him they were moving. Besides, there had been none of the sensations of descent down a gravity well. He was well travelled enough to know that.

He was in the hands of monsters, but he had no chains, and the cell was far more pleasant than anything provided by the slavemasters of the Black Ship. The cell seemed enormous after the cramped conditions of the hold, though it was smaller than the least of his wardrobes in his mansion at home.

He sat a long time on the bed, uneasy at the comfort of the mattress, always looking at the door, wondering what his fate would be. Once his exhaustion overpowered him, he slept properly for the first time since his capture. This was at first restful, but descended into a nightmare of shadowy figures with burning red eyes who stood in the corners; crowds of them receding into distances the room lacked the dimensions to contain.

He woke, and the shadows were still there, and they immediately began to move towards him, flickering as if the lumen was failing, though its light remained steady. He cried out, and pressed his hands into his eyes, and curled into a ball.

'Emperor save me!' he cried, and fainted.

When he came to again, the shadows were gone, and he slept some more. When he awoke finally, he saw that a meal had been left on the step.

Captivity aboard the Black Ship had made him feral. He fell upon the tray, snatched up the food, guzzling it with his filthy hands, almost choking, not tasting it, the experience of weeks of battling over scraps overpowering his reason. Only when he finished did he see the silver cutlery, and realised from the flavours lingering in his mouth that the food had been of good quality.

He wept.

After some time he crawled back onto the bed, and fell asleep again. This time, the shadow beings let him be.

Time passed. Days, probably. He could not tell. The light was always on, and there was no change in the ship's machine hum. No real way to gauge the hours except by his hunger, and the regular provision of meals, always delivered when he was asleep. When he slept, sometimes the shadows came, and when they did he enjoyed no moment of peace. He found himself grappling with them in his dreams until he woke. On those occasions they crept out of his sleep and lurked in the shadows at the corner of his cell, always looking at him, waiting for him to slip, exhausted, back into slumber, whereupon they rushed forward and bit at him.

It was real. They were there. He woke with their toothmarks on his body. Only when he focused his mind and willed them away did he repel them. They were not defeated, only driven off a while, but he found then that his hated gift offered some use.

That could be it. He had heard stories, of seers and witches who fended off wicked spirits when the gaze of the Emperor was elsewhere. His gifts were returning slowly. The sense of energy, the vitality borrowed from somewhere else. His thoughts quickened.

Or he could just be going mad. The titter that came out of his mouth at the thought did not help him dismiss that line of reasoning.

Clothes were left for him when the fourth meal came, and though simple and rough compared to his habitual garb, they were blessedly clean, and he eagerly donned them, ignoring the strange sigils embroidered into the cloth. Once he had removed his old clothes he became acutely conscious of how much they stank, and that led him to realise his body was filthy. He was still covered in the effluvia of the slops. His legs were caked with his own waste. Lice crawled about in his body hair, and when he saw them he became miserably aware of their itching bites. He had not noticed before. The arcane devices of the Black Ship had dulled more than his witch-curse.

He felt ashamed. He looked about for some means of washing himself, but there was none. The only water he was given was provided with his meals. The ablutorial had no supply. Feeling disgusted by himself he took up the glass from his next meal, and dashed the contents over his face and hands, although he was terribly thirsty. It removed a little of the dirt, that was all, leaving him feeling filthier than before. Then he knew for sure that his strength was returning, because he was gripped by an all-consuming anger.

'Hey!' he shouted up at the ceiling. 'Hey! If you must detain me here, then provide me with the means to wash.' A little of his superiority returned, though it was but an echo of old arrogance.

There was no response.

With nothing else to do, he slept again.

Chapter Fourteen

LESSIRA

THE SAINT ASTER

MEETING MESSINIUS

'Are you feeling alright?' Yassilli Sulymanya asked Fabian. She shouted over the engine noise of their little shuttle. Her eyes strayed up to Fabian's hands, which gripped the hanging straps with white-knuckle tenacity.

He noticed her looking, and loosened his grip.

'I'm fine,' he said.

He wasn't fine. The shuttle was tiny. There was no grav-plating. Footlocks held him to the deck. When he'd come aboard, he couldn't help but notice how thin the hull was. It was a six-man conveyance. He and Sulymanya had the ship to themselves, the rest of the historitors remaining aboard the *Interlocutor* as it made its way to its own anchorage.

'You do not need to lie to me, Fabian,' she said. Sulymanya was an exceptionally beautiful woman, with skin as dark and smooth as a perfect night sky, patterned with glowing constellations of electoos, framed by a vast halo of black hair. She was also frighteningly competent. Fabian found her a little too cocky, which amused him, if only because she reminded him of himself. 'I am of rogue trader stock,' she said.

Which I know, thought Fabian, *because you never shut up about it,* though decorum forbade him from saying so.

'And I know that some grounders find it hard to adjust to life in the void. It is nothing to be ashamed of.'

'I am fine,' he said, and affected a more relaxed air, though in truth he was close to jumping out of his skin every time the little ship dipped to avoid another craft. It was going far too quickly for his liking. What she had just said registered a little slowly. 'I'm sorry... grounder?'

'Yes. We have a lot of names for people like you.' She smiled a brilliant flash of white, infectious with mirth. 'There's rock-born, well-dweller...'

'Alright, I wish I hadn't asked. I get the picture,' he said.

'...planet-hugger, sky-frighted...'

'Yes, fine, Yassilli,' he said. 'I think we're coming in to dock.'

She cocked her head, ostentatiously listening to the engines. 'I think you are right,' she said.

Before Fabian could stop her, she had swung her arm out, her whole body following balletically in the micro-G. Yassilli wore no footlock, and flicked the toggle that activated the viewport shutter.

It slammed up hard. Planetshine flooded into the transit bay. Through armaglass so clean it might as well have not been there, Fabian looked out over Lessira. The system sat over one of a number of nexus points where stable warp currents had come to rest after the upheavals caused by the opening of the Cicatrix Maledictum. An early target for reconquest during the crusade, the few years since its taking had seen it transformed into a hub fortress, and its skies were full of warships, new orbitals and chartist vessels.

A buoy bearing a single lumen beacon flashed by the window, dazzling Fabian.

'Don't be so jumpy,' Yassilli said. 'We're passing through the cordon delineating the orbital zone set aside for Battle Group Iolus of Fleet Tertius. Standard procedure in anchorages this crowded.'

The ships were packed in close together and Fabian saw four cruisers around what had to be the *Saint Aster*. Its escorts were racked up in dry-docks as closely as canned piscids. There were more groupings of ships beyond, surrounding the planet to a depth of thousands of miles, each boxed into small spaces by ranks of flashing buoys. Shipping lanes were similarly marked. He supposed Yassilli had it right, and it would help to control such a dense amount of traffic, but Fabian could only think the buoys cluttered the space further, making it even more dangerous.

'Don't the ships look a bit close to you?' he asked Yassilli.

She shrugged. 'It's closer than you'll usually find void craft. How dangerous it is depends on how good your pilots are.'

There was a moment of silence.

'How good are the pilots of Battle Group Iolus?' he asked.

She grinned at him again.

The shuttle slowed a little to transmit its permission codes. They were received quickly, and it sped up again, dipping down under the vast warships, out of the light of Lessira and into shadow. Against the blue glare of the world it was hard to make out detail on the vessels, but even so it was clear all the ships were damaged. Paler areas hinted at patched hulls. There were large sections absent of light, indicating widespread power failures, or places where decks had been vented into the void.

They flew under the last of the capital ships, and back into the light, and there Fabian got a look at the *Saint Aster* itself.

It was no longer than its sisters, but it was certainly of higher mass, with more heft about the waist. It was nominally of the Overlord heavy cruiser class, a rare beast as Fabian understood it, but it had been heavily modified. The broadside gun decks were extended much further out than was standard for its kind, to support additional pairs of lance turrets, which would have brought the total from two up to six, if one of the dorsal mounts had not been empty. The extension of the gun decks afforded the *Saint Aster* more space for anti-fighter turrets and additional void shielding, so it was a formidable-looking ship, though much battered. Bathed in the full light of Lessira and its sun, the *Saint Aster*'s injuries were plain to see. Black scoring marked its grey hull. Twisted spars of metal reached out into space. The mount of the missing dorsal turret was buckled enough to distort the shape of the spine. Many of its decorations were missing, but then they passed over the top, and the figurehead of Saint Aster mounted at the front of the command spire shone gold in the sunlight, and it seemed as if nothing could defeat the ship in that moment.

They dipped down. The figurehead disappeared out of view, and the ship again seemed tired. The pilot adjusted his flight path to avoid maintenance barges, forcing him to dive steeply, before executing a sharp turn upwards to arrive in a hangar. Fabian's guts followed each bank and swerve with enthusiasm.

They put down with a flourish, Yassilli would have said, or too hard, in Fabian's opinion. Red lumens strobed the transit bay. Atmospheric balancers hissed. By the time the side hatches opened, Fabian had just about composed himself. He smoothed down his uniform, and stepped out.

A single Space Marine waited for them. He was a veteran of the Firstborn type, with two fifty-year service studs bonded to the bone of his forehead. His armour bore the white livery and heraldry of the White Consuls Tenth Company captain, but this had been diminished in size to make way for Fleet Tertius markings, and in some places the crusade badges had supplanted his Chapter iconography completely. He wore a green half-cloak over his reactor pack.

'Lord Lieutenant Vitrian Messinius, I presume?' Fabian asked.

'You are well informed, historitor,' said Messinius.

Fabian scrutinised him. In his files, Guilliman had good words to say about Messinius, and so Fabian had hoped for one of the rarer sort of Space Marine who retained his human sensibilities. But Messinius' countenance was stern, unused to smiling, he guessed, and he had that slightly dead look found in the eyes of so many Astartes.

Fabian continued smoothly, nevertheless. 'Lord Guilliman recommended you to me. I am glad that you are here to welcome us. I was hoping to seek you out anyway, to record the testimony of your actions during the crusade.'

'I do not have much time,' Messinius said. 'Is this interview part of your official processes?'

'It will be for the primarch's eyes,' said Fabian.

'Then I shall make time,' the Space Marine said, albeit reluctantly. He saluted, fist across his chest. 'It is noisy here,' he added. 'I apologise. The battle group is undergoing repair. We are about to commence full drydock work, but the crew is already doing what it can. You must be careful.'

'I shall, although I do not worry about my associate here.' He indicated Yassilli. 'This is Yassilli Sulymanya, historitor elevate. She was raised aboard ships.'

'You are a scion of the Sulymanyan rogue traders?' Messinius asked.

'I am,' said Yassilli. 'I was.'

'I know your house,' said Messinius. 'I fought alongside one of your ancestors. A fine warrior. Come, this way,' he said, and led them out of the hangar. Once they were on the other side of the blast doors it was much quieter, though they had to squeeze past reparator crews who had the corridor deck plating up for stretches of twenty yards and more.

'It is not far to the command deck, but the lifters in this

section are non-functional, so we must walk a way,' Messinius said.

'When was the last time the group put in for repair, lord lieutenant?' Yassilli asked.

'Fully? Not since the start of the crusade,' said Messinius. 'Fleetmistress VanLeskus has been racing to secure as much of Imperium Sanctus as she can, and has prioritised swift advance over all things. Many of the Tertius battle groups are in a similar situation, it is only this diversion back into the Segmentum Solar that allows us this brief respite.'

'And how long have you been with the fleet?' asked Fabian.

'Since the beginning. Five years, two hundred days, fourteen hours, according to Fleet Tertius time, though according to our battlefleet chronolog, that figure is months out in the positive range when compared with battle group time, and even more so when tallied against the passing of days on Terra,' Messinius replied. He frowned. It was a slightly hostile expression. 'These are questions related to military matters. Are you all this inquisitive? It seems dangerous to share such information.'

'We are to record all things. You have a historitor in this battle group,' said Fabian. 'Don't you speak with her?'

'I avoid her,' said Messinius.

'Because she is inquisitive?' said Yassilli.

Messinius almost smiled at that, Fabian could have sworn.

'I was actually expecting Historitor Serisa Vallia to meet with us when we arrived,' said Fabian.

'I have no idea why she did not,' said Messinius.

'Can you tell me a bit about Athagey?' asked Fabian.

'Groupmistress Athagey is an able commander. She has been appointed ranking officer for this campaign of containment in recognition of that.' Unlike Lucerne, Messinius made no allowance for the pace of mortals, and the historitors were almost trotting to keep up. 'Full records of our fleet engagements will be provided.'

'I understand her story must be fascinating, but could you tell me what Groupmistress Athagey is like, lord lieutenant?'

'What is she like?' Messinius repeated the question back. The Firstborn glanced down at the historitor, his face blank.

'As a person?' ventured Fabian.

Messinius looked thoughtful. 'She is a little reckless, but then bravery is a laudable trait. The crew are loyal to her. We Space Marines follow her willingly. That is the highest mark of respect.'

'Yes, but I mean is she amusing, is she erudite, ill-tempered? I like an idea of my subjects before I meet them.'

'Are you going to subject her to similar questioning?'

'It is our role,' replied Fabian.

'I see.' He gave an unreadable expression. 'I would not know,' said Messinius. 'I am not a good judge of unaltered human character. I am sorry.'

They turned a corner, moved around a trio of hard-linked servitors wielding tools, and reached a set of lifters.

'This bank is operational,' said Messinius, and he called to the machine-spirit to summon a car. He was silent for a moment. 'If you really want an impression of Athagey,' he said, 'she is a singular individual who you can only experience for yourself.'

Again, there was a flicker of a smile. Fabian realised far too late Messinius was simply avoiding speaking ill of his commander. The mistake was his own. Space Marines were as individual as other people. Messinius was still quite human, he was just not the same kind of human Lucerne was.

Athagey was going to be difficult.

'Ah,' said Fabian.

Messinius gave Fabian a meaningful look. The lifter arrived. They got in.

'Correct provisions have been made for the Logos,' said Messinius, 'although I have little idea why it should fall to me to provide this information. Should you have any issues or requests, please direct them to First Lieutenant Finnula Diomed, the group-mistress' second. I advise you not to bother Athagey. Or me.'

The lifter stopped. They went up a narrow corridor covered by machine-governed weaponry, then through a heavy gate into the silent command deck. Many of its work stations were in pieces on the floor being pored over by red-robed trans-mechanics. The large command dais that dominated the front of the deck was empty and powered down. A detail of Naval armsmen watched over the Adeptus Mechanicus, but other-wise the place was devoid of human occupants, and seemed huge as a result.

'Up here,' said Messinius, pointing aft. He led them up stairs to the back of the deck, to a round, armoured door. It chimed in recognition as he approached, and rolled open.

'Historitor Majoris Fabian Guelphrain, Historitor Elevate Yassilli Sulymanya,' Messinius announced in his Space Marine's battle-honed voice, and stepped aside.

Ears ringing, Fabian and Yassilli stepped right into Athag-ey's line of fire.

Chapter Fifteen

LORD GAVIMOR

A BATH

TO SERVE THE POWERS TRULY

A woman's voice woke him by calling his name. 'Lord Gavimor.'

He started, body filling with adrenaline, ready to fight. He was alarmed at how deeply he had slept. The woman stood in the open doorway, affording him a glimpse of the corridor outside for the first time. This appeared to be of the same featureless black metal as his cell. Red lighting limited his view. Bloody shadows crowded his guest, as if hovering around her shoulders and waiting to be let inside, like those of his dreams. He half expected to see their glowing red eyes.

'You are awake.' She entered. To his immense relief, the shadows did not follow her. 'That is good.'

The woman looked like she might have been beautiful, but had taken steps to destroy her looks. Her face was scarified with symbols and looping patterns. She had extended the line of her lips with a cruel downward curve, and had stained the scars a dark purple, giving her the appearance of some savage xenos. But these knife cuts were not so barbaric as the piercings that covered her body. There were many fine rings from which silver chains hung from her nose, the corners of her eyes, her ears, her lips and her bald scalp, where they were especially concentrated in close-spaced ranks like mail, so the chains swept back over her head in place of hair. She wore a low-cut robe, showing more chains hanging in the valley between her breasts, and lower, disappearing under the cloth below her navel. She must have had hundreds. When she moved, it was to a gentle, metallic tinkling.

She turned back to the door. A timid thought that he should attempt to escape flashed through Gavimor's mind, but he remained where he was, propped up on his elbows on the bed.

'Aren't you going to get up?' she said. He saw her tongue was pierced multiple times, and tattooed purple like her lips.

Wordlessly, he stood. She wrinkled her nose at his smell.

'Enter,' she called over her shoulder.

From the corridor came two large males carrying a bath between them on poles, like a sedan chair. Gavimor's heart twinged at the sight, for he had once had such a chair, in his lost life. The serfs set the bath down, went out, and others brought in a table. Another man arranged a jug upon the table fashioned from a large, rainbow-hued shell, soap, a razor, three ewers of steaming water, a large sponge and a comb. More serfs carried huge amphorae in and filled the bath. They were mute. All were hairless, with tattooed slave marks on their heads framed by curving designs. They all appeared dead, but alive, as if no soul inhabited their flesh. He had never seen such broken men.

'Leave us,' said the woman. The serfs bowed and departed. The door slid shut and locked behind them.

'What is this?' asked Gavimor, so scared by this change in circumstance, he half expected it to be a ploy of the shadow men.

The woman looked at the steaming surface of the water, then at him.

'It is a bath,' she said. 'I was informed you were of noble birth. You know what a bath is, don't you?'

He nodded numbly.

'You asked for a means to cleanse yourself. Yes?'

'I did.'

'Then get in and be cleansed. My name is Tharador Yheng. I am to attend you.'

He hesitated.

'Do not be bashful,' she said, and beneath her cruel scars she smiled. 'Your nakedness means nothing to me. You were used to servants. Let me serve you. Think of me as you thought of them.'

He stared at her.

'Get undressed, then.'

He stood, lifted the robe over his head, leaving himself feeling exposed and even more afraid.

'Are you going to get in?' she said, amused.

He got into the water. It was hot enough to make him gasp, and it stung the sores left by his manacles, but as he sat down and allowed it to rise up over his hips, the heat became pleasurable. He shivered, and lay back, tentatively relaxing, though the smell coming off the water, already turning grey, was disgusting. The woman evidently thought so too, because she went to the table, fetched a bottle, and tipped in a measure of perfume.

'Do you like your accommodation?' she asked. 'You are comfortable?' She went back to the table.

'Yes, yes I am.' He turned his head to watch her gathering items up from the table.

'Then do I not deserve thanks for my hospitality?' she asked.

'Thank you,' he said weakly. The perfume in the water made his head buzz, and he realised it was drugged, making him feel pleasantly numb.

'I...' he began. His mouth was dry. 'I have been having nightmares.'

Her nod was the tinkle of stars shattering. 'The dreams here have teeth,' she said. As she moved, her outline blurred, and he could not focus upon her. 'You are close to the warp, close to holiness. We are visited by beings from the othersea. We welcome them, and we are protected from their more violent attentions by the power of my master, and the faith of his servants. The things that visit you are lesser beings, jealous of you. They wish to taste your glory.'

'Glory?'

'You are our honoured guest,' she said, affecting surprise. 'You have been chosen. You know no glory yet, but you will be gloried. The shadows have a presentiment of that. They hunger for your coming power.'

She turned around. In one hand she held the jug fashioned from the shell, in the other a cake of soap. She had a sponge wedged under her elbow, a strangely domestic sight on someone so exotic. He saw past her adornments, and decided that she was still beautiful, and that her mutilations accentuated rather than hid her perfection.

'Chosen for what?' he said. The drugged perfume worked on him further. The world seemed to recede. His mind dulled, yet was uplifted.

'Chosen to serve the gods,' she said. She stepped closer. Her dress was slit up to the top of her thigh. Her legs were very long, very shapely. 'Chosen to serve the great Tenebrus, the Hand of Abaddon himself.'

'Abaddon? Abaddon...' He turned the name over in his mouth. 'Do I know that name?'

'He is the Warmaster, son of Horus, the true heir to the Throne of Terra.'

'Horus? But then, you are the enemy,' he said. He frowned. 'I saw the Adeptus Astartes on the ship. They were no servants of the Emperor.'

'No, they were not, and you should be glad it was so,' she said. She poured water onto his head, wetting his hair. He shut his eyes, collapsing into the sensations of the bath, her touch, and the scented steam. 'Nor am I. The Emperor is a monster. He is the enemy of the true gods, the Powers.'

He opened his eyes a crack. 'He is the protector of mankind.'

'He is a tyrant who would deny us the truth of reality, keep from us the power that exists in us all, and have us all enslaved,' she said. 'You were a rich man. You had power where millions around you had none. Money, food, fine clothes. No doubt your every whim was obeyed.' She poured more water onto his head.

Memories flitted through his mind as she spoke, and he smiled. 'I did.'

'He gave you these things when He gives billions nothing, and perhaps you could have been content with that, but everything was taken away by the Emperor because you are blessed with a measure of His power. You have a profound connection with the warp, a sacred thing, but He is jealous. He wants all power for Himself, so He calls you unclean, and decries you as a witch. He would slay you because you enjoy a morsel of holiness.' More warm water washed over his head. 'Why does He treat those born with the ability to touch the warp so poorly, when He is a witch Himself? Why should there be one law for Him and another for you? Why, indeed, should there be one law for you and another for me? I was born into poverty, deep under the ground. Our world was supposedly sacred, steeped in the love of the Emperor, but there was no love for the likes of me. We were persecuted, starved, beaten, exploited, forced to live in the graves of others and driven out of them when we were found. He took away all you had. He denied me everything from the moment of my birth, even the sight of the sun. I was not blessed like you are, and yet now I have power that is greater than yours. I have power because I stopped listening to the priests and the lawmen and my so-called betters.' Her voice hardened. 'I have power because I took it.'

She put the jug down, and worked the cake of soap between her hands. When she had a thick lather, she began to massage it into his hair.

'Then I should take power.' He became glum. 'I had power, though, and it was taken from me. It could be taken from me again.'

'You had false power. Temporal power. My masters offer true power, eternal and glorious. If you were to serve them, you too would enjoy their generosity.'

'I couldn't,' he said, discussing the rankest blasphemy as easily as if he talked over the hunting season with his friends, but the narcotic steam soothed him, and the feeling of her hands on his head was so pleasant. 'I would be betraying the Emperor, the Lord of Mankind.'

'Do you know what the Emperor does with psykers like you?' she asked. She continued kneading his scalp. Where the suds dropped into the water, it turned black. 'Do you know why witches are taken by the authorities in the first place?'

'No,' he said, thinking aloud. 'There are the astropaths, and the other Imperial servants. I saw a sanctioned witch once, at a regimental raising. He had medals. They have to come from somewhere.' He was half-aware that he was talking like a child, but he couldn't help himself, and like a child being bathed by its mother, he was comforted by the woman's touch.

'This is true,' said Tharador. 'That is their fate, my master tells me, but only of some. Let me ask you, how many psykers have you seen in total, in your entire life?'

He frowned, trying to think through the effects of the soothing, narcotic steam. 'A handful. A dozen maybe.'

'And how many were on the ship you were imprisoned upon?'

'I don't know. I didn't see all the ship,' he said. Fear rose in him at the memory of the hold, making him angry.

She laughed when she could very easily have become offended by his tone. 'How many in your hold, then?'

'Hundreds. There were hundreds,' he said.

'Then you can guess that there were thousands on that ship. There were three Black Ships in the flotilla you were part of.' She picked up the shell again, and got up, going to the table to fill it with clean water. 'So if only a tiny number of those aboard are destined to become like these psykers that you saw, ask yourself, what happens to the rest?'

She returned, and poured water over his head. When it coursed over him and into the bath it was still black with dirt. She fetched another scoop of water, and more soap.

'I don't know.'

'They are taken to Terra in ships full of suffering. Those that survive the journey are judged by callous men who care nothing for their pain. Those they deem powerful enough according to their measure are forced through excruciating rituals and made to live a life of miserable servitude, holding together an empire that despises them simply for existing. The Adeptus Ministorum preaches hatred of all kinds of witches, but without them – the Navigators and the astropaths and the rest – the Imperium would die. Not forgetting the greatest witch of all, the Emperor Himself.'

More water rushed over him. He felt his sins running into the water along with the ship-dirt.

'Those that are chosen are of the sort that you met during the course of your privileged life – the slaves, the soul-bound, the despised mutant. And they are the lucky ones.'

With the fourth scoop she rinsed his hair clean.

'Lie back,' she said.

He obeyed, and she knelt again, and began to carefully wash him tenderly with the sponge.

'What does happen to the rest?' he said.

'They are taken into the Emperor's Throneroom, and they are consumed. Their souls are fed to the monster at the rotten heart of the Imperium. They die slowly, in agony, and in the process their immortal essences are annihilated. I know this because my master, another who has true power, power he has taken and cultivated himself, told me. You have a minor talent. You are not strong enough to have served them. You would not have been chosen for slavery. You would have become food for their evil god.'

Through the fug of the drugged perfumes, Gavimor tried to deny this, but part of him accepted it as complete truth. Tharador Yheng seemed to fill his universe. The feel of her touch, the sound of her breathing, the gentle, lovely notes of her chains as she moved.

'But if you chose my masters,' she went on, 'you would exceed your gift, and become a sorcerer, like I am becoming. The warp would be yours to command. Immortality would be your reward. There would be no constraint, no morals to hold you back. You would be like you were before – rich, above the ignorant masses, but better, more mighty, perfect in form and thought. More powerful. And this time, you would win this power for yourself, it would not be given. That makes it all the sweeter. You would be a vessel for a glory you cannot comprehend. Does that not sound magnificent? Do you wish to be a vessel for glory?'

He leaned back as she soaped his chest with the sponge.

'I have power. I have power over you. Can you feel it?'

She had strong, sure hands. He let out a little moan. She leaned close to his ear. The chains that served her as hair brushed against him, and he shuddered at the touch.

'Does that please you?' she said.

'It is a long time since anyone has touched me so.'

'Does it please you?' she whispered, more urgently.

'Yes,' he said, his mind by now awhirl, all his senses intoxicated by Tharador's presence and the drugs in the water.

'If you wish more of the same, all you must do is commit yourself to the true gods. Agree to serve them, body and soul, and know pleasure and power of the like even you, in your gilded cage, could never have dreamt of.'

Her touch was electrifying. He succumbed.

'I will.'

'Swear it!'

'I swear!' he said, though a small part of him shouted up in dismay at what he promised. 'I swear to serve the Powers.'

She laughed sensuously. For a moment, her fingers seemed to be crueller than iron claws, her chains dripped blood. Her eyes were depthless holes, but the sensations were fleeting, the fear they caused swallowed swiftly by pleasure.

'Then see how the Powers reward those who serve them well,' she whispered, and her hands moved lower.

Chapter Sixteen

GROUPMISTRESS

A REGRETTABLE NAME

THE PROBLEM WITH STIMMS

Fabian found Groupmistress Athagey to be a woman of around fifty, notwithstanding the effects of any anti-agapic treatment she might have had, though from her general attitude Fabian suspected she suffered no vanity, and looked her actual age. She was short-haired and slender, with strong features of a sort the unkind might call plain. She was dressed soberly in standard Naval attire, without the flamboyance some groupmasters affected, except for a single streak of magenta in her greying hair.

The conference room was dominated by a long table. At the end was a large, elaborate chair for the ship's master, but Athagey sat at the side of the table, not at its head. The room was luxurious, appointed with natural, lustrous wood furnishings and trim. A life-sized copy of the ship's figurehead occupied a niche in the wall opposite the door. Saint Aster was pouring water. The work made some allusion to her myth, the details of which were hazy in Fabian's memory, but which involved some sort of thirst-defeating miracle. A water bringer. Saints fitted neatly into a handful of categories.

Two other things Fabian noticed right away. Firstly, Athagey was something of a sybarite: she had a faintly rakish air despite her sober manner of dress. She was enjoying a big drink, and smoking a black lho-stick whose ash she carelessly dropped around an ashtray. Secondly, she was clearly very angry.

'Well then, are you coming in or are you going to stare at me like some kind of zoological specimen?' Athagey barked. 'Haven't you seen a woman before? I don't have all day. I bet you don't have all day. We're all bloody busy. There's a crusade on, remember?'

'I apologise, madame groupmistress,' said Fabian.

He looked at Messinius. The Space Marine pretended he hadn't seen. Very human, decided Fabian.

'Forgive my manner,' Fabian said. 'It has been a long and rough voyage through the warp.'

'Aren't they all?' she said, and blew out a stream of smoke.

'Madame, historitors, I shall leave you to your conference,' said Messinius. 'I have much to attend to.'

'Yes,' she said curtly.

Messinius dipped his head in salute and left without a look back.

'Come, sit,' she demanded, gesturing at the chairs opposite her. Athagey got up as soon as Fabian and Yassilli took their places, going to a cabinet at the back. She retrieved a decanter and two fresh glasses from inside. 'You'll take a drink, of course,' she said. She slopped liquor into her own glass with little care. Fabian saw that her hand was shaking. She glanced up and saw he'd noticed, so took her time pouring the others.

She left the decanter out, sat down, and shoved the glasses across the table. It was highly polished, and the glasses slid to a slow, spinning stop.

She sipped her own drink. 'So you're Fabian Guelphrain.' She spoke at him, not to him.

'I am, and this is Yassilli Sulymanya, my aide,' Fabian replied, slightly shocked at her behaviour. When she looked at him again he saw the redness in her eyes, and the dryness around her nostrils, then he thought he understood. 'I will be here for a while, but will afterwards move–'

'Right,' she interrupted. 'Come here to fill up my warships with bloody civilians writing poems and getting in the way with their imagifers.'

'Our role is not quite that–'

'I do not really care, historitor. I do not hold with allowing civilians into military hierarchies. Frankly, it's a security risk.' She ground out her lho-stick in the stone ashtray. 'In case you haven't guessed by my delicate manner, I am not best pleased by this. Non-military Adepta have no business in a theatre of war.'

'The Logos Historica Verita is not an Adeptus,' said Fabian, 'but a division of the Officio Logisticarum, which is a superordinary affiliate of the Adeptus Administratum. We're a paramilitary divisio. We have military training.'

'Then I'll have civilians with guns roaming around? Even better,' she said.

Fabian spoke calmly. 'We have training up to the strategic level. A lot of our information retrieval missions are dangerous. We are no strangers to battle, or to planning combat operations.'

'You are also no strangers to poking your noses into business that does not concern you,' she said. She took a long drink from her glass, then filled it up again. The decanter's neck rattled on the lip of the glass.

'Madame groupmistress, I promise you the Logos is not here to get in your way,' Fabian said. 'We have a great deal of experience working alongside the Navis Imperialis and every other branch of the Imperial war machine. Military objectives take precedence under nearly all circumstances.'

Her eyes narrowed. 'I don't care either way if you think you will be a hindrance or not. That is not the issue. Let us not dance around this. I know what you're about,' she said. 'You're the primarch's spies.'

'I'm sorry?' he said.

'All this talk of writing a true history and documenting the war so it can be won more quickly.' She jabbed a finger at Fabian as he began to speak, silencing him. 'Don't gainsay me,' she said. 'I have been subjected to the propaganda and have seen through it. The primarch is a great lord, and it is thanks to the Emperor he has returned to lead us.' She said this in a way that led Fabian to think she didn't believe it. 'But he can't look over all of our shoulders all the damn time. He should let us get on with the war and trust it will be won.'

'Forgive me if I seem presumptuous, but I have spent a good deal of time with him, and I'm sure making every decision for you is not his intention.'

'Isn't it?' she said. 'They say he is a god. If he is, he's the god of petty rules. Codex this, codex that, all to be followed to the letter, although that doesn't apply to him. If it doesn't suit him, the rules change. Where's that leave the rest of us?'

'Madame, we have got off to a bad start here, if I may just–'

'They took the bloody name of my fleet, do you know that?' she said. 'This was Strike Group Saint Aster, named for my ship, which I have commanded these past fifteen years. We were absorbed by Tertius after Machorta, and I got to serve under the kind of glory-hungry commander Lord Guilliman imposes on officers like me, who have done nothing but serve the Imperium faithfully. At least then, for a while, we were Battle Group Saint Aster, and it was a proud name, well respected. It had a ring of destiny to it. It honoured the thousands of lives lost on these ships. It meant something, Throne damn it all.' Her eyes were reddening further. She wiped at her nose. 'That is, until the Battle of Xeriphis, when Battle Group Iolus was all but destroyed by the Word Bearers. They were merged with my group, under my command. But did I get to keep my designation, that proud name steeped in the blood of the faithful?'

'Madame,' Fabian tried again. 'I do not see the relevance of this to our mission with–'

'Let me finish!' she snapped. 'I'll tell you – no, ser, I did not get to keep my name. I did not get to keep my honour! Bloody rules, alphabetical designations all round, enforced by the oh-so-officious Officio Logisticarum. And I thought the Adeptus Administratum were bad! So now our victory roll is appended to that of a bunch of people who were bad enough at their jobs to get themselves killed. How's that for a true history?' She raised her glass and smiled harshly at him. 'And as much respect as I have for the primarch, does he really think he can rule us with this amount of pen-pushing micromanagement? What does he think he is going to do, take on every heretic, fallen Space Marine, ork, aeldari and Emperor alone knows what else personally? It's a big galaxy. He can't be everywhere at once.' She slugged down her drink. 'So,' she said acidly, 'don't you tell me you are not here to spy on me, because I don't believe you.'

They looked at each other. Even ever-confident Yassilli was stunned into silence.

'Right then, now that is out of the way.' She tossed a couple of vox-beads across the table. 'These are tuned to the battle group network. Use only them, not your own equipment. You'll upset my tech-adepts. Contact my purser, he'll see you to your quarters.'

'Lord Lieutenant Messinius said–'

'That will be all! You're dismissed, historitors. Thank you ever so much for coming.'

She swivelled her chair around so she was facing away from them. Fabian wasn't quick enough in standing.

'That means get out,' she said. 'I'm busy. Drinking.' She waved her glass around.

Fabian and Yassilli shared a glance.

'Thank you for your time, Madame Athagey. I look forward to a fruitful collaboration,' said Fabian.

Yassilli had a very good line in hard looks. She gave him one then. They left the ready room. The armoured portal remained rolled back, so when Yassilli spoke she did so under her breath.

'What was that all about? That was almost heretical.'

'Wounded pride, and...' Fabian leaned in to Yassilli and whispered into her mass of hair. 'Didn't you see?'

'What?' she asked.

'The shaking, and how red the whites of her eyes were, the redness around her nostrils?'

'Do you think...?' Yassilli said, leaving her question unsaid.

Fabian nodded. 'I think Groupmistress Athagey might have a bit of a problem with stimms.'

Chapter Seventeen

CANTATUM BELLUM

BAD AIR

THE WILL OF THE EMPEROR

The *Cantatum Bellum* had taken itself away from the fleet mustering grounds over Lessira. Black as the void that it sailed, it hid amid the second of the system's three asteroid belts. Lucerne found it lurking in the shadow of a wrecked mining station far from the main shipping routes. He ordered the *Solemnity* to approach slowly, broadcasting standard Imperial brotherhood hails every three minutes. The *Cantatum Bellum* remained silent.

They came to within four hundred miles before Lucerne ordered a halt.

'Still no response, my lord,' the master of vox informed him.

'Keep trying,' said Lucerne. He had his helmet off, displaying his concern for all to see. His left hand gripped the hilt of his sword.

Lucerne stared at the *Cantatum Bellum* knowing his ship could not take her, if it came to it. The *Solemnity* was a small vessel of new design; another one of Cawl's contributions to the crusade. It was fast, and heavily armed for its size, but it wasn't much larger than a Cobra-class destroyer; far smaller than the Vanguard-class strike cruiser that housed the Angevin Crusade.

'This does not bode well,' said Techmarine Avias, who watched with Lucerne and Apothecary Lycopaeus. It was standard practice for torchbearer missions to convey one of each specialist to Space Marine groups being reinforced. The Techmarine to integrate new wargear into a Chapter's armoury and to set up a process for manufacture, the Apothecary to introduce the technology for the creation of Primaris Space Marines. It was also standard practice for the Unnumbered Sons to replace their livery with the badges and colours of the Chapters they were on their way to join, part of the ritual of changing brotherhoods, but in this case, Lucerne decided that would be provocative, and they were garbed still in yellow.

The three of them were the sole transhumans on the command deck. The other brothers were in their quarters. Avias leaned onto a guard rail over the central hololith pit. Specialised lenses in his helmet whirred, enhancing the display of the craft.

'Their communications arrays are all intact. I see carrier waves. Their signum is broadcasting loudly.'

'Then they can hear us,' said Lucerne.

'They can hear us perfectly,' said Avias. 'They are choosing not to reply.'

'Why do they not answer?' said Lycopaeus. 'Do they not trust our cyphers?'

'You are being generous,' said Avias. 'I'd say this is a calculated snub.'

'Try them again,' said Lucerne.

Cogitators chittered as the hails were repeated. They waited a moment. Vox-communications at that close range should have been instantaneous. There was no reply.

'Throne preserve us,' grumbled Lucerne. He clumped down

of the small command deck. 'Move aside,' he told the master
of vox. The crewman got up from his station. Lucerne almost
crushed his chair as he leaned onto the back, and stabbed his
armoured finger onto the open frequency rune.

'Cantatum Bellum, by the grace of the Emperor and by the
command of His last loyal son, Lord Roboute Guilliman, Lord
Commander and Lord Regent of the Imperium, respond to our
communications. I am Brother-Sergeant Lucerne of the Unnumbered Sons of Rogal Dorn, here with Primaris reinforcements
and technological materials to strengthen your crusade. You
will respond immediately.'

They waited again.

Lucerne stood up from the vox-desk. 'I will go over. I will
make contact with them directly, and report back.'

'You are going alone, brother-sergeant?' said Lycopaeus.

'I am,' said Lucerne.

'I would offer my opinion,' said Avias.

'Do so, but quickly,' said Lucerne. 'Bring me my helm, my
weapons!' he called to his servants.

'If this lack of response is any indication of the welcome you
will get, it would be imprudent to go alone,' said Avias.

'You are right, but it is better I risk only myself.' A pair of serfs
offered up his helmet, and he took it and placed it over his head.
Ceremonial manacles were closed around his wrists, though he
left the weapons chains dangling, and kept his chainsword and
bolt pistol at his belt. 'Shipmaster, take the *Solemnity* to safe
distance, out of their weapons arcs. Void shields to remain up.
Maintain position for an escape vector. All crew to remain on
high alert. If there is any sign of aggression from the *Cantatum
Bellum*, you are to withdraw immediately, send word to the primarch and inform Lord Lieutenant Vitrian Messinius of Fleet
Tertius. You are not to engage or to attempt to rescue me under

any circumstances. If it comes to battle, you will be lost. This ship will not stand against the *Cantatum Bellum* alone.'

'The Black Templars ship will not be able to put up much of a fight, it is scarred by war. Much of it looks uninhabitable,' said Lycopaeus.

'An injured wolf is the most dangerous,' said Avias. 'I am seeing clear power readings around their weapons. Appearances can be deceptive.'

'Do you seriously believe Space Marines will fire on their own? We are brothers come to help them,' said Lycopaeus.

'You are naive, brother,' said Avias.

'In these dark times, anything is possible,' said Lucerne.

Lucerne took a Thunderhawk over. It was not far in void terms, but he had the pilot approach the *Cantatum Bellum* from the aft, where the ship had fewest weapons. He rode in the cockpit, watching all the way as the engine block grew. The fires were out, giving the strike cruiser an air of abandonment.

He found himself absorbed by the giant orbital the cruiser sheltered beneath. Whenever it had been built must have been a long time in the past, for its hull was worn paper-thin by the particular erosion of the void. The large asteroid it was tethered to bore the straight gouge scars of macro-harvesters. These were the only clues to its purpose. The station's form was unknowable, reduced to a complex filigree of broken plating and projecting spars, hollow and fragile as a dead apian nest.

They flew into the station's shadow, and the pilot swung out from the aft of the cruiser, bringing them alongside the ship and giving them a clear view down the barrels of its cannons.

'I cannot attempt a landing on their hangar deck, brother-sergeant,' the pilot informed him. 'The doors are shut.'

'Then hove in to the side by the twelfth deck access hatch,' Lucerne said. 'Dead stop. Transmit a request that a docking corridor be extended, in the name of the returned primarch and Rogal Dorn.'

'As commanded, I obey,' the Space Marine said.

Jets puffing white gas, the Thunderhawk stopped alongside the ship. The pilot transmitted Lucerne's request. The hatch was white in the black hull, surrounded by neatly nested rectangles of the retracted docking corridor, each part of the mechanism clearly delineated in the hard sunlight found in the void. The edges of the door, the corridor sections and the surroundings were chipped down to dull metal, distorting the outline, while the templar cross on the door was worn away, only a hint of allegiance, not a bold display.

'No response. Nothing is happening...' began the pilot, before interrupting himself. 'No, wait. I have an energy reading. They are letting you in, brother.'

'That is a start,' said Lucerne.

Silent in the vacuum of space, the long metal corridor emerged from the side of the ship, section by section. The Thunderhawk pilot made a few adjustments to align with the corridor, until it was close enough that docking mag-locks could pull the gunship in.

The corridor clanged into place around the Thunderhawk's side hatch.

'The seals are faulty. There's no atmospheric pressure the other side,' said the pilot.

'When I go below, seal off the lower deck forward compart-ment, draw the atmosphere,' said Lucerne. 'As soon as I am aboard, disconnect and stand off in the shadow of the station.'

'Yes, brother-sergeant.'

Lucerne got out of the co-pilot's seat, left the cockpit and went down to the forward compartment, where he waited by the side door in the prow of the ship. The pilot shut the rear door. Seals engaged, and the air was sucked out. The noise became tinny, then vanished, leaving Lucerne alone with the sound of his breathing. Lumens on the wall flickered from green to red, indicating the air mix had been removed.

He opened the door onto the docking corridor. There were biolume panels built into the sections, all dead. He shifted his helm sight into infrared, finding holes in the sides of the corridor as dark blue spots of cold. The door to the *Cantatum Bellum* glowed a lighter hue.

He activated his mag-locks, and set out, reaching the ship without incident. As he approached the end of the corridor, a panel button lit up green to the side of the door. The button yielded to his push, and the airlock opened, allowing him within the *Cantatum Bellum*. The door shut behind him, teeth locking into their grooves on the threshold. Flickering lights informed him that the seals were good, so he waited while the chamber filled with air.

He opened vox-channels back to the *Solemnity* and the Thunderhawk. There were no attempts to jam him. 'I am aboard,' he said.

The cycling lights in the airlock turned green. 'Brother Dimus, you may depart. Stand off,' he ordered the pilot. The *Cantatum Bellum* shook a little as the gunship disconnected. Unoiled machinery ground all around him as the tunnel wound itself back in, making the deck tremble.

He keyed the inner door open and stepped inside the *Cantatum Bellum*.

The ship was in even poorer repair than he had expected. The same extent of damage visible on the outside was apparent within. Panels had been removed from the walls, allowing the guts of subsystems to hang out. Some of these bore evidence of rough fixes, others seemed to have been judged beyond help and had simply been left.

'I am Brother Racej Lucerne, sent by the primarch. If any

hear my words, declare yourself,' he called, upping the amplification of his voxmitter, so that his voice bounced from the
walls. There was no answer. Cautiously, he advanced down
the corridor into the body of the ship, resisting the temptation to draw his weapons. Every instinct his transhuman body
possessed urged him to violence. The few functioning lumens
flickered. Water dripped from the ceiling ahead of him.

His battleplate warned him that the air mix had too high a
concentration of carbon dioxide, and traces of toxins given off
by burnt plasteks. He opened his breathing slits nonetheless,
the taint to the air being dangerous to a mortal but not to him,
as he wished to scent his environment.

The ship's interior smelled of ruptured pipes, a mingled aroma
of oil, human waste and machine fluids. He caught the stench
of death, and the acrid tang of plasma-seared metal. He smelled
people, unwashed, some very sick. Beneath it all was another
scent, high and false and faint, but all-pervasive: the musky per-
spiration of transhumans laced with engineered biochemicals.

He was not alone, then. There were Space Marines still on
board.

He lost their scent. The odour of the dead overwhelmed his
finely tuned senses. As he neared a side room it became almost
unbearable. He looked within.

Inside were piles of corpses in shrouds, heaped on shelves
made of welded metal. Each shroud was stitched tight around
the body, and decorated with templar crosses and strips of
parchment. There were dozens of them.

'You have found our honoured warrior-serfs, my lord,' said
a voice.

It was all Lucerne could do not to draw his weapons. He
stopped his hand halfway to his gun, and made himself relax.

Somehow, an unmodified human had stolen up on him to
stand in the middle of the corridor ten yards away. He wore a

heavy black habit with white robes underneath, with a white tabard bearing the fluted templar's cross over the top. He was armed: a Chapter-serf, not a thrall, as the Black Templars' nomenclature had it. At his left hip was a broadsword, at his right a holstered autopistol. Out of necessity he wore a breather mask to filter the tainted air. In most respects he resembled a member of one of the Adeptus Ministorum's monastic orders, with tonsured hair and devotional tattoos.

'It is not wise to approach a member of the Adeptus Astartes so stealthily. I could have killed you,' said Lucerne.

'I have no need to announce myself. The Emperor is my guide. You did not kill me, because the Emperor did not will it. I have faith He shall preserve me, especially from His Angels.'

'Then tell me your name,' said Lucerne. 'Now that I have seen you.'

'I am Alcuin, servant to Castellan Beorhtnoth. I have been sent to greet you.'

'Why do your masters not come?' said Lucerne.

'They are at prayer.'

'Is this why they did not respond to our hails?'

'It is one of the reasons. They will be finished shortly. I will take you to them, my lord.'

'You are a warrior-serf?'

'One of the last. Most of the crusade's mortal warriors are dead. Only Angels remain,' he said, with the assurance of the truly devout.

'I am Brother-Sergeant Racej Lucerne, of the Unnumbered Sons of Rogal Dorn.'

'We know who you are, my lord,' said the serf. 'The Emperor reveals all to His most faithful. Please, if you would follow me.'

Alcuin took him up through three decks of the ship. Everywhere were signs of long campaigning. The damage was extensive, and he saw only a few mortal crew.

'The will of the Emperor,' Alcuin answered. 'My masters have been fighting alone for a long time now. We have known many victories, but they come with a cost.'

'Then the crew are also dead?'

'Many are. Only a few thousand remain,' said Alcuin. He spoke with total acceptance of the deaths, as if they could not be any other way. 'Most of the serfs and thralls have passed on to the Emperor's light with them. *Felix ille est qui moritur in ministerium*,' he added in High Gothic.

Fortunate is he who dies in service, Lucerne translated into the low speech. 'Have your masters also died? How many of them remain?'

'Fourteen,' said Alcuin.

'How can they continue to make war with so few?'

'You are not used to our Chapter. We fight until we have won.'

'Why?'

Alcuin looked back at him, eyes bright above his breathing filter. 'Because the Emperor wills it to be so,' he said.

They ascended the decks by stair. None of the lifters were working. Such was the disarray he saw, Lucerne wondered if Guilliman's concerns were justified. It could be that the Black Templars had simply been unable to link up with the torchbearers sent to them. The ship seemed barely voidworthy. Alcuin appeared unconcerned, even when they took a corridor where the temperature plummeted. The end was walled off by blast doors. A fierce cold radiated from them.

'We must go up through the service ways,' said Alcuin. 'The hull is open to the void here.'

Alcuin took Lucerne into a narrow staircase, by means of which they attained the ship's processional along the spine of the vessel, and there Lucerne encountered something that he had not seen before on a Space Marine vessel.

The heart of the *Cantatum Bellum* was occupied by a cathedrum. A wall of carved stone as ornate as any place of worship found on a shrine world filled the breadth of the ship. There must have been a thousand statues on it, all about a foot high, each occupying their own niche in the facade so they stood in vertical crowds, dense as a colony of seabirds. They were all mortal, so far as he could see: a host of saints.

There was a gothic arch in the centre, fifty feet high, with five archivolts heavily carved with hand-sized Space Marines engaged in battle. They framed an immense pair of wooden doors. These were also carved, with hundreds more small figures. A smaller wicket, big enough to admit a transhuman in armour, was set into the left gate. Alcuin opened it, and they went inside.

Chapter Eighteen

THE PENITENT KNIGHT
A CHAPLAIN'S ANGER
HELP REFUSED

Lucerne stepped into darkness, his entrance preceded by a gust of foul air that set the candles around the walls flickering. A single strike of leather scourging flesh echoed around the cathedrum, but whatever was in train there was halted by the snick of the latch on the door.

In the centre of the dark nave, before giant statues of Saint Sigismund and the Warrior-Emperor, twelve of the brothers of the Angevin Crusade stood in a circle around a single shaft of white light. They were a mixture of veterans and battle-brothers in the main, with only a single pair of neophytes. All of them were armoured and armed, and all of them were heavily marked by war.

The crusaders turned to look at him, red helm lenses glinting. The eyes of those who were helmless narrowed in the dark.

Alcuin bowed. 'My lords,' he announced. 'Lord Sergeant Racej Lucerne, of the Unnumbered Sons of Dorn, sent here at the primarch's command to–'

Lucerne strode past him, his boots ringing from the stone paving, so that he could see into the circle.

'Who is in charge here?' Lucerne demanded.

The remaining two members of the crusade were at the centre. One was their Chaplain, and he stood over the last, who, alone in being unarmoured, was kneeling, facing Saint Sigismund's effigy, head bowed and hands penitently clasped. His robes were in a pile at his side, his bare skin glistening with sweat and blood under the shaft of light. The Chaplain held a thonged whip in his hand, whose caress had laid many wounds upon the penitent's tattooed back.

'You interrupt our worship,' called the Chaplain. His skull helm was surmounted by a halo of spikes. His eye-lenses glowed with the working of the helm's machinery.

'Forgive me,' said Lucerne. 'I come to you on an errand of some urgency.'

'How can you ask for forgiveness when you do not understand the nature of the insult you have given?' said the Chaplain. 'There are few of us among the Adeptus Astartes who have seen the glory of the Emperor's light. You are shadowed, ignorant of the divinity of the god that made you. How, then, can you know the depth of your sacrilege?'

'I know,' said Lucerne. Very deliberately, he walked to the chancel, where stood the great altar flanked by Saint Sigismund and the Holy Emperor. There, he went to his knee, and made the sign of the aquila, his head bowed in silence.

'What are you doing?' demanded the Chaplain. He thrust the bloodied whip at a thrall, took a towel, and wiped his gauntlets clean. He stepped out of the circle, and took up his crozius from one of his brothers.

Lucerne stood. The Chaplain stopped before him. His black armour was covered with skulls that glared accusingly at the Primaris warrior. Lucerne reached up and undid his helm, exposing himself fully to the poisonous atmosphere of the ship.

'I ask forgiveness from the Emperor, and from the most holy Saint Sigismund, foremost of the sons of Dorn, he who saw the light, and sought to drive back the darkness, and took the oath of the Crusade Eternal.'

'First insults, now mockery.' The Chaplain responded by activating the disruption field of his crozius. It crackled loudly. 'You wear ritual chains for your weapons. You bear the cross of Sigismund. By what right do you carry these emblems of our faith?'

'By the right given me by the Emperor,' said Lucerne. 'I have taken Sigismund's oath, which is why I wear these oath-chains. I wear this cross,' he said, picking up the carved stone amulet hanging from his pauldron, 'in honour of his faith and his sacrifice.'

'You will pay for this effrontery,' said the Chaplain. 'None but the Black Templars may carry these symbols.' His crozius buzzed loudly.

Lucerne stared into the red eyes of the Chaplain.

'If faith in the Master of Mankind is restricted to your brotherhood alone, then you had best strike me down,' he said. 'For I have faith.'

The others in the crusade were looking to each other, eyes questioning.

'So be it,' said the Chaplain, and hefted his weapon.

When the Chaplain moved as if to strike, another voice rang out.

'Hold, Mortian!'

The kneeling Space Marine got to his feet, and moved from the circle. He was hard-faced, green-eyed, short by Space Marine standards, even those of the Firstborn, but broad across the shoulder. His head was fuzzed with blond stubble. A scar ran diagonally across his face, wide and smooth, breaking the nose as it crossed it.

'You say you believe. Explain,' he said to Lucerne.

'The simplest explanation is the truth,' said Lucerne, keeping his gaze locked onto the Chaplain's eye-lenses. 'I do believe. I believe in the divinity of the Master of Mankind with all my soul. I believe that He was sent to save us all from the darkness. I believe that He watches us now, and protects us. I believe that He suffers for us, to keep us safe. He burns with the light of agony to hold back the dark. That is why I serve Him.'

'Lies,' said the Chaplain. 'This cannot be so. You are an infidel, a thing of Cawl's.'

'Be at peace, Mortian,' said the other Space Marine. He held up a placating hand, though the hostility on his face told another story. 'Explain further.'

'There are those among the Primaris who believe as you do in the divinity of the Emperor. I am one of them. Before I was taken by the agents of the archmagos, I was training to be a priest with the Missionarius Galaxia. The changes wrought upon me did not blunt my faith. I have fifty others of similar conviction with me, all true believers, sent by the primarch to reinforce your crusade. We have a warship to add to yours. I mean no disrespect, but you are few and you need our aid.'

A snarl escaped the Chaplain's voxmitter. 'We are the true servants of the Emperor. We need no aid but His.'

'Peace, Brother Mortian!' said the other, more forcefully now. Serfs came with robes and a habit. One of the neophytes joined them, and together they helped the whipped Space Marine dress. The warrior showed no evidence of pain as the rough cloth dragged over his wounds, then he looked to Lucerne again.

'He is correct, stranger. The Emperor is our guide and our brother-in-arms. We require no help from the primarch. We answer only to the highest authority. We thank you for your efforts in reaching us, but decline your offer. Take your men, and leave.'

Lucerne switched his attention from the Chaplain to the Space Marine.

'You are Castellan Beorhtnoth?'

'I am he,' said Beorhtnoth.

'It took three days to locate your vessel. Why do you not muster with the rest of the fleet at the prime world of Lessira?'

'The Emperor alone dictates our path,' said Beorhtnoth. 'We follow our own destiny. We fight alongside this fleet for now, as He decrees. When He has other tasks for us, we shall move where He decrees.'

The neophyte went back to his place among the others, throwing Lucerne a troubled glance as he did. Lucerne noted it, and decided to seek out the boy later. He did not return the look, but affected that he had not seen, and held instead Beorhtnoth's eye.

'Then you will know that all the Space Marine Chapters are to receive reinforcements, at the order of the primarch, Roboute Guilliman, Lord Commander of the Imperium and Imperial Regent, by the will of the God-Emperor Himself.'

'Is that so?' said Beorhtnoth. A thrall handed him a cloth. Another brought a silver bowl full of scented water. He ritually cleansed his hands and face before he spoke again, muttering prayers, making Lucerne wait. When he was done, he continued. 'The Space Marine Chapters are independent. They are beholden to no authority but their own, by the order of your primarch, ten thousand years ago.'

'He is not my primarch. My gene-father is Rogal Dorn, the same as yours.'

'Your gene-father is Belisarius Cawl,' growled Mortian.

'This is ridiculous,' said Lucerne. 'The son of the Emperor Himself has sent out orders, and you ignore them?'

'We take them under advisement, as is our right, if indeed it is he risen from the dead.'

'You doubt it?'

Beorhtnoth shrugged. 'How can such a thing be so? The enemy has many weapons. Lies are one of their strongest.'

Despite being prepared for intransigence, Lucerne found he could not believe what he was hearing. 'It is no lie. I have served Lord Guilliman myself. He is the son of the Emperor returned again. Your own High Marshal Helbrecht has decreed that all Black Templars crusades are to accept Primaris reinforcements and technologies immediately. All crusades currently in contact with the Officio Logisticarum have taken their oaths of fealty to the Imperium and accepted the Primaris technology. All,' he stressed, 'except yours.'

'But we have been sent no reinforcements,' said Beorhtnoth.

'A torchbearer fleet was despatched to your warzone four years ago.'

'It never reached us.' Beorhtnoth handed back the towel. The thralls bowed and departed.

'We have a message from your Marshal Angevin saying that it did, along with his oath of fealty.'

'They reached our system, yes. There was but a single ship, badly damaged by transit through the warp, and overwhelmed by enemies,' said Beorhtnoth. 'We never met face to face. Is that not so, Mortian?'

'It is so,' said the Chaplain.

'I am here now,' said Lucerne.

'And I still decline, as is my right,' said Beorhtnoth.

'You are a castellan. Where is Marshal Angevin? This crusade carries his name.'

Beorhtnoth bared his teeth, an expression that was not quite a smile. 'He enjoys his reward in the next life, sat at the right hand of the Emperor, amid His army of champions.'

'He is dead then.'

'He died trying to save these so-called reinforcements. Had they not come, he would still be alive,' Beorhtnoth said. 'This conversation is over. You may leave now.' As if his words were a trigger, his men began to move towards the door. Power armour whined.

'You defy the wishes of the primarch?' Lucerne called after the departing men.

'He is not our primarch, Lucerne, as you forget.'

Mortian extinguished the power field of his crozius, and pointed the inactive head at Lucerne. 'If the Emperor desired us to have your kind in our ranks, then we would already have them. The fact that the earlier fleet failed is an expression of His divine will.'

'His divine will in what, exactly?' said Lucerne.

'That we retain the purity of His original design,' said Mortian. 'We are the work of the Emperor. You are the work of Belisarius Cawl. We are His Angels. You are not.'

'Mortian, you have said enough. Come,' said the castellan.

'I am, then, a false Angel?' said Lucerne.

'Those are your words,' said the Chaplain. He stared at Lucerne a moment longer, then he too turned his back upon him.

'Go in peace, Lucerne. Fight your war elsewhere with honour,' said Beorhtnoth.

'Wait!' Lucerne shouted. 'If it is the will of the Emperor that you seek, let us ask Him to give His judgement.' The Space Marines did not stop, but moved insolently, slowly away from the Primaris Marine. 'I demand my right to trial by combat!'

The small group of Space Marines stopped. Beorhtnoth remained facing away from Lucerne.

'By what law do you claim this right?' he asked. His voice boomed around the nave. 'You are not of our brotherhood, and have no standing here.'

Lucerne lifted up his right hand. 'I wear the chains. I have taken the oaths of Sigismund, the great saint and your founding master. By the decree of your High Marshal and the will of the Avenging Son, I am a Black Templar.'

'You do not wear our colours,' said Beorhtnoth.

'In deference to you only,' said Lucerne. 'I would rather be given them by my new brothers than take them.'

'You will not have them. You are no brother of ours.'

Beorhtnoth made to go, but one of the others half turned. He wore the red-trimmed livery of a Sword Brother, one of the Chapter veterans.

'He has the right,' he said.

'What?' Beorhtnoth asked him. 'Why do you speak up in his favour, Sword Brother Alanus?'

'Because he has the right,' said Alanus. 'He is of Dorn's line. He has taken the oaths. He may be misguided, and if he is then the Emperor will show us, but let him prove himself by the sword trial.'

'He has no right as a Primaris.'

Alanus glanced at Lucerne. 'That vote was not unanimous. There are those of us who remain uncomfor–'

'Silence!' Beorhtnoth shouted, and his rage was swift and fierce.

'I will not be silent,' said Alanus. 'I believe him to be wrong, and you to be right, brother-castellan, but if he makes the plea of challenge, it must be answered. That is our way. We have afforded this honour even to xenos, in the past, whom we hate and abhor. He may be impure, but he has the right.'

Beorhtnoth looked to Mortian. 'What say you, lorekeeper?'

Mortian paused before speaking, and when he did, it was with reluctance.

'Brother Alanus speaks wisely. The challenge must be accepted.'

Beorhtnoth turned back around to speak to Lucerne, his face a snarl. 'Then you will fight me, and when I kill you, your brothers will go.'

'No. When I best you, we join this crusade,' said Lucerne.

Beorhtnoth's face twisted with an insane rage, and it looked

like he might attack right there, but instead he nodded slowly.
'Agreed. Under the gaze of the Emperor and the saint.'

Chaplain Mortian took his crozius in both hands. 'So be it,' he said. 'Let it be decided by the Emperor's will.'

Chapter Nineteen

DUEL

MERCY

NO TRIUMPH

They faced each other across a chipped black circle painted on the ship's deck. Statues of dead Space Marines looked upon the duelling ground, and in the dark they swelled the spectating crusaders into a crowd.

Facing the warriors past and present of the Angevin Crusade, Lucerne was alone.

Lucerne's lack of support was irrelevant. He concentrated on the duel to come, the feel of the deck under his feet, the size of the space they had to move in, seeking out anything that might give him an advantage. According to the rites of the Trial of Blades, neither he nor his opponent wore armour, but waited bare-chested at opposite sides of the ring. Lucerne was bigger than them all, difficult for the Black Templars to garb. They had found him trousers that nearly fit, and a pair of leather boots that didn't. The discomfort was of no consequence. He did not think it would affect his ability to fight, but it was another small variable that had to be accounted for. The most pressing factor was Beorhtnoth himself, how skilled he would be, how strong, how fast. Lucerne tried to gauge these things as he watched him pacing back and forth like a caged felid, his expression fierce, tattoos rippling with the movement of huge muscles. His hatred was there, bright as fire in his eyes, brazenly displayed. Was that hatred for all Lucerne's kind, or just for him?

He had to get to the bottom of what had happened to the torchbearers, but first he must focus. He had to beat Beorhtnoth. He had little doubt the Black Templar would kill him if he could. Lucerne had to be merciful if he could. That was a disadvantage.

Mortian came forward, his skull helm grim. The others were barefaced, their expressions more guarded than their leader's, but hostile nonetheless. Even the statues seemed to judge Lucerne poorly. He wondered what the crusaders had seen, and what they had done. He thought that Lord Guilliman might have been right. When he looked at these men, at their fanatical faith, he saw the potential for treachery.

'Since the dawn of our Chapter and before, to the days of the sacred Seventh Legion, the sword has been the ultimate arbitrator,' Mortian said. 'The Primaris Marine Lucerne, by the gene-seed he bears and the loyalty he professes to He on Terra, has rightfully challenged our castellan, Brother Beorhtnoth, for a place in our crusade.'

Beorhtnoth's neophyte went to his master's side, a pair of thralls came to Lucerne, and they equipped the opponents with identical broadswords. Lucerne opened his right hand to receive the sword. The hilt was placed in his palm. A heavy manacle was closed about his left wrist. He looked down when the thralls pushed the locking pin in place, and attached the short chain coming off the manacle's staple to a loop on the pommel of the sword. The thralls were malnourished and sickly. Their skin was jaundiced, and they had sores around their mouths where their respirators irritated their skin. They smelled as bad as they looked. They lacked Alcuin's confidence, and neither of them dared look up at him, but focused solely on their task before withdrawing, bowing, their eyes averted. He also watched Beorhtnoth's neophyte, sure he was avoiding eye contact. Lucerne's attention seemed to bother him greatly. Lucerne wanted to know what was behind the warning glance he had given him in the cathedrum.

'A Black Templar's weapon is a part of his body. It is a part of his soul. It is his honour. It is his life,' Mortian said. 'You wear Saint Sigismund's chains as we do, Lucerne, therefore I grant you the privilege of doing so here in this duelling ground. It is not an allowance given lightly.' He turned the glowing skull eyes of his helm from Lucerne to Beorhtnoth.

'There is a matter in dispute. Let the Emperor decide. Be forced from the ring, and forfeit the duel. He who yields or is slain shall admit his error, in the eyes and the judgement of the almighty Master of Mankind, who watches all we do, and guides us in our service to Him.'

Lucerne adjusted the metal cuff, and made a few experimental passes with the sword. Air hissed over the razored edge. He swivelled his ankles, balanced upon the balls of his feet, finding his centre.

Mortian stepped back to the edge of the circle. He raised his crozius. Beorhtnoth continued to pace. Lucerne shifted his weight, coming into a low guard position, sword held off centre in a double grip below his waist, point up. Beorhtnoth kept his blade loose in his hand, letting it sweep back and forth, like he were clearing weeds on some backworld agricolum.

Lucerne slowed his breathing. His twin hearts thumped slowly in his chest. When Mortian let his weapon fall, Beorhtnoth would come for him. The Black Templar was rousing himself to anger. Where his skin was not darkened by the black carapace plates, it was flushed with increased blood flow. He was breathing fast. He was calling on his Emperor's gifts to make him strong and fast.

Lucerne would fight with calm. Let Beorhtnoth's choler burn him out, he thought.

He must win. If even this one, insignificant group of Space Marines rejected the Primaris Marines, others would surely follow.

'Begin!' Mortian screamed suddenly, his vox-amplified voice filling the chamber. The head of his crozius thumped to the deck.

As Lucerne expected, Beorhtnoth wasted no time in attacking, sword blurring into a high arc and sweeping down as he charged.

A shift in Lucerne's posture, an adjustment of his arms, and his blade rose to meet the castellan's. They connected with jarring force, sparks chipped from the edges, the ring of metal on metal pure and high. The contact was violent but fleeting, and then Beorhtnoth was past Lucerne.

Lucerne pivoted around and back. Beorhtnoth turned fast, almost instantaneously following the move, sweeping his blade one-handed out at arm's length. The blade buzzed through the air, missing Lucerne by a hair's breadth.

Lucerne switched to the middle guard, point forward, aimed at Beorhtnoth's head as they paced in slow circles around each other.

There was no talk. Both the combatants were stern, eyes locked.

Hatred was not Beorhtnoth's alone. The others stared at him with loathing, except, perhaps, the youth.

Beorhtnoth feinted, once, twice, three times, each stab and swing bringing him closer to Lucerne, until the fourth strike was made in earnest, and Lucerne caught it in good time but with poor form, not clearing the weapon, and their blades remained locked. Beorhtnoth leaned into the blow, upsetting Lucerne's balance. His blade rasped down the length of Lucerne's as he pushed him back. Lucerne regained his poise before they reached the edge of the black circle, and turned Beorhtnoth and his blade. The swords slid up and down each other as the warriors sought advantage. Steel kissed steel. Finally, quillions locked, and Lucerne used his greater strength to twist Beorhtnoth's blade, almost disarming him. The First-born Space Marine kept his grip but, at a disadvantage now, was shoved back by Lucerne.

They parted, and circled again.

Both of them were perspiring, and more profusely than a mortal man, as their bodies sought to keep cool under the stress of heightened metabolisms working hard. Lucerne's hearts ran faster, their twinned, offset beats kept his pulse racing. Man-made organs secreted synthetic hormones. The tang of ancient science rose from warriors' sweat.

He thought of calling out to Beorhtnoth to see sense, but the look on the Black Templar's face dissuaded him. This duel would end in blood, one way or another.

Again Beorhtnoth attacked, a low swing turning to a high cut, which, though parried, got him nearer to Lucerne than the Primaris warrior would have liked. Another crossing of blades, this time at chest height. They pressed close, like wrestlers, face to face, so close that Beorhtnoth's spittle spattered Lucerne's cheeks. Muscles strained with effort, both warriors seeking to force the other back and out of the ring. Suddenly, Beorhtnoth changed his strategy, pushing himself away, using Lucerne's strength to help throw himself back. The sudden release had Lucerne stumble slightly. Taking advantage of this tiny opening, Beorhtnoth swung his sword around his head, releasing the hilt from his hands, and using the honour chain to lengthen his reach, swept it at Lucerne.

It was a wild move, and one that Lucerne did not see coming. The sword could have hit him on the flat, and done him no harm. He might even have trapped it against his side. Neither of those things happened: instead, the point, rotating like a drill, hissed towards his head. Lucerne leaned back awkwardly, turning his head, but the tip caught him. So sharp, he felt the cut only as a cold caress that turned hot as flesh parted down to the bone, and his engineered blood pattered to the floor.

The sting was a rebuke, not pain as a man would feel it, but the agony of dishonour.

A lesser opponent might have taken the time to gloat; not Beorhtnoth. He yanked his sword back, its length bouncing along the floor, took the hilt into his hand, and attacked again. Lucerne let out a wordless shout, took Beorhtnoth's sword with a high, downward, circular parry, swept it aside and found the termination of the move in Beorhtnoth's thigh.

Lucerne's sword bit deep. Beorhtnoth grunted, a little of his strength going from his right leg, but he did not fall. Instead he drove his head forward hard into Lucerne's face, flattening his nose. Bone cracked loudly. Lucerne's vision starred. Now, that did hurt.

They parted again, Beorhtnoth limping, blood sheeting from a flap of skin and muscle hanging from his thigh, Lucerne staggering, part dazed.

'That is two blows for one, Primaris,' said the castellan. 'Do you yield? Take yourself away from here, and find a life with another Chapter. There is no dishonour in owning defeat. It is by our errors that we learn, praise the Emperor.'

Lucerne shook his head. There was a hole in his cheek letting in air. Blood from both wounds coloured his lips, but already they were clotting.

'No dishonour except my existence,' he said. 'Do not deny your hatred for me. I see it on every face in this room.'

'You are mistaken,' said Beorhtnoth.

'I was speaking to your Chaplain,' said Lucerne. 'He hides nothing.' He spat out a mouthful of blood. 'What occurred with the torchbearers, castellan? Why will you not accept the Gift of Cawl?'

'Nothing occurred,' said Beorhtnoth, 'but a tragedy of war.' His wound was ceasing to bleed now, though it was deeper than Lucerne's. 'Maybe they had honour and skill. I see both lacking in you. You must prove you are worthy, and you are failing. Your kind is trumpeted as bigger and stronger. Better than us. Where then is the Emperor's blessing upon you? Why do you bleed?'

Beorhtnoth attacked again. A blur of blows were traded between them, each one delivered with enough force to send displays of sparks spraying over the duelling ground. Again their blades locked. They pushed closer, and closer. Beorhtnoth grunted with the effort. His wound leaked as the effort split the clots.

'Will you yield to me?' Lucerne said.

'Never!' spat Beorhtnoth.

'You must. You must yield to me. You must yield to the primarch, the Emperor, and the needs of the Imperium.'

Slowly, slowly, Lucerne's extra height and strength told. His skin rippled with the efforts of the sinew coils, an enhancement the Firstborn lacked, and he forced Beorhtnoth down. He hissed through his teeth. The wound on the castellan's leg played its part, and Beorhtnoth was pushed to the ground.

'Yield!' said Lucerne.

'Never,' said Beorhtnoth.

Their swords pinned between them, they sank to the deck. Lucerne got his elbow onto Beorhtnoth's neck. The castellan got a hand free, and hooked his fingers into Lucerne's cheek wound, ripping it wider. The pain of the tearing was intense, and Lucerne let out a growl that turned to a shout. The edges of the swords were cutting at them both, leaving thin wounds on their chests, but still he bore down, choking the air from his foe.

'Help him, Chaplain!' Lucerne heard someone say.

'That is not the rite. They must fight alone,' said Mortian. 'Stay your hands, all of you!'

Transhuman blood was engineered to soak up more oxygen. A Space Marine could go for minutes without air. It took an agonisingly long time for Beorhtnoth's eyes to slide closed, and his bloodied hand to come free of Lucerne's open cheek.

Lucerne stood. His cheek was hanging free of his face, exposing his teeth and gums.

'I win,' he managed to say, bringing forth a great welling of blood.

Mortian looked to the castellan. 'He still lives. You must finish him.'

'I will not sully myself with so dishonourable a kill. He cannot defend himself. I win. The Emperor has spoken,' Lucerne said. His front was covered in his own blood, from his face, nose and the long blade cuts that lacerated his chest.

'He must yield, or he must die. He has done neither,' said Mortian.

Lucerne held up his right arm. Gripping the sword pommel in the left, he pulled his hands apart, reddening with the effort, until with a plangent noise the chain broke. He cast aside his sword, and it clattered over the duelling ring. Then he bent down, took Beorhtnoth under the armpits, dragged him from the ring, and dropped him.

'There. I have proven myself,' said Lucerne. 'I will not slay a loyal servant of the Emperor while he lies helpless. That is not the way of the faithful. He is out of the duelling ground. By the laws of the Trial of Blades, I win, and I claim my prize. My brothers and I shall reinforce you, and we shall fight together, for the greater glory of the Imperium.'

He stared at the Chaplain, who matched his gaze with the bulbous lenses of his skull helm. All in the chamber looked on, waiting for a conclusion to the contest. Finally, the Chaplain spoke.

'Very well. You may join us. But you alone.'

'That was not the pledge,' said Lucerne. Speaking was getting harder. His face burned with pain. His muscles cramped. Each word was a chewed wad of bloody cotton.

'You have bested the castellan and shown your prowess. Your brothers have not. Every one of them would have to fight us to win their place.'

'That is senseless, and it is not what we agreed. We are here to help you. Let us fulfil our oaths.'

'It is our rite, not yours,' said Mortian. 'By the authority invested in me by the Adeptus Ministorum, through whom the will of the Emperor flows at its most pure, I deem it so. Be not affronted. You have proved your worth and will fight by our side. Take up your place, or do not, but your brothers shall not be admitted to our crusade while I live.' He turned to the others. 'Neophyte Botho, see to your master. Neophyte Hengist, show Brother Lucerne to his quarters.'

The crusaders went into action.

'Where is your Apothecary, to see to my injuries?'

'He is dead,' said Mortian. 'Gone to the Emperor's side as all the righteous are fated to do. You must tend to your wounds yourself.'

Hengist tarried, waiting for him as the chamber emptied, leaving Lucerne the victor.

To Lucerne, it felt like no triumph at all.

Chapter Twenty

DIOMED PAYS A VISIT

BETTER TREATMENT

BAD SPIES

Fabian's quarters aboard the *Saint Aster* were ridiculously opulent. He was expecting an officer's cell like he'd had on the *Dawn of Fire*, but instead he and Yassilli were shown to a suite of rooms by the purser, a fussy little man who ran about everywhere straightening the cushions before scurrying back to his office.

'We are going up in the world,' said Yassilli, after he'd gone. She caught Fabian looking oddly at her. 'What?'

'Compared to me, you were raised in a state of unimaginable wealth. Aren't you used to places like this?'

'I was, but I have spent most of the last few years bunking with other historitors in the barracks while you got your own room, so I think I'm allowed to comment.'

The floor was a beautiful parquet. There were bookcases, barred to keep the books in place, a well-stocked drinks cabinet contained within an antique globe of Mars, shelves with carefully chosen artefacts illuminated by individual lumen beams, and a bed large enough for four.

'I suppose I shouldn't get used to this,' said Fabian. 'I'll be moving on soon enough. Not everywhere will be so grand.'

'I was wondering what the facilities would be like in Imperium Nihilus,' said Yassilli with a grin. 'Sadly, I won't be finding out, because I'm staying here. What a shame.'

'Don't you have somewhere to be?' Fabian said. 'The others are coming.'

'They are,' said Yassilli. 'Historitor majoris,' she said. She bowed and left him alone.

Fabian discovered the quarters had a bathroom bigger than his old quarters. He took a bath. It felt sickeningly wasteful of water, and he was still feeling guilty as he went through his papers later that evening, when there came a knock at the door.

'Enter!' he called.

The door opened. A woman in a high-ranking officer's uniform came in. Fabian was by that time rather tired, and his heart sank when he saw that she didn't look happy. Unhappy faces meant long conversations, if not argument.

'Hello,' he said. He got up, self-consciously tightening his robe. 'Forgive my attire. I was rather filthy after our journey here.'

She didn't seem to care.

'I am First Lieutenant Finnula Diomed,' she said. 'Groupmistress Athagey's second-in-command, and shipmistress of the *Saint Aster*.'

'I am Historitor Majoris Fabian Guelphrain,' he said. 'Please call me Fabian.' He held out his hand. She ignored it.

'How nice,' she said. Her teeth weren't gritted, but they weren't far off.

'I'm sorry if that sounds glib,' he said. 'I mean it sincerely. Rank gets in the way, doesn't it? Not that I demean yours. First lieutenant, and I'll wager that Groupmistress Athagey only has the most competent people by her side.'

She stared at him blankly, like he were gabbling in the deep cloud dialects of Venus. She was quite pretty though, he found himself thinking.

'Are you alright?' she asked him.

Fabian blinked, realising he'd been staring.

'It was a difficult voyage getting here. I'm still not over it. Sorry. Is there something I can do for you?'

'I would be grateful for a few moments of your time,' she said.

'Of course,' said Fabian, managing to recover some of his poise. 'It is our role as historitors to act as bridges, if we can. Would you like a drink?' he asked. 'A little wine, maybe? Nothing too strong, I'll wager? You don't look like the kind of woman that drinks on duty.'

She gave him a frosty look. 'A little wine would be welcome.'

He went to the drinks cabinet. 'I'll say this for you, you're treating me far better than even Guilliman himself did.' He selected a bottle, and two glasses. 'Please,' he said, 'sit.'

There was a round table with four chairs in one corner of the room beneath the portrait of a glaring admiral. He gestured to that, and she sat. There he joined her, and poured them both some wine.

'Is this about my work here? I assure you, we try to cause no problem. We do try to smooth over the worst friction, if it occurs.'

'Your work is your work. It must be done. We all must serve,' said Diomed. She let out a tense breath, put her hat down on the table, and smoothed back her hair.

'I've already spoken to the groupmistress about it,' he said. 'If she gave you the impression that we...' He stopped. Diomed looked pained. 'Hang on a minute,' he said. 'This is about my meeting with Groupmistress Athagey, isn't it? If you've come here to ensure that I know we're not welcome, she made herself quite clear on that score.'

'It's not that. It's difficult. A rather delicate matter.' She hesitated. 'Look, I would not have let you meet her alone if I had had notification of your arrival,' said Diomed. 'I received the news too late.'

'You would have stopped her seeing me? Sounds like you don't like historitors very much.'

'That is not the case. It's the groupmistress. I wanted to make sure she was sober,' said the first lieutenant bleakly. She gulped her wine – a shame, as it was a fine variety. The poor woman must have felt disloyal, he thought. 'But she is wily, and she will speak her mind, something that I advise her against often. I have come here to be frank with you. Eloise is a brilliant commander, but she can be a little indiscreet. She does not mind who she offends. Her opinion is worth more than her life to her. She will tell you so, if she decides to speak to you again. If she does say anything like that, please ignore it.'

'I see,' said Fabian neutrally, sure there was more to come. There was.

'I know why you are here. The primarch has ordered the expansion of the Logos. The groupmistress may make this more difficult, but I can prepare the way for you.'

'I suppose you want something in exchange for this service. What is it?'

She looked guiltily into her wine. She seemed very tired, thought Fabian. There was a certain vulnerability to her that he found touching...

What am I thinking? he thought.

'I should ask you for nothing,' Diomed said. 'It is my duty to aid you in your task. The primarch commands this be done, and he is the living hand of the Emperor. So it will be done.'

'But you still want a favour,' said Fabian.

She gave him a slightly desperate look.

'Whatever offensive nonsense Groupmistress Athagey said to

you in the Dead End. The ready room,' she added, responding to Fabian's questioning expression. 'We call it the Dead End. Whatever she said in there, do not put it down in your histories. She is an asset in battle, but a liability in diplomacy. She deserves no censure. I should have been there. Her rudeness is my failure.'

'How do you know she was rude to me?' asked Fabian.

'I know her very well.'

'You mean she's rude to everyone.'

'Will you help me? She is my friend. I do not wish to see her castigated. I want her rougher edges overlooked. I'll do what I need to do to protect her.'

Fabian looked at her with fresh respect. He didn't doubt her words.

'No wonder the Imperium is full of corruption,' he murmured.

'I'm sorry?' she replied, and looked scared. It was an emotion out of place on the face of this battle-hardened woman.

'Fear,' he said. 'It's supposed to keep us all in line, but all it does is help us exploit each other.'

'Perhaps,' she said. Her lips went thin. She was waiting for his decision. He hurried to put her out of her misery.

'She's addicted to combat stimms, isn't she?'

Diomed went white. 'I beg you not to–'

Fabian held up his hand.

'I don't mean that as some sort of sinister preamble before I extract more favours from you. I mention it only so that you know I noticed. I mean, it is clear as the void.'

'It's only when we're not fighting,' Diomed said. 'Eloise requires constant stimulation. She gets bored so easily.'

'Well,' said Fabian. 'Her behaviour is interesting to me purely as historical colour. We are not spies, first lieutenant.' He smiled awkwardly. 'We are not the Inquisition or enforcers of the Lex Imperialis. We document things. We are not here to judge individuals. It's systemic failures that interest us, not personal, moral ones, and as long as she keeps winning battles I would not worry too much. The Logos' main role is reassembling the history of the Imperium so the primarch can see what went wrong. Writing a history of this crusade also falls under our remit, but it is secondary. Spying on particular individuals, or reporting lapses in judgement so they may be punished, is not what we are for. Though of course, if you were to start working for the enemy, or proved to be monstrously incompetent it would be different.' He was still failing to put Diomed completely at ease. 'You have commissars for that anyway. It's not my job.'

'Sorenkus,' said Diomed. 'He is our Navis-Commissar. He's easy enough to control. He only cares about results.'

'Winning battles, see? You were worried my arrival would upset finely balanced arrangements?'

She nodded. 'The Logos is regarded with suspicion. I hear rumours about the primarch. I hear that Guilliman brooks no disagreement. There are some who say he wants to instal himself as Emperor.'

What she said was dangerous, but Fabian didn't care about that, it was a common enough opinion in certain circles. 'Do you believe that?'

'No,' she said.

'Good. He has no time for disagreement, because he's nearly always right. That's why he doesn't tolerate dissent, unless it is well reasoned, and true, then he listens, but most of the time it's all down to him. I worry about him,' he said.

She looked surprised.

'He's not a human being like you or I, or the Adeptus Astartes,' he explained. 'Even the Custodians don't come close to what he can do. He's like a...'

'A god? That is what the Adeptus Ministorum say he is.'

'Not like a god exactly, he is a man, but he's like a man

concentrated. Everything that makes a hero is in him, but to excess – a hundred heroes, compressed to fit a human shape. He's...' Fabian ran out of words. 'If you imagine light,' he gestured vaguely up at the stateroom's chandeliers. 'He's like a sun to a lumen bulb. It's all still light, but... not. He's human, but more intense. And he is not all-powerful. He had brothers. Now he's alone. The fate of us all rests on his shoulders. It can be nothing but crushing.' He drank some more wine. 'He's not like other masters you may have served. He is our only hope. If he wishes to become Emperor, well, I've seen no proof of that. He's here to save us. It is that simple.'

'Then the groupmistress will not be censured for her lack of diplomacy?'

'Neither for that nor for her taste in stimulants,' said Fabian. 'Not from me, anyway. Not from anyone else either, if she continues to win as many battles as she has.'

Only now did Diomed seem mollified.

'Though she was very upset about the name change.'

Diomed rolled her eyes. 'Terra's dry dust, not that again!'

'I thought it a bit sad actually. She did have a point. It's that kind of thoughtless bureaucracy that grinds us down. Lord Guilliman is not perfect. He is a genius. We are not. He cannot make us all as clever as him, so he gives us rules to live by. But what are human beings going to do with rules other than misinterpret them, try to work around them, or just break them? He has a thing about rules. It's the way he was made.'

'You speak so familiarly of him,' said Diomed.

Fabian shrugged. 'Trust me, the first time I met him I felt like I was being pinned to the ground by a mountain every time he looked at me. But humans are adaptable. We adapt.' He smiled again. This time, she didn't look like she wanted to kill him. 'So, now I've revealed myself to be no threat, I suppose you're going to make my life miserable?'

She gave a brief laugh.

'No, I will help you. I will make sure the historitors are properly established in Battle Group Iolus. I'll help you with the other groupmasters here in orbit around Lessira. You'll find most of them sympathetic anyway, but there are always quicker ways of getting things done.'

'Indeed there are,' said Fabian.

'You will have to be quick,' said Diomed. 'We'll be here for six weeks, but the others are beginning to disperse. You are later than we expected, and the enemy is raising rebellion after rebellion throughout this part of the Segmentum Solar. There is no time for rest. We suspect a major offensive from the Heretic Astartes soon. Fomenting rebellion followed by multiple-system invasion fits the modus operandi of the Word Bearers. It began at Talledus, not far from Sol itself. Fleet intelligence believe the Word Bearers were waiting for the majority of crusade fleets to depart before they began their attack there, provoking a revolt on the cardinal world. They worked with the Iron Warriors there too, like at Gathalamor. They might have been stopped on that occasion, but it was only the first. Seven cardinal worlds have risen up, their populations turned against the light of Terra. There have been many other attacks besides.'

Fabian nodded. 'We'll record it all. I have yet to meet the historitor currently with the battle group. I should start there. Can you get a message to her? I expected her to meet with us, in fact, when we arrived, but she didn't.'

Diomed drummed her fingers on the table.

'I'll take you to her.' She stood up abruptly.

'Now?'

'Why not? We can talk a little more on the way. Would that do?'

Fabian considered. He was exhausted, but doubted he'd sleep if he retired now. Besides, when opportunity presented itself, it was best to grasp it. 'Absolutely. Just let me get dressed.'

Diomed put her cap back on, and adjusted it until it was properly seated. 'It's funny what you say about you not being spies.'

'How so?'

'Because I've often thought if Historitor Serisa Vallia is a spy, she's a lousy one,' said Diomed. 'Or, by appearing to be so incompetent, very effective. I've considered both possibilities. I'll help you, but in your records note down that I still do not trust you.'

'Believe me, it's already in there,' said Fabian.

Chapter Twenty-One

LIFE OF PLENTY

TO SERVE TRULY

CHANGER OF THE WAYS

Gavimor's existence became one of indulgence. Yheng came to see him often, bringing with her new and undreamt-of pleasures. She showed him some of the sorcerous arts she had learned, and told him he too could learn them, if he remained true to his oath.

Narcotics, drink, warm bodies, fine food, Gavimor enjoyed them all. Yheng taught him mantras of command that would allow him to exert his will over the lesser spirits of the warp. She gave him visions of faraway places and times, and he learned more of the evil of the God-Emperor. The old him, jaded as he was, would have been horrified, but now it just seemed obvious that something as oppressive as the Imperium could only be the work of a monster, and he lamented those who would never know.

When he said this to Yheng, she put a finger to his lips.

'Speak not of the weak. The Emperor follows the same law as the rest of we enlightened – to the strong go the spoils. His greatest crime is not that He takes power for Himself, that is the natural order of things. His crime is that He pretends other- wise. Hypocrisy is His greatest sin.'

Time passed in a blur. How long he was on the ship he did not know. The progression of events collapsed into fragmentary moments. Taken as a whole they seemed to make sense, but when he stopped to think about the days, they were frighteningly dis- jointed. Tharador was with him, then she was not. It was dark, it was light. One second he seemed to be asleep, the next he was peer- ing through the veil of reality into unknown worlds. The shadow men were there sometimes, though now they only watched from respectful distances. They dared not attack him any longer.

Finally, abruptly, it ended. Tharador came to him with two muscular serfs, empty-eyed and silent as the rest.

'Tonight is the time,' she said to him. 'Tonight you will ascend and embrace your potential as a servant of the gods.'

'Tonight?' he asked, disbelieving.

She smiled. 'Tonight.'

He was cleaned, and fed fine foods. Tharador plied him with wine. She took him through the words he must say, making sure he knew them. Then he was dressed in robes worked with gold, and led out of his cell for the first time. The corridor beyond was foreign ground, and resisted his presence. It swam in and out of perspective, refusing to reveal itself. It was nothing but a corridor, he reassured himself, but he felt he wandered into forbidden realms. If he was on a ship, it was like none he had ever set foot on before. He passed from the place of his impris- onment into raging factory levels, where the heat beat at him in time with the hammers of the forges. Through these domains, where strange beasts howled as they were trapped in bodies of steel, he came to the place of his doom.

Another corridor, the duplicate of the first and just as uncertain, then brass doors inscribed with the sigils of the Great Powers.

They opened to him. Tharador's serfs led him into a room, very tall but narrow. The walls were decorated with sinuous curves like those Tharador had carved into her flesh. Eight humans, enlightened sorcerers like Tharador, stood in a circle. An unlit brazier was placed between each. There was a ninth place that was empty; Tharador's, he assumed.

A pulpit was raised over the ring. In it was a stooped, spindly figure. Where the others were recognisably human, this one was not. As Gavimor drew near, even in his drugged state, he saw that the man was a mutant of gross kind.

He halted. The two serfs stopped.

'Do not be alarmed,' Tharador whispered into his ear. 'This is my master, the sorcerer Tenebrus. You see the marks on him? They are the signs of his favour with the gods. He will lead the ritual that will bring you your rewards. Only he can do this. Do not be afraid.'

Either side of Tenebrus were two large hourglasses. Their sands were not contained by the usual bulbs, but held in multi-sectioned glass chambers which together made a sigil Tharador had told him was the mark of wise Tzeentch. One glass held pink sand, the other blue, and while the pink sand rested in the lower part of the device, the blue sand was gathered at the top of its glass in defiance of the ship's gravity.

Gavimor was led into the centre of the circle, into a pool of warm light. Tharador left him and took up her place with the others. A serf hurried up to her and put a heavy staff in her hand. He felt lost without her. But he must be brave. *Only the strong are deemed worthy,* he reminded himself.

Tenebrus looked down upon him. He had a broad smile. Too broad.

'Gavimor, welcome,' he said. 'You wish to break free from the dead hand of the Emperor and realise your potential? You wish to give yourself to the Powers and serve them, so that you may serve yourself?'

He looked to Tharador; she nodded. A gentle chant began. It soothed and electrified simultaneously. He was standing on the shore of a new, wild sea.

'I do. I pledge to serve the pantheon,' he said, fighting to keep the quaver from his voice.

'Today you shall be given to the great Architect of Fate, what do you say? Do you go to him willingly? Will you allow yourself to be filled up by his glory?'

'I will.'

'Then call to him,' said Tenebrus.

Gavimor spoke the words Tharador had taught him. They were faltering at first, then came quickly and strong. 'I come here to greet many-hued Tzeentch, Watcher of Destiny and Changer of Ways. I give myself freely to him, so I may partake of his wisdom, and know the twisted paths of the future, and the past.'

Tenebrus nodded paternally at him, as if proud of what he had done. 'Good. Good.'

The chant rose. Gavimor felt a sudden pressure in his wrists and ankles. Bindings of light gripped him, as solid and unbreakable as those of iron that had bound him on board the Black Ship. They spread his arms and legs and pulled him into the air.

'Tharador!' he called, suddenly panicked.

She ignored him, looked steadfastly ahead, chanting with the other sorcerers.

A door opened, and a wailing came out of it. Men armed with curved blades and whips forced in a group of Imperial priests, all of them abused, their faces bruised, robes torn, flesh cut. They were goaded into place behind the sorcerers, forming a second circle.

The chanting rose. Tenebrus shouted words in a language that hurt Gavimor's soul to hear, and raised up a golden rod. The brazier fires roared up, bright greens and pinks, azure and gold.

As one, Tenebrus' servants cut the throats of the priests. Blood poured onto the floor, soaking into the robes of the sorcerers. More victims were brought forth, these willing, for they knelt in the vitae of those who had gone before, and shouted praise to the Changer of the Ways as the knives flashed. Again blood flowed. The chanting grew louder. The rod Tenebrus held shook, its outline blurring.

A third group of sacrifices were brought in, these all manner of people, all ages, unwilling but terrified into submission and led like beasts to the slaughter.

Tenebrus' invocation reached a crescendo. The chant became a solid wall of sound. The flames howled in a many-coloured vortex. The sorcerer gripped the rod in both hands, and with a roar, wrenched down with unearthly strength. The rod cracked, spitting sparks from delicate workings. Evil spirits raced around Tenebrus, claws raking, hands beseeching, mouths mocking, eyes weeping.

Gavimor felt something huge approach, stealing up on him from behind, then into him.

Tharador Yheng's promises were fulfilled, for he knew power. He saw all of time displayed before him, past and future revealed in all their terrifying, infinite run. He knew pleasure also, pleasure at the power, pleasure at the knowledge.

Power and pleasure were fleeting. Madness came first as his mind shrivelled under exposure to eternity. Pain followed quickly. Truly, glory did fill him. His flesh stretched, his bones warped.

As he screamed with agony, before his soul was snuffed out, Gavimor learned what it meant to truly serve the gods.

The vortex of flame blew out, buffeting the sorcerers. From the bloody ruin of Gavimor, a pillar of crystal shapes twisted up into being. From each of the dancing facets, avian eyes peered.

The shapes drew in with the sound of shattering glass, taking on the form of a giant. It was twin-headed, with two bird's beaks that snapped and gabbled. Long limbs stretched out, clothed in thin, dry skin studded with iridescent quills. A portion of the crystal twisted itself into a staff topped with a book.

The crystals writhed away, leaving in their stead Kairos Fateweaver, the Oracle of Tzeentch, the Vizier of Change, Master of the Well of Eternity.

The chanting ceased. The last of the sacrifices fell to the ground, their lifeless bodies piled in pools of blood.

There was a moment of silence. Yheng heard a quiet hiss. The sands had started running. When the sands ran out, their time would be done. Before the daemon's coming, the sand seemed ample, but now there seemed so little.

Kairos shook his twinned heads, flinging the last scraps of Gavimor into Tenebrus' acolytes. Yheng's body reacted to the creature's manifestation. Her skin trembled. The chains set into her skin vibrated at painful frequencies. The daemon gave off a dusty, dry smell, like parchment, with a potent ammoniac reek that stung her eyes and caught at the back of her throat.

Kairos was tall yet bowed, his back bent by the weight of his knowledge. His two heads swung about, taking in all aspects of the chamber, until they fixed on Tenebrus within his pulpit. Recognition flashed in Kairos' eyes. He shifted, clawed feet clacking on the stone floor, wrapped his hands around his staff and rested his immense weight upon it.

Then Kairos spoke, and Yheng teetered on the brink of insanity. Every word brought an overwhelming vision of a million futures and an unrecognisable past. Her fellow acolytes moaned. Blood wept from the corners of their eyes. Only Tenebrus seemed unaffected, looking at the invoked demigod the same way he looked at everything: amused, curious and faintly condescending.

'Hand of Abaddon, sorcerer of Chaos, lord of the warp, we

greet you gladly, great ally,' said the rightmost head, and it inclined with courtly manners.

'*Peon, fool, manipulator, you dare much to call us forth from the Changer's side,'* said the head on the left, beak snapping with contempt. The heads spoke simultaneously, each delivering their supposed truths over the other. Concentrating on the twin voices ripped holes in Yheng's sanity, but they both had to be heard and heeded.

Kairos reached out a hand towards the sorcerer. Silver sparks rained from his talons, and he withdrew.

'*Protected!'* hissed the left head.

'Forgive the insult, Great Lord Kairos,' said Tenebrus. 'I have you ninefold bound, Seer of Seers. I would gladly offer myself to you for all the knowledge you may impart, but I must resist temptation's call. The war in the materium hangs in the balance, and Lord Kor Phaeron, Dark Cardinal, seeks answers to a pivotal riddle.'

'*Wars no balance make,'* said the first head.

'*Defeat is ever-present on certain paths. Tip the scales as you will, victory is no certainty,'* uttered the second.

Then together, they said, '*You ask for yourself, not for him. All things are known to us. Lie to the liar and be destroyed.'*

'*What is it you truly desire to know?'* asked the right head.

'*Your death?'* said the left.

'*Your life?'* said the right.

They spoke together again. '*The fate of your immortal being.'*

'*Yes, immortality is what concerns this mortal,'* said the left head, nodding. The daemon pointed a claw at Tenebrus. '*The mother of insanity is the urge to break the wheel of life.'*

'*No, power is his wine,'* said the other. '*Power first, then eternity. He would intoxicate himself on both.'*

'*Let us see what will be,'* they said together. '*Let us see if he will succeed.'*

'I desire to know none of this, oh great Weaver of Fates, but more and greater rede I seek,' said Tenebrus.

'Speak, then,' said the right head.

'We shall listen,' said the left.

'We know, we know,' said the right head. *'What you seek. Visions of a golden child trouble you.'*

'We have seen it also,' said the left head. *'In the past.'*

'And the future,' said the right.

'The warp trembles with the news of its coming,' said Tenebrus. 'I would know what it is. I would know where it is.'

'Anathema,' said the right head. *'Bringer of unity under a name long unsaid.'*

'Mutant,' said the other. *'The herald of the end. It brings lies, and victory to the Four under the hand of the Shaper. Much power shall be all-knowing Tzeentch's.'*

'All shall fail,' said both.

Yheng watched the hourglass out of the corner of her eye. The sands raced towards their destination, leaving few grains behind. Their audience was nearing its conclusion.

'What is this name?'

'I do not know,' said the right head.

'It cannot be said,' said the left.

'You must know,' said Tenebrus. 'You are the keeper of the Well of Eternity. Everything is known to you. You deny me, against the terms of my invocation.'

'Not so,' said the right.

'Exactly so,' said the left.

'It is hidden by a great power, one stronger than all others,' said the Fateweaver's right head.

'It cannot be told to the likes of you,' said the other head. *'It cannot be uttered by the likes of me.'*

'Is it as Kor Phaeron fears? Is the Emperor returning to the material realm in a new form?'

'*What is whole can return,*' said the right head. '*What is not, cannot.*'

'*Has He the desire?*' said the left.

'*It is impossible,*' said the right.

'*He bides His time,*' said the left.

'*He is out of time,*' disagreed the right. '*It is not He.*'

'When, and where?' Tenebrus demanded.

'*It cannot be seen, so I do not know,*' said the right head.

'*I know, but I cannot tell you,*' said the left. '*Doom comes upon all who attract His attention.*'

'I can find out though, can I not?' said Tenebrus. 'I am not the only one to presage its coming. The news of this spreads far...'

'*There are some who may know,*' said the right head.

'*But do they see what is to be seen?*' said the left.

'*Or only what they wish?*' said the right.

'And of these,' Tenebrus persisted, 'where would I find one who knows where this child may be?'

Kairos shook his great heads and bowed them, unwilling to speak, but bound to do so by Tenebrus' spell. The daemon struggled a moment against the compulsion, and the braziers roared bright fires.

'*Srinagar, the world is called,*' said the right head, beak clacking as the words forced themselves out.

'*Asmormen is the place,*' said the left, with equal reluctance.

'If I went to Srinagar, would I find what I sought?'

'*You would find the path to knowledge,*' said the left head.

'*You would find the path to ignorance,*' said the right head.

'Asmormen would yield the same result?'

'*Yes,*' said the right head.

'*No,*' said the left.

With a silvery, delicate pattering, the last grains of sand ran out. Simultaneously, Kairos' heads swung outwards, one to look at the glass of the future, the other to look at the glass of the past.

'*Time is done,*' they said together.

'*The future meets the past...*' said the right head.

'*...in the present,*' said the left.

'*And there we have no dominion,*' said both heads, speaking together again. '*Your audience is over, little sorcerer, your power over us is gone.*' Kairos lifted up a claw. '*Behold the benevolence of Tzeentch! Take a gift, in recognition of your mastery over the warp.*'

'*Suffer the curse of the Changer, for your impudence in summoning us,*' said the right head.

Multihued lightning burst from Kairos' hands and eyes. The members of Tenebrus' cabal threw up their staffs, calling on their own powers to protect themselves, and some were successful. Four were not, and died; all the warrior-serfs who had wielded the sacrificial knives fell along with them. Surrounded by purple-and-green fires, these acolytes collapsed, flesh running, skin melting. Their bones liquefied, what noises they could make turning from screams into gurgling bleats as their bodies warped into new, monstrous forms. Clothes unravelled into ropes of sentient thread that slithered away into holes in the deck. Eyes popped free of sockets, rolled onto the floor, sprouted legs, and ran madly about. One man split into two identical versions of himself who shouted together, drew knives from under their robes, and drove them home into each other's hearts.

Yheng had her staff held horizontally before her. Blue witch-fire played along its length, holding back the screaming light that Kairos projected, but she was failing, her magic was fading, while Kairos' warp flames grew stronger and stronger.

'*Beware, Tenebrus, of your ambitions,*' Kairos hissed. Which head spoke could not be seen, for the daemon's form wavered behind the energies of change. '*You may succeed in attaining them.*'

A thunderclap resounded throughout the chamber. Kairos vanished, taking his warping fire with him. A shockwave threw everything aside. The surviving sorcerers slammed into the walls along with the bodies of their servants and their victims. Yheng skidded through a lake of blood and bubbling flesh, fetching up against the mutated corpse of an Imperial priest. For a minute, the survivors lay stunned, unable to move, then came one moan, and another.

Yheng picked herself up. Tenebrus' pulpit was empty.

'Master!' she called. She ran as best as she was able through the slippery mess.

She found Tenebrus unconscious at the bottom of the pulpit steps. His face was bruised. He appeared more human that way, at peace, the unnatural width of his mouth concealed. She grasped his wrist, and to her relief felt his pulse, faint, thready and birdlike, but he was alive.

His eyes opened.

'Master?' she asked.

'My staff,' he whispered. He tried to get up.

'Wait,' she said. She found his staff and handed it to him, and he used it to push himself to his feet. When Yheng moved to support him, he gratefully accepted her arm. 'My lord, are you hurt?'

Tenebrus turned his pallid face up, his laconic shark's grin on display.

'We are all hurt, Yheng. We mortals die a little by the day. Why else do you think I chase such power, when the risks are so easy to see?'

There was a movement under the sorcerer's robes. A black, pointed tentacle poked out from the hem, and rolled over, glistening with protective slime. Tenebrus hissed and it vanished.

'My lord...' she said, eyes wide. 'The Great Changer has touched you. You are blessed!'

'Blessed? I suppose you could see it like that. Every usage of power has a cost,' he said, 'or brings a boon. It is all a matter of perspective, my acolyte. This is what worshipful fools like Kor Phaeron never understand. One cannot serve Chaos and one cannot master it. It consumes those who worship it just as it destroys those who think they can control it. Chaos is a primordial force. The primordial annihilator, the aeldari call it, and although Chaos is not so old as that name suggests, it is an apt term.'

With difficulty he walked beside Yheng, with her help. He moved differently. She wondered then how much Kairos had altered him, and her sense of worship was tainted by fear.

The surviving sorcerers were picking themselves up off the ground. Four remained whole. All were covered in gore. Serfs trooped in from outside, their dead eyes speaking of men and women inured to such horrors.

'We must be masters of our own destiny,' said Tenebrus. 'Chaos comes from within as much as it influences from without. We direct it as it attempts to direct us. These impulses are in perpetual competition with each other.' He continued to limp along. 'Whatever this universe is, it is undoubtedly broken. Whatever path was intended for us is lost. All we can do is to survive, and attempt to prosper in the world fate has given us. We are locked forever in a game with gods that would devour us. A game where we are both cat and mouse. They are our nightmares. Without us they cannot survive, but they would be our masters, and they have grown strong enough to consume us. You must not let them control you, Yheng. True power is to be found on the dagger's edge between submission and mastery.'

He stood taller, his pain subsiding, his twisted body accommodating his new mutations. The movement under his robes shifted, then ceased. He breathed deeply, rejuvenated.

'We cannot rule Chaos, and we cannot beat it. There is only one sure way to prosper in this ruin of a universe,' he said.

'What is that?'

'To survive Chaos, one must become Chaos. I seek immortality,' he said. 'To transcend the limitations of mortal flesh and become one with the warp. Only then do we have a chance at preserving our souls. You don't think I care about Abaddon's victory, do you? Or how it is achieved? I don't, nor do the Powers – for them the struggle is the game. But imagine,' he said, 'to kill a god. Slaying the Anathema, what power would that buy?' He coughed, and his robes undulated, making her tense. 'That is what motivates me. However, our plans are somewhat postponed by the advent of this child. If the child is what Kor Phaeron fears it to be, then it would not matter if we burned the Emperor on His Throne. We must deal with this emergence, quickly. Better we find it first. Kor Phaeron may do something foolish. The right kind of victory, eh, Yheng? The right kind for us.'

She glanced at him. He was smiling at her. Those were the words that Kar-Gatharr had used. He was telling her he knew what task the Dark Apostle had set her.

But was that her purpose now? Who was her master?

'Shall I prepare our followers to go to the worlds Fateweaver spoke of? If we can get our cultists to them first, perhaps we can outpace Kor Phaeron.'

Again, Tenebrus flashed his wide, wide smile.

'There is no need. Tzeentch himself guides us. We have agents already on Srinagar, and we will need Kor Phaeron.'

'Then you knew already where to go next.'

'Oh no,' he said. 'I did not. The daemons of Chaos are cunning. Kairos is as deceitful as he is truthful, he speaks verities and lies equally. But it is clear to me that the Great Changer wishes us to know where we should go. We have Tzeentch's favour, despite Kairos' reluctance. We go to Srinagar, because it is a relay nexus of one-fifth of the Segmentum Solar's astropathic network. Asmormen is a rock. The choice is obvious.' He licked sharp teeth with his black tongue. 'There are more kinds of knowledge than those that can be prised from the mendacious mouths of daemons,' he said. 'Sometimes, my dear Tharador, simple, mundane fact is all we need to triumph.'

Chapter Twenty-Two

THE WARS OF FLEET TERTIUS

AN OFFER REBUFFED

SERISA VALLIA

Finnula Diomed took Fabian in an officers-only transit car down the *Saint Aster*, banishing the two ensigns already inside when they boarded with a sharp look, leaving them free to talk. Fabian activated a pocket vox-thief to record her words. It was one of his favourites, but worked off crystal storage blocks of an annoyingly specific kind, whose scarcity forced him to be sparing in its employment.

The ride took ten minutes, so they did not have a great deal of time, but Fabian managed to coax a breakdown of the battle group's war out of her. She outlined the dangerous voyage to Hydraphur, the Battle of Machorta Sound, then the system-hopping campaign to the warp nexus at the abandoned world of Olmec, the mad race to Lessira, ordered by Fleetmistress VanLeskus to beat Fleet Quintus to its target. The battle there had been brief but fierce, with many losses.

'That's when Iolus began to fall apart,' said Diomed. 'And Commodore Athagey to rise. She'd already made a name for herself at Machorta. Then there was Evuldi of course, and the xenos incursion there. While she was riding high, Iolus lost half its capital ships at Lessira, before being destroyed at Xeriphis.'

'She was honoured by promotion to groupmistress of an existing battle group, which was merged with Saint Aster.' Fabian frowned. 'That's how it works isn't it? That ad hoc battle groups are subordinate to the pre-established?'

'Generally,' said Finnula. 'When is anything ever simple? The honour is a double-edged sword, as is this posting leading the efforts against the rebellions here.'

'Could you explain?' asked Fabian. He enjoyed speaking to Diomed. There was something about the curve of her jaw and the way her eyes were set in her face that arrested him. The feeling was enjoyable, if alarming. Fabian had had little experience with women.

'We're firefighting,' Diomed replied. 'For all the scale of the threat of the Word Bearers to the Segmentum Solar, there is more glory to be won liberating systems than stabilising ones that have already been reached. It's police action.'

'I did get the impression that Athagey is not happy.'

'You don't say.' Diomed sighed. She was sitting ramrod straight, knees together out in front of her, cap high on her head. She did not look comfortable. Fabian wondered if she ever was. 'It's VanLeskus. Like any alpha leader she likes to keep the greater share of the honour for herself. Eloise was a little too successful for our glorious Cassandra, may the Emperor bless her thrice. Groupmistress Athagey blames the bureaucracy for the removal of the Saint Aster name when the groups were merged, but I think it was a calculated snub from VanLeskus.'

'Have you thought of telling her that?'

'Are you actually mad, or are you an idiot?' said Diomed. 'You've seen her. She'd explode.'

'At the moment she is angry with the Imperium's most powerful man,' countered Fabian.

'Better she's angry with a distant primarch. I'm sure she's using Guilliman as something to rage against because he is safely far away. She knows.' Her smooth forehead frowned. 'I think.'

'I'll never understand women,' said Fabian.

Her eyes narrowed. 'Is that supposed to be funny?'

'No, it's supposed to be true,' said Fabian. 'I spent most of my life buried under paperwork. The sexes were separated stringently in my divisio. I barely even knew my own mother.'

'There were no female adepts in your department?'

'Oh, there were lots, but we were segregated. Last thing you want in a place like that is a population explosion. They added supplements to our food to keep us focused on our work, if you get my meaning.'

'I see.'

'You know,' he said, 'I would like to write this history myself. Can I interview you further? You're a little more approachable than Athagey.'

'Should we do it over dinner?' she said with wide-eyed innocence that took Fabian in completely.

'Well,' he stammered. 'If you–'

'Don't understand women but want to perform a little fieldwork so you can get to know us better, do you?' Diomed said. 'Have those drugs worn off? Looks that way.'

'I–' Fabian blushed.

The train car slowed. Points snickered under the cabin as it was shunted off onto a siding.

'This is your stop. I'd revise your seduction technique. Better yet, stick to history completely,' she said. The door opened. 'It's deck seventeen, section four-C. Vallia is in with the Munitorum liaisons and the like. If you get lost, just ask for the historitor. They all know her.'

'Of course.' Embarrassed, Fabian got out, but made himself turn back to face Diomed. 'I am terribly sorry,' he said from the small platform. 'I meant no–'

'Save it,' she said. 'And I'll think about the interview. I'll even think about dinner. Life's too bleak to take offence, and much too short.' She slammed her palm against the departure stud, and the car drove off, electric motors whining.

He watched it go, unsure of what to do.

Thoroughly off balance, Fabian went to find Serisa Vallia.

It took Fabian half an hour to search out the historitor. Her quarters were deep within the administrative zone of the ship, which in pre-Rift days had been some sort of magazine, if the markings trapped halfway between its warren of retrofitted floors were anything to go by. The adepts he ran into were over-worked and ill-tempered, but gratifyingly, they recognised him for who he was, saluted and got out of his way.

He found Serisa Vallia's door and knocked on it.

The voxmitter embedded in the wall by the door lock hissed. *'Go away,'* she said. *'Busy.'*

The vox snapped off. He pressed the button again.

'This is Historitor Majoris Fabian Guelphrain of the Found-ing Four. You will open this door, immediately.' He stood up, then had second thoughts and pressed the button again. 'That is an order,' he said apologetically.

The door clattered away into the wall. A red-faced woman appeared. She wore a pair of Ardenian monoculars that mag-nified her pupils to comical size.

'Historitor Guelphrain!' she said, then snatched the visual aid away. 'My apologies. Please. Come in. Come in.' She backed up clumsily, knocking a pile of papers onto the floor. She cursed under her breath as she tried to pick them up.

The room was small. A cot took up most of the floor space. A small sink protruded from the wall by the door, making entry difficult. A desk filled nearly all of the rest of the space, leaving only a small passage between the furniture. Bookshelves secured to the wall by scavenged military mag-locks were piled high with untidy sheaves of paper.

'They really have tucked you out of the way here,' he said.

'I upset Groupmistress Athagey,' Vallia muttered.

'Easily done,' said Fabian. He looked down. 'Let me help you with that,' he said, getting down on his knees. As he helped pile the papers they bumped heads, mortifying Vallia.

'I'm sorry. You shouldn't be doing this. It's my fault, sir.'

'What shouldn't I be doing?' said Fabian.

'Picking this up.'

'Why?'

'Because you are Fabian Guelphrain, *the* Fabian Guelphrain,' she said. 'A founder.'

'And because of that I shouldn't be on the floor, helping you pick up spilled papers?'

'Well, no, I mean...' She blushed.

Fabian sat back on his heels. 'Once, I would have agreed with you. Before I was a historitor I was very full of myself, but when you are one Septicentio-grade paper shuffler among three hundred thousand, you cling to what little dignity you can find.'

'What did you do before?'

Fabian handed her the last sheet of paper, got up, and offered her his hand.

'Mostly ignored the pleas of dying worlds,' he said. 'Pompously. You?'

She took his hand and he pulled her up. 'I was an instructor at the Academia Administratum of Sud Afrik,' she said. 'Comparative tithing, exacta calculation and interplanetary obligation. I got into trouble for my professorial thesis. They were going to execute me for economic heresy.'

Fabian nodded. 'I had a forbidden pastime.'

'What?' she asked.

'The truth,' he explained. He looked around her room again, and gestured at the bed. 'Can I sit?'

'Yes, please,' she said, and rushed to clear a space.

'So,' he said, once he was seated. 'First of all, you know me, but I don't know you. As the Logos has expanded, the notes on our operatives have got briefer.'

'There's not much to tell,' she said. She sat on the chair at the desk. The quarters were so cramped their knees brushed. 'I was saved days before my execution, shipped out from Terra to Battle Group Delphus, Fleet Sextus. I was trained by Edet Sukhima, who was trained by Viablo of the Four. Do you...?'

'A good friend.'

'Of course. I've been here for three years. Transferred from Delphus Sextus when it left Terra, then to Saint Aster Tertius, which is now Iolus Tertius. And I've done nothing. Nothing at all.'

'This doesn't look like nothing.'

She shrugged. 'I've tried to assemble an account of the fleet's actions. VanLeskus wouldn't speak with me. Athagey gives no support to me. I'm on my own. The Logisticarum adepts are too harassed with other duties to help, but I've been speaking to whoever will listen to me. The Logos seal works better on some than on others, but I've not been able to gather any information to add to our primary brief. I've been off this ship twice.'

'That's disappointing,' Fabian said, and frowned.

His words kindled a little fire in Vallia. 'There's only me. You've no idea how difficult it's been working under these circumstances.' She stopped. 'I'm sorry, sir,' she said. 'I don't mean to-'

'No, it's fine,' said Fabian. 'Throughout Fleet Primus the Logos is respected, by the will of the Imperial Regent.' He looked around the tiny cabin. 'But his will only goes so far, mighty though it is. It's no wonder you are dispirited.' He got up. 'Pack all this up.'

'Am I being dismissed?' she said.

'No,' he said. 'I have fifteen other historitors with me. I am not here to judge your efforts to this point, but to make sure your future is a damn sight easier than your past has been. Guilliman has sent the Founding Four out to spread the Logos. Get your belongings. Things are changing, I'm starting with you.'

Chapter Twenty-Three

DEAD MAN'S QUARTERS

ANGEVIN'S TOMB

CALL TO WAR

Lucerne was put into quarters once occupied by a serf officer. It still contained the effects of the previous inhabitant: a great-coat on the hook on the back of the door; an unfinished letter; a rack of candles before an idiosyncratic collection of idols; a series of miniature oil portraits on wooden board no bigger than Lucerne's thumbnail. There were other articles spilled on the floor. A handful of things, each one deeply personal.

For Lucerne, the cabin was vexatiously small. His wound needed tending to, and he had concerns for his armour, but there was no space for it inside. That, at least, had been pro-vided with a proper stand in the ship's armoury, but he was suspicious of his hosts, and he did not trust them not to meddle with it.

The usually buoyant Lucerne found his humour deserting him as he perched on the tiny chair and attempted to fix his cheek in place with flesh-bond. Such fine medical work was beyond him, and he cursed as his fingers adhered and the flap of skin and muscle remained unattached. He looked at the damage in the dead man's tiny mirror. His nose was squashed, yellow bruising spread all round his eye sockets. He could not judge if he had been a handsome man before, but he was certainly less so now.

He got his fingers free and shook his hands out. He could return to his men, and leave this band of fanatics be. They were fighting for the Emperor, at least, and extinction would claim them soon enough if they did not take Cawl's Gift. What did it matter? But then he thought back to his conversation with Guilliman, and he realised that it mattered very much. The Primaris project was vital to the Imperium's survival. Even one small group rejecting the new Space Marines posed a risk. And there were the crimes they had undoubtedly committed.

He sat back, gathering his wits and his emotions both, before attempting the dressing again. Someone rapped on the door.

'Enter,' Lucerne said.

The lock wheel spun, and the door squealed open. Basic maintenance was lacking wherever Lucerne looked. Beorhtnoth's neophyte, Botho, came in. He was young still, without his final black carapace implant, but he carried himself like a veteran.

'Neophyte Botho?' said Lucerne.

The youth was shy, and only managed brief eye contact when he spoke.

'I beg your leave, master, but I thought you might wish a little help with your wound.'

Lucerne searched the youth's face for falsehood, but found none. 'Thank you,' he said. 'A wound like this can be difficult to tend to oneself.' He struggled to speak. His face burned with pain.

Botho nodded and came to Lucerne's side in an almost apologetic way. Lucerne looked aside. The youth examined the injury with an experienced eye. He moved the flap around.

'This looks worse than it is.'

'Maybe. But I have little skill with the flesh-bond.'

'Then I shall do it for you. Once the wound is closed, your Emperor's gifts will heal you quickly.'

Lucerne picked up the dispenser.

Botho shook his head. 'It must be cleansed first. Do you have an irrigator?'

Lucerne indicated a device on the desk with his eyes.

'Is this necessary?' he asked, as Botho rinsed out the wound.

'Adeptus Astartes are resistant to infection, but I was taught that resistant is not the same as immune.'

'Are you training to be an Apothecary?'

'No, but I have had some training by the Apothecaries. Our crusades sometimes find themselves without medicae support. It is the duty of every neophyte to tend to the needs of his master, wounds included.'

Botho reached out for a box of sterile swabs, and used one to blot up the water. It came away pink.

'Now I will take the flesh-bond, if I may, master.'

Lucerne held it up. Far more delicately than Lucerne could manage, Botho ran thin seams of the glue within and around the injury, then carefully pressed it closed.

'What happened here, neophyte?' asked Lucerne. 'Where are the crusade's Primaris reinforcements?'

'We did not receive them, master,' said Botho. He released Lucerne's face, gave the wound one last critical look, then handed him a sheet of sterile, plastek flimsy. 'This will not adhere to the flesh-bond. Hold the wound closed for three minutes, until the bond has set.'

Lucerne did as he was asked. 'Thank you.'

Botho bowed. 'It was nothing, my lord.' When he stood straight again, he almost made to go, but halted himself. 'My lord, I do not wish to speak out of turn, but you should leave. Go back to your ship. Forget us. Let us follow our own road to the Emperor's light. Our path is nearly done. We will not live much longer.'

'What happened here?' Lucerne asked again. 'What happened to Marshal Angevin?'

Botho looked away. 'Just leave, my lord. It would be better for us all. Go back to your brothers.'

'I am not going anywhere until this crusade accepts the will of the primarch.'

Botho bowed. 'Then may the Emperor watch over you, master.'

Lucerne let him go. The nerves were cut in his cheek, he had no feeling there, and had to prod it with his fingers to make sure the bond had set and the wound was closed. He felt the stirring of the Belisarian Furnace. A few hours asleep under its influence and he would have nothing but a scar to remind him of the duel.

He did not have a few hours. Lying unconscious would be dangerous. He closed his eyes, meditating to still the implant.

When the heat in his chest subsided, he went to fetch his armour.

Lucerne moved unseen through the ship. So many of the subsystems were down and so few of its crew alive that he had little concern he would be seen.

The Black Templars were a fleet-based Chapter that rarely gathered together. Many of them fought in large company-sized forces, but there were numerous smaller warrior bands like the Angevin Crusade scattered across the galaxy. Although they maintained an unknown number of Chapter keeps, to act as armouries, training facilities, archives and the rest, each force needed to be completely self-sufficient, possessing everything to replenish their numbers, maintain their equipment and lay their dead to rest.

Sergeant Lucerne was on his way to the vessel's mausoleum.

The corridors were dark. The few mortal crew members he encountered bowed their heads as he went by, and though his armour's noise echoed loudly in the ship's corridors and halls, none of the Adeptus Astartes came to challenge him.

The mausoleum was under the ship's cathedrum. It had a hexagonal plan, with niches for bodies stacked twelve high. For the crusade's most honoured dead, there were six sarcophagi arranged around the middle of the room, heads towards the centre, feet pointing to the walls. Their lids were flat, and the battle gear of the deceased was laid out on top, held in place by brass hoops. The lack of permanent decoration reflected the fluid nature of the crusades, as the bodies would one day be transferred to more permanent resting places. Three of the sarcophagi were occupied. Marshal Angevin's armour lay on the one facing the door, sword clasped hilt up, with the point resting on his knees.

Lucerne used his armour's sensorium to scan for vid-thieves. He found nothing. There was a honeycomb rack full of servo-skulls opposite the entrance, but every one of them was inert. The lack of power extended to the lumens. He lit a candelabra so he might better see, and by its uncertain light he examined Angevin's armour.

The plates were broken, not repaired, the fragments held together by breach-sealant, paste and wires. The underlying layers were visible everywhere, and in three places broken right through to the undersuit. These points of damage were large, made of overlapping impacts, and the surroundings were deeply chipped. Lucerne had seen this kind of damage many times before; it was caused by boltgun fire. This was not unusual. The enemy's fallen Space Marines used the same weapons as their erstwhile brothers.

But still he wondered who had fired the bolts.

Bones rattled in their sealed niches. The *Cantatum Bellum*

trembled. The main drives were firing up. He felt the sure push of motion as the ship rose up and away. Contra-forces dragged at him. They were accelerating dangerously quickly.

He set the candelabra down and left the mausoleum in search of answers. In the wide corridor outside were only statues of the dead, eyes downcast. He tried his vox, but got no reply, either from the Black Templars or his own ship.

He ran down towards the command deck, and entered it unchallenged.

All the crusade were present. The last of the human officers went about their tasks. The oculus shutters were grinding closed, the asteroid belt dipping away below the bottom of the window. Holo displays were snapping on. On the main tactical view, he saw the *Solemnity* rising up behind them on an intercept course.

'What is happening?' Lucerne said.

'Rejoice, brother,' said one of the crusaders. Lucerne had been given none of their names. 'We have a target, our crusade goes on.'

'How?' Lucerne said. 'Where does this order come from?'

'I have been given His guidance,' said Mortian. 'The Emperor calls us to battle.'

The unmistakable noise of the warp engines coming online shivered the command deck, followed by the unpleasantness of activating Geller fields.

'You are going to make a jump? Here? That's madness. We're nowhere near a Mandeville point. Mass interference from the asteroids will tear us apart!'

'We will be safe,' said Mortian. 'He shows us the way. The Emperor protects.'

To the scream of overworked warp engines, the *Cantatum Bellum* tore open the veil of reality, and fell roughly into the empyrean.

The tear crackled shut, leaving the pursuing *Solemnity* behind. Gravitic shear rippled across the fabric of space and time, a great swell that upset the Primaris ship and put out its engines. By the time the *Solemnity* had recovered, it was too late to follow.

Sergeant Lucerne had gone.

Chapter Twenty-Four

TZEENTCH'S GIFT

OPERARIUS TOLMUN

A PASSENGER

Tenebrus undid the fastenings of his robe, pulled his arms from its sleeves, and let the top of the garment fold down, leaving him naked from the waist up. He cupped the gift Kairos had given him, letting the black tentacles squirm over his fingers.

Yheng forced herself to look. Tenebrus' body bore fewer marks of divine favour than his face and hands. His skin was pale and marked with sores, and he was terribly thin, but his physiology was human-looking enough, which made the nest of tentacles sprouting from his left side all the more disturbing. The contrast accentuated the mutant nature of his wide mouth, black eyes, and deformed fingers so that for a moment she felt she looked upon a thing purely of the warp, and not a man.

Tenebrus grinned his shark's smile. The spell broke. He was still human, she reminded herself, just.

'Come, Tharador Yheng, do not be afraid,' Tenebrus said. 'The mark of Chaos is not a disease you can catch. One must work hard to be so blessed.'

He looked back down to the tentacles. There were seven or eight of them, the exact number hard to tell, because they squirmed about, lengthening and shrinking, and when they pulled in tight to his side they almost vanished, becoming indistinguishable from the smaller polyps that surrounded them. They were segmented, and small mouths gaped open and shut at their tips, like the corpse-eating annelids that dwelled in the catacombs of Gathalamor.

She approached him, the objects on the board she carried shaking with her nerves. She attempted to steady her emotions, to drive out her disgust, telling herself that the mutations her master bore were not very different to the marks she had made on herself. They were expressions of individuality, of devotion to the pantheon, and of power.

The worm-limbs writhing at Tenebrus' side said that she was wrong. Tenebrus examined them neutrally, like a man prodding at a cancer he had accepted would kill him.

'Come closer!' he said. 'I cannot do this without you, my acolyte. My tolerance for pain is great, but it is not boundless. You must do the cutting.'

She put the wooden board down on a table of dark green glass that grew directly from the ship's deck. Aboard the *Paracyte*, what was made by technology and what was made by sorcery was indistinguishable. The board was warped with age, forcing the three planks that comprised it apart. It had been painted red once, but most of the paint was gone, leaving a faint pink stain in the lignin and a few scaly patches where the colour had survived. On the largest of these fragments, the curve of gold letters could be made out. It was impossible to tell what they said, or what alphabet had been used.

The board carried a number of handmade silver nails, a hammer with a head of grey stone chipped white by impacts, a folded gold cloth, a small plasma torch, a metal bowl, a sharp hook set into a bone handle, and a lascutter.

'Do what must be done,' said Tenebrus. He held his hairless head up stoically, and for a moment he looked ridiculous, like a diseased beggar striking the pose of a heroic statue. 'You remember your instructions?'

She nodded. Her chains jangled.

'Then get on with it.' He turned to his left, so the new mutation was closest to the table block.

Hesitantly, she reached out, and grasped the largest of the tentacles. It wriggled in her hand with surprising muscularity. Perhaps aware of what she intended, it attempted to withdraw itself into Tenebrus' torso, but she squeezed tighter, digging her nails in, dragging it out and placing its thickness upon the glass. She groped for the hammer. Tenebrus picked up a nail, and placed it on the skin just below what Yheng could not help but think of as the tentacle's head.

'Strike now, Yheng,' he said.

The hammer wavered in one hand. In the other, the worm pulsed in her grip, its slime acidic on her skin.

'Strike!' he commanded.

The hammer fell. A spark leapt. The nail pierced the tentacle's flesh, but met with unexpected resistance and did not penetrate fully. Pink fluid spurted from the mutation, and it thrashed about in an attempt to retract, but Yheng held it fast.

'Again!' Tenebrus said, through teeth gritted with pain. 'Do it with conviction.'

She hit again, harder, and this time the nail sank easily through muscle and the glass, as if both were made of some other, more yielding matter.

'Now the others, hurry!' Tenebrus said.

Together, they wrestled the uncooperative appendages onto the glass, where Yheng pinned them with nails. The smaller ones had to be winkled out of Tenebrus' side with the hook, an operation that caused the sorcerer much pain, and he hissed as Yheng worked. When it was done, Tenebrus leaned back a little, stretching his mutations out to their fullest lengths so they could move no more, but quivered helplessly in the air like bowstrings, dripping mucus.

'Quickly, quickly, before they tear free!' he chided.

Yheng picked up the lascutter, but her hesitation saw Tenebrus snatch it from her hand.

'What the Great Changer inflicts by his will, I purge by mine,' he snarled, and thumbed the activation stud.

A short blade of light shone. Tenebrus sliced down. Vile-smelling smoke boiled off him. The first tentacle came free, but lived still, flopping about from its nailed head. When Tenebrus cut the second, he grunted and faltered. The tentacles screamed, a high-pitched squeal issuing from each opening. Tenebrus sagged, going paler than ever, and dropped the lascutter.

'Yheng,' he gasped. 'You must do this. The pain... The pain is...'

'Yes, master,' she said. She picked up the scalpel, and began to cut.

Tenebrus and his worms cried out in agony. She did not stop, continuing even when he passed out.

Rostov stared at the wall. All of the city throbbed with hidden industry. Every human world had a similar intrusive beat, and though each settlement played its own subtle variation, the rhythm was recognisable, the symphony of mankind.

It was not the only song Srinagar sang. He could feel the relay, even behind its layers of wards and baffles, even behind the thick rock that separated the mountain from the city. A choir of minds, thinking out to the stars, binding the Imperium together. He meditated on it, feeling the different resonances of the individuals who made it up, all burning away at a great rate. The astropathic network was costly in souls to maintain, and had become more so since the Rift.

He wondered at the sensations he experienced as he felt the power of the choir. This was something new. Was it down to the strength of the relay, which was one of the largest in the segmentum, or was it the consequence of the Rift opening? He could not be sure, but it might be that he was changing too. He would have to watch himself, in case he became a threat.

His vox-bead chimed.

'We've found him,' said Antoniato. They were taking no chances, utilising Rostov's own verbal cypher as well as the usual encrypted vox-channels. *'Matches exactly what we learned. Cinquento-grade maintenance operarius, right face, right job, right name. He's low-born, but his Administratum profile says he's intelligent. He fits. Frustrated, aiming for power. The usual story. I'd lay money on him being the main contact for the local network.'*

'Where is he now?' Rostov asked. He dragged his glove down his face, letting the rasp of the leather and the motion of his skin pull him back into his body. The sense of the beacon receded. Physical sensation rooted him in the moment.

'He's in the Administratum district, on his way to work. We've got eyes on him. Do you want us to move in and detain him?'

'No,' said Rostov. 'Keep him under observation. I want to watch him for a while. I shall track him myself.'

'Whatever you say, inquisitor.'

'I am on my way.'

The worms cut from Tenebrus smelled like the fish oil they sold by the bucket in Gathalamor Imprezentia's docks, and they would not stop squirming. At first, she tried to use the implements on the board to prod them into the bowl, but they wriggled their way free of tong and spatula. After she almost lost one down a crack in the floor, she gave up and resorted to her fingers and the hook. Their slime burned her hands, their stink seeped into her skin, but finally she had them all in the bowl, around which they flopped pathetically, unable to crawl up the steep sides. It was with great satisfaction that she poured the sanctified promethium on them and set them on fire with the plasma torch. Their stench intensified as they burned, and they squealed with disturbingly human voices. She let neither distract her from the incantation she had to speak while they turned to ash.

Tenebrus lay on a couch. After his collapse, she had finished the cutting on the floor while his shades hissed and rattled around the ceiling. The daemon-servitors had minds little better than animals, a blend of butchered human brains and lesser Neverborn, but they were protective of the sorcerer. She was half-convinced they would attack her, mistaking her actions as an assault on their master, but she'd ignored them, and finished her task. She'd needed to bring lumens in close to see better, and the light had shown up the rawness around Tenebrus' mutations, and the translucency of his skin.

After she was done, she dressed the wound. It went deep, a wide scoop of flesh taken out down almost to the ribs. The cutter had cauterised it, there was little bleeding, but she wondered if he would survive the excision. When his breathing stabilised, she took him to the couch at the side of the room. It was hard work. Tenebrus was much heavier than he looked, as if the larger part of his mass was not visible.

The couch was finely made, of rare cloth, though dirty. Tenebrus himself was a creature of filthy habits, and his quarters were poorly kept, but his taste was that of a lord. Yheng could not decide if that was a weakness.

She returned her attention to the task in hand. She took the glass stopper from a decanter of yellow wine, and mixed it slowly into the ashes of the worms. Dilution lessened the smell in intensity, but it lingered on the air. She could taste it and it clung to her clothes. She thought it would be a long while before she was rid of it. More incantations were required, all of a minor sort, to ensure the purity of the mixture. After ladling most of the potion into a brass goblet, she took it to Tenebrus' side, trying as well as she could to ignore the rising warning rattles of the daemon-servitors.

'Master,' she said. The cup was warm in her hands. The vapours rising from it made her giddy. 'Master, it is ready.'

Tenebrus stirred. His features were slack, the wide mouth gaping partway open. She became aware of the pounding of the *Paracyte*'s machines then, for the first time in a while. At that moment, Tenebrus' rooms were simple quarters on a ship, and not some uncanny realm. His power ebbed.

'Master.'

His eyes flickered open. His skin was almost pure white now, and the contrast with his entirely black eyes was striking. He grimaced as he sat up, holding his side. Blood oozed through the dressings where the burned flesh cracked.

'Yheng.'

'Master, are you in discomfort?'

He nodded, his characteristic superiority eaten away by pain. 'I am, no matter. The ritual must be completed.'

'The wound is severe, master,' said Yheng. 'Perhaps you should call on Xyrax's flesh-techs?'

'Perhaps,' he said. Hissing, he got to his feet. 'But not now.' He hobbled over to a chair, and eased himself into it. 'The potion, quickly. While I was unconscious I wandered far along the strands of possibility. A moment of divergence approaches. I must witness it.' Feebly he waved her over to his side. 'The potion. Now.'

She handed him the goblet. His hand was shaking, a display

of weakness that alarmed her, but he got the goblet to his lips and drained it, showing no distaste at the flavour, and handed back the cup.

'Tzeentch has shown me the way,' he said, some of the steel returning to his voice. 'By drinking this potion made of my own transmuted flesh, a rare opportunity beckons. For a while, I will live through the mind of another, and by doing so I will see what awaits us on Srinagar.'

'Whose eyes will you steal?'

'One of our agents'. I prepare them for such use. They crave it.' He smiled. 'My servants believe they are performing a holy act, allowing themselves to be possessed by the divine.' He chuckled. 'Who knows, perhaps they are right, and through the caresses of my spirit they know a little of the Powers' grace.' He gripped the chair arms, and began his spell. 'Lord Tzeentch,' he said. 'I make sacrifice of myself. Make nothing of distance. Make nothing of time. Let me see what was, what is, what will be. Lend me your divine insight.' His words became something guttural and inhuman.

Yheng felt the air change. The shades became utterly still, utterly silent. Once more, the rumble of the *Paracyte*'s forges faded away. Tenebrus looked stronger. Pale witch-light flickered around his shoulders and his head.

The sorcerer ceased speaking. He closed his eyes.

Weather trumpets sounded over the crowded streets of Srinagar, warning of the coming storm. The intensity and timing of the weather was encoded into the tune: heavy-particle sleet, three-day duration. Gilber Tolmun paid it no mind. There were off-worlders in the cavern city, for whom the whims of Srin and Gar were frightening, unfamiliar things. Not for him. Though not from the world originally, he had been there long enough that he wasn't concerned about the weather, not any more.

He was late for his shift and hurried. Hab-blocks carved directly from the planet's soft grey stone made grim boundaries to the road, like the tombstones of anonymous soldiers. The main passage was gridlocked; the workers' omnibuses lined up tight as train carriages. A collapse on the periphery, he'd heard. Another sinkhole.

Gilber Tolmun did not mind. He liked to walk.

As the trumpets blew, heavy plasteel shutters were squealing into place over the ceiling lights, obscuring the blue sky, and lumens were coming on to bathe the roads and alleys in a sickly yellow glow. He watched them work with a critical eye. He was part of the maintenance crews tasked with ensuring the shutters' operation. One broken shutter could mean a lot of lives lost, if it happened in a storm. Collapses were an ever-present peril in Srinagar's cave cities, but the suns were far worse. His was an important role.

Although maintaining the weather shutters was his job, it was not Tolmun's vocation. That was another thing entirely, a path far loftier, and replete with solemn responsibility.

Tolmun was going to save mankind. Tolmun was a missionary of the Word.

Just thinking about his mission sent a frisson of excitement through him. As he threaded his way through the crowds towards Access Tube 29, he looked upon his fellow citizens with pity. He knew the truth. The whole edifice of Imperial authority was constructed to keep the common man down, and the elite in power. He knew that the Emperor was a false god, and that His son was a false prophet. There were greater powers, gods that paid attention, who would reach out to those who beseeched them. There were gods in the galaxy who would answer your prayers.

He had seen miracles with his own eyes.

His faith was dangerous. The tiny cult tattoo he wore hidden on the web beside his smallest toe alone would condemn him to death. But he persevered. People deserved to know. They deserved freedom. Tolmun cared about his fellows. The Great Powers could make their lives so much sweeter, if they were strong enough. It was a hidden calling. Small cells that met infrequently, all unknown to one another. Every one of them put their lives at risk to ensure mankind could tread the path to enlightenment.

He reached the access cylinder to Tube 29. A code punched into the runepad opened the way to the stairs inside. Down were the city's service levels that his departmento shared with a hundred maintenance clans. Up were the more exclusive ceiling tunnels and catwalks of the shuttermen.

The voxmitter in the pad came on. A voice spoke out from it against a constant background hiss.

'*You're late, Operarius Thirty-Six-Seven.*'

'Many apologies, watch-master.' Gilber Tolmun offered no explanation for his tardiness.

'*There's a fault in the bearings of shutter forty-seven. See to it. The tech-priests will talk you through the rites of replacement via vox.*'

'Yes, watch-master.' He hid his contempt for the Adeptus Mechanicus beneath a servile tone. Theirs was another false creed. He did not need their guidance for such a simple task, but patience was a virtue in a cult magus. He played their game, while he must.

Gilber went into the cylinder. The door swivelled back into place behind him, and he ascended.

Rostov kept his distance from the target. The streets were heaving thanks to transport failures. Srinagar was a cavern world of reasonably civilised standards, but relative peace didn't mean the transit system worked. The signs of decay were everywhere:

soot-caked statues so corroded by pollution they were but nubs of stone, broken lumen poles, flowstone frills of calcium leached from rockcrete. The slab-habs were overcrowded. There was a smell of rubbish. The local diet couldn't have been up to much, most of the inhabitants of the city were shorter by a head than Rostov, and pale. It was a typical troglodytic population. Nothing he had not seen before.

He kept his hood up as he went, extending that part of his talent that could shroud his presence, ensuring he went unremarked upon, if he was seen at all. Trumpets blared. His wrist slate provided him with a translation of the weather-horn's wail. Not relevant. He kept his full focus on his quarry. Inquisitors were the hunters of men.

The shutters finished closing all over the city. Outside breezes ceased. Sunlight was cut out. The smell got instantly worse. Mechanical atmospheric-cyclers rumbled into action, and lumens flared, taking over the role of natural forces. Shut in, the hubbub of the city redounded on itself. Noises lost their clarity, became a babble. It was claustrophobic in a very particular way. Rostov examined the sensation dispassionately. He had been taught to treat all experiences the same, good and bad, interrogating them for usefulness. He filed the odd sensation the cave-city evoked away. Another world visited. Another comparator to employ, one day, where it might help him fulfil his role in the Emperor's service.

The target reached an access point into the city's workings. Rostov stopped and watched him go in. The door shut. After a few moments, Rostov followed. A tumbler-cracker had the lock disarmed in a second. Unobserved, he went inside.

'I am in pursuit,' he voxed in code. 'I am entering the undercity.' With the vox-waves blocked, he switched his equipment to the emitter network laid throughout the maintenance shafts: receivers and transmitters keyed into hardlines.

The stairs curled in a tight spiral in both directions. He closed his eyes and concentrated. Rostov was not a conventional telepath, beyond his gift at removing himself from people's perceptions; his powers had needed physical contact until recently. But all a witch's gifts sprang from the same place; they were different branches of the same tree, and like he could feel the emissions of the relay, he found his skills growing in other areas – more change, more cause for concern. He caught the psychic spoor of Gilber Tolmun with worrying ease. The operarius was heading up.

He could have had Tolmun apprehended immediately. The planetary authorities on Srinagar were compliant, the large Astra Militarum garrison upon its moon saw to that. It was an important planet, closely watched. But it was best to observe first, gather what information he could. Rostov was not a blood-and-thunder inquisitor. By nature he preferred more subtle means. If he could, he would insert himself into this world, and withdraw, unseen as the thrust of a stiletto blade delivered from the cover of a cloak.

Rostov found himself in a half-place trapped between the ceiling of the cavern city and the stony underside of the world above. There were unexpected voids there, and doors out to the surface. He passed a scratched glass window, centuries old, looking out from a hillside over a plain of nodding blue grasses, where large beasts grazed. Humanity's domain intruded into theirs by way of towers and machinery poking up through the ground, and huge shafts bored through the rock. Between cooling vanes a dump spilled detritus from sharply piled mounds. Around it pollution had killed off the vegetation. Yet away from the cities, the planet was oddly untouched, its surface too toxic for men to frequent. Humanity was a meek guest on Srinagar. Even there, so close to the principal settlement, the beasts grazed, the grass grew. The light was changing, becoming brassy. The storm would hit in minutes, soaking everything in poison, yet the beasts, immune to the furies of their star, had no concerns.

He passed the window.

He found Tolmun working in a gallery around one of the shutter assemblies. He had already removed a long access panel, jacked apart the runners, and was in the process of removing bearings as big as his fist from their track. Whatever else he was, he knew his business.

Rostov smothered all sign of his approach, dulling the man's senses, approaching to within a few yards. He was dangerously close, so found a shadowed spot on the far side of a cone of lumen light, and hid himself there. He sent a coded pulse signal to Antoniato. *I see him.* Acknowledgement pulsed back.

Gilber Tolmun murmured machine prayers, soothing the shutter's motive spirits as he pulled out their innards. Rostov observed him for several minutes, seeing what he could glean from Tolmun's character. He wondered, as he always did, what had driven this man into the arms of the Imperium's inimical enemies. Rostov understood the misery of human life, but the alternative was worse, and though the full truth of what the warp represented was occulted, the dangers of damnation were widely known. What arrogance, he thought, could convince someone they were exempt from the evils of xenos, Chaos or wicked men, that they could take their poisoned gifts and suffer none of the inevitable consequences?

Rostov had seen enough. For the sake of the city's people he decided to let Tolmun finish his work before apprehending him. He wasn't going anywhere.

But then he felt something move through the warp; another mind. To Rostov, Tolmun's simple soul had a candle heat. This newcomer was a blowtorch, and it closed in on the mainte- nance worker. Tolmun stiffened, gave a little cry. The bearing he was taking out thumped from his hand and rolled across the floor. He sagged, grabbed at the rails.

When he hauled himself up, he was another man entirely. He abandoned his work, and strode directly towards Rostov.

The inquisitor pulled back into a cavity between thumping machines, and pressed himself against bedrock. Whatever rode in Tolmun's flesh was of a different order of power to the cultist, and Rostov exerted all his will to shroud himself.

Tolmun's footsteps slowed as he approached Rostov's hiding place. The inquisitor's hand went to his pistol.

Tolmun peered intently into the dark. He was staring straight at Rostov. The inquisitor could feel the mind possessing him, operating him like a driver would a conveyance. A sense of great psychic power radiated off the conjoined entity. It knew there was someone there. Tolmun's face creased in suspicion. The entity found a stablight on Tolmun's tool belt, unhooked it and snapped it on. The beam shone in Rostov's face.

Slowly, Rostov eased his pistol free, all the while exerting his skill to hide himself in plain sight. Possessed man and psychic inquisitor stared right at each other for a second.

The stablight snapped off. Tolmun withdrew. Rostov held his breath until footsteps were no longer audible.

'He's on the move. Find him, pursue him,' he voxed his retinue. 'Do not let him out of your sight. Gilber Tolmun is hosting a passenger.'

Chapter Twenty-Five

TREMORS

AN ASSASSINATION

LACRANTE PURSUES AGAIN

Trumpets sounded with increasing frequency, warning of the imminence of the particle tempest. The tremors started soon after. They were slight at first, and hardly noticeable under the throb of the underground city's machines, but Rostov sensed them, for they were each preceded by a bow wave of psychic energy. These were initially weak, but as he stalked Tolmun through the network of tunnels and walkways threading the ceiling of Srinagar, they grew stronger, until the pulses of the warp were enough to affect even non-psykers, if in subtle ways. He saw it when he passed galleries looking down on the streets; people stopping dead and looking around in confusion, not knowing why they felt the chill of death on their souls.

Tolmun left the undercity network by another official stair, and went out through busy streets. He was making no effort to hide himself, but walked easily through the people, eyes forward, certain of where he was going. He headed unerringly west, and Rostov suspected he was heading for the mountain roots of the astropathic relay.

Tolmun was moving quickly, and the city was small. Before long they came out into the great square that marked the edge of the cavern settlement: the beginning of the domain of the Adeptus Astra Telepathica.

The mountain was largely cut off from Srinagar Civitas. The main access route was overland, up a long, steep set of monumental stairs that headed through a pair of gargantuan armoured gates, and into the mountain a mile away. The stairs rose up from a wide plaza within the city, backed by cliffs to the south, and the city to the north and west, contained in a vast, artificial, cubic cavern, out of which the stairs led up a perfectly formed incline cut into the planet's crust. Currently, the stairs were blocked, covered over by the largest shutter Rostov had yet seen. The stairs were all beautifully carved and surrounded by exquisite statuary, in good condition, unlike elsewhere, but the shutter was ribbed and ugly, forged of rusty plasteel, entirely utilitarian.

The stair road was closed, but people still needed to get into the mountain. On the cliffs to the east were subsidiary stairways that climbed via a series of steep switchbacks to three small tunnels, all heavily defended, that went underground to the mountain and the relay within. These were crowded and getting more so as people abandoned the main flight. Huge queues of functionaries and workers were forming, stretching back from these lesser gates and down into the square. At the top, enforcers of the Lex assisted Adeptus Astra Telepathica troops in performing laborious security checks.

Tolmun was heading up the cliff stairs, pushing his way through the queues. Rostov increased his pace, and was soon shoving into the thickening crowd.

A psychic jolt rolled out from the relay. When it hit Rostov it was like a lumen bulb burning out in his mind. For a moment, he heard the thoughts of the crowd around him, bringing on a spell of dizziness he fought off with difficulty.

The ground shook again. He assumed the tremors were unusual; they were alarming enough to the citizens of Srinagar that they stopped and looked up. There was the collective short intake of breath that humans make when peril presents itself: a surprised, fearful sigh.

He continued elbowing his way forward through the uneasy populace.

'Cheelche, where are you?' he voxed.

'Out of sight,' she replied. She always got surly when obliged to keep hidden. She wanted to walk freely abroad. As on most Imperial worlds, that was not possible.

'Concentrate,' he said. 'We are working here. Report now.'

'I'm following you, Leonid. I'm up in the walks above the main way. I can see you both, you and the target.'

He glanced up. From beneath, the network of pipes, walkways, conduits and the general miscellany of Imperial infrastructure seemed to infest the cavern ceiling like vines.

'Can you get into a position for a clear shot?'

'Always. Do you want me to take him?'

'Hold for my order,' he commanded.

'Yes, Leonid.'

'Antoniato?' he voxed.

'I'm following you, following him. If you need backup, I can be with you in about five seconds.'

'Never mind me. Eyes on Tolmun. Make sure he doesn't slip away.'

'Understood.'

'Out of my way! Official business!' Rostov said.

The crowd was thickening. Progress was slowing. The queues to get into the mountain knotted themselves up into snarls. Angry faces turned to him. When they looked into his eyes they saw his authority, and tried to get out of the way, but it wasn't enough to force passage. Soon he might have to reveal his office, and then the game would be up.

His vox-bead chimed with Lacrante's signifier.

'*Inquisitor.*' Lacrante sounded wary.

'I hear you,' Rostov said. Tolmun was making his way up the steps, not paying attention to the people he pushed his way through, but looking upwards, always towards the mountain. He reminded Rostov of a rich man who had travelled years to see a particular cathedrum or set of ruins, and once the object of his pilgrimage was in his sights, wandered direction-less towards it, caught between great joy and lassitude now his quest was over.

'*It might be nothing, but I've spotted someone else who is trailing Tolmun. What are your orders?*'

Rostov was seized by an intense curiosity, so much that he had to check his impulse to turn about and search the crowds.

'Are you sure?'

'*Sure as I can be. He's no expert – looks shaky, too obvious, maybe. I could be wrong, he could be nervous about something else, but I think he was following Tolmun, until he hit the square. He has a hand vox-set, sent something. He's turned back now. Do you want me to break off and pursue?*'

'I trust your instincts,' Rostov responded. 'Tail him.'

A great swell in the warp sent sparks shooting around Rostov's vision. He stumbled, and the frightened babble of the crowd closed over his head like water. His view of the world cut out, to be replaced by a great orb of fire, a seated figure silhouetted before it. The vision made him gasp. When the image cleared, he was on the floor, pinning a minor adept to the ground.

The man shouted something at him. Rostov heard nothing but a ringing in his ears. He got back up, reeling. He searched the crowd for Tolmun, seeing him getting closer to the weather entry to the mountain, but staring past it still, like he could see through the stone to the beacon beyond.

The ground shook hard. Alarms rang from multiple quarters. Stressed metal sang as it parted high above in the tangle of pipes and catwalks. A shower of bolts rained into the crowd. Screams punctuated the worried murmur of the people, which itself was rising in tone and volume.

Another tremble in the fabric of being. This one was huge, a rogue blast of storm wind terrifying in its strength and unanticipated speed. The hairs on Rostov's neck prickled with foreboding.

'Something significant is about to happen,' Rostov voxed his followers. 'Be ready.'

The weather trumpets blared a sharp, frantic tune. Rostov half-caught the translation on his arm slate: a *horribilis* scale astral event; all caution urged.

The psychic wave hit him first, lifting his soul up and threatening to tear it free of his body to drown in the depths of the empyrean. The vision returned tenfold in strength, smiting him to his core.

Burning into his third eye, the warp eye that hid within the spirit of all creatures, was a vision in gold. It was a person; it seemed to be a child, but at the same time a man and then a woman, fully grown, then a babe. The features were indistinct, multiple variations existing on top of each other, so that Rostov could not be sure what he looked at. As before, the figure was seated, surrounded by a halo of brilliant flame, though it too burned with unbearable fires, and then it stood from a seated position, and opened its arms, and a great emittance of light radiated from all around it, smiting Rostov with a physical force that had him cry out.

The earthquake followed hard on the heels of the vision, rolling out from the mountain and across the land. With a squealing roar, part of the infrastructure came free of the cavern ceiling, and fell at a ponderous rate that seemed contrived. When it hit the ground the people screamed, scattering from it and trampling each other in their panic. Rostov was shoved in every direction, still half blinded by the vision. Metal folded itself up, and laid itself down, crushing people to red smears against the square.

Rostov was lifted from his feet and carried back by a surge-tide of panicked humanity, and almost dumped on the floor, where he would surely have been crushed. One of his gloves was ripped free, and his fingers trailed across cheeks, reading secrets, sorrows and private joys. They came in such fast succession, once more the empyrean threatened to overwhelm him. From the peril he found his strength.

'Stop!' he shouted. A wash of psychic force burst from him, stunning the people around him. They toppled as one, falling in stacks like piles of dropped index cards. Rostov was mired in them, and struggled to escape their tangled limbs.

He got up onto the pedestal of a statue. People were scrambling for escape, running blind. This was not solely the result of the earthquake; he could feel their fear. They had seen what he had seen.

An aftershock rumbled. One of the ugly hab-blocks collapsed with a shattering roar and a cloud of dust. Servo-skulls were sweeping down from ceiling roosts. Throaty engines growled as units of enforcers and emergency medicae teams tried to push their vehicles into the crowd. There was screaming coming from the southern edge of the stair plaza, where the crowd had funnelled itself into a series of small doors to escape, with predictable results.

A grav-skiff hissed overhead, bearing a team of four local Lexmen. Sanctioners, peacebringers, lawgivers, whatever they called that grade of heavily armed headbreaker on Srinagar. Three servo-skulls flanked them, and a cherub carrying a heavy voxmitter that broadcast the voice of one of the enforcers out to the crowd.

'*Halt. Cease all movement. The danger is passed. The danger is passed. Halt, cease all movement.*'

Rostov looked up the stairs towards the weather tunnel entrances. Many of the people between had crouched down, frightened or dazed by what they had experienced. This afforded him a view to the top. Tolmun was looking right back at him. The mind that puppeted the operarius was powerful. Rostov could feel that, and in return it recognised him for what he was: inquisitor, and witch.

A gunshot rang out. The crowd flinched. Splinters flew from the wall by Tolmun, and he ducked. The enforcers banked round on their skiff. The men around the vehicles at the edge of the square began shouting, and fanning out, then bludgeoned their way into the crowd. Another shot followed, and this one found its mark.

Tolmun went down.

'Cheelche, hold fire!' Rostov voxed.

'*It wasn't me, it wasn't me, damn it all!*' said Cheelche. '*I would have hit him first time. It came from the other side of the plaza.*'

Rostov looked to the north, over the marble square and the lower flights of the grand stair. He saw nothing but the dull, uninspired local architecture. Then a flash in a window caught his eye. He turned to it just as the window blew out on an orange pillar of fire.

'*Gods of old waters, the shooter suicided himself,*' said Cheelche.

This last act had the enforcers in uproar. They were moving through the crowd to the fallen operarius, and forcing their way to the blast site with a characteristic lack of gentleness.

Rostov cursed under his breath. The situation was escalating beyond his control.

'Antoniato, get to the shooter's position. Show them your

credentials. Stop the local Lex wrecking the evidence. I'll get up to Tolmun. Cheelche, disappear back to the lander, the last thing I need is a shoot-out between you and the law.'

'*Oh, Leonid...*'

'Save your complaints, Cheelche. Get our weapons ready. Prepare my armour. Whoever was riding Tolmun was here for a reason. This world is a target, and this is now a combat operation. Lacrante?'

He received no reply.

'Anyone seen Lacrante?'

'*He was chasing down your tail,*' voxed Cheelche. '*I watched him head off north, out of the plaza, into a street near the blast zone. Vox reception's patchy out that way. A lot of induction machinery pumping water for the geotherm plants.*'

'Keep trying him,' said Rostov. 'I'm going to be busy. It's time to let them know the Inquisition is here.'

He shoved his way through the dazed people, only then making the bottom of the steps. They mounted up before him, carved into the rock. He got up the first three flights before an enforcer stepped in front of him, shotgun aimed to kill.

'Be about your business, citizen.' The muzzle of the gun prodded Rostov's chest. 'There is an active investigation in progress.' Beyond the Lexman, others worked, rounding up the locals. Servo-skulls buzzed over the murder scene.

Rostov opened his hand. His Inquisitorial seal hung from its chain, ruby winking.

'You will find I have my own investigation, and it is of higher priority. I am Leonid Rostov of the Emperor's Inquisition, Ordo Xenos, and you will let me pass.'

The man Lacrante was trailing had peeled away and set out back into the city by the time the first psychic pulse hit. Being a non-psyker, Lacrante did not see what Rostov saw, but felt the wave as a nauseating unease that rolled up and through him from his bowels, hitting its height at the back of his throat. The following tremor shook the buildings. Flakes of rock split from bare walls and hab-blocks alike. There was a market off in a square to the side, and open-fronted shops whose slanted, closable fronts mimicked the great sky shutters. Srinagar's subterranean nature prompted a love of light among its people, and there were a great many lamps for sale that jangled and chimed as the earthquake passed through them.

The tremor caused Lacrante's target to look back. He caught sight of Lacrante, his eyes widened in fear and he sped up.

'Throne take it, I've been made,' he voxed. He got a jagged magnetic warbling instead, then realised he was close to the district power plant. He was on his own.

His target was a small man, bald, thickening about the middle. He looked to be reasonably wealthy by the world's standards, with a well-cut suit of clothes that had enough luxury trim to mark him out. The most conspicuous thing about him was a cravat of a soft yellow held in place at his throat by a large diamond pin. The weather trumpets were blaring their warnings, and verbal notifications were broadcast from vox-towers at the corners of a junction down the street, but the road was busy with people living their lives; a good deal of them looked to be workers turned back from the mountain road going home early. They were heading in the same direction as Lacrante and the fugitive, but with that treacly slowness of people with no urgency, who are used to the risks of their own environment. People always seemed to Lacrante to have no clue how short life was, how little time they had to get anything done, and it angered him. He went sideways, prising gaps open with his shoulder, warded off muttered complaints with a scowl.

The target glanced back again with that half-hopeful look of the pursued that their hunter has given up. On seeing Lacrante again, he hurried himself.

Lacrante pushed on.

As he neared a junction, the second psychic pulse burst its way through the city's collective soul, and everyone in the crowded street felt it. That time, Lacrante caught a glimpse of a painful light, and a figure seated, staring at him from a featureless face. It hurt him to see, migraine stars exploded in his mind, and his legs nearly gave out. He had to stop a moment, brace himself against a tenement wall and pinch the bridge of his nose. He shook the lights away.

People had stopped everywhere, dazed, not a few of them wearing slack expressions of horror. The target was clutching his head, but still staggering forward. Lacrante shook off the after-effects of the pulse and shoved the crowd aside.

'You,' he shouted. 'Stop!'

The tremor hit, and his target ran.

Lacrante swore.

He sprinted down hardtop that convulsed under his feet like a serpent. Glass shattered in windows. A stall of cloth collapsed. Alarms clamoured from every quarter. He heard something break in the square behind him, and screams, thin at that distance. Let the others deal with that, Lacrante's attention was on his target. The little man was fat, but fast, impelled by fear.

'Wait!' Lacrante shouted. 'Hold there! I need to talk to you!'

His words only sped the man on.

The tremor subsided. The man took a sudden turn to the right, ducking under coloured awnings into an alleyway hidden between two buildings. The klaxons of Lex enforcement vehicles honked down the road. Heavy transports grumbled past as Lacrante turned into the alley, and found a narrow set of stairs rising up into an archway carved into the stone.

The target's lack of fitness was beginning to tell. He was

slowing, stumbling on the worn steps, and slipping in accumulated garbage.

'Just stop!' shouted Lacrante. 'I'm not going to hurt you!'

The man didn't believe him, probably with some justification; it was a promise Lacrante could not keep. The target reached the top, where he vanished off to the left. Lacrante ran after him. He passed the corner warily, cautious of ambush, but the man was intent only on flight, and panted off into a tunnel, very roughly carved into the rock, barely wide enough for Lacrante to move down without scraping his knuckles on the sides or banging his head on the ceiling.

Part of it had collapsed. He caught the man trying to burrow his way through the rockfall, a task that was clearly beyond him.

'You there.' Lacrante pulled his laspistol. 'Turn around slowly, and I'll go easy on you.'

A rock clattered down the pile of broken stone. There was a gap at the top big enough for an infant to wriggle through. The back of the man's head angled up. There was a hopeful tension in his body.

'Don't even think about it. You're not going to get through there. Turn around. I only want to talk. I don't want to shoot you.'

The man let out a little whimper that could have been a laugh or a sob.

'They all say that.' The man turned around. He was caught, and not going anywhere, and he knew it. 'That's what they told me you'd say, when you came for us. And now you're here!'

'Why were you following Gilber Tolmun?'

'Was I?' he said. He made the strange little noise again. He was faking courage. Tears were gathering in the dust at the corners of his eyes.

'Don't be stupid. Why were you following him, and my master, Inquisitor Rostov?' He threw the name in to see what happened.

The effect was remarkable. The little man's face crumpled.

'An inquisitor? Oh my, oh no, oh this is it. This is the end. This is...'

He licked his lips. An amount of fortitude showed on his face. He moved his tongue in his mouth.

'For the Ever-Living Emperor!' he said.

He bit down hard. There was a crackle of glass, and a wisp of acidic steam escaped the corner of his mouth. With a weird sob he fell back on the stones. The sob turned to a scream that turned to a disturbing gargling. Froth bubbled up from his lips. He thrashed about, then lay still. By the time Lacrante pressed his fingers to the man's neck, he was already dead. Something oozed out of his dissolving flesh, burning Lacrante and making him swear.

'Acid capsule?' he said in disbelief. He wiped his hand on the stone. 'Rostov, Rostov, can you hear me?'

His voice was flat in the small space. Damp stone and chemical poisons made his nose run. He felt claustrophobic. The man's face was collapsing into itself from the mouth outwards. His skull was softening, deforming, spreading out to coat the rocks.

'Rostov? Antoniato?'

The rising and falling of the magnetic pumps sang over his vox. Cursing, he pulled the man's cravat away, careful of his fingers this time. The cloth was melting, and came apart. He expected to find another amulet showing this man to be a servant of the Hand, but instead he wore three amulets around his neck, all approved by the Imperial Cult.

'Not a heretic then,' he said. 'Not of the usual sort.' By now, the man's head had dissolved into a flat, glistening mass, like a mould growing over the stone. The smell of it burned his throat and made him want to vomit, and Lacrante held his breath as he went through the dead man's pockets. He was carrying no form of identification, so Lacrante took out a blood-draw spike, drove the needle into the dead man's arm, filled it up, then carefully put the ampoule back into its protective case.

As he was coming out from between the buildings back into the street, Antoniato's voice got through the thrum of interference.

'Lacrante, where are you?' Antoniato asked.

'Still alive and coming back. The tail is dead. I caught him but he took some kind of acid capsule. His head's soaking into a rockfall. It wasn't pleasant.'

'Any idea who he was working for?'

'No identification, but I don't think he was working for the Hand. Someone else has an interest here.'

Tenebrus came around gasping for breath, hands flailing. Yheng went to him, gripped his wrists, and hushed him until his eyelids ceased fluttering, and his soul was back in his body.

The spasms subsided. Tenebrus took in one last gasp. His gaze focused.

'Yheng,' he said. Perfectly black eyes bored into her soul.

'My master,' she said.

Tenebrus bonelessly sank into the chair. Yheng relaxed her grip on his arms, but did not let go.

'Did you find what you sought?'

'I believe so. I saw a vision, a golden being standing from a chair of fire. There is a powerful mind at the heart of the astropathic relay. It sees this being clearly. As it moves in half slumber, and the violent stars of the system stir the warp, so the visions leak out. I think they are beheld by all in the city there, would you believe. A powerful, powerful mind. I saw it.'

'The child?'

He nodded. 'It was a child. It was a man, a woman. It was everything.'

He pulled up his hands and ground the heels into his eyes.

The movement pained his side, and he hissed. Serous fluids stained his dressings.

'Now shall I send for Xyrax's flesh-techs?'

He nodded, then caught her as she went to leave.

'You are good to me, Yheng.' He moved to make himself more comfortable. 'Get a message to the Dark Cardinal. Tell him I do not have the location of this being we seek, but the mind in the relay will know more. It is as Kairos said. But we must hurry. My host was executed. There is an inquisitor there. I saw him. They may know of this movement in the warp themselves. We have to assume they do, and be swift. Events are moving apace. We will not reach this prize uncontested. The Word Bearers must bring war to Srinagar.'

Chapter Twenty-Six

MISTRESS AND COMMANDER

SRINAGAR DESCRIBED

SETTING SAIL

The next time Fabian met Eloise Athagey, she was briefing her fleet prior to departure, and he found that Athagey in public was a different woman to Athagey in private.

She addressed the chief officers of her battle group from her dais on the *Saint Aster*'s command deck with a rare sort of steady-eyed authority. Her words had an inspiring force that went beyond fierceness and conviction. There was a solidity to them. She was not saying what she wanted to happen, or what she hoped would happen, but what *would* happen. The miserable, aggressive woman he'd encountered a few weeks before was gone. Her uniform was crisp. She wore a meticulously maintained haptic glove and a monocular eyepiece so closely fitted that he would have taken it for an augmetic, had he not seen her without it. There was no sign of stimm abuse, and although a glass of some spirit or other was close at hand while she spoke, it gave her a rakish air rather than suggesting dependence.

Fabian found himself absorbed by Athagey-as-commander, and made copious notes on his serica tablet. The historitors recorded everything. A command band nestled in Yassilli's extravagant hair guided a servo-skull around the groupmistress. For all Athagey's disavowal of the Logos initiative, she appeared to be playing up to the chroniclers, full of theatrical gestures, knowing looks, and half-smiles that hinted at innuendo.

'Lords and ladies of Tertius Iolus, we must bid farewell to the safe haven of Lessira, and strike out again, a little earlier than planned. The Emperor's war is never done, and neither is ours.' She picked up her glass and sipped decorously. 'However, we go into battle with great confidence. We have learned that the enemy is making another move,' she said. 'Unlike before, this time we have advance warning and will be ready for them.'

Half the personnel were present by hololith, their glowing ghosts hanging at various heights in the air. In a flight of poetic fancy, Fabian saw them ranged around Athagey like judging, lesser gods, and she addressing them as a spirited mortal in defence of her soul. Fabian found the mismatches in size and focus fascinating. Some chose simple facial captures, others appeared on thrones surrounded by all the trappings of power. There was much to be gleaned from a person's choice of holo-phantom.

'Tactica displays, please,' said Athagey, in way that made it sound like a joke between friends.

The main tactical light pit ignited. A true-pict representation of a medium-sized world fizzled into being, a large moon in close orbit. They were both life bearing, with the surfaces appearing little marked by human avarice. Orbitals garlanded them, a sign of extensive activity, but the forests and seas spread wide, and there were few signs of urban canker.

'Srinagar Primus,' Athagey said. 'Alpha-class cavern world, Solutio Tertius exacta grade. So what? you will ask. I shall respond that this world is more important than it at first appears. It hosts a Zeta-class astropathic relay, one of the Ring of Fifty around the Throneworld. This, my friends, is a lynch-pin in the governance of the entire Imperium, and as such is under close supervision of the Adeptus Astra Telepathica. The Word Bearers will attack soon. No, it does not fit the profile of other worlds attacked by the Word Bearers in recent months. Yes, the relay makes it a valuable strategic target. However, as none of you people who serve under me are idiots...'

There was much laughter at this, some of it rather forced, thought Fabian.

'...you will ask how we can be sure that Kor Phaeron's traitors will strike here. That is a good question. This is how.'

She moved her hand dramatically, her haptic glove pinch-ing data from a gel screen to be displayed as a large light weave beside the global true-pict.

'Firstly, this message from Srinagar, sent two months ago, standard Terran time, six weeks by fleet reckoning. They have some kind of seer there, and it is the interpretation of the wise magi of the Adeptus that her words predict imminent inva-sion by Kor Phaeron himself. This would not be enough for me. This is.'

Another message, laid over the first. There was no time to read these things, they were displayed only for effect.

'This is a message from honoured Inquisitor Rostov. Anyone remember him?'

More laughs. Fabian gathered this Rostov had spent time with the fleet.

'Rostov has been away from our gentle company for a year now, but we remember him fondly.' She smiled in bawdy fashion.

Fabian found himself writing quickly. Athagey really was an outlier in behaviour. There were some officers who were this showy, but not very many. Most of them guarded their dignity like they would their fortunes. From what he'd heard she was much alike to the Lady VanLeskus in character. No wonder they did not get on.

'His astropath contacted us the day before yesterday, fourth watch, to inform us of anomalous psychic phenomena, perhaps connected to his ongoing mission, and various other, classified details,' Athagey said. 'Again, this would not be sufficient cause for me to order the battle group to Srinagar, but together, they make a compelling case. I have had our own astropaths consult their tarot, and after much very considered prayer...'

The laughter this time was strong and genuine. Athagey was not a devout woman then, judged Fabian.

'...the Emperor Himself commands that we go there.' Her tone became more serious. She activated another display. 'This will not be an easy fight. Particle effusions from the system stars are a genuine danger. Any ship without active void shields will find itself taxed by stellar flares. These are predictable, but not regular, and have the same effect as a directed neutron beam – devastating for organic life. Any ship without shields will lose most of its crew, should we find ourselves there at the height of an emission.

'Warfare on the surface will be difficult. Srinagar has its own standing regiment of the Astra Militarum, barracked upon its moon. They have adequate protective gear for surface fighting, even in the teeth of the particle storms. Our Militarum troops, on the whole, do not. Therefore, an army of Space Marines under Lord Lieutenant Messinius will head to the planet with Adeptus Mechanicus skitarii support. I deem this to be only a precaution. Kor Phaeron has had his own way for too long in this campaign. They will not get close to Srinagar, because our battle group will meet them in the void, supported by all of Battle Group Quartus Delphus. I have led you to victory many times before, and I shall again.' She smiled wickedly.

'And this time, we stand to take a fine head indeed, none less than that of the Dark Cardinal, Emperor damn him for all eternity.'

Chapter Twenty-Seven

PETTY MEN

AN OVERESTIMATION OF INFLUENCE

AN IMPORTANT NAME

Rostov spent a difficult night dealing with the aftermath of the shooting. He was convinced that the enemy would move soon against the world, and getting that information out became his priority. Rostov's seal opened every door, including that of the planetary governor, who needed little convincing to agree to mobilise her forces, and revealed that they had sent their own message on the advice of the Adeptus Astra Telepathica some weeks before.

Yet despite his ease in dealing with the planetary authority, his request to see Tolmun's superior was responded to sluggishly. It was only when Rostov's meetings with the governor were concluded that he could turn his attention to why. When his requests became a command, the maintenance guilds stopped obfuscating and invited him immediately to see the man. By then two days had passed since the shooting, and when Rostov went to see Watch-Master Hephaeus the planet was in a frenzy.

The watch-master received Rostov at his offices in the Sector

Administratum of the city, where all off-world and on-world governmental agencies were housed. Srinagar's semi-subterranean existence required a large amount of machine support, which bred a large bureaucracy, so the sector was substantial, and the maintenance guilds powerful within it. Initially, Rostov considered the delay was due to them throwing their weight around, somewhat dangerously, in order to extract some advantage from him, but the moment he met Hephaeus, he discounted that.

Watch-Master Hephaeus tried to be nonchalant when Rostov came in. He almost managed. He was pretending to look over some papers, and took his time to look the inquisitor up and down, as if he were of a sufficient grade to appraise a man like Rostov. It was a sham. The man's fear filled the room like a bad smell. Rostov knew then that the watch-master was hiding something, and he adjusted his techniques accordingly.

'You look official,' said Hephaeus, taking in Rostov's battle garb.

'I am unofficial, in most senses,' said Rostov.

'That what's I mean,' said the watch-master with forced lightness. 'I was expecting something less showy from the Inquisition.' The word caught slightly in his throat, and he cleared it with a cough. 'I wasn't expecting the armour, or the weapons. Are you trying to frighten me? There is no need. I will cooperate fully.'

'My panoply is not to intimidate you, watch-master. War is coming here,' said Rostov. 'It does not suit my purposes to go unseen any more. I will have to fight. And I do not have to frighten you, because you are frightened anyway. You are afraid because you know what I am.'

'You are an inquisitor.' Hephaeus tried to shrug, but his mouth betrayed him, drying around the title and gluing his lips. He licked them moist and reached for a glass of water on his desk. He kept his tone level, but his shaking hand betrayed him. 'Of course, I will tell you whatever you need to know. You have authority. I understand that.'

'I do not only have authority, watch-master, I have the *ultimate* authority,' said Rostov.

The man persisted with his show of courage. It was so important to these petty men that they keep face, Rostov thought, for the sake of their own self-image. Every master of drains and king of cabling was the same; stubborn in the face of their own insignificance. It was tedious, but Rostov knew the game well.

He pulled out a chair without waiting to be asked or asking himself. There were papers on it. There were papers everywhere. Rostov picked them up and dumped them on a pile of others. He could have swept them on the floor, but that, in this circumstance, he judged too much. He would not need to be violent. He sat, and stared into Hephaeus' eyes.

'You have a difficult job,' he said, with a trace of sympathy. 'Men with important roles like the ones you oversee can be difficult. I understand your show of bravery. You must appear strong. I appreciate that. The Imperium is built upon the strength of men like you.'

The man's shaking spread to his head, making it wobble.

'I meant no insolence. I said I will tell you what you need to know.'

'One way or another, you will, yes,' said Rostov, and his words sent the watch-master paler still, so he was whiter than the sheets of paper waiting in his in-trays. 'I am telling you I understand this charade you are performing. You live in a small world of obligation and counter-obligation. In the context of this planet, your role carries weight, but there are many men above you. Your so-called betters do not understand the pressures of your role, and what you must do to keep them safe. You are responsible for the shutters. Your men understand their worth, and they will not obey a weak man, while your patrons will not respect someone who bows immediately to off-world authority. You could lose your employment. You could lose everything. Your office can be sold on, so you must look strong.'

Rostov tugged off his gloves and laid them on the desk, crossed his legs and clasped one of his knees. It was a simple postural change, and he sat as one would in the company of friends, but his eyes and tone remained ice-cold and stone-hard.

'But you are afraid. You are afraid that Tolmun's treachery will taint you. Is this not the case?'

'His treachery is nothing to do with me,' said Hephaeus, a little too quickly.

Rostov looked at him until he began to sweat. 'You know what I am.'

'I said. I said! Yes. You are an inquisitor.'

'"My lord",' said Rostov. 'That is the correct form of address. You speak with a representative of the Golden Throne of Terra. You will not meet a more important man than I in your life.'

'My lord,' said Hephaeus, more of a wheeze than words. He licked lips that had dried again. He did not reach for his water this time.

'What am I besides an inquisitor, Watch-Master Hephaeus? What makes me suited to my role of prising secrets from men like you?'

There was a flicker of disgust in Hephaeus' eyes. He could tell Rostov was a witch. The psychosphere of the room vibrated with his terror.

Hephaeus mumbled something.

'Louder,' said Rostov.

'I said you are a wi...' He stopped himself before the fateful word could emerge, and straightened his posture. 'You are a psyker, my lord.'

'I am blessed by the Emperor Himself.' Rostov lifted up the small effigy around his neck and dangled it. 'Thanks to His grace, I can tell you are afraid simply by looking at you, and if I do this...' He grabbed Hephaeus' wrist. The other man yanked back, but Rostov held him hard. 'I can feel the shape of your fears. If I were to hurt you, badly, I would be able to see exactly what you are thinking. I would see through your eyes. Not one of your memories would be safe from me, every confidence betrayed, every dark thought, every passion, I would know them all. Do you wish me to hurt you badly?'

Hephaeus shook his head. 'N-n-no, my lord.'

'Do you know what else I can do?'

Hephaeus' face was screwing up. There was a hint of tears at the corners of his eyes, though Rostov had done nothing more than hold his wrist, and he exerted no painful pressure.

'I can tell the worth of men, and I can tell that you, Hephaeus, are not a worthy man.'

'It's not true, I do my work, I serve Him on the Throne, I...'

'You are lying,' said Rostov. 'You are lying about something.'

Hephaeus nodded hesitantly. He was crying freely now.

'Then do not lie to me again. Your subordinate, Gilber Tolmun. What do you know of him? Who did he serve?'

'Tolmun...' Rostov felt the familiar swell of fear, of a man searching for something to say to make the inquisitor go away. 'I... Nothing. He's often late. He abandoned his post a few days ago, but... but... I know nothing else. He was arrogant. Difficult. They're all like that, these shuttermen.'

'You do not know who he served?'

Hephaeus shook his head mutely. Curious, Rostov thought. He was telling the truth.

'Think. Was there anything strange? Any long absences? Traitors have been passing information to the enemy that has caused much trouble to the Imperium,' said Rostov. 'That is why war is coming to this world. Your entire populace and the service you provide to the Imperium is at risk. This is the fault of Gilber Tolmun.'

'Tolmun was one of those people?'

Rostov nodded. 'Death is the fate of all traitors, Hephaeus. Tolmun is dead. Are you a traitor?'

There was a shifting in the panicked swirl of Hephaeus' thoughts. Whatever he was hiding, he did not know about Tolmun's unfortunate choice in faith. The two were not connected. That was disappointing.

'He was a link in a chain,' Rostov said. 'These cells the enemy stitch into the fabric of our world work by passing orders from mouth to ear. It probably made him feel important. I assure you he was not. He was a pawn. Do you know who his masters might have been? Who were his friends, his associates?'

'I-I-I don't know!'

Rostov squeezed hard. Years of combat made him strong. Bones closed in Hephaeus' wrist. A little pain sharpened his reading of the squirming man. The watch-master did not know about Tolmun, but details of bribes, and violence, appeared and vanished in the torrent of his fear.

'Then find out,' said Rostov. 'You will have his associations on file whether you know it or not. You watch your workers. His was a position of responsibility.' Rostov released him.

Hephaeus fell back gasping, his face red.

'Yes, yes, we do.'

Rostov tossed a small silver sphere onto the table. 'This is an encoded, limited use vox-bead. When you have the information, use the bead to contact my servant Lacrante. He will come to you, and you will give him the names of everyone who worked with Tolmun, in this departmento and outside it. Do not tell anybody why you are gathering this information. If you do, it is a death sentence for you, and for them, and for anyone else I deem a threat to the Imperium.'

'Yes, inquisitor, anything!' said Hephaeus.

'There is one other thing.' Rostov rested his hand on the butt of his pistol. 'I possess the authority of the Emperor of Terra Himself. If I were to command it, this entire planet would be burned to ashes without question. Passing judgement on you and enacting my punishment would take a heartbeat of my life, and I would forget it a moment later.' Rostov snapped his fingers. 'Yet your existence would be over, and once you were cast from this life, the Emperor would turn you away from His light if I said it should be so.'

Hephaeus trembled all over. His lips wobbled like a child's. His voice was thick. 'My lord, I... Please, my lord, I...'

Rostov pointed at him. 'I have seen, in your thoughts, the actions you perform to ease your own existence. Some might overlook this. I will not. Every act of extortion is another cell in the cancer that chokes our civilisation, and I will not abide it. So I advise you, watch-master, to live your life in scrupulous honesty from now on. You are rewarded enough for your work. Seek no more. I shall make it my business to return here one day, and when I do I shall visit you. If I do not like what I find, I shall not be so merciful again.'

Rostov tugged his gloves back on.

'Get the information I need to my servant Lacrante. Get it today.'

Once he was back out amid the power coils and hissing moisture conduits of the Sector Administratum, Rostov contacted Lacrante himself.

'How did it go with Hephaeus, my lord?' Lacrante asked.

'Typical mid-ranking official. Dishonest, violent and greedy. He tried to stall us only to show he wasn't scared, which he was. The fool was hiding some low-grade criminality. He knew nothing. I put the fear of the Emperor into him, and told him to furnish you with a list of Tolmun's associates. As soon as you have it, chase down anyone on the list whose name we do not already have. You and Antoniato are to proceed with interrogations.'

'Yes, my lord. The Adeptus Administratum Officio Census representatives got back to me,' Lacrante said. *'I got a full list of Tolmun's family from them. There's only a few people on there that we haven't already arrested. Antoniato and I have been to the courthouse again and spoken with the magister. He gave further promises of cooperation from the Adeptus Arbites planetary precinct, and though there's not many of them here, they're sending squads out now. The local enforcers are making good on their offer of unconditional support and are rounding up the last of Tolmun's friends, the ones we knew about already. A few have gone missing, but we're closing in,'* said Lacrante. *'I've had to flash the seal a few times, but the enforcers are doing their best.'*

'Try to be on hand to apprehend remaining suspects yourselves if possible,' Rostov advised. 'The ones that have gone missing are likely to be the most dangerous. Local Lex is open to bribery. The last targets will have plenty of warning of our coming, and it may provoke them into being rash.'

'Then I will go out. Antoniato is in the archives, seeing if he can track down the man I chased and the shooter. They take gene tags here. They're partial, restricted to samples taken during the course of investigation, but it covers about sixty per cent of the population. Emperor willing, he will have a name today.'

'It is fortunate they maintain records,' said Rostov. 'It is less fortunate it took us two days to access them. That might be the result of fear, like Hephaeus, but it could indicate something more sinister. Keep alert for what's missing as much as what is revealed. Assume there are agents in the government. Make sure Antoniato trawls for recent deletions.' Rostov passed under a gurgling pipe six yards in diameter. Heat burned off it. Machines beneath shook the walkway he travelled. Srinagar Civitas was not a pretty place. 'Keep me up to date. Tolmun's cohorts will be easy to run to ground, I feel. Once we have what we need from them, it's a simple matter of cult expurgation that we can pass on to the local authorities. But these others are of interest. I want to know who ordered the killing of our target, and why. I shall pursue that as soon as you have names. You concentrate on the Tolmun links, and make sure Cheelche stays out of sight.'

'*Yes, my lord. Shall I send her back to the* Res Fugit?'

'Keep her on-world. If she makes a fuss, have her remain in the shuttle, but she is to stay. We shall need Cheelche's skills soon enough. No matter how quick we are, we will be here when the fighting starts, and it would be better for us if Cheelche and her guns were by our side. I have had word from the ship that Battle Group Iolus of Fleet Tertius is coming here. They have further information from the Adeptus Astra Telepathica that makes Athagey believe an attack is imminent. I am going to send DiFerrius away to hide at the system's edge. *Res Fugit* is fast, but not suitable for battle against Heretic Astartes.'

'*Well, I've spoken to the magister about Cheelche in any case,*' said Lacrante. '*I suggested that they give her an icon of permission, which he did, but only when I said if they didn't you might get involved personally. He wasn't happy.*'

'Happiness is not the lot of the Imperial citizen, duty is. We still have our mission to perform. Keep yourselves safe. For the Emperor.'

'*For the Emperor.*'

He cut the link, and walked on.

Rostov used the time it took to cross the service district to think. There were evidently two separate cults at large on Srinagar, and they were at war, but either of them could prove a risk to the defence once the Word Bearers came, and either could lead him back to the Hand. He wondered once more what the mind who rode the dead operarius was looking for, and what it had to do with the Hand of Abaddon. When he considered that the Hand could be a sorcerer themselves, he wondered if he had just looked into his enemy's eyes. If so, what was he doing here? What did it have to do with the astrotelepathic relay, and what was the significance of the golden figure? Was it a projection of the enemy, or something else?

He saw a beach in his mind again. Heard the laughter of carefree children at play. It made him suspicious. Children did not laugh like that on many worlds.

Why were the Word Bearers coming to Srinagar?

The relay was the key. He resolved to go there next.

Crowds of workers were gathering at the edge of the service zone, forming lines to board evacuation lifters that would take them deep down into the planet, below the level of the city, into shelters built to protect them from the worst of the solar storms. A constant barrage of announcements and klaxons assailed his hearing, and when Antoniato contacted him, it took three attempts for them to hear each other. Gene matches on the shooter, and from another individual, retrieved from skin flakes on a burned-up piece of shirt.

When he deactivated the channel, the rest of the game was set.

Antoniato had given him a name.

Chapter Twenty-Eight

ANCIENT EVIL

A SENSITIVE TASK

KOR PHAERON

Messinius was in his private office when Areios was shown in by his servants.

'Captain Areios,' Messinius said. He got up from his desk to greet his protégé. They clasped arms, wrist to elbow.

Areios had a few inches on the Firstborn Messinius. Neither of them wore their armour. Messinius was dressed in simple robes, Areios the off-duty uniform of short-sleeved tunic and trousers common to all the Unnumbered Sons. You could see the difference between the bloodlines when they were out of their armour. The paleness of the Raven Guard, that made light-skinned men milk-white and dark-skinned men grey. The influence of Sanguinius that recast every kind of face in beauty. The burning eyes and coal-black hue of Vulkan's progeny. The square jaw and searching eyes of Guilliman. Areios had that, although his attention was solely confined to threat. Messinius examined the captain's face for signs of awakening humanity, but found no more than the last time they had spoken. So many of the Mars-born Primaris Marines were like that, so altered and wiped clean in mind by Cawl's long sleep they appeared almost devoid of soul. Messinius regarded calling their humanity back his most difficult duty.

Still, Areios was a valuable asset.

'You wished to see me, lord lieutenant?' Areios asked.

'Yes. Sit. Talk with me.'

Areios did as he was asked.

'You will take some refreshment?'

'Water, please,' said Areios. 'I approach the point of dehydration. Too long in the fighting cages. Too many things to do.'

'We must attend to our bodies' needs, Ferren. A blunt weapon is no use to anyone.' Once, Messinius had encouraged Areios to drink other things. Even a Space Marine needs some stimulation in his life, a little flavour, a touch of joy. His suggestions had fallen on deaf ears.

Messinius poured Areios a cup of water, and fetched himself some wine. His beakers were simple things cut from sections of a tasgen's horn, a rare and ferocious beast.

'The mission. You are the most exemplary warrior within the Unnumbered Sons attached to these two battlefleets. The role you have been given is of crucial importance.'

Areios nodded. Not proud or pleased, simply acknowledging Messinius' statement as fact.

'You did not say this in the mission briefing with high command, nor did you elaborate on what I must do. Why?'

Messinius drank from his beaker. 'Can you deduce the reason?' the White Consul asked.

Areios stared straight ahead, hardly moving. His arm lifted like it was a mechanism separate from the rest of his body. He drained his cup, and set it down. No pleasure, not even at the relief of thirst. He was a machine servicing itself.

'Groupmistress Athagey does not believe the Traitor Legion

will make landfall, she deems it even less likely that they will make their way through the troops under your command into the astropathic relay. She intends to stop the Word Bearers in the void, and is confident that she will do so. I judge that her strategic evaluation is correct. Therefore, you felt no need to go into detail of my role in the coming battle. The deployment of my men is a backup, intended to deal with any unforeseen eventualities.'

Messinius nodded. 'That is a fair and mostly accurate deduction. But it is not the whole of it.'

Areios' face changed by the absolute minimum required to convey an unspoken question.

'Pride, Ferren. Do you remember it?'

'I feel it still. I am proud. I am proud to serve. I am proud to be a Primaris Marine. I am proud to be a son of Roboute Guilliman.' He stiffened almost imperceptibly.

'Did you choose any of those things to be proud of?'

There was a moment's pause. Areios shook his head.

'Groupmistress Athagey is proud. Her pride is dependent on her choices, and so she leaves herself open to failure. She is volatile. She recognises that your deployment is necessary, but if she were to acknowledge that, it would cast doubt over her battle plan. In her eyes, if in no one else's.'

'Explain,' said Areios.

Messinius sighed. 'I have tried to teach you, Ferren. So many of the first Primaris brothers are like you. Cawl made you mighty, but the payment he exacted was steep. He took too much of your humanity.'

'I am loyal to mankind. The preservation of the Imperium is my first and only goal,' said Areios.

'You misunderstand me. I do not question your devotion to our species. I am, however, pointing out your lack of empathy for the motives of natural-born humans. One day, you will no longer be an Unnumbered Son. One day, I am sure, you will be elevated to high office within a Chapter. You might even become a Chapter Master yourself. You will be called upon to fight alongside baseline humans on many occasions. It is vital that you relearn some of what you have lost. Diplomacy, tact and insight to the actions of others will be as important weapons to you as your bolter is.'

Areios continued to stare ahead, but nodded slightly. 'You have said before. I will attempt to address my shortcomings, lord lieutenant.'

'They are not your shortcomings. They are the fault of Cawl. Sometimes I think Guilliman asked for legions of Space Marines, but was given legions of machines. Thankfully, not all of you suffer this, and there seems to be little difference in temperament between the Firstborn and the Primaris raised as new intake by the Chapters, but for the Mars-born and for you especially, Ferren, it is an obstacle to overcome. Be mindful of people like Athagey. Try to learn what motivates them, what they are frightened of, what their ambitions are. Only then will you be able to serve them properly as an ally, and protect them.'

Again, Areios nodded. Messinius wondered if he really understood.

'Is that all, lord lieutenant?'

'No, brother, you must listen. It is likely that the enemy will not breach the relay. They must deal with two battle groups, then effect a landing, fight their way through myself, our brothers, and an entire regiment of specialist Imperial Guard. They cannot make teleport attack on the relay. The psychic turbulence will confound any locus lock.'

'So I am a fail-safe, as I said.'

'You may be more than that. What do you know of Kor Phaeron?'

'He is ancient,' Areios said. 'Lord Guilliman has revealed that he was the adoptive father of the traitor primarch Lorgar. He is among the Imperium's greatest enemies.'

'He is also a potent sorcerer, greatly favoured by the Dark Gods. If there is a way into the relay, he will find it. If he finds it, he will likely lead the attack himself, or send in his most powerful lieutenants.'

'This is a warning?' said Areios.

'Be careful, Ferren,' said Messinius. 'You and your men are among the very best that I have, but you are not finished, not even now. You will rush in to attack, confident in your abilities, and find yourselves up against a foe of uncommon sort. Facing heavy odds, you will sacrifice yourselves without a second thought because you believe it is the right thing to do. Do not do this. You are not expendable. You are not mechanisms. Too many Primaris have died because they lack the capacity for reflection. A Firstborn Space Marine knows his worth, he will withdraw rather than throwing his life away.'

'We are to let people die, to save ourselves?'

'Sometimes, yes. That is our burden. Sometimes one world must burn so a dozen more can live. Judge the risk carefully, act accordingly.'

'I understand,' said Areios. 'I have been making progress in instilling the values of the Firstborn into my men. You need only review the combat logs to see how our fighting style is adapting. We have improved.'

Was that defensiveness? wondered Messinius. If so, it was a good sign.

'I am not sure you do understand. Your role in this battle is containment. If the enemy makes their way into the relay, you are to call for reinforcement immediately. Hold them in place. Under no circumstances are you to engage their sorcerers alone. If needs be, you must retreat. You must be prepared to forget your pride. You must judge if the battle is lost, and if it is, you must leave before you are too.'

'Why must I not face them?' said Areios.

'Because Kor Phaeron's champions have ten thousand years' experience fighting Space Marines. Because they have a measure of warp power that makes that of our greatest Librarians seem mean in comparison. I ask for caution, Ferren, above all other things, because if you face one of their high priests, they will kill you. Contain them. Confound them. Do not underestimate your foe. Do you understand this as well?'

'I understand,' said Areios. Another pause, that of a cogitator calculating. 'You also did not wish to say this in front of high command because you do not want them to feel we value human lives less than our own.'

'You are learning, good,' said Messinius. 'When we break warp, I am sending you in ahead, with the historitors. They are going before the ground troops to begin the retrieval of Srinagar's astrotelepathic archives. These stretch back thousands of years, and contain much useful data for the Lord Commander's Logos initiative. You will attend with them.'

'So that I might make an early survey of the mountain's defensibility?'

'That, yes, but mostly I want you to watch. You will be present as a symbol of unity within our forces, a message to the Adeptus Astra Telepathica there, should one be needed, that the historitors' mission has the full backing of the fleet, the Adeptus Terra and the primarch, and will not be hindered. This is only a precaution, a subtle reinforcement for those people in the fleet as much as for those on Srinagar about the Logos' worth. But for you, it is an opportunity. Watch how Fabian and his men interact. Listen to what they say. Try to understand them a little more. You are a fine warrior, Areios, but Lord Guilliman had more in mind for us than war. It was always his wish that Space

Marines rise above violence, that when time permits we will help baseline humanity achieve what it can. My Chapter, the White Consuls, believes this completely, and throughout our territories before we lost Sabatine we upheld the primarch's ideals. We have many gifts, Ferren. They do not have to be solely for killing. I want you to learn this. Try to remember what it is to be a man.'

'I will try,' said Areios.

Messinius looked into Ferren Areios' eyes, and wondered what manner of person he had been before Cawl's creatures had transformed him. Was there anything of him left?

'I am sure one day you will succeed,' said Messinius. 'You may go.'

Chapter Twenty-Nine

HIGH TELEPATHICUS
A HOLLOW MOUNTAIN
RICH ARCHIVES

Four days, the trip took in the end. The *Saint Aster* dropped them a day's sailing out from the prime world, and Fabian led the delegation down. He got a good view of the planet and the moon through the shuttle's vid-feeds. The stain of humanity on them both was a little more evident than in the hololith, but then so were the dark green of its forests, and deep blue of its grasslands, and the shattering white of the ice caps.

Yassilli Sulymanya, Serisa Vallia and Captain Areios had come with him. Nobody said much on the trip. Sulymanya sat with a blank expression on her face for the entire passage, her mind somewhere else. Vallia, by contrast, was so nervous that she had not stopped fidgeting, asking lots of questions, then lapsing into silence, then repeating the process, like an avian singing its refrain.

Ferren Areios said nothing and did nothing. Being far too large to use the seats, he was mag-locked solid to the centre of the transit bay, occupying the majority of its volume. He was so still he could have been an empty suit of armour, or an inconveniently sited statue. Now this was a Space Marine whose humanity had been scraped out and replaced, thought Fabian, completely different to Lucerne. He spoke only when addressed. He was concerned with the waging of war and nothing else.

Srinagar Civitas was situated forty degrees south of the equator, where a small massif, almost square in shape, thrust up through the blue prairies, rippling them into hills south and east, and deforming the crust into fractured badlands at the foot of a great sheer scarp to the west. The city was easy to pick out to the east of the massif, smears of grey around a geoformed mountain, the prairie punctured by starkly black, rectangular holes, as if the world were a house full of unglazed windows. The largest was huge, big enough to put a heavy lander down in, with a highway-sized flight of stairs leading up from below.

They swept down to one of several exterior landing pads occupying a flattened ridge halfway up the side of the mountain housing the relay itself. Approximately half the mountain's height had been carved into geometric shapes, and it was covered in arcane machines that fizzed sparks into the afternoon.

Claws kissed rockcrete. The shuttle settled down, engines whooping and dying. When the safety lumens clicked to green, Fabian and his fellows unfastened their restraints. Fabian stretched tiredly. It had been a sleepless voyage through the warp, and the shuttle was too uncomfortable to let him rest on the last leg through the void.

'Let's make a good impression,' he said. 'By that, I mean let me do the talking.' He edged round Areios and banged on the cockpit door. 'Let us out!' he said.

Atmosphere cyclers huffed. Something rumbled in the wall of the bay, tasting the air for toxins. It blurted out its report in a jarring squeal none of the historitors could understand. If Areios did, he gave no indication.

Locks disengaged, and the ramp opened onto Srinagar's open
skies.

A welcoming party of officials had gathered to greet them
dressed in the full regalia of their office. The contrast between
the Logos' sober, military-style uniform and the ostentation of
the other Adepta was stark.

The Logos' uniform was the same for all ranks, only a few pins
and coloured piping to set them apart. This was not the case
for the Adeptus Astra Telepathica. The basic garb was simple
enough: a green robe for the astropaths themselves, a robe or
uniform with green flashes for their servants, but as soon as rank
and specialisation became involved, it got complicated, and when
rank was filtered through ten thousand years of competition for
influence, ego and vanity, the results tended to the outrageous.

He found himself confronted by a number of people whose
sex, age and even humanity was hard to discern beneath layers
of stiff brocade. The signature green of the Adepta was reduced
to the merest hint among clashing threads of gold, copper and
silver. Emeralds were favoured for the colour, but they had
precious friends of every other hue. The characteristic hoods
on the robes of the higher astropaths were reduced to decorative flourishes; instead they wore elaborate headdresses that
might have had some kind of use in the wearer's duties, but were
more likely stylised versions of practical items. These people
were frail, drained by their onerous service, yet the clothes they
wore would have doubled the weight of some of them, and no
matter that every single one of the psykers was astropath-blind,
their garb was a visual feast.

The most extravagant outfit belonged to an elderly adept
wearing a huge headpiece and cloth-of-gold coat over multi-
layered robes in five shades of green. He occupied an equally
extravagant eight-legged spider-chair. All the astropaths carried
slender staffs; they were a practical aid as well as a badge of

office, but so important was the psyker in the chair that he had an indentured man holding his staff for him.

'I feel underdressed,' Fabian whispered out of the corner of his mouth at Yassilli.

'You realise most of these people are telepaths?' she said back.

'Then it doesn't matter if they hear me, does it?'

The ramp clanged down fully. Fabian came down out of the lander flanked by Yassilli and Serisa. Areios came to mechanical life and lumbered after them, as subtle and welcoming as some crimelord's protection-automaton. Cold wind hit them. Fabian's face burned with it pleasantly.

A herald in a winged helm came out from the group, and bowed. 'Greetings, Historitor Majoris Fabian Guelphrain. The most clairvoyant High-Telepathicus Wesu Sveen bids you welcome to our humble planet, and this magnificent facility.' He indicated the elderly man in the spider-chair, then the carved rock rising up over them.

A strange mental pressure pushed at Fabian from the mountain, like a form of heatless warmth. His teeth tasted of metal. His field of vision seemed unaccountably different. It was hard for him to put into words the effect of psychic power, but he recognised witches hard at work.

'I thank you for your kindness,' he said. 'These are my associates. Historitor Designate Vallia, and Historitor Elevate Sulymanya. They will be aiding me in the recording of your archives.'

'There are more aboard, I assume?' said the herald, peering into the dim hold of the shuttle. 'Our archives are extensive, and precious to us.'

'In the next ship. I have a team of sixteen more, as well as their ancillaries, and our equipment,' Fabian reassured him. 'That is every historitor available near Srinagar. We realise the importance of the relay's libraries, not only for their historical importance, but also in furthering the successful prosecution of the crusade. We will work night and day to ensure that this information is gathered and protected. Now...' He turned to the Space Marine looming over them all like the Emperor's own judgement. 'At the behest of Captain Messinius, lord lieutenant of Fleet Tertius, I am accompanied by Captain Ferren Areios of the Unnumbered Sons of Guilliman, First Chapter, First Company. He will lead the defence of the mountain. There is a third vessel carrying fifty of his brothers coming in behind us. A larger force, led by the lord lieutenant himself, will be arriving very soon to repel any attack on the city, should it come to that.'

'Let us hope it does not.'

Every time the man spoke, Fabian felt something tickling in the back of his head, and he realised that though the words came out of the herald's mouth, he was not formulating them. Sveen was telepathically manipulating him.

'First Transliterator Rumagoi will act as a liaison.'

An adept dressed slightly less ridiculously than his fellows came forward, a younger man close by his elbow. Like the herald, they were sighted, and probably not psykers. Both bowed to Fabian.

'A pleasure to meet you,' the older man said. 'I and my aide Colus will be your official helpers here. If there is anything we can do to expedite the process of safeguarding our archives, then you must only ask.'

'Thank you,' said Fabian.

'We have already begun preparations,' said Rumagoi. 'Please follow me. High-Telepathicus?'

The astropath bowed his head once, not directly at Fabian. It didn't seem meant for the historitors, and was instead a gesture of recognition at someone on the far side of the platform, or a motion sparked by a suddenly recalled memory. Whatever it meant, the dignitaries turned around all together, and they proceeded up the ridge towards the relay's entrance.

* * *

The landing zone had no direct access into the mountain, to prevent it being used as an avenue of attack, Areios judged. It was still a weakness. The procession shuffled along only as fast as the clicking legs of Sveen's spider-chair could carry him, and the Space Marine had plenty of time to survey the site. He found the defences lacking.

Their route was a path only a few yards wide, warded by railings, whose every fourth pole was topped with a flashing, beeping lumen, as if that were necessary to warn people of the precipitous drop. Most of Srinagar was out of sight underground, the rectangles in the surface visible from orbit revealed to be great aperture lights that led from sloped ferrocrete housings into the ceiling of the settlement below. Data inload acquired before departure told him that these were shut at times of high stellar activity. Currently, particle bombardment was in the null-phase, and they were open. To the south-west, the city's greater edifices and certain machineries poked up into the open air, and further off were the landing fields of the primary space port. Between these buildings the despoliation mankind inflicted upon its worlds was clear to see in tox-scarring, quarrying and piles of unsorted refuse dumped on the surface. But when they rounded the spur of the landing ridge, they could see south to the horizon over an unspoiled wilderness of rolling plains punctuated by crags, where herds of large, dome-backed beasts ambled, unaffected by their proximity to the city.

Areios remembered Messinius' orders. He turned his attention to the delegation. Fabian was making conversation with the first transliterator.

Engage recording, he instructed his battleplate's machine-spirit, then tracked through all aural input, scrubbing out everything until Fabian's words were crystal clear.

'I understand that Srinagar's surface is dangerous to humans,' Fabian was saying. 'Something to do with the weather?'

'It is periodically dangerous,' explained Rumagoi. 'Although it appears from here we have but one sun, we are a binary system. Our suns, Srin and Gar, are mismatched in size, Gar being the smaller, and in a very tight orbit with Srin. The gravitic effects of Srin on Gar cause perturbations in its solarsphere, which result in bursts of dangerous subatomic particles. So when we speak about the weather, we are referring to these eructations from the secondary star,' he said. 'Predicting our solar storms is a complicated art, but we are dependent on it here.'

'What about these native creatures?' Fabian asked. 'How do they survive?'

Areios panned his view out over the plains. Threat indicators in the median range flashed around the beasts when he zoomed his auto-senses in to them. Already he was formulating kill-tactics.

'It's very interesting,' said Rumagoi. Areios noted a change in tone: enthusiasm, he thought. Rumagoi was warming to his subject. 'The local life is well adapted to the bombardment, but the particle sleet is deadly to the human form, and so when the star spits, we must hide underground. We live as much under the open air as we can, but we must be careful, and there are sometimes mistakes. The local life can stand it, because the species here possesses a very dense gene-code. If I may explain?'

'Go ahead, don't worry about patronising me. My knowledge is broad, but shallow. I live to learn,' said Fabian.

'The human form houses a double gene strand,' said Rumagoi. 'Theirs has twenty-eight. Our genetors established a long time ago that this is an effective defence mechanism against neutron bombardment. If part of their genetic make-up is corrupted, it is deactivated, and another part, identical, takes over. There is multiple redundancy built into their being. We humans don't have that. They have other adaptations as well, you see their high backs, the thick skin?'

'I do,' said Fabian.

'They have blisters of super-dense liquids throughout, hyper-saline, saturated with iodine. This also keeps them safe. Furthermore, they possess a magnetic sense that helps them predict the storms some hours before the brunt hits. One of the first arts our astrameteomancers learn is observation of our animals. For example, when they sink low, there will be a shower. When they make burrows, they are preparing to wait out a long storm. They can last for a year or more if they have to in a form of hibernation. It is supposed that life must have arisen here long before the stars' orbits neared, and evolved over time to cope with the particle effusions of Gar. They're quite fascinating. I have numerous treatises, if you are interested.'

'We historitors are interested in everything,' said Fabian. 'They are close to the city, and there appear to be a lot of them. Are they not exploited?'

This questioning confused Areios. Most of what Fabian was asking was freely available on the ships. He thought at first the historitor had been lax, then he saw the look on Rumagoi's face: pride at being useful and knowledgeable. He looked to Fabian. The historitor wore an encouraging smile.

Tactical assessment, he said to himself. *Hypothesis. Fabian Guelphrain is doing this deliberately. He is putting the other man at his ease.*

Areios had a flash of his time as a youth, a memory fragment that came from nowhere. Playing with the little ones, telling them stories, praising their small achievements to fill their hearts with good feelings and encourage them to better efforts. He barely recognised the memory as his own, but was this what Fabian was doing? Areios thought it was.

'Their biology makes them practically useless for any purpose other than a few esoteric technologies,' Rumagoi responded. 'They are all highly toxic, and cannot be eaten. Some are harvested for their salts, but they are fierce, their adaptations to the sun serve equally well as armour against attack, so the risks outweigh the gains. Besides, Srinagar is well blessed with resources that are much easier to gather. We use those to fulfil the exacta, which is low thanks to our special status as a relay hub – we exist here primarily to serve the Adepta. There are few settlements on the world, and therefore no need to kill the beasts. Live and let live, I say.'

'Any intelligent xenos?'

They crossed the ridge now, and Areios saw the massive stairway that cleaved up from the plain. There was no vehicular traffic on it, only pedestrians and small, legged, personal conveyances, but a great throng of people was moving between the mountain and the city. This was a major weakness in the defences. Areios took a pict-capt and marked it for urgent conveyance to the lord lieutenant, because it appeared an even greater vulnerability when seen close than it had on the mission files. Beneath, after a long drop, there were lesser stairs clinging to the cliffs; entrances to the mountains, more weaknesses. A cordon of Guardsmen in planetary defence and Adeptus Astra Telepathica uniforms kept part of the main stair clear for the dignitaries. Cyber constructs swept back and forth overhead, scanning the crowd for potential assassins. They were taking a risk greeting Fabian's party so openly.

Politics, Areios thought. *A display of power.*

'Ah now, that is interesting,' said Rumagoi. 'None extant, but there are archaeological ruins on the southern continent that date back to antiquity. Local legend has it that they were struck down by the Emperor Himself for their deviant ways.'

'You're a very knowledgeable man.'

Fabian's compliment made Rumagoi even prouder, but he waved it away.

'I only try to read as widely as one can. I believe a man serves the Emperor best when he is best informed, though that is not a popular opinion.' He looked at Fabian. 'I assume it is safe to say that to someone like you. It isn't always wise to admit to curiosity.'

'No, it isn't,' agreed Fabian. 'But you're safe with me.'

A promise he cannot keep, thought Areios. *But not insincere.*

They went down a path that joined the main stairs near the top, where they were broad and flattened out. Areios marked every strength and weakness he could find. The gates to the mountain were as thick and strong as those of any fortress, and they were closed. They looked formidable, but their position meant they would be easily targeted by ground artillery fire. The group went inside via a side gate guarded by yet more security personnel, and he judged this yet another weak point. Once inside, the group broke up. Sveen took his leave of them, and departed with the majority of his dignitaries. Rumagoi told his own servants to show Vallia and Sulymanya to the complex that would house the administrative part of the historitors' efforts. Areios watched the delicate dance of pleasantry and command, until he was called and directed over to the military officers of the mountain.

The group of Astra Militarum and Adeptus Astra Telepathica personnel lined up and stood to attention as he approached. He deactivated his vid-capture function. Despite the thickness of the main gates and the martial displays outside, this would be a hard place to hold if it were attacked. He would have to tell these people. He would have to heed Messinius' lessons on tact while he did it.

He tried his best. It didn't work.

After that, his real work began.

'I shall show you to our archives,' Rumagoi said to Fabian. The first transliterator was a little pompous, but his obvious enthusiasm for knowledge made the historitor like him.

Fabian received word that the rest of his people were arriving, and voxed orders that the Logos begin landing their equipment.

The day was moving up a gear. There was a lot of work to be done and already it appeared that the relay was preparing for invasion, for there were a great many soldiers within, and he realised many of the people moving up and down the great stair were preparing to evacuate. Inside the mountain, the sense of powerful minds at work was stronger, a psychic background radiation that made Fabian's soft palate itch.

Rumagoi pointed out various areas of interest as he took Fabian deeper underground, explaining its construction, with the choir housed in a duratanium sphere at the centre of an artificial cavern, and the adepts' tabularia all around the outside. Power was geothermal for the whole settlement, and he gave troop numbers, defensive batteries, and many other facts and figures. He obviously wanted to impress Fabian, so Fabian obliged with encouraging noises and follow-on questions.

By several long stairs they reached a hall deep beneath the surface, its high ceilings held up by a forest of pillars. Much of it was empty, and dimly lit, but lumens shone at the far end where a run of iron railings between the pillars divided the hall in two.

'We are directly below the choir here,' Rumagoi said quietly, as if the astropaths could hear him. 'This is the most secure part of the complex, so if the enemy do come, you shall be safe.'

'The archives are better fortified than the choir?'

'Absolutely. Astropaths are easier to replace than information,' Rumagoi explained. 'There is ten thousand years of data kept here. The stories of the xenos may not be true, but this relay does go back to the foundation of the Imperium. I have the proof of that.' Rumagoi caught the look in Fabian's eyes. 'It's exciting, isn't it?'

Beyond the bars lay tantalising banks of wooden cabinets and bookshelf stacks forty feet high. An enormous lock held the gate closed. A man in simple green robes sat behind a pulpit within touching distance of the gate. There was nothing on the sloped board before him, no screens or buttons, but around his neck he wore a key of such size and weight that it bent his posture into a permanent bow. A visored helmet was bonded to his skull, and had been there for some time by the looks of it, his skin having grown up into rough ridges around the edges.

'Archivist!' Rumagoi called. 'Open the gate. We have a special visitor.'

The archivist mumbled something under his breath, and came out from behind the desk. His feet had been replaced by a wheeled unit, and he glided to the gate.

'The vault of knowledge is always open to you, oh vaunted one,' the archivist said. With some effort, he lifted his giant key, placed it in the lock, and turned.

Latches snapped back all the way up the gate, the archivist gave it a gentle push, and it groaned open.

Rumagoi bowed formally. 'Historitor Majoris, by the permission of the Adeptus Astra Telepathica, the archives of the Srinagar astrotelepathic relay are open to you, for the glory of the Emperor, and the returned primarch.'

Fabian looked upon the rows of cupboards and shelves, each one brimming with secrets. His heart beat a little quicker. He was very different to the adept plucked from obscurity by Guilliman, but he still coveted information.

'I shall take a look around, if you would give me a brief tour, so I can consider the best plan of attack,' said Fabian briskly. 'We won't have time to pack all this. You must help us prioritise the physical media you wish to evacuate. Do you have data-looms?'

'We do. Most of this is recorded upon them, or so it is believed.' He gestured at the scrolls, books and miscellaneous data storage. 'The looms are this way. Shall we go there first?'

Fabian nodded. 'I will summon the others. We shall begin work immediately.'

Chapter Thirty

ROSTOV HUNTS
THE EVER-LIVING EMPEROR
CONGREGATION

Colus was the man's name.

Rostov had a list on his person, a small, select band of citizens who included the man whose face Lacrante had watched melt, and the assassin who had taken down Tolmun. They called themselves the Church of the Ever-Living Emperor, a legitimate, if fringe cult who had passed the last round of Adeptus Ministorum accordance assessments comfortably.

Rostov was almost certain they were not what they said they were.

The inquisitor and his retinue were heading to root them out of the deep hab-zones of sector aleph-7 when the warning sirens rose up from the mountain.

'That doesn't sound good,' said Cheelche, waddling as fast as she could to keep up with her human comrades. She cradled her favoured weapon in her upper arms, a square-profiled t'au-built plasma carbine, carried stock up, finger covering the trigger guard ready to snap fire. Her lower arms were on show, not hidden as they usually were. She had paired chikanti las-grips wrapped like knuckledusters round her clenched fists. Though they were something of a signature weapon for her species, she didn't use the grips much. Cheelche preferred a mismatched set of xenos pistols ordinarily, but the grips were a good choice for the warren of hab-blocks, being broad-spread weapons that put out a laser fan big as a shield. More like lascutters than guns, their focal point extended no farther than a few feet, but they would slice an armoured warrior in two should he be foolish enough to stand within that range.

'There is another storm coming in,' said Rostov. 'A big one.'

Lacrante and Antoniato shared an uneasy look.

'Now?' asked Lacrante. 'That'll make things difficult for the fleet.'

'The stars do not govern themselves according to human wishes, no matter what the priests have to say,' said Rostov. 'Ignore it. Focus on our task.'

They were making for a location four blocks away and three levels down, out of the main caverns. There the character of Srinagar changed. It was darker, dingier, ripe with the smell of leaking sewer pipes from the city above. The corridor-streets were both narrow and low, and the rooms opening off them appeared to have been carved into the rock with little regard for planning, making the sector a kill-zone of angular traps and cover. There were piles of rubbish everywhere. Even in a small city like Srinagar, on a planet blessed with relative wealth, there was always space for deprivation.

All that part of the city was deserted, the majority of its civilians having already been evacuated. They saw no one but a single patrol of enforcers sweeping for stragglers. After a brief challenge, Rostov sent them on their way, though they shot black looks at the chikanti as they moved off.

'Keep a low profile, go back to the ship,' Cheelche muttered to herself. 'Hey, Cheelche, now you've been sat in a dark hold for a week, why don't you just roam about the streets with a big sign saying "I'm a filthy xenos" on your back?' She kicked a rusted food container out of her path. 'How is that keeping a low profile?'

'Hush, Cheelche,' Rostov said. 'We are near.'

They slowed. They readied their weapons. There was a heavy clunk and the whine of plasma coils charging. Antoniato had blacked out the glassite with heat-resistant paint, but it was already beginning to burn off, and intense blue light shone through the gaps. Rostov drew his power sword. Lacrante had his lasgun, sword and laspistol, standard Astra Militarum issue. They were quotidian next to the arms his fellows carried, but he liked his old kit.

Rostov gestured with the blade of his hand, sending Lacrante ahead. There was only one approach to the church, and they were forced to move in together. Lacrante's role was to check the mean, stone-carved hovels lining the way for ambush. If anyone had been there waiting, he would probably have died, but his death would give his comrades a chance to react. He obeyed Rostov's order without question.

There was no one in any of them. Lacrante made a junction where the ground sloped into the cavern housing the church, where natural cavities had been extended and joined into one large space. The walls housed rock dwellings, the uneven floor a shanty. Though poor, it too had been evacuated, and a ghostly stillness lay on it, only the faint blare of the weather trumpets disturbing its peace.

Lacrante bobbed his head about, trying to hug the cover and remain unseen while scouting the cave for Colus' friends. The church was slightly off centre on the far wall. It was the largest rock building, though that was not saying much, it being two storeys of oddly placed windows and a single crookedly carved door. He saw nothing, no movement, no signs of life; never-theless, he suspected he had been seen.

He waved the others forward. Rostov came to stand behind him. He was silent, and so close his breath tickled Lacrante's neck. Lacrante felt something else, in his mind, as Rostov extended his warp senses into the cavern.

'They are watching, and have seen us,' Rostov said. 'There are one, maybe two psykers in there with them – not powerful, but I will not be able to approach shrouded.'

'Full-frontal assault then,' said Antoniato. He peered over the inquisitor's shoulder. 'I don't like this. That's a good defen-sive position.' His plasma gun hummed, the heat of its readied charge warming the back of Lacrante's legs.

'Nevertheless, we must take it. Cheelche, cover. Lacrante break left, Antoniato, go right. I will advance, and trust to the Emperor to shield me. May He watch over you all.'

Rostov flicked a switch at his belt, drew his pistol and stepped out. The moment he did, a shot winged down from one of the windows and struck at him. It was a good shot, targeted on the head. Jagged daggers of light flared around the inquisitor as his refractor field took the brunt of the force. Refractors were better against energy weapons than solid shots, so it didn't halt the slug, only slowed it. Power spent, it skimmed Rostov's cheek, leaving an angry welt.

Lacrante sprinted under fire, the shots all going wide. Anto-niato disobeyed Rostov's order to stop partway to cover. Firing from the hip, he let free a stream of plasma that splashed against the rock church with a blowtorch roar. He hit one of the windows, clipping the sill. When the stream snapped off, fires were burning inside and molten stone dripped down the front of the building. Someone was screaming, a full-throated expression of agony that didn't stop, not even for breath, but went on and on.

Lacrante crashed into the wall of a shanty, making it wobble.

He blinked after-images from the plasma stream from his eyes. He was looking back towards the cavern entrance where Cheelche crouched, snapping off beads of plasma from her fancy xenos carbine. Gunfire was coming from all over the cave now, not just the church. There were cultists hidden in the shanty.

He took a deep breath, waited for Antoniato's plasma gun to roar again, then threw himself out into the winding alleys that divided up the shacks. Las-bolts and slugs greeted him. He felt the sting of a bullet whipping across his bicep, caught a glimpse of Rostov shooting calmly, refractor field making a bladed light show around him, before he dived down a side street. The clatter of a light autogun came from ahead, where someone was attacking Rostov from the side. In a half-crouch to keep himself out of the firing line, Lacrante moved up to intercept.

The cultist fired his gun like it was distasteful to him. He certainly didn't know what to do with it, holding it unbraced and with his arms oddly bent so that his whole torso shook and the shots went wide. He was in danger of breaking his wrists.

Lacrante whistled. The man's inexperience showed again when he immediately turned, and Lacrante put a las-bolt through his neck. He fell, choking on the smoke of his own vaporised flesh. Lacrante ran over, covering him. Blood pooled under his head, his eyes frightened. He was trying to talk, but no longer could; then he died.

He was richly dressed, far out of his natural habitat, thought Lacrante. He wore a yellow ribbon tied around his right arm, the same colour as the cravat worn by the little man who'd killed himself in the tunnel. Must be the cult marker, he thought.

He heard running footsteps coming at him, turned round too slow. Another man was charging, face grotesque with aggression, undisciplined, but in the right place at the right time. His gun came up, ready to fire, and Lacrante was caught off guard.

A slash of red light cut the man in half, another strike tearing his leg off, a third ripping his skull in two. The force of the last hit flipped his corpse into the scavenged plasteel walls of a shack with such force that he brought it down. It was a messy death, spread wide. Lacrante wiped brain matter off his cheek. He looked back to find Cheelche, her t'au carbine slung over her shoulder, the emitters of her chikanti las-grips gleaming ominously. She rolled her eyes at him.

'Do I have to do everything for you, ape?'

'I thought you were supposed to be covering us,' he said.

'And I thought you were supposed to be a soldier,' she replied.

'Come on,' he said, and they went deeper into the tangle of alleys, making the far side as Rostov was approaching the church. The whole upper storey was ablaze. Plasma burns had carved liquid scars into the rock. A trio of men were breaking from the shanties, firing behind them, heading into the church. Lacrante dropped one with a shot in the back. Antoniato hit another of them full-on with his plasma gun, the man burning up as a miniature, human-shaped supernova.

Lacrante threw himself against the church wall by the door. A couple more shots came streaking out of the dark. Cheelche unslung her rifle and pumped a number of bright bolts inside, silencing whoever was in there. No more gunfire came.

Rostov joined them.

'Did we get them all?' Cheelche asked.

'No,' said Rostov, moving forwards.

'Wait! Wait for us!' Cheelche said.

Rostov strode directly at the door.

'Can't he just bloody wait a minute?' Cheelche moaned.

Antoniato came out of the shanty. His plasma gun was wailing unhappily, cooling vents blasting steam. He hit the quick release on the shoulder strap and dumped the overheated weapon on the floor.

'Throne-cursed thing will be the death of me,' he said.

Rostov motioned to Lacrante. Lacrante nodded, unhooked a frag grenade from his belt, pulled the pin, then tossed it inside. He waited for the explosion, and ducked inside before the dust had cleared.

A fire burning in the back gave him enough light to see by. It looked like a pile of rags, but the Sanguinalia-feastday smell coming off it informed him it was a corpse. The room was bigger than he expected; longer than it was wide, leading to a door at the back where some steps lit by a couple of oil lamps in alcoves headed up and down. The place was a mess of smashed furniture and scattered books. It looked like people had tried and failed to set up barricades in there.

He went forward, gun up, switching from shadow to shadow, finding no targets. Sparks were falling from the floor above. Heated stone ground and split. *Give it half an hour,* he thought, *and the whole place will come down.*

He reached the head of the stairs, covered the upper floor. No one came, then he heard the prayers below.

He looked back, signalled Rostov. The inquisitor came forward. Cheelche was kneeling, facing out, sweeping her carbine back and forth across the cavern. Antoniato peered inside, pistol gripped in both hands, pointing at the floor.

'You and I together, Lacrante,' said Rostov. He held up his gun. 'I shall go first. Take them alive, if we can. If it comes to it, prioritise Colus.'

The stairs were steep, burrowing down even further into Srinagar's crust. Lacrante wondered just how far underground the delvings went. He went slowly, making an effort to keep his breathing level, turned a corner, found a further run of stairs terminating in a patchwork door of salvaged plasteel. He looked back at Rostov. The inquisitor's face was a collection of shadows dancing in the light of his power sword. A curt nod from Rostov, and Lacrante kicked the door in.

'Nobody move!' he shouted.

There was a chamber half the size of the one above. He counted fourteen people of all ages. They looked rich, but were otherwise diverse, though all had something in the cult's deep yellow on their person. They stood in a circle, hands linked, around a well-made statue of the Emperor and the Golden Throne. It was strange to think of it that way, because usually the Emperor and the Throne were inseparably melded when depicted together, but this effigy of the lord of all humanity differed in one important respect.

The Emperor was standing tall, chest out, proud, one hand just brushing the armrest, having left the Throne behind. The congregation looked upon their god with fanatical adoration, made all the more feverish by fear. It was then he recognised Colus from a pict Rostov had.

'Brothers! Sisters!' one of the throng shouted, her voice trembling with emotion. 'Today is the time! Today is the day we ascend!'

Simultaneously, they tore pendants from around their necks, and held them up.

'Until the return of the Ever-Living Emperor!'

Lacrante knew what came next. He moved his aim, fired, hitting Colus on the wrist and blasting his hand to charred ruin. He cried out as his fellows bit down on their suicide capsules, flooding their mouths with potent acids. They stood in place, shaking with ecstasy and pain as the fluid ate down and out through their throats, spilling smoking, bloody slurry down their perfect robes. Fumes seared their lungs into uselessness. They screamed, then gurgled, their dissolved flesh filling the room with choking, searing fumes. Lacrante coughed, temporarily incapacitated, and for a moment he thought he was going to lose his lungs. By the time Rostov pushed past him, most of them were dead.

'Lacrante, get yourself in order,' Rostov said, seemingly unaffected by the acrid steam or the horrors that filled the cellar.

Lacrante coughed, got his gun up, found he was covering corpses. As he got a better look at them, it became obvious this group represented the last of the cult, those too old, too scared or too weak to fight. Only Colus remained alive, cradling the remains of his ruined hand. He was weeping.

'I should have gone with them, it was my time. Why did you stop me?'

'You'll get to meet the Emperor soon enough,' said Lacrante. He spat. His throat was raw, and his eyes stung.

'You have time to redeem yourself,' said Rostov. 'If you tell us what is going on here.'

'You won't have her!' burbled Colus through his tears and snot. 'It's too late.'

Rostov pulled off his glove, and rested his bare skin against Colus' forehead.

'I won't have who?'

'No one,' said Colus.

'Listen to me, I know what you believe you are doing here. You do the Emperor's work, yes?'

'You know nothing. I know. You are trying to trick me,' spat Colus. 'I won't tell you anything. You're an inquisitor, one of His tormentors. You'd rather crush out the light to keep the darkness you know alive for fear of change, and damn us all in the process.'

'Then enlighten me. Show me the way to redemption.'

'I'm not talking!'

'I am afraid I do not have time to be gentle,' said Rostov. With his free hand, he reached down, grabbed Colus' ruined fingers, and squeezed.

Colus screamed. Rostov's back arched, and he clamped hard

onto Colus' skull. His breath shuddered from him. Suddenly, Rostov released Colus.

'You have a prophet,' he said. 'Mistress Sov.'

Colus let out a strangled cry. He was sobbing now.

'We're not your enemy,' said Lacrante.

'Everyone's our enemy. Everyone but the Emperor.'

'She is in the relay, yes? She is the focal point. You know this because you work there. The assistant of the first transliterator.'

'You'll get nothing more from me.'

'I can hurt you more, then you will tell me everything. You are risking the lives of hundreds of loyal Imperial servants, so I will have no mercy for you. Only if you speak might your sins be absolved.'

Colus curled his arms up around his hand.

'You understand nothing. I hope you rot in the worst hell the Emperor can find for you.'

Lacrante raised his gun. Rostov pushed it aside.

Colus began repeating 'The Emperor protects' over and over, and nothing Rostov did to him got him to stop.

Rostov got up. 'I know what I need to know for the time being.' He looked back to the mountain. 'Lacrante, get him upstairs. Tell Antoniato to get him into the shelters. Keep him alive,' Rostov ordered. 'Do not take your eyes off him, we will interrogate him more thoroughly later. Then you, I and Cheelche are going to the mountain.'

Chapter Thirty-One

COME WITH ME

INQUISITION

PROPHET

Late on his second night on Srinagar, Fabian was woken by a hammering on the door. He'd managed to block out the weather trumpets that blared every hour with growing urgency, but a knock like that was another thing, loud as artillery fire, and more insistent.

'Resilisu!' he croaked. 'Resilisu!'

It took him a moment to remember his servant was gone.

'Throne preserve me,' he moaned. Groggily, he hauled himself from under his covers. It was warm in there, and cold outside. For a cavern world, Srinagar was chilly, and he resented being dragged from his slumber. His quarters were modest, chosen for their proximity to the mountain stair and his work in the relay rather than their comfort.

More knocking boomed from the door. As he came down the stairs he could see it juddering in its housing.

'Alright, alright, I am coming!' he said. 'What are you doing, smacking it with a power fist?' he muttered, and keyed it open.

It moved aside. He found himself staring at a Space Marine's belt buckle. 'Ah,' he said.

'Historitor Majoris Fabian Guelphrain.' The warrior, anonymous behind his mask, wasn't asking. 'You are to come with me. Inquisitor Leonid Rostov of the Ordo Xenos commands you attend him immediately.'

'That's a heavy knock you've got.' Fabian ran his hands through his hair and yawned loudly. The cavern shutters were open still, and a freezing wind blew in from the surface into the square, stirring bits of trash lying on the flagstones. He wondered when they'd be shut, and whether it would be for the enemy first, or the weather. It was strangely serene. The evacuation was coming to an end and the city was deserted, empty of all but a few military vehicles.

'You are to come with me. Immediately,' repeated the Space Marine.

'I heard you.' Fabian looked down at his nightwear then back at the Space Marine pointedly. 'I assume I can put my trousers on first?'

Fabian was taken deep into the mountain, upwards this time, into parts he had not yet seen, towards the relay itself. There were many soldiers there in the green garb of the Adeptus Astra Telepathica and the blue uniforms of the Srinagar XV, come down from the moon, their bodies bulky with radiation-shielded armour and heads lost in huge, inhuman bubble helms. They manned strongpoints built into the structure, and new barricades of prefabricated sections placed across the major access points. Areios' warriors reinforced them in ones and twos.

As Fabian went within the hollow peak, the sense of pressure emanating from the relay grew. He already had a headache by the time he was shown into a room where Rumagoi paced nervously, and a blond man with reddish skin dressed in carapace armour sat staring directly at the door, as if he were expecting Fabian to walk in at the very instant that he did.

'Historitor Majoris Fabian Guelphrain,' he said.

Fabian recognised the look in his eyes. Inquisitors came from all manner of backgrounds and in appearance no two were the same, but they all had that look. Fabian would have known Rostov was an inquisitor even if he had not been summoned; he would have known were Rostov not wearing his burnished carapace, the Inquisitorial 'I' stamped crisply in the chest piece. Rostov could have been in rags. Fabian had seen that look in the eyes of refined old men, giant warriors, introverts, extroverts, the faithful and borderline heretics. Warriors, scholars, maidens and scoundrels, whatever their origins, inclinations or methods, all inquisitors shared that look.

A look of absolute power.

Space Marines had scared Fabian in the beginning, and Roboute Guilliman scared him still, but inquisitors were far more frightening than primarchs and their progeny.

Inquisitors scared him because they were fully human, and therefore fully flawed, and would exercise their power with complete, unwavering conviction, right or wrong.

'Inquisitor Rostov, I presume?' he said.

Rostov inclined his head in the affirmative, and opened a gloved hand at a chair.

'I have a few questions I must ask you,' he said.

'Of course,' said Fabian. His mind was racing. The Logos and the Inquisition had been at loggerheads more than once. Hardly surprising: the Inquisition sought to hide knowledge, the Logos to illuminate it. Their relationship was a fine example of the disruption the primarch's return had wrought across all Imperial organisations, with his need for haste crashing repeatedly into bureaucratic inertia. As for the Logos and the Inquisition, it had not yet come to blood, but Fabian expected the day was close.

'My lords, perhaps I should wait outside while I conclude my–' began Rumagoi.

'You will wait there,' said Rostov. He held up a finger. Rumagoi halted his pacing. 'Roboute Guilliman sent you here. Why?' Rostov asked Fabian.

'I am here to ensure the Logos Historica Verita has a proper level of support throughout the crusade fleets. We are in phase two of the expansion of our organisation.'

'But why you, why here, why now?' asked Rostov.

'I am not sure of the direction of your questioning, inquisitor. I am here because I am the most senior historitor closest to this sector, I command a cadre of historitors. This world has a valuable archive of astropathic messages stretching back through the history of the Imperium that would be useful to our ongoing mission, and must be protected from the enemy, and though it is incomplete, it is a precious primary source.'

'There is more,' stated Rostov.

'There is always more,' said Fabian. 'From a personal point of view, the safeguarding of the archive is a good opportunity to demonstrate the utility of the Logos as a fully functioning arm of Imperial governance to those who remain sceptical of it.'

'You have no investment in personal glory?'

Fabian had nothing to hide, so spoke freely. 'I have no real desire for glory, no. Knowing things is what motivates me, I think, if anybody can objectively examine their own motivations. Once, when I was a mid-ranking adept, I dreamed of acclaim, but my life has moved so far beyond where I thought it would go that I find myself detached from ambition. What I want to do now is serve the Emperor, properly, meaningfully. I want the Logos to be a success. I want the primarch to have what he needs to save our miserable lives.' He looked up at Rostov. Piercing blue eyes stared into the back of his skull.

'You are telling the truth,' Rostov said.

'You are a psyker,' said Rumagoi. 'I thought it so.'

'Yes,' said Rostov.

'Fascinating,' said Rumagoi, appraising Rostov anew.

'Now,' Fabian said. 'It's late. Why have you summoned me here?'

'The archive,' Rostov asked. 'Have you noticed any kind of pattern in the messages? The recent messages?'

'We have had no time to do anything but try to save them, inquisitor,' said Fabian. 'We've evacuated the most precious physical records, but our main task is exloading the contents of the data-looms. That will take time. Once we are done, we can run searches on your behalf if you wish. However, these are astropathic records. They incline to the abstruse.'

'When can you do this?'

'Not for a day or two. If you could provide us with para-meters, it would make our job easier.'

'I shall. Soon. First I have to be sure what I am looking for.' He flexed his fingers. Leather creaked. 'The Word Bearers are coming here for a reason. They are looking for something, and I believe it is inside this mountain.' He turned to Rumagoi. 'There is a powerful mind, unusual. It is broadcasting fragmentary visions. Mistress Sov?'

'Where did you hear that name?' asked Rumagoi. 'The iden-tities of the astropaths here are guarded.'

Rostov did not answer, but pulled out a tightly rolled cyl-inder of paper from a pouch.

'Do you know any of these people?'

Rumagoi read down the list. 'No,' he said. 'No, no.' He evi-dently expected to see nothing familiar, so his lips were partway towards forming another no when he came to a name he very obviously did know. His jaw hung slack.

'Colus?' he said. He looked up, shocked.

'You know him,' Rostov said.

'He's my aide.' The strength left Rumagoi's arms. They flopped down by his side, and the paper slipped from nerveless fingers. He knew what it meant to be connected with an Inquisitorial suspect. He was as good as damned himself.

'What is this about?'

'Serendipity,' said Rostov. 'Now where do you think he is?'

'When you called me, I summoned him, but he didn't arrive. I thought it was something to do with the attack. He would have been ordered into the shelters, and though I asked him to remain available, I didn't think it was unusual. Cross-city communications aren't that good here, especially after a big particle wave like we had the other day. It can take a week or more to get the hardlines up and running.'

'Don't you have vox?' asked Fabian.

'We're underground. If you're not keyed into a relay, it doesn't work, and the channels are reserved for the military when we are under danger of attack. I sent a runner, but I haven't heard anything from him.'

'Doesn't he live here?' asked Fabian.

'In the mountain? None of us do,' said Rumagoi. 'The psychic exposure is too great. It's alright when you are awake and fighting it, but going to sleep, letting our unconscious minds be exposed to all this? We'd be dead in days. Working here is bad enough. Our lives are shorter because of it, but we serve.'

'I have spoken to Colus,' said Rostov. 'I have seen the visions emanating from this mountain. There is something happening here, something unusual.'

'I am sure this is only a misunderstanding,' said Rumagoi. 'Colus is one of the most devout men that I know.' He then added, after thinking, 'Though I must protest my own innocence. Whatever he is mixed up in, if he is, I have nothing to do with it.'

'We shall see,' said Rostov. 'He is in my custody now.'

'What?'

Rumagoi nodded. 'Yes, many things, but the unusual has become the usual since the Cicatrix Maledictum split the sky and until the tremors started we didn't–'

'Slow down,' said Rostov. 'If you have nothing to hide, you have nothing to fear. I need specifics. Tell me. Take your time.'

Rumagoi blinked, and swallowed. 'Many messages recently have been corrupted with the same thing. A glorious child. An angel, sometimes bright, sometimes dark. The same thing, over again, scattered in the information content of the teleprayers. It started some months before the Rift, and has been gradually increasing in frequency since. These interruptions became visions. There were tremors associated with the visions. There's no point in denying it.' He sighed, and threw up his hand. 'It's all centred on her. We are taking all the relevant precautions. Mistress Sov is an asset. She has–'

Rostov silenced him with a glance.

'You don't need to plead her case,' he said. 'I have not come to kill her. She is under the Emperor's seal and approved by the Adeptus Astra Telepathica. As of this moment, I do not deem her a threat. I only need to speak with her.'

'She doesn't speak other than to deliver teleprayers, and lately, visions. She's tanked. She's ancient. You will get no sense from her, inquisitor.'

'I will be the judge of that. Take me to her.'

Rumagoi looked to be on the point of disagreement, thought better of it, and meekly nodded his head.

'Of course, immediately,' said Rumagoi, although he did not look pleased at the prospect.

Rostov looked at Fabian. 'The historitor is coming with us.'

Rostov set a pace that Rumagoi struggled to match, and the first transliterator was florid and sweating by the time they reached the innermost part of the relay. Rostov moved unerr-ingly, already sure of where they needed to go, and passed through the various checkpoints with impatience. For his own part, Fabian experienced a mix of curiosity and trepidation. He had never been into an astropathic relay before; few people had. He felt the psychic pressure coming from the choir growing weightier by mathematical square with every ten yards they went. Rumagoi's insistence on reiterating the danger of what they were doing worried him.

'You don't have the training,' Rumagoi kept saying. 'Have you been tested for psychic ability? Never mind, never mind!' he asked when they reached the final portal, but broke off before Fabian could answer, exchanging worried whispers with the guardian of the last door.

They entered the centre of the relay. Rostov turned down the protective equipment, flashing his Inquisitorial seal when the offer turned to insistence. A concerned Rumagoi wore a strange, almost decorative helm made of crystals and wire. As Fabian lacked the training that Rumagoi was so concerned with, he was encased in a combination helmet and full torso chest- and backplate that thrummed to strange frequencies, and occasion-ally gave off outgassings of corposant that curled unpleasantly behind him.

They crossed a spindly bridge from the inner surface of the sphere that led to a pearly orb mounted on an extrusion of cables and struts reaching up from the sphere floor. Rostov strode forward, unbothered by the crushing presence of so many powerful minds. Fabian felt like he was far underwater, and not in any tranquil place, but one troubled by currents that threatened to tear him away. The bowed plastek faceplate resonated with his own breath, which competed weirdly with the thrum and snap of the relay machines. He felt isolated from himself, lifted up and away, like his mind were a float tethered to his body. He struggled to process his surroundings, with its bizarre geometries and imprisoned psykers. They were seated on thrones, held in place by manipulated gravity and strong iron bands. Their empty eye sockets stared at the Pearl at the centre, ghostlights flickering in the shadows where their eyes should have been. All of them had their mouths wide open. All of them were silent.

Fabian had the impression they were screaming nonetheless.

He was barely conscious by the time they reached the centre, his protective gear trailing corposant from the psychic bleed-over. Bizarre machines gathered around an aperture above the Pearl, and they were watching him through their arrays of mirrors. Rumagoi seemed to be judging him, tutting, comically wagging his finger, then the door opened, he staggered in and Rumagoi was nowhere near him, but engaged in a conversation with Rostov that Fabian did not recall them starting.

'...not usual to have a relay so close to a civilian population centre, but we take precautions. The mountain is baffled, the rock helps, the population is small and rigorously screened for psykers.'

Fabian opened the faceplate, letting the yellowing plastek dangle on its hinge. 'Why?'

Both Rostov and Rumagoi looked at him like they'd forgotten he was there.

'Why what?' said Rumagoi.

'Why are they sited where they are? Far away from people, I mean.'

'Oh, a few things,' said Rumagoi irritably. 'Daemonic possession, psychic overspill, reality collapse, that kind of thing. Nothing very serious.'

'Help me get this off,' said Fabian.

Rumagoi grumbled his way over and helped unclip the heavy device. The pressure was much less in the Pearl, even though it was the focal point of the whole relay; Rumagoi had told him that. He couldn't remember why it worked that way, or when he'd been told.

'This one is closer than most. We need the population to service it,' said Rumagoi, answering a question Fabian didn't recall asking. 'Putting it in the void exposes our people to the stars' mercy, the same with placing the city at a safe distance on the ground. The risks of the stars outweigh the risks of having people close to the relay.'

Rumagoi pulled the equipment off. Fabian groaned in relief, and bent down with his hands on his knees.

'Do you need to sit?' Rumagoi asked.

'I'm fine,' he said, waving him away. 'If the particle effusions are so dangerous, why is it here in the first place?' Fabian asked.

Rostov, who was standing with his hand on his chin looking at a dark glass cylinder, answered.

'The warp is affected by what goes on in reality. It is not simply our spiritual nature that moulds it, but matter and gravity. Large mass objects warp the empyrean's shape. Certain physical phenomena can open up calm channels in the endless storms there. The activity of the stars poisons human life, but creates a conduit of rare conductivity in the warp. Messages sent from this place travel far and sound loudly. That is why the relay station is situated on Srinagar. Correct?' he said to Rumagoi.

'A touch simplified, but yes,' said the first transliterator. He reached out to touch a wall stud. Amber light flooded the inside of the cylinder. 'This is Mistress Sov,' he said reverently.

'She is the cause of the earthquakes and of these visions. The enemy are coming for her. Why?' Rostov asked.

'She's always been very powerful,' said Rumagoi. 'She started strong, she used to transliterate her own teleprayers, no need for help. Her talent grew over time, until she had become the most powerful of her kind in all the sector, an epsilon-level on free. All this is in our records. She's old. She was ancient when I was a boy, tanked long before I was born.'

'An unusually long lifespan for an astropath,' said Rostov.

'She's survived far longer than most,' Rumagoi agreed. 'Most of them die after a couple of decades of service. But not only has she survived, she's grown stronger, and she's getting stronger still, evidencing increased telekinetic ability. The tremors, you see. They are new, and she causes them.'

Rostov looked at him with such intensity Rumagoi was forced to look away.

'Have you noted a greater incidence of psykers in the general population?'

'Yes,' said Rumagoi. He frowned. 'An increase of five points, and the ones we are seeing are higher on the Assignment. Being an astropathic outpost, we scale them ourselves before handing them over to the League of Black Ships. It was rare we'd see anything higher than a Zeta once every ten years. Since the Rift, we've come across many more.'

'How many more?' asked Rostov.

'Seven,' said Rumagoi fearfully. 'A little over two a year.'

'I know nothing about the statistics of witch births,' said Fabian. 'But that's a lot, right?'

'It is a terrifying amount,' said Rumagoi.

'It is happening everywhere, a great awakening of the mind,' said Rostov. 'Many of my colleagues are concerned.'

'I don't think it's just humans, either,' said Fabian. 'Fleet Primus spent much of the last couple of years fighting the orks in Ultima Segmentum Sanctus. There were reports of powerful ork witches and battlefield-wide manifestations of psychic activity.'

'It is the Rift,' said Rostov. 'I am sure of it. But that is not why I am here. Not directly.'

'What do you hope to learn?' Rumagoi asked.

'I do not know,' said Rostov. 'I must see, and to do that, I have to touch her.'

'Why?'

'It is the nature of my gift.'

Rumagoi was disturbed. 'The only way to do that is to drain the tank. You put her at risk. You could kill her.'

'She is putting us all at risk. I have to see what she sees, directly. That's a command, first transliterator. I have the authority.'

Rumagoi was shaking. 'Very well, very well. Just be careful, please.'

'You have affection for her,' said Rostov.

'Respect. She has done much good,' Rumagoi said. His hands hovered over a bank of controls, unwilling to descend on them. 'She is revered. She has given her life in service to the Emperor. Her talent and her actions have saved millions of lives. I do not want to see her killed before her time, to satisfy some inquisitor's hunch.'

'Drain the tank. I will be swift,' said Rostov.

Rumagoi muttered to himself darkly as he activated the draining sequence. Skulls descended from the ceiling to count down the procedure and utter dire warnings. The light in the tank turned red.

'Ready to purge support medium,' a toneless machine voice said.

'You will be quick?' Rumagoi said.

'I will be quick,' said Rostov.

Rumagoi stabbed the last button.

'Purging. Purging. Purging,' said the voice.

The milky liquid drained away. As the level fell, Mistress Sov became only a little clearer. Amnion was glutinous, and ran thickly down the inside of the tank. She was a shadow that crumpled without the support of the fluid, falling against the glass with a thump, and squeaking helplessly down the inside of the cylinder. Her breathing tube and mask went taut, then pulled free from her head to dangle as she sank to her knees.

Rumagoi watched in a state of high agitation. A mechanical sucking noise finished the draining.

'Quickly!' the first transliterator said. 'You will have to catch her.'

Rostov knelt by the tank.

Rumagoi keyed another button. The cylinder split open on nearly invisible seams. The smell of the amnion flooded into the room: a gluey smell, rendered fats and tallow. Mistress Sov half fell out of her prison into Rostov's arms. Beneath the slick of the fluid she was heavily wrinkled, her breasts were flat points on her chest, and her skin sagged under her arms. She looked like she was five hundred years old. She moaned.

'You have come,' she said.

'Now, now, hurry, for the love of the Emperor!' Rumagoi said.

Rostov tugged off an amnion-smeared glove with his teeth.

'Forgive me, mistress,' he said, and laid the back of his hand upon her cheek. 'I have to be sure.'

Behind Fabian's eyes, everything went white.

Chapter Thirty-Two

VISION

THE SEA, THE SKY, THE SUN

A CHILD

Inquisitor Leonid Rostov felt warmth on his face, and sand between the toes of his bare feet. A strong wind blew. His eyes were closed, his vision pink and patterned with veins.

He tried to open his eyes. But it was not his face. It was not his sight.

What are you showing me, Mistress Sov? he thought.

She gave no reply.

The face of the person he was seeing through moved. Rostov's consciousness followed it, but not exactly, sliding afterwards as if reacting a half-second too late. But he could feel. His awareness stretched through the being. It was a man, face itching pleasantly with a beard full of salt. He was strong, with muscles that moved easily, and he was content. He let out a long breath, and opened his eyes.

Whiteness at first, before his sight adjusted, showing Rostov a brilliant indigo sky, hardly a cloud to mar it. A beach of sand whose colour approached that of snow stretched away from him, curling around a boulder, and sloping steeply down to an ocean as dark as the sky. Wind-sculpted ridges of sand gave way at the tideline to smooth wetness. The steepness of the incline called abrupt breakers that jumped up from the water before crashing almost immediately down. The air smelled of salt and dimethyl sulphides. A world rich in life. When the man turned to the left, he looked upon a spiny forest, marching almost down to the high water mark.

Time jumped. The man was walking. He carried a pole over his shoulder, a cloth bag dangling from the end. The pole was worn smooth by his touch. It was many things to the man, important, as familiar as part of his body. It was a fishing rod, a weapon, a tent pole, an aid on rough ground. In his other hand, the man carried a pair of sandals. He wore a short chiton. His skin was a deep brown. Bits of the environment leapt at Rostov. Fragments of seaweed on the beach, the trees in the woods, the colour of sea, sky and sun, but there was nothing that gave him a clue where he could be.

The surf pounded. The sun was hot.

Another jump. The man rounded a boulder. The shore bent back into a bay three-quarters closed by a spine of rock. The little island dipped under the water, becoming a reef, leaving only a narrow channel, perhaps a dozen feet across. A perfect natural harbour. Outside the bay, the sea was stirred up into choppy whitecaps by the wind, and crashed on the beach over and over, but in the bay the water was green and still, and a flotilla of canoes rode wavelets placidly.

In a clearing on the hill, a group of houses occupied the rocky ground, well out of the way of the worst storm tides. Wood and leaves on stilted platforms; undistinctive. He could have been looking at any one of a hundred thousand worlds. Then he heard the bell-like voices of children at play, laughter and shrieks broken up by the wind, always returning.

This was the world he had seen before.

The man's stride picked up pace, moving directly to the houses. A few men working on nets at the shore waved at him and called out, and he waved back, answering their hails with their names. Their dialect was far from standard Gothic, unintelligible.

The sand gave way to warm rock. The man climbed stairs smoothed by generations of feet, that curled up through the houses. The village was small, a dozen shacks. The man stopped at the last. He put down his sandals with others on grass matting, took down his pole, opened the sack, took out a carved wooden animal, and put the rest neatly aside. He climbed a rope ladder onto the hut's veranda, then pushed back another mat serving as a door, and went inside.

The house was very dark after the blaze of the sun. It seemed larger inside than it had from outside. There were numerous bedrolls rolled up by the wall, clearing the room for the needs of the day, but one was out, and occupied.

There was a woman, sleeping. There was a baby close by, a bundle on the floor, small hands twitching in its dreams. A baby, but so much more.

The man moved forward.

Contact was broken.

Fabian got up off the floor with the worst headache he had ever suffered. Rostov was cradling the astropath, Sov. Her lips were moving, and Rostov was bent low to listen, but Fabian could not hear what was being said over the wail of the alarms.

Rumagoi consulted a shielded scope.

'The enemy are here,' he shouted into Fabian's ear. 'We will begin shutting down the relay and moving the astropaths out. We must leave.' He looked at Sov. 'Help me get her back into the suspension cylinder.'

Rostov stood.

'It's too late,' he said. He did not shout, but they could hear him. Somehow his voice cut through the clamour. 'Mistress Sov is dead.'

The three men could not speak easily until they had left the chamber, but once they were divested of their protective gear and in a quieter place Rumagoi rounded on the inquisitor.

'What have you done?'

'She did what she had to. She was glad to give her life for this. It may be nothing, but she did her duty. This is troubling.'

'What did she tell you?'

Rostov ignored him. 'Fabian, I advise you to get your historitors out of this facility and into shelter.'

'We have not finished copying the archives.'

'Then I leave the choice to you, but be warned, the enemy will be coming here one way or another, into this relay. She told me.'

'We have to finish,' said Fabian. 'I shall put Captain Areios on high alert, but if we leave now, then all our efforts will be wasted. If the enemy do come, the archive will be lost. We have to finish.'

'Why do you think the enemy will come here?' Rumagoi asked. 'We were told to expect bombardment, not invasion! What did she say?'

Finally, Rostov answered him.

'She said, "He is coming."'

Chapter Thirty-Three

MOVES MADE
DOMINANT WILL
OTHER MEANS

Athagey met the foe with a savage grin.

'Here they come. The heretical bastards walked right into our trap.'

The Word Bearers fleet sailed through the void in crescent formation. The rays of the suns shone off their hulls, lighting them up like motile stars. Athagey gauged their distance by their relative brightness. It was peaceful, and beautiful, like all void battles were in their opening moments, before the shooting began.

The sharp, clipped murmur of orders passing back and forth across the command deck made her spine shiver with pleasure. Only victory outdid anticipation. There was a delicious pride to be enjoyed of a strategy laid out, of fleets in formations before they were disrupted, and vessels torn apart. Battle, at its height, was a manifestation of chaos. But the start was pure order, thousands upon thousands of human beings working towards one collective goal. Organised violence at scale brought out the very best in mankind, she thought.

It was all hers to command. Dozens of ships, hundreds of thousands of lives, the fate of a world in the balance. A lesser mind would shy away from such responsibility. Perhaps if she had suffered more defeats, she would have been reluctant to shoulder the burden, but she enjoyed the power. She enjoyed the potential for disaster that she would turn into triumph.

Athagey feared no defeat, because she never lost.

She paced up and down her command dais, the short heels of her dress boots clicking on the metal.

'Tactical hololiths on,' she ordered. 'Enginarium to begin acceleration to quarter speed.' She looked out at the approaching stars, growing brighter with every moment. 'I see no munition swarm ahead of the Word Bearers. Have they cast out preceding mass shot?'

Screens were consulted.

'Negative, groupmistress,' one of her deck officers reported. 'No munitions detected. Negative on mass perturbation of void space. No energy signatures for either cannon fire or torpedo engine engagement.'

'Frame distortion?' Athagey said, lifting up her chin and staring at the command deck's ceiling. There was a winged saint up there she liked; it wasn't particularly well rendered, but it seemed to pay special attention to her. She half-fancied the Emperor watched over her through its inlaid stone eyes, when she was feeling pious.

'Enemy fleet are at negative four light minutes,' the officer reported.

This was the great challenge of void war. The first rounds were pure strategy, for what each side saw had already happened.

Athagey wandered around the circuit of the dais, peering over the shoulders of her lieutenants working at their stations.

'Give information immediately should fire be detected.'

'They mean to come in fast,' said Diomed. 'They don't want

to outpace their own munitions. They haven't launched them yet, and they won't until they are closer.'

'Probably, Finnula my dear, probably,' said Athagey. She turned to her fleet liaison.

'Hainkin, give order to Iolus to spread formation. If the foe are preparing for a full charge, let's not crash into them, shall we?'

A bell clanged. A klaxon honked. The orders rippled down from the dais to the comms desks, and were sent out into the fleet.

'Advise moving task force one turn full broadside to present guns to the enemy,' said Diomed.

'Not yet.'

'We are not going to cast out our own mass cloud?'

'Oh yes,' said Athagey. 'Like them, we're just going to wait a little. Are task forces Quartus Delphus One and Two in position?'

'One is hiding in the moon's shadow,' another officer reported. 'Two reported position taken up at system's edge five minutes ago.'

'Stellar weather?'

'Particle count climbing. Major eructation predicted in minus one hour, fifty-nine minutes, potential duration four to six hours.'

'Enemy contact?'

'One hour, thirty-five minutes.'

'Perfect,' said Athagey. 'Let's refrain from casting out our mass shot until they are nearer. That way they'll assume they're dealing with some idiot dunderhead like Dionis, Emperor rest his soul, rather than I, Eloise Athagey. We'll keep them off guard until we're ready to strike, and they can reckon with the suns and the guns of the Emperor at the same time.' She smiled, gaze fixed on the oculus. 'Kor Phaeron, eh? Jolly good. Let's see that old witch VanLeskus keep me on back line duty once I've blasted his sorry arse out of the cosmos.'

She took her throne, and rapped her knuckles on the armrest.

For the time being, she ignored the hard press of the stimm box in her breast pocket.

'Is it just me, or is today a mighty fine day to be sailing for the Emperor?'

The bridge of the *Dominant Will* resounded to the quiet praises of the thousand priests arranged in tiered balconies at the back of the deck. Kor Phaeron sat enthroned upon a pinnacle of dark rock shot through with veins of deep red. From his position he could survey all.

Tharador Yheng stood beside her master upon a contra-grav stage, watching Kor Phaeron from the corner of her eye. Never had she been in the presence of such dark majesty. The aura of his power shifted in her witch-sight. Ten thousand years he had fought the Long War. He was steeped in the approval of the gods, mightier than her master Tenebrus. He appeared... pleased, in an unforgiving sort of way. She thought he approved of what he saw: the devout at work, prayers always on their lips as they prepared ancient weapons to destroy another fleet. He said little. The Dark Apostle Pridor Vrakon stood to the side of his throne, and it was he who delivered what few orders were necessary. There was no idle chatter. Kor Phaeron's crew worked silently, speaking only when absolutely necessary. Mortal holy men and Heretic Astartes priests both patrolled the deck, looking for infraction against the Rule of Lorgar. They would find none; the people aboard served with all their hearts. The *Dominant Will* was a temple of the gods, and the command deck its sacred tabernacle.

Such peace. Such purity of thought and deed. Seeing this serenity, this purpose, all bent to the will of the true gods, Yheng wondered if Kor Phaeron's way were a better way, as he himself insisted. Tenebrus was injured, warped by mutation, but not Kor Phaeron. He sat enthroned, a great champion. She could feel the favour of the Powers on him. He made Tenebrus seem like a thief, stealing from their table, when the Dark Cardinal was invited to dine with them in honour.

But that was the choice. No power came without a price. Tenebrus' position was more precarious, but she wondered how free Kor Phaeron was. Did he serve himself while serving the gods, as Tenebrus did, or was he simply a tool of greater beings?

'The enemy do not appear to be doing very much,' said Tenebrus. His voice was weak. There were dark pouches under his black eyes. The rituals he had undertaken had enfeebled him. Yheng began to understand why Kor Phaeron had summoned the sorcerer to his side. She judged that the Dark Cardinal was perfectly capable of the same feats that Tenebrus was, but in having her master perform them, he had delegated the risk.

'You have no understanding of what you witness, sorcerer,' said Kor Phaeron. 'You know nothing of void warfare.' He did not look at the sorcerer when he addressed him, but stared out into the dark of space, his time-weathered face left in profile. Vrakon turned his helmed head and gave Tenebrus a long warning stare. The sorcerer ignored him.

Tenebrus bared his mutant's teeth. 'I am a student of all things, my lord Kor Phaeron, though I admit that the working of magic is my forte. One cannot be mighty in all things. I am curious to learn.'

'You are weak enough that you must admit your weakness,' said the Dark Cardinal. 'I have been conducting war since the Emperor walked the stars, spreading His lies wherever He went.'

'Perhaps, oh great and puissant lord, you would explain, for the benefit of my acolyte?'

Kor Phaeron's face barely moved when he spoke, leaving it as severe and fixed as a death mask. 'This is the calm. Soon all will be light and thunder, and we shall give the gods great sacrifice.

Now, be silent. If you would learn, watch, and witness. Give me the enemy's numbers,' he demanded of his crew.

'We count eight capital ships, my lord – two battle cruisers, three cruisers, three light cruisers,' a doleful voice intoned. 'Twenty-two escort craft.'

Kor Phaeron looked out across to the line of the enemy, arrayed to meet him in a two-deep wall of ships.

Tenebrus watched expectantly. Yheng risked a glance directly at the Dark Cardinal.

'They knew we were coming,' Kor Phaeron stated eventually. 'Yet they meet us with only one of their crusade battle groups. This is an obvious trap.'

He said nothing more, but Pridor Vrakon spoke. He did not need to explain, but something moved him to. Yheng prayed to the Four it was some small measure of favour for her that made him speak.

'Their presence in this number, and so well ordered, suggests they were expecting us,' Vrakon said.

If Kor Phaeron disapproved of Vrakon's explanation, he did not show it, but continued to stare at the enemy. Occasionally he would make the smallest movement of claw or eye, and his crew would rush to obey orders that were obscure to Yheng, but perfectly clear to them.

'It is possible they also anticipated my lord Kor Phaeron's involvement,' Vrakon continued, his voice loud and strident through the ancient emitters of his warplate. 'He is a great prize for them. This system presents an opportunity for ambush. Technological means of detection are limited by the activity of the stars. Access to the warp is limited by the power given off by the relay, and the trans real-warp phenomena that allow it to operate. We will be ambushed.'

This was all presented as simple fact. Neither Vrakon nor Kor Phaeron were perturbed. The Dark Cardinal did not move.

He called no alarm nor bade his warriors rush to arms, while Vrakon spoke slowly, almost in a trance, like a stone oracle delivering dooms.

'They will have another of these fleets waiting in hiding. The positioning of the visible force is a provocation. They are asking us to fight them.' Vrakon lifted up his massive power gauntlet to point at the tactical hololith. 'There will be forces stationed midway between sun and star, in the planetary auspex shadow. If there is another, I expect them to be waiting in interplanetary space. This visible force is a blockade, to keep us away from the world. If we alter course, they will match us, engaging us at long range, holding us until one or more of their supporting forces can execute an approach, or harry us directly into their path.' Vrakon looked up to the top of the oculus. 'They will come from above or below the plane of the ecliptic, maybe from the rear. They mean to trap us, and destroy us.'

'So, how then will the prize be won?' said Tenebrus. 'You cannot invade. You cannot teleport from this far out, and you will not be able to get close enough to take down the void shields protecting the city. You cannot use sorcery either, I am thinking.'

'No,' said Vrakon. 'Even with the shields down, the emyprical rip caused by the psyker beacon would scatter our souls to every corner of the warp, whether technology or sorcery is employed.'

'Then I am intrigued to hear your solution.'

Yheng looked surreptitiously at the parties present, Tenebrus, Vrakon and Phaeron. It was Kor Phaeron who answered.

'Your sorcery would not suffice, Hand of Abaddon. Mine will. I am the blessed of the gods, bearer and protector of the Word. To the truly faithful, the Powers grant other means.' He raised his voice, a tiny amount, but the effect was instantaneous, sending his crew into a rush of activity. 'Begin the attack.'

* * *

Third Lieutenant Basu looked up from his station. 'Energy signatures indicate full burn from all approaching Word Bearers ships, my lady. They are accelerating to maximum attack speed. On current course they will pass right through our formation within the hour.'

Athagey nodded, visible eye narrowing as her data monocular fed information directly to her left retina.

'That is not a viable invasion approach. They know we are going to ambush them,' she said baldly, then began to speak rapidly and with purpose. 'Increase depth of formation, concave bow, four-thousand-mile depth at apex,' she commanded. 'Iolus capital assets prepare to launch torpedoes, one volley, turn starboard, ninety degrees, to present port broadside, *Lux Eterna* and *Exeunt Malus* excepting. Captains Godrick and Zenobius stand ready. Escorts, hearken. Torpedo vessels give fire on my command, to fore. Scimitar spread, groups split by alphanumeric designation. Even group, six thousand miles plus superior ecliptic. Odd group, six thousand miles minus inferior ecliptic. *Lux Eterna* and *Exeunt Malus* prepare nova cannons for immediate firing. All carrier craft, reserve strike craft launch until further notice.' She paced as she spoke, a small flock of cyber-constructs trailing her, vox-thieves snatching up her words for storage in the log.

Bells rang and the chatter on the bridge increased. Her orders were repeated word for word as they were passed out to the other ships and into stations deeper within the *Saint Aster*. Coordinating such large and unwieldy vessels effectively was difficult, but Athagey's crews were well trained, and worked smoothly. As return notifications came back, officers spoke up from their stations to Athagey directly.

'All ships report torpedoes ready to launch,' said one. 'Broad spread, scimitar pattern as requested.'

Athagey waved her hand theatrically. 'Then launch them.

Give those traitorous, daemon-loving bastards a taste of the Emperor's wrath. Make sure the *Saint Aster* is out ahead of the others, master ordinatum, or what's the point of being the bloody flagship?'

The ordnance crew responded with gusto. 'Aye aye, group-mistress!'

Klaxons whooped. The ship grumbled as tower-long torpedoes eased their way from the prow. They always looked like they were moving so slowly, almost lazily, struggling to haul free of the ship, but they pulled away, to be joined by swarms of others, the blue lights of their plasma drives losing themselves in gaily illuminated groups.

'Hard a-starboard!' Athagey yelled. 'All ships turn contra to prime world orbital path. Present port batteries to the enemy!'

Tocsins whooped. The *Saint Aster*, mighty beast that she was, grumbled and moaned as her manoeuvring jets forced her around. The void-scape shifted, sweeping the command deck's oculus across the stars, tracking all along the right flank of the enemy's formation. The view moved away from the foe, until the right side of the window glowed with the light of Srin and Gar, far off and out of sight. Srinagar was slightly off to their starboard, visible in the lower right quadrant of the oculus as a thin crescent of light, its massive moon hogging near space, the orbits between scattered with the glimmer chaff of inter-lunar orbitals. There was another rumbling from the ship's lateral thrusters, from the starboard side this time, and – metal groaning – the *Saint Aster* came to a slow stop. Sunlight gleamed on the figurehead, forever stooped in the merciful act of delivering water to the thirsty.

'Get me a view of the enemy on the main hololith. True-pict, enhanced data vision!' Athagey commanded.

The main pit glowed with the light of awakening scoptic plates, then the air turned into a miniature representation of the battlesphere, jewel-sharp images of ships crowded with data-tags.

'First Lieutenant Diomed,' said Athagey, snapping out the words like gunfire. 'How are our big guns?'

'Groupmistress, *Lux Eterna* reports nova cannon online and ready to fire. *Exeunt Malus* reports nova cannon ready to fire. Requesting targeting data.'

'Convey the following. Centre formation, four-hundred-mile spacing. Targets of will.'

'Conveyed.' She waited. 'Accepted.'

'*Lux Eterna* to fire nova cannon now.'

The order was passed on. On the tactolith, the tags appended to the Mars-class cruiser flashed. A streak of light shot from its bow, brilliant white on the display. The graviometric impellers of a nova cannon accelerated a plasma shell to a significant fraction of the speed of light, and it outpaced the torpedo swarms in the blink of an eye. The shell exploded to a fuse timed to the smallest fraction of a second. Nova cannons were devastating, but at that speed, even a small error could result in a shot far off target.

'Report!' Athagey commanded. 'Time to visual confirmation.'

'Fleet light distance, two minutes,' Lieutenant Basu replied.

'I want damage information the moment it is available. *Lux Eterna*, reload. *Exeunt Malus*, fire!' Athagey shouted. Spittle flew from her mouth in her excitement.

A second nova cannon shell raced through the void.

'*Lux Eterna* reports four point five minutes to reload. *Exeunt Malus* commencing reloading now,' Diomed reported.

'Keep up steady fire rate, five minute intervals, double shot spaced by thirty seconds. I want any ship that loses its shields to suffer the second hit. Do we have that report?'

'One minute, two seconds,' Basu responded.

'Damn it. Too slow,' Athagey said, and rapped her knuckles

'Prepare an augur sounding, wide soak. All
ships prepare to give broadside fire as soon as targeting information is disseminated.'

There followed a tense wait. Athagey took out her snuff tin
and took a pinch of stimm. The narcotic was fine grade, vitadandum, taken from the supplies given to her strike pilots.

'I can feel you looking at me, first lieutenant,' she said to
Diomed. 'Eyes on your station.' She sniffed the drug, and felt
her pulse quicken. 'Do we have that hit data or not yet, Lieutenant Basu?'

'Coming in now, groupmistress. Visuals in six, five, four...'

'Put it up on the vid-screens. I want to see this,' she said.

'Three, two,' Basu counted down. 'One.'

The fuse was timed well. Athagey watched the explosion
bloom in the centre of the enemy's formation on screen and
holographic representation. False sunlight washed around the
port edge of the oculus, casting hard shadows across the deck.

'Integrate augury data. Give me the results!' she snarled, her
pulse racing under the influence of the vitadandum. Everything
looked sharper, clearer. She felt like she could break the spine
of a Space Marine with her bare hands.

The tactical hololith rippled as it reconfigured under the input
of new data.

The shell had exploded off centre of the enemy, slightly
behind their leading ships. Data-tags blinked for attention, and
they could see the results themselves on the vids; oily light and
fire as void shields died.

Another brief sunrise swept across the deck, as the first of
the *Exeunt Malus*' shells detonated. More data. More hits. More
shields flickering to nothing.

'Excellent work, excellent!' Athagey shouted. Cheers went
up. 'Augury command, disseminate data. Fleet Gunnery, coordinate fire on ships with shield failure. Rip out the centre.'

'Enemy will be in long lance range in thirty-two seconds,' Lieutenant Ashmar reported.

'And so will we. Lances lock on. Stand by to open fire, all broadsides, wide mass spread. Let's have these bastards striding into the teeth of the Emperor's Navy!' Athagey said.

The tactolith shivered as the *Lux Eterna* fired its nova cannon again, its shot streaking away to a location as yet unknown.

'All ships report targets acquired.'

'Enemy is within lance range!' Ashmar shouted.

They felt the hits exactly as they saw them, twinkles on the approaching fleet turrets, focused beams cast at the speed of light. Their void shields boiled; the enemy were better provided with lance weapons than the Imperials, for their ships were of older, superior patterns.

'Return fire!' Athagey shouted.

The *Saint Aster* shuddered with the release of its main guns. Lance beams flicked on and off, almost too quick to see, the damage already done before the sight had registered. A wall of torpedoes, mass shot and explosives hurtled towards the enemy, a wall they could not hope to avoid, but must weather as best they could, as the closing ships traded lance fire.

'Twenty-five minutes until close range,' reported Basu. 'Forty-nine minutes until weather front hit.'

Athagey took another snort of snuff. The fires in her brain roared higher.

'I do hate to employ cliché,' she said, 'but today I think I shall indulge myself.' She smiled a special smile, one she reserved for battle; a smile her crew feared as much as her enemies did. 'So it begins,' Athagey said.

Chapter Thirty-Four

A NEOPHYTE'S TUITION

BOARDING TORPEDOES

THE MASTER'S RUN

The *Cantatum Bellum* floated in the void, dead as a corpse in the water. It ran with minimal power, even its oxi-technomantic and heat dispersal systems offline. They were in the full light of the sun, and void temperatures were high. Heat seeped into the ship's shell, and the already foul air thickened.

The enemy fleet passed by underneath the Black Templars ship, following the plane of the ecliptic to cut towards Srinagar as directly as possible.

Lucerne's autoreactive lenses darkened to near-total opacity as another nova cannon shell detonated. The enemy were in reversed spearhead formation, not the kind favoured for rapid planetary assault, which puzzled Lucerne. The nova cannon's photon wave ripped through the closely packed vessels, bringing curling displays of void shield displacement from them, and lighting up ovals of warp fire around each ship.

A couple lost their protection entirely.

'That one,' said Botho, pointing through the armaglass at a medium frigate. 'The shields are down.'

'We will die,' said Lucerne. 'The Imperial fleet is firing double nova cannon bursts, optimal spacing. If we board that ship, we will be consumed when it hits.'

The other Black Templars looked at him. His presence was still unwelcome.

Beorhtnoth was not one of those that looked at Lucerne, but he agreed. 'He is right. Pick another, neophyte.'

'This is madness. The boy lacks the experience,' said Lucerne.

'This is how we train our brothers, Sergeant Lucerne,' said Beorhtnoth. 'How is he to gain experience if he is not exposed to risk, or to choice? So he will choose, and he will choose well.'

'I do not agree,' Lucerne said.

'You may have bested me in combat, but I still lead here. You wish to be one of us, you must follow our customs,' said Beorhtnoth. 'Botho, choose. You must be quick. In a few minutes, the ships will be out of range. Which one do we board?'

Botho watched the fleet sail by. He was not flustered or shamed by the conversation, but watched carefully.

'That one,' he said decisively, and extended an unwavering finger at a ship some way out on the left flank. It was a sleek hunter, an unusual-looking vessel.

'Justify your choice,' said Beorhtnoth.

'It is smaller than the others, so the complement of Heretic Astartes aboard will be lesser, but it is not so small as to be a pointless prize for us to take.'

'Go on,' said Beorhtnoth.

'Its shields are on the brink of failing. The next nova cannon hit, if it is on target, will take them down, but it is too far out from the core of the formation to be badly damaged, meaning we shall be safe. The Imperial admiral is targeting the centre. Provided they continue to do so, and their shots remain so well placed, we will be safe. We will be able to cripple that ship and withdraw without being destroyed.'

'In what way should the destruction be accomplished?'

'We are few, so we should strike at the enginarium.'

'What foes can we expect to face?'

'A complement of one hundred and fifty Word Bearers, maximum. Perhaps twenty thousand mortals, but they will not be fighters – the slaves of the enemy make bad warriors.'

Beorhtnoth nodded and turned to Lucerne fully.

'What say you, brother-sergeant?' Beorhtnoth's words carried a tinge of malice. 'You have given us your opinion already. I assume you have another to share with us all.'

'I follow your lead, lord marshal,' said Lucerne.

'Come now, bashfulness is no warrior's virtue, especially when you have already been so forthcoming.'

Lucerne looked over the craft. 'I cannot argue with the boy's assessment,' he said. 'Though I add that he has neglected to factor warp-xenos into the ship's fighters.'

'You do not need to use the old euphemisms with us,' said Mortian. 'We know these things for what they are – daemons of the enemy.'

'Neverborn then,' said Lucerne. 'These are Word Bearers. There will be Neverborn.'

'Then you will not accompany us, because the boy missed one detail?'

'No. I will accompany you. I am of your number. I would be regarded as your brother. I will fight by your side, for the Emperor. I merely point out what he has missed. For his edification.'

The oculus flared with another searing blast of plasma.

'That was the second,' said Sword Brother Alanus. 'They are firing paired shot, thirty-second separations, at five-minute intervals. We should prepare, and set out after the next round to avoid being caught in the plasma wave.'

Lucerne watched the ships of the enemy fleet. They were moving at speed, but in the hugeness of the void seemed to crawl by like clouds in a soft summer sky.

'So be it,' said Beorhtnoth. 'Warriors of the Angevin Crusade, to the boarding torpedoes.'

The jolt of expulsion was always a shock when it came, even though it was expected. It was also never pleasant. There was nothing Lucerne could do but wait for it, in the dark, hemmed in by armour and the cramped, tubular space of the torpedo, watching the marker lumens change colour and his helm display count down.

It came with the roar of short-burn motors, a gut-punch acceleration. Launching from a boarding torpedo tube at full burn was a spine-compressing experience that taxed a Space Marine's body to the limit. A standard human could not have withstood such aggressive velocities. Gravitational force equivalent to several Terran-G pushed at his chest. Lucerne's lungs could take in no air. The pressure was so great that he felt the fused box of his ribs creak. Enhanced though Lucerne was, the crawling fingers of unconsciousness scrabbled at the borders of his mind. The torpedo punched out into space with near-terminal violence, but in the punishing speed lay all the advantage. The cruiser shot three torpedoes simultaneously. The energy expenditure of the launches was so small and brief that it was not picked up, and so the *Cantatum Bellum* remained hidden, a splinter of metal lodged unnoticed in the flesh of eternity. The torpedoes were tiny motes of solidity in the endless black, so inconsequential they would only be seen if they were actively scanned for. Against the rising barrage coming in from the Imperial fleet they were invisible. The EM pulse of the nova cannons blinded augurs for minutes after detonation, and the battlesphere filled with the demi-empyrical backwash of straining void shields.

The engines cut out. Acceleration ceased. The pressure vanished. The torpedoes were dumb-fired like common bullets. Only in the last seconds of flight, when they were too close for the enemy to do much about them, would their correctional thrusters fire and drive them at their target.

Poor-quality vid captured by the torpedo's augur lenses showed their target in grainy monochrome. Weapon flare frequently whited out the image. Without the engines burning, the torpedo was eerily quiet. The suck and hiss of Lucerne's breath through his underhelm respirator mask dominated, punctuated by the regular peeps of distance markers.

'Be ready, my brothers!' Beorhtnoth said.

'We are ready!' the others said. The torpedo was a medium-class five-man conveyance. Brother Alanus rode the prow point. Behind him went Beorhtnoth. Then Botho, his Scout armour exchanged for a full carapace void-rig. An Initiate named Sciopus occupied the next restraint cradle, then Lucerne. All of them were held in place by padded bars, boots mag-locked to the floor. It was narrow, their weapons held awkwardly so they could be used as soon as they arrived, but they had to be kept clear of the restraint bars.

'Sixty seconds to impact,' Beorhtnoth said.

Lucerne's counter sped down to zero. The enemy ship was huge in his thumbnail view.

'For Saint Sigismund!' the castellan said.

'The founder of our order, may he judge our actions with pride!' the others responded. Lucerne, who did not know the call and response, listened.

'For the Imperium of humanity!' Beorhtnoth called.

'We of Terra are the pure, the rightful lords of the stars,' the others responded.

'Death to the traitors!' Beorhtnoth said.

'They are the deniers of the light, the polluters of purity.'

'For the Emperor of Terra!'

'The most holy, the most pure, the one true god.'

'Guide us into the light of your being.'

'And we shall know no fear.'

Five seconds to go, and the torpedo fired manoeuvring thrusters. Lucerne's guts rose in his chest cavity as the ship swerved, its motion giving a nominal feeling of up. Something, somewhere, finally noticed them. Flak exploded around the craft, rattling it with shrapnel. A direct hit from anti-ship burst cannons or las beams and they were all dead.

At one second to impact, the melta-cutters ignited.

'No pity! No remorse! No fear!' they all shouted, and Lucerne knew this battle cry well.

The torpedo hit hard. Lucerne was thrown forward in his restraints. The torpedo juddered and bucked, its mechanisms burrowing it deep inside the enemy craft. Melta-arrays roared, cutting their way inside. The Space Marines were thrown around every foot of the way, until the little craft's machine-spirit trilled a fanfare, the torpedo slid to a halt, and the front blew off with an ear-splitting bang. Smaller charges shattered their restraints, and they were shoving their way out of the buckled torpedo through tangles of metal.

Alanus was first, his shield up. There were slave-warriors of the enemy waiting for them, and he went out into a crossfire of autogun bullets. Alanus and Beorhtnoth were slaughtering the last few by the time Lucerne had shouldered his way out. He thumbed on his chain sword and identified a target, but as soon as he had spotted it, Botho had blown the man to pieces with a single bolt.

Molten metal cored from the hull cooled on the deck. Foam wept down the side of the breach. The seal wasn't complete, and air escaped with a high-pitched squeak. Blood-steam rose from the shattered foe, drifting until caught in the air current, where it was sucked away into space.

Beorhtnoth opened the company vox. 'Chaplain Mortian, Sword Brother Vengis, report.'

'We are aboard, castellan,' replied Mortian. *'Brother Vengis sits with the Emperor. His torpedo was shot down. All his men are lost.'*

'As the lord of man deems it should be, so it is,' said Beorhtnoth. 'Split your unit. Send two on the Master's Run. The rest of you secure us transport out of here, target designate Angelus. We make to target designate Baraqiel. Target Cassael is hereby abandoned.'

'The enginarium is this way,' Alanus said. He angled his shield to cover as much of his body as possible. 'I take point.'

Beorhtnoth nodded. 'Lead the way. Expect heavy resistance.' They set out.

'Botho,' Lucerne called. The neophyte turned back to face him. 'What is the Master's Run?'

'Cause havoc. Draw attention away from primary objectives. Destroy targets of opportunity,' the neophyte answered. 'It is a glorious assignment.'

'It is a suicide run?'

'Yes,' said Botho as Lucerne fell in beside him. 'They will not be coming back. And if the Emperor is with us, neither shall we, but we shall go to Him and be with Him, in the light, and His glory, forever and ever.'

'If He wills it, so be it,' said Lucerne, already half thinking that was what the Emperor intended.

Chapter Thirty-Five

ATHAME

ANOINTED

TO THE CENTRE

The two fleets met in a tempest of violence. The Word Bearers plunged like a sword tip towards a breastplate, lance turrets lashing out at the ships as they passed through, broadsides unleashing full payloads in both directions with rippling flashes of light.

The Chaos fleet was travelling so fast that the contact lasted less than half a minute before both sides had cleared each other completely. For those thirty seconds the universe was upended. All space was torn up into a maelstrom of deadly energies. Shields gave out with blasts of radiation. Shells slammed into unprotected hulls. Lance beams on sustained fire tore great furrows in the metal skins of the ships.

Through all this, Athagey shouted orders.

'Escort craft and light cruisers ignite engines, begin acceleration to pursuit speed. Prepare to give chase as soon as the enemy are past the main line. All main-line ships, prepare to give starboard battery fire, accelerate to quarter speed. Change heading to planetary approach vector, run parallel to the dogs and hammer them from behind.'

The *Saint Aster* trembled to the beat of its own guns. Its void shields flared, dumping mass and energy into the warp, turning the shields purple, blue and magenta with discharge that swirled around the ship and obscured the battlesphere.

Then the Word Bearers were cutting like knives towards Srinagar. Their lance turrets fired behind them, but they were out of the arc of their main guns. They left trailing fire, shield-corposant and lines of debris. A number of smaller ships were rolling wreckage, and these were now the focus of the Imperial fleet's fire, as they tried to blast them into small enough pieces that the void shields could take their impact. One Chaos cruiser was ablaze from stem to stern, short-lived explosions bubbling out of its sides in the airless void. It was heeling over, pushed off course by plumes of vented gases, dying.

The tactolith shivered. It showed the two fleets moving apart from each other, the Word Bearers having passed through the Imperial Navy like shuffled cards. Dotted lines showed predicted trajectories of vessels, munitions and wreckage. Alarms whooped. There was a haze of smoke on the command deck, diffuse, blown in by the atmospheric recyc systems from a burning, unsealed compartment somewhere.

'Damage reports!' Athagey shouted. 'Ship first, followed by fleet. Tell me what they have done to my girl, second lieutenant!'

'Fires on decks six, seven, nine and nineteen, groupmistress. Several hits to portside batteries. Lance targeting arrays offline. Void shields two and three still down. Void shield one operational. Full motive capability.'

'Fleet liaison!' she said. The *Saint Aster* was turning, rumbling still as it cast explosives and energy beams after the receding enemy. 'What's the rest of the butcher's bill?'

'*Coming Light* has no shields, moderate damage, full void

through twenty levels, but they are contained. *Unmerciful* reports reactor problems and is unable to join pursuit formation. The rest...' He scanned the list. 'Minor scrapes, my lady. Consolidated crew casualty figures estimate fifteen thousand, six hundred and rising. Navis armsmen and Militarum attachments report no attempts at boarding by the enemy.'

'Our tally?'

'A brace of raiders, three more light support craft, and the cruiser, corrupt ident reading, silhouette match suggests *Master of Fate*.'

'What is the status of the stars?'

'Activity is rising. Emission soon.'

Athagey's eyes narrowed as she thought.

'Send additional repair crews over to *Coming Light*. Get those shields back up, or they'll be sterilised by the solar storm. All able ships begin pursuit. Captain Ladinmoq, *Vox Lexica* may begin launching strike vessels as soon as the weather front has passed over us, not before. The same stands for other carriers.'

An alarm rang, then another, then a third.

'What by the dust of Old Earth...?'

'Augur margin readings suggestive of imminent reactor failure, *Master of Fate*!' Basu shouted out.

'All crew, shield eyes! Brace for debris impact!' Diomed commanded.

They saw it on the tactolith first, a perfect sphere of white that grew, flared, and died.

A second later, a wash of racing energy hit the ship. Once more the void shields blazed, dragged out into a long, glowing teardrop. The explosion was bright as a dying star, even with the *Saint Aster* turned away from the light.

'Total destruction,' Basu reported. 'Debris cloud expanding

at eighty miles per second. Impact in six minutes. Debris size is small, and should not penetrate the shields. Threat rating null.'

'What effect on the enemy fleet?' Athagey asked.

'Minor void weakening.' Finnula squinted at her screens. 'Wait. They are firing manoeuvring thrusters.' She stood up, looked out of the oculus. 'The enemy fleet is breaking apart.'

Athagey called up a flat real-time vid on her throne hololith. The enemy fleet were accelerating and scattering. She frowned around her monocular.

'What are they doing? One cruiser kill shouldn't make them run.'

'They are no longer heading for the planet,' said Diomed.

'I can see that. I want to know what they are doing, not what they are not doing,' said Athagey. She thought a moment. 'Send a coded pulse to Task Force Quartus Delphus One. Have One come out from behind Srinagar. I doubt they'll see battle now, but I want to put the pressure on. They'll be too far out to contribute, but it will discourage lone vessels from making passing strikes on Srinagar – one good volley will lose us the main settlement and the relay. Keep the enemy from the planet if we can. Inform Captain Hustulin of Quartus Delphus Two that he should be ready to move in rapid intercept from the system rim. If these dogs are going to scatter, we can put a few of them down as they run, at the least.'

'Hustulin is forty minutes out by vox,' said Athagey's chief vox-officer, Lieutenant Gonang. 'Quartus Delphus Two is in a broad net. It'll be two hours before they're all apprised and moving together.'

'Then get on with it!' Athagey's spirits deflated a little. It would be harder to achieve true victory with the Chaos forces moving apart. 'Track Kor Phaeron's ship!' she barked. 'And Diomed, please try to come up with some sort of explanation as to what the hell they are trying to accomplish!'

* * *

Bells tolled slow alarms throughout the *Dominant Will*. The shields had been reduced to a quarter efficacy, and lumps of debris, munitions and energy beams were passing through. With every impact the ship jangled, so many were the chains and sacred ornaments hanging from the ceilings.

'It is time,' said Kor Phaeron. He got up from his throne, and walked the steep stairs down to the deck with solemn purpose. The ship shook and rumbled around him as it came about to a new heading. 'The Imperial dogs begin their pursuit. While they are focused on our destruction, we shall take our prize from under their noses.' He raised his enormous fist at the oculus. Through the images of the gods graven into the armaglass, bright engine flare of accelerating spacecraft refracted, surrounding Khorne, Slaanesh, Nurgle and Tzeentch with scintillating displays of rainbows.

'Ah,' said Tenebrus, floating down beside Kor Phaeron on his grav-stage. Yheng could tell he enjoyed every moment of discomfort he inflicted on the priest. 'So now you will tell us how you intend to gain the surface?'

'I will show you, apostate sorcerer,' Kor Phaeron snarled. He gave Tenebrus a savage look. 'I will show you what real devotion to the gods brings. I will show you how they serve those who serve them best,' he sneered at the sorcerer.

The Dark Cardinal stepped down from the final step with a mighty tread. Vrakon followed. The deck plates creaked under his weight. He walked around the great promontory of his throne spire, and into its shadow. Priests came forward, muttering prayers, billowing incense from spouts implanted into their backs. The sweet, heady scents of putrefaction, spices, blood and musk enveloped them.

Gathered by the throne platform were twenty of the Anointed, all helmed, their hulking Terminator armour making them seem as daunting as the gods themselves. It was darker than it should

have been there, where shadows gathered thickly in silent conspiracy, cloaking the Terminators, so that the words on their
armour were illegible, and the planes of the plates indistinct as
distant mesas viewed through heat shimmer. Their eyes glowed
steady though, a bright and dangerous gold, a light of knowledge and of certainty, of vistas beyond mortal ken known and
comprehended.

'I shall show you something that few are privileged enough
to witness,' said Kor Phaeron.

With great care, the Dark Cardinal extended a finger. His
claws hinged away from the back of his gauntlet, allowing
him to press at a small panel set into the thick armour of
his thigh. Green gases vented from the compartment. The
panel slid up, and aside, revealing a blade in a velvet-lined
niche. It flickered and changed before Yheng's eyes, settling,
though with no great certainty, on a dagger with a hilt much
too small for Kor Phaeron to grasp, and a blade that looked
like knapped flint.

Kor Phaeron's eyes dilated. His breathing changed. Viewing
this object gave him great pleasure. Some mechanism beneath
the knife raised it up, and then Kor Phaeron passed his hand
over it. The skin of the materium quivered to the touch of magic,
and the blade floated to his hand. With exaggerated care, the
Dark Cardinal gripped it between thumb and forefinger.

'This is the means of traversal,' he said.

'Other means,' said Tenebrus, feigning interested surprise,
though both he and Yheng knew what it was.

'This is one of the athames chipped from the blade of the
sword that wounded Horus Lupercal himself,' said Kor Phaeron,
holding up the blade to his greedy eyes. 'Ten thousand years
ago I was deemed worthy by the gods of receiving a part of
that most holy instrument, and I have guarded it ever since.
The anathame was the bringer of enlightenment, the glorious

tool of the gods. In this fragment is invested part of its limit-less power. It can clear the vision of the blindest pagan so that they might see the truth. But it has other properties. You would see them, Hand of Abaddon?' Kor Phaeron was so exulted by his handling of the blade that he looked upon Tenebrus kindly for the moment.

'I would, gladly,' said Tenebrus.

'Warriors of the Anointed!' Kor Phaeron declaimed, and of a sudden there was a hissing of supplementary muscle fibres and the growling of armour joints as the Terminators came to life. 'Prepare to wage war for the greater glory of the Powers!'

The priests chanted loudly, joined by choirs caged beneath the floor.

Kor Phaeron cut down. The athame's whisper through the air culminated in a sobbing shriek, and the very skin of the mat-erium split wide.

A cut in reality like an opening eye, or the gape of a birth-ing canal. It was wholly two-dimensional, and the same from whatever angle it was looked upon. Yheng moved around it. It obscured whatever was behind it, but the view through the hole did not change. She saw into an interior space, a building, unlit, its darkness accentuated by trembling lines. Everything was split, as if through a prism, like each portion of the spectrum was vibrating at a different frequency to the others, making multiple layered images that slid queasily over the tops of each other, but all made of qualities of darkness, not of light.

'Go, my warriors, and bring me victory,' Kor Phaeron said.

'As the Four demand,' Pridor Vrakon said.

So saying, Vrakon stepped into the breach. His warriors followed in single file. They were indomitable, but durability came at a cost of speed, and it was a full minute before the last was through.

'You next, sorcerer,' Kor Phaeron commanded. 'Fulfil your

duty to the Warmaster. Bring me what I desire. Find the source of these visions. Return with information, or not at all.'

Tenebrus looked the rift up and down. 'Remarkable,' he said. With that, he stepped through.

Yheng watched him, expecting to see him and the others standing in that other place, perhaps distorted, yet she saw nothing but the room. She was frightened.

'You hesitate,' Kor Phaeron said to her. 'I sense conflict in you. You are better than your master. Purer in faith. Go. Perform your service for the Powers, and you too shall know enlightenment of a kind that Tenebrus never shall.'

She dared look at Kor Phaeron then. His cold, ancient eyes glimmered at her like stars trapped in a cave. 'Faith,' she said. 'I will have faith in the gods.'

Closing her eyes, she took the road through the warp, and the slit in space-time closed behind her, leaving only the faint and fading sound of softly tinkling chains.

A horrible cacophony of screaming filled Yheng's every sense: sight, touch, taste and smell as well as hearing. She had not expected this. She had expected to step through, and be in the promised place, but she was not, and she began to panic.

There was something blocking their way, a terrible burning being that wordlessly forbade her passage. It had no features; attenuations of limbs trailed away into streamers of fire. It was in pain, its back arched, wings of light spread behind it as if they strained for release from the body, but it saw her. She could feel it, and it would not let her pass.

Around her, she felt questing minds, hungry things, with ideas for teeth and appetites that knew no satiation. She tried to push forward. She drew on her own powers, hard won from cruel gods, but made no headway.

Something had her about the arm; long, spindly fingers that

gripped with iron strength. The something heaved, resisting her attempts to fight it off. The vision shifted. The whispers died. She was on the stone floor of an office, papers sifting through the air. She could not think. She was in that room and somewhere else. Her head rang, and her vision danced, still blurring like the image she had seen through the tear. The burning being occupied her mind's eye to the total exclusion of all else. It was all she could see clearly, hanging over her, vortices of power curling from its twisted body.

Tenebrus stepped in front of the being. He was there with her. They were his fingers on her arm, the fingers she dreaded being touched by, but now found salvation in.

'Yheng! Yheng!' He shook her, making her chains jingle. She looked at him dazedly, unable to focus, staring past him at the looming guardian and the curls of fire. Her retinas stung with its presence. Her soul charred. Then she felt something at her lips, cold and hard, the lip of a flask. Tenebrus grabbed at her chains, and dragged her head back; the pain in her scalp as they pulled on her piercings helped focus her.

'Drink!' he commanded, and he tipped some foul-tasting liquid into her mouth. She spluttered. 'Drink!' he said, and forced her head back further.

The potion burned its way inside her, not only into her stomach, but outwards, into her wider system, calming the insane vibrations of the atoms of her being and hauling her soul by painful increments back into its shell of flesh.

She gulped the liquid down, and Tenebrus released her. The golden being vanished. She fell, and grovelled on the floor.

Cold from the stone seeped into her hands. The building was shaking. The first thing she thought of was an animal quaking with terror. Then she realised it was her. She was trembling, from the soles of her feet to the top of her skull.

'Yheng?' Tenebrus said.

She looked up, eyes and head sore.

'My master,' she said, and vomited all over the floor.

'You display your weakness. Stand, Yheng, servant of the gods, and be strong,' said Tenebrus. He bent low, and helped her up. She saw he used only one hand. The other was cradled against his wounded side, and that was now dark with freshly spreading blood.

'I am sorry.' She wiped her mouth with a shaking hand. Her gorge rose again, but she forced it back. 'I have failed you.'

'Have you?' said Tenebrus. He looked around the room, spotted his staff, and retrieved it. 'That passage was testing. I do not think if Kor Phaeron were here with us in this room, he would be bragging still about his mastery of the warp. We were opposed, Yheng. The thing we came here to find does not wish to be found.' He looked at her. 'He didn't come, did he?'

She shook her head.

There was a burst of boltgun fire somewhere not very far away.

'The Word Bearers have a fight on their hands in the materium also. The Dark Cardinal is not so confident of success as he pretends.'

'What are we going to do, master?'

'Our duty, to the gods and to ourselves. We find the soul that sees the vision. This whole mountain is a resonant device designed to channel and amplify psychic energy through a single focal mind. So where do we go, but its heart?'

Chapter Thirty-Six

DATA-LEECH

BOLD HISTORITOR

AREIOS TESTED

'How is it coming?'

Fabian paced back and forth. The books dulled the noise of his footsteps on the stone, but they still annoyed his underlings, rapping across the deep, warbling hum of the data-looms they clustered around, their serial linked data-saints greedily sucking up every last bit of information from the relay noosphere via leechcodes.

'It is not much progressed from the last time you asked, historitor majoris,' said Serisa Vallia, who along with a junior adept was manning the primary data-leech control. Three rune boards were in front of her, all marked with the secret signs of the Mechanicus.

'The archives are extensive,' said Rumagoi. He was more nervous than Fabian, and kept looking around the stacks and their irreplaceable logbooks as if they would disappear the moment they were out of sight. He'd already lost Sov, and was downcast. Losing the archives as well might break him. 'You are attempting to copy thousands of years of data in hours. I would have thought it impossible, but...' He trailed off, looking at the historitors' machines. What he couldn't say was that though their equipment was advanced, crafted to the highest Mechanicus specifications, it might not be enough to save Srinagar's memories.

'Just give me a time,' Fabian said, barely restraining his temper.

'You asked them last a minute ago. Let them be, Fabian,' said Yassilli softly.

'See for yourself, sir,' said the adept, Guilin. 'The completion indicators have moved only a little.' In his heavy goggles, three bubble tubes of yellow liquid were reflected. Tiny skulls floated in each one, the liquid rising higher as the information was drawn out of the machine and copied into the Logos' equipment.

'He's right. Leave it to us,' said Vallia. 'At least we have their most prized hard copies away.'

'Right,' said Fabian. They'd taken hundreds of boxes out of the place, but so much remained it looked like they'd removed nothing. He watched the machine nervously. Guilin paused the inload while oblong data-crystals were swapped out from the leech array. They came out burning cold. Moisture from the air froze on them as gloved historitors packed them into crates. 'I have the most awful feeling of danger,' he said privately to Yassilli, making sure Rumagoi did not hear.

'Don't spook them,' she replied. 'They're doing their best. Five more minutes, that's what the indicators say.'

Fabian nodded. The weight of millennia of records pressed in on him, silently begging to be saved. As much as Rumagoi, he did not want to lose this information. They had had time to remove only a fraction of storage media in the archive, but nearly everything that had ever passed through the relay was contained in the ancient machines beneath it. It was a huge amount, millions of scrolls' worth, at a conservative estimate. It was vital they retrieved it.

'I wish we could take all the hard records with us as well,' he said, glancing at Rumagoi. The transliterator was glum with the coming loss.

'With luck, they'll be here in ten thousand years still,' said Yassilli. 'We'll just have to be satisfied with the noospheric records, won't we? This is a precaution. They'll never get this far. Athagey will either destroy them or they'll turn tail and run.'

An alarm began to sound – far off at first, some levels above, but the shrieking machine wails spread, heading towards them, until emitters hidden somewhere in the high ceiling joined the chorus.

'Oh, Throne!' said Rumagoi. 'The enemy. They're here!'

'You were saying?' said Fabian. He strode to the leech array. 'Hurry!' he told the technician.

'We can go no faster, sir,' said Guilin.

'Three more minutes, that is all,' said Vallia.

Fabian clenched his fists.

'Fabian,' Yassilli called to him. The fear in her voice had him turning about quickly.

She pointed to a light moving through the data-hoard. Soundless flames of cold plasma danced slowly down an aisle, heading towards the iron railings cutting the cavern in two five hundred feet away, then the light wavered back, and headed off obliquely to the north, passing with ethereal facility through the stacks lining the aisle. Where it touched paper, the edges glowed and riffled themselves, stirred by draughts in something other than the air.

'You had to say something, didn't you?' said Fabian. 'Never tempt fate. Especially in a place like this.'

'How's this my fault?' Yassilli said.

'Careless words call gods,' said Fabian. 'We're going to have to follow it. Guilin, Serisa, finish the exload. You...' He pointed at two others. 'Get the data-crystals already in the transit cases loaded up, then get them out of here.' There was a pile of open crates by a grav-sled. Half were already stacked on the flatbed.

'Where do we take them?' one of them asked. 'We can't get into orbit, if the enemy are here.'

'I don't know. We've got to hide them. Get them to the forces outside the city on the surface, maybe.'

'The weather,' said one of Rumagoi's aides. 'The storm is coming.'

'What do you suggest, Rumagoi?'

The adept looked helplessly at him. 'I don't know.'

'Then use your initiative,' Fabian snapped at his men. 'You're historitors, aren't you? Just get it finished and get that loaded.'

Fabian drew his weapons, depressing the activation stud on his power sword hilt.

'Anyone else not doing anything, come with me,' he said.

A squad of the Srinagar XV had been assigned to the group. Half a dozen historitors produced pistols. A few of them had brought short-pattern lascarbines, and the room filled with barely audible whining as they brought their charge packs to readiness.

'What do you think it is?' Yassilli asked. She had fetched her own weapon, a bolt pistol that she had to carry with both hands, though it was small calibre, designed for standard humans to use. 'It's beautiful,' she said, watching the cold fires dance.

'Beautiful, but nothing good,' said Fabian.

He signalled that the group spread out and follow the fire. Fabian headed down into a cross aisle and matched pace with the cold plasma. The flames dithered, turning in a wide spiral, passing within feet of Fabian, giving off an audible crackling and the scent of sulphur, then zipped off at high speed, passing through several sets of cupboards and shelves with short, sharp cracks.

'Find it!' he shouted, running after it, and not seeing it.

'Over here!' someone called. The voice was muffled.

Fabian took a left at a run. The fire had come to the centre of a crossway where six aisles met. There was a circular void there, a seating or study area, but the ancient furniture was buried under boxes of mouldering fibreboard. On the other side, the plasma was moving in a tightening spiral, the shifting lights dancing more quickly. A deep thrumming that set Fabian's teeth on edge started up.

Yassilli joined him. 'It's stopped?'

'Whatever is going to happen is about to happen,' he said. 'Take cover and stand ready!' he shouted.

The thrumming grew louder, shaking his innards.

The air ripped, like paper rent in two, and from the gap between shone a hellish golden glow, and a shape came forth. It was hurled out of the space behind the world so fast they could not see what it was at first, but it was big. It bounced off the floor, crashed through a heap of wooden crates, scattering dusty codexes, hit a set of shelves, punching through and bringing the whole lot down before it landed, and skidded, rolling over twice with a clatter that Fabian recognised as the sound of ceramite hitting stone.

'Heretic Astartes!' he shouted.

Las-beams stitched bright trails into the dark. The historitors were all chosen for their minds, but their bodies had been honed to make them fit for their purpose. All had had military training. None of them missed. The Srinagar XV were even better.

A strobe of red and blue las-fire glanced off the angles of its plate. The warrior was buried under piles of books and scrolls, and struggling to right itself. It was on its back, Fabian thought – rocking from side to side until it rolled, and got a knee under itself. Then with great difficulty it stood. Only then did Fabian see what they were fighting, and his stomach turned to water.

Heavy armour made their enemy taller than a regular Space Marine and much heavier, grisly trophy racks crammed with skulls over a high cowl taking his height over ten feet. The warrior was clad in Terminator plate, all but impervious to the lasweapons Fabian and his men possessed.

'Throne of Terra!' Yassilli shouted over the bark of her bolt pistol. Her shot exploded harmlessly on the warrior's stomach. 'Is that what I think it is?'

The heavy sound of rapid-fire bolt cyclers chambering rounds clattered through the archive. The historitors scattered.

The chugging roar of a twin-linked bolter firing on full automatic drowned out all else. The sound of it was ear-splitting, filling up the great void as thoroughly as pumped rockcrete. Fire flash lit the giant warrior as he tracked his weapon from right to left then back again. Bolts hammered into the boxes at the centre of the reading area, blasting them apart. Paper rained down like confetti scattered on an Ascension Day parade. Wood splintered, the innards showing pale under centuries of black polish. The bolts flared as they burst through the shelves, solid-fuel rocket motors setting the archives ablaze. One of the Srinagar XV was hit square in the side of the ribs. One moment he was a living, breathing servant of the Emperor, the next there was a space a man used to occupy, the gruel of his innards rolling stickily down the shelves. The paper fell red.

'How long?' Fabian yelled into his vox-bead.

'Two minutes, twenty-five seconds,' Guilin responded. *'Then we've got to get the last of the crystals on the grav-sled, and get it out of here.'*

Fabian cursed. 'I've got the only weapon that can get through that armour,' he said.

'What?' Yassilli screamed at him. 'You don't stand a chance!'

'I'm not going to fight him,' said Fabian. 'I'm going to dis-tract him.'Then he was running, head low, keeping out of sight of the Terminator as best he could, and still the giant fired on.

Alarms blared all through the relay. The enemy were appearing at random throughout the facility, dropping out of holes in time and space. How the traitors had got inside, Areios did not know. There was no warning. There were no landing craft. Teleport should not have been possible, and there were no augury spikes telling of teleport flares. Nevertheless, they had suddenly manifested all over the facility. The odd spread of them suggested to Areios that something had gone wrong, and it was indeed fortunate all of them had not appeared together, for a force of twenty Terminator elite gathered would have been unstoppable by the force he commanded.

The boy Ferren of Hive Daner 50 would have lost his nerve at the sight of these monsters stepping from the dark, hard though he was, born into the pits of poverty and weaned on violence. The boy would have crumpled, and begged for mercy. The warrior Ferren Areios felt no fear. He would not kneel, or beg, only fight.

They rounded a corner on the path to the archives, and found a foe in the corridor, a Word Bearers Traitor legionary, wearing an ancient variant of Indomitus-pattern Terminator plate. He knew its strengths and its weaknesses. He automatically and unconsciously compared it to other marques of the battleplate. He felt he had known this information since birth, so thoroughly had Belisarius Cawl woven it into his being. It was more important to him than the corpses of Telepathica adepts lying around the corridor, their blood splashed up the walls.

At twenty yards they were within a second of close melee range. But Areios reacted coolly, and so did his men.

'Squad twenty-two, spread and give fire.'

Eight of them were with him, all clad in Ultramarines blue but bearing the markings of the Unnumbered Sons of Guilliman, First Company, First Battalion. They split fluidly, exhibiting the same coordination as a flock of avians evading predators, bolt rifles aimed, but it was not they who opened fire first.

The first of Areios' warriors went down before he could loose a shot, breastplate shattered by five perfectly aimed bolt-rounds, both hearts obliterated. The traitor was already moving on to the next Intercessor as the Sons of Guilliman returned fire.

The corridor filled with the flame trails of bolt-rounds. The Terminator carried a twin-linked pattern of antique sort, and was firing in burst mode, conserving his ammunition. Even so, the gun had a ferocious appetite, and the Terminator advanced as he fired, wading through the storm of shrapnel to engage at close range. Another of Areios' Primaris Marines made the ultimate sacrifice to the Emperor.

The Terminator's weapon ran dry, and he charged. It was pointless trying to fight the traitor with combat knives, so the Intercessors fell back by twos, firing constantly at the warrior until his plastron was a cratered, smoking mess of shattered ceramite. One of Areios' men made the mistake of pausing to reload while he was too close, and paid with his life. The Terminator lumbered into him, lightning-wreathed fist swung in a hammer's arc, hitting the warrior on the pauldron. The combination of impact and disruption field obliterated the Space Marine's left side, so much energy liberated that his fire partner was thrown into the wall. He failed to get up in time, and the enemy stamped his arm flat, pinning the warrior to the ground, and finished him with a punch to the head.

Areios ran at the traitor as he straightened from the downward blow, let himself drop, skidded past the Terminator in a shower of sparks. As he passed he tossed a krak grenade at the enemy's leg, its mag-locks clamping it in place.

The device imploded, shattering the armour and the leg beneath, and the Terminator toppled to the ground. Areios scrambled back to his feet, jammed his bolt rifle into the space between cowl and helm, and emptied his magazine. Shrapnel stripped armour of paint, cratering it to the point of compromise, as Areios fired and fired. The traitor's head snapped back and forth, fires caught in his battleplate, and he moved no more.

Areios stepped back from the dead Word Bearer. Alarms rang in his helm, from the relay, from his squad. Mortis runes sang their dirge. There was nothing coming in from outside, and his attempts to contact Messinius' larger force on the surface went unanswered. Stellar particle emissions chattered voice-like static in his ears. Inloads from the rest of the combined force in the mountain flooded his tactical displays, corrupted by dropout, but the picture was clear enough.

'The enemy are all over the relay,' he said. 'Stellar weather is disrupting our communications. We must assume a landing is taking place as well as this teleport assault. Squad, split. Sergeant Covarn, take Meketo and Sobelius with you down to the historitors. See that they and their records are evacuated from the mountain.' He switched his vox-channel to the wider company net, and shouted into the static of the shrieking stars that, even down there, beneath thousands of tons of stone, was tearing apart the electromagnetic spectrum. 'Command cadre lead a demi-company to meet me at the entrance to the main sphere, Hall of Utterances. The rest of you, sweep the mountain for intruders, five-man squads only. Do not engage alone.'

He looked to his men.

'For the Emperor and the returned primarch,' he said.

The group split.

Chapter Thirty-Seven

FOR SIGISMUND, AND THE EMPEROR

NEVERBORN

ONE OF US

There were running firefights all the way down to the enginar-ium decks. Mortals came at the Black Templars at first. They did not have the discipline of the armsmen of Imperial ships, but they were no mob. There were hints of military formation in their uniforms and standardised weapons. They had no officers, being led by howling priests, chanting liturgies of hate and pain as they charged. Easy to kill, they were not easily routed. Fana-ticism gave them courage.

To Lucerne, they were a surprise. He had fought various forces that worshipped the gods of the warp, including some drawn from the old Legions, but he had never seen this level of organisation in mortal followers. Regiments of Astra Mili-tarum turned from the light lost their shape quickly. Corrupt Space Marine Chapters often broke up into bands of reavers; the very nature of Chaos was opposed to order. The Word Bear-ers defied that. He expected a ship defiled by the warp, but found instead that it was a dark mirror to the *Cantatum Bellum*, a church-vessel, full of religious art and other signs of faith. The walls were deep reds and purples, decorated with solemn daemonic faces and the effigies of the Dark Gods in their myriad forms, while here and there, in niches lit by flame, statues of dead champions looked out.

The mortals could not stand before them. Lucerne watched with interest how the Black Templars operated. They fought in mixed groups of neophyte, Initiate and Sword Brother. He assumed this was because of their numbers, but saw from the way they supported each other in combat that it was natural to them, and effective, though their mode of battle was completely different to the regimented tactics of the Primaris Space Marines.

When they faced a group of Word Bearers legionaries, he saw this at its most pronounced.

Five of the foe were waiting for the Black Templars, holding the far side of a bridge over a trench full of pipes. All were equipped for close-quarters combat, as if they wished to test themselves against the knights of Dorn and had sought them out for the purpose. The bridge was forty yards across, almost square, so perfect a duelling ground it could only have been chosen.

'Slow!' Beorhtnoth said. The Black Templars went from a jog to a stride, walking out onto the bridge. Botho raised his boltgun to his shoulder, but Beorhtnoth pushed it down. All the Black Templars, with the exception of Botho, carried blades. Beorhtnoth and Alanus had power swords, Lucerne and Sciopus chainswords. Alanus' left arm was occupied by a tower shield sheathed in energy. Botho had his boltgun, the rest carried bolt pistols.

The two groups approached each other on the bridge. Neither side spoke, but arrayed themselves against each other. Lucerne found himself facing a monster with a double-handed chainaxe. No signal was given. Combat began.

Sword Brother Alanus went in first, his power sword held like a gladius at chest height, point forward. His opponent wielded two powerblades, and he slashed with astonishing speed, bringing up a wall of lightning from Alanus' storm shield. Alanus crouched, weathering the battering rams of the warrior's swords, waiting to lunge.

Lucerne saw no more. His attention was fully occupied with his own opponent. He was tall, this one, his power armour modified to accommodate bulging muscles. Inward-curving metal horns almost touched above his head, exaggerating his height. Icons of all the Dark Gods hung from cords around the roots of the horns, jangling as he swung his axe.

It was a massive weapon, slow, but Lucerne was wary of parrying it, judging that the warrior's strength and the axe's weight would smash right through any blade defence. He back-stepped out of range of the first cut. The axe head slammed down into the bridge deck, diamond-hard teeth ripping up the metal. A plume of white-hot sparks bounced around the duellists' feet. Lucerne stepped in while the Chaos Space Marine was wrenching the axe out, bringing his sword down. The warrior yanked his weapon up, catching the blow on the haft of his axe. Lucerne pressed in, weapon sawing down into the metal, and skidding up and down between the traitor's hands. Lucerne leaned in, his superior Primaris strength no use against this brute, and they were locked in place. His chainsword whined as it cut into the haft of the axe.

The warrior turned, twisted his axe two-handed. Lucerne's chainsword skidded down the axe, catching on the Word Bearer's knuckles. They were apart a moment, before the Word Bearer slashed out, the first blow in a walking assault, the axe cutting at Lucerne, forcing the Primaris Marine back. The Word Bearer advanced with each strike. Lucerne counter-attacked, and the spinning chain tracks of the weapons met, and locked.

The warrior pushed two-handed. Lucerne braced his pistol arm against the flat back of his chainsword. The axe dipped down, until Lucerne's chainsword was level with his foe's face. He slid his arm up the weapon, smashing the butt of his pistol into the warrior's helm. The Word Bearer held fast, and before Lucerne could hit him again, he gained the upper hand, and swept Lucerne's sword aside in a wide circle, and smashed the howling axe into Lucerne's pauldron. Ceramite filings flew everywhere as it bit into the shoulder armour.

Lucerne dropped his chainsword, letting it swing by his honour chain. He grabbed the axe below the head. His foe tried to pull it back, but Lucerne held it fast, and pushed his bolt pistol into the gap between gorget and faceplate.

'For the Emperor,' he said.

Four bolt shots shattered the traitor's helm and blew his head clean off. The headless corpse dropped, axe stilled.

The skirmish was coming to a close. Alanus still fought the enemy with two swords. Beorhtnoth was fighting a pair of them, sword a blur, deflecting their weapons. He punched one foe in the face, sending him back, reversed his sword and rammed it through the chestplate of the other. Lightning crawled all over the Word Bearer's armour. His helm lenses burst, and he slid off the end of Beorhtnoth's sword. The castellan parried a blow from the second warrior with his vambrace, smashing it aside. He slammed the pommel of his sword into the traitor's breathing grille, then again; kicked the side of his knee, bringing him low, before twirling the sword round and driving the point into the gap between helm and torso armour, then dropping to his knee, the twist cutting the sword down savagely through his breastplate.

Alanus decapitated his foe, but Sciopus was dead, his own opponent lying on the ground before him, armour broken open by bolt shots. Botho had his gun up, smoke venting from the barrel.

Beorhtnoth stood. 'We are close,' he said.

They paused a moment among the bodies of the dead. Staple ladders for mortal maintenance crews ran up and down into the darkness. There, Lucerne saw the first signs of corruption, lurking out of sight of the gilded temple ways: slime running down the walls, corroded ducts, and yellow eyes that stared then vanished.

The castellan went to Sciopus, took a krak grenade from the fallen warrior's belt, and clamped it to his neck.

'What are you doing?' Lucerne asked.

'We have no Apothecary. No way of retrieving his gene-seed. It is best the enemy do not take it, if we should fall.'

He stepped back. The grenade went off, obliterating Sciopus' head and the progenoid glands in his neck and chest.

'Plant charges here, Botho, then wait for our return,' Beorhtnoth ordered.

'But, brother, I will follow you unto death! Do not leave me here.'

Beorhtnoth went to his neophyte, and for the first time Lucerne saw tenderness in this most fanatical of warriors.

'Neophyte, I do not ask you to stay here to dishonour you. Someone needs to hold this bridge. It is our way off this vessel once our mission is done. This is a vital task.'

Botho nodded hesitantly.

'Yes, brother,' he said.

'We three then,' said Beorhtnoth to the others. 'The enginarium, and victory.'

The three Black Templars slaughtered their way towards the ship's stern. They caught another unit of Word Bearers unprepared, and cut through a press of mortals. In the approaches to the reactor, they encountered shambling cyborg things, sent into battle by adepts of the Dark Mechanicum. All perished before their guns and blades.

They reached the semidecks around the reactor core: hollow, circular platforms that encased the heart of the ship, which beat within a magnetically sealed fusion chamber three hundred feet high. Pipes broke the decks into small, awkward spaces crammed with machinery. Plastified cables snaked everywhere, emerging from holes then plunging out of sight. The space throbbed to the power of the reactor. It was hot, and claustrophobic.

The three warriors went into the semidecks slaughtering everything in sight. The crew in the deeps were pallid, nervous things, many bearing the dubious blessings of Chaos, and were easily slain. Their bodies soon lay in broken tangles at the base of the machines that had enslaved them.

'Find the main polarity moderator,' Beorhtnoth told Lucerne. 'Deactivate it, destroy it if possible. I shall overload the fuel feed. Alanus, guard the door.'

Lucerne knew the machine he was looking for, and found it quickly, although no two voidships were the same. Two adepts of the Dark Mechanicum scuttled away from him as he approached the iron baldachin that sheltered the device. The half cog and daemon skull of the Mechanicum was stamped into everything. Mutant rats started up from nests of cables and raced before him, undulating like serpents.

Lucerne went to the machines. A bullet sparked off his power plant. He turned, and blew away his assailant with a single bolt-round from his pistol.

Some sort of matter covered the controls, and he scraped this away to read the dials and reach the switches. He knew enough about the workings of a voidship reactor to destroy one, and reset the magnetic resonators which held the plasma core from the walls of the containment flask. Somewhere deep in the strands of half-flesh enwrapping the device, a red lumen blinked. The settings altered, Lucerne smashed the instruments with his fist.

He returned to the others.

'It is done,' he said. 'We have sixteen minutes before the reactor collapses.'

'The fuel overload will ensure a large explosion,' said Beorhtnoth with grim pleasure. 'Let us go.'

A single warrior waited for them in the great space outside the reactor, a soaring, vaulted hall large enough to accommodate an entire Chapter of Space Marines.

'What are you doing on my ship, corpse-worshippers?' said the warrior.

Alanus and Beorhtnoth reactivated their power swords.

'Sending it into the hells where you belong,' said Beorhtnoth.

The warrior laughed at them. 'What do you know of hell? I am Xhokol Hruvak, a follower of the word. I know the truths of many heavens, and many hells. Let me show you something of them.'

Three animal shapes coalesced from nothing in front of him.

'Atraxiabus, Phezondamus and Shriabanda will be your teachers,' he said.

The things moved fast. Lucerne had an impression of skinless muscle, lidless eyes, tentacles whipping over raw shoulders. Lucerne and Beorhtnoth fired, but though their bolts were true they seemed to pass right through the creatures. Then the beasts were drawing their legs together and springing powerfully into the air.

The beast hit Lucerne hard, almost toppling him. Sabretoothed jaws clamped around the wrist of his sword arm. The thing bit down with such force his armour creaked and threatened to burst.

He jammed the boltgun into its side and fired. The bolts passed through it as if it were made of smoke, yet the jaws remained clamped tight around his arm. He switched his target, jamming the barrel into one of the thing's many eyes. This got a reaction, and it screeched and let go. Lucerne fired at it, and kicked it. His boot connected. He heard bones crack, and it skidded back across the deck, claws out, and kept its distance.

It was like a xenos creature in some respects, except the lack of skin, and its inconstancy. He recalled the type.

'Warp beasts,' he said. 'Khymerae.'

'And I am their master,' said Hruvak. An electro whip unfurled, bright magenta in the gloomy vault. Lucerne aimed his gun, but the whip wrapped around his wrist, the charged length ripping through the chain, and yanked it free. The bolt pistol clattered to the deck.

Alanus was down, wrestling with a khymera. It crouched on his storm shield, the Black Templar's head sliding about in its jaws. Beorhtnoth impaled his own attacker, and it roared, and slipped off the sword to the deck. There it ceased moving, and began to vanish.

'You killed one,' said Hruvak. 'A shame. They are difficult to train.'

He threw out his left arm. A single retractable power claw snapped out from its housing on his vambrace, activating as soon as it was clear.

'Never mind. I shall find more. There are always more.'

A small jerk of his head sent the khymera at Lucerne again. The whip slashed out at the same time as it jumped, snaring Lucerne's sword. Pulses of electricity burst into his armour, disrupting its systems and causing joints to lock randomly. He was poorly positioned to take the beast's charge, and was nearly floored by it. Ironically, it was Hruvak's whip that stopped him falling. Lucerne folded his arm to his chest as the beast leapt, allowing him to lever it out when it hit and send it back down to the floor before it could get a grip with its jaws.

The other khymera still had Alanus. Its sabred fangs sank into the soft seal below the Sword Brother's helm. Beorhtnoth drove his sword through the side of the beast, sending it back whence it came, but as it faded from view, Alanus did not rise.

Beorhtnoth went from the side of his dead brother, opening fire with his gun. Bolt-rounds slammed into Hruvak, distracting him just enough that Lucerne could yank on the whip, ignoring the pain from its charge-pulse, and disentangle himself from its length. Beorhtnoth came in fast towards Hruvak. The Word Bearer turned, taking the strike of the castellan's sword on the edge of his single claw. The impetus of Beorhtnoth's attack put him in danger, and Hruvak punched him hard in the face with his whip arm.

The castellan staggered. Lucerne moved in to help, but again the surviving khymera attacked him, driving him away from the fight. He got his arm around its neck this time, and it squirmed in his grip, and it felt more like a snake or giant fish than the cat it resembled.

'By the grace of the Emperor, by His holy light, I banish you, Neverborn!' he yelled, and smashed his chainsword guard into its face. It roared, and he hit again, bursting two of its yellow eyes. With a mad wriggle, it leapt from his grasp, and ran off into the dark.

Beorhtnoth and the Chaos champion were trading blows, moving back and forth as they each gained and lost the advantage. Beorhtnoth was keeping close to stop Hruvak employing his whip, but that deprived him of the benefit of his sword's reach, and put him at risk of Hruvak's serpent-tooth blade.

Lucerne heard voices coming from the far side of the grand vault. He switched through his visual filters, calling up heat-sight that revealed the approach of enemy in power armour. Strange, uncertain things moved through them.

'Castellan! Word Bearers and Neverborn moving in.'

Lucerne fetched his gun, and aimed at Hruvak, just as the Word Bearer found an opening and punched the blade up under

Beorhtnoth's breastplate. The power field tore out the inside of the castellan's chest cavity. Fire leapt from his neck.

Lucerne fired. He walked forward as he shot, emptying his pistol into Hruvak. Ceramite broke. Blood spattered the floor. Finally, a bolt penetrated his side, and the champion fell.

He looked at the Black Templars. Both were dead. He hesitated a moment, wondering what he should do, when bolts began fizzing through the air around him. Fired at range and by moving warriors, they were inaccurate, but were getting closer.

'Emperor watch over your souls,' he said. Then he ran.

At the bridge Botho waited for him.

'My master is dead, then,' the neophyte said.

'In combat, glorious and unafraid.'

Within the clear visor of his void armour, the neophyte's face dropped. 'It is for the best,' he said. 'Lord Beorhtnoth was not suited for this era, but made for older days of faith and certainty.'

'There is still faith, brother, and through it we can bring certainty again. Let us escape this place, so we may add our efforts to those of the returned primarch and his holy father, the Emperor, and serve a little while longer.'

'Praise be to that,' said Botho. They left the bridge, and Botho activated a remote trigger, blowing explosive charges that dropped the bridge down into the dark, pipe-filled chasm. As it clanged away into darkness, Lucerne ran a short-range auspex scan.

'No enemies ahead. The loss of the bridge will hold them, if only for a few minutes,' he said. 'We go.'

They ran, the howls of daemons at their heels, heading out to the hangar Mortian had been ordered to take and hold.

Chapter Thirty-Eight

COVARN

BAD ODDS

INTO THE SPHERE

Fabian's only hope was to stay behind the Terminator, out of his fire arc. Their heavy plate made Terminators virtually invulnerable, but they were slow, and lacking agility.

'If I can stay behind him, I will live. If I can stay behind him I will live,' Fabian panted. The Heretic Astartes tracked him with its gunfire, ignoring the las-shots smacking into its armour fired by the historitors and the Militarum unit.

'If I can stay behind him, I will live,' Fabian said. A stream of bolts chased him, obliterating everything they hit. Splinters stung him. He was running faster than he ever had in his life. The Terminator was focused on him. Fabian was the only one of the historitor group with a weapon that could conceivably penetrate the traitor's armour, if he was insanely lucky.

'The greatest threat,' he muttered. 'Who'd have thought it?'

But it was working; he was leading it away from the others.

A bookcase took several bolts. Wood exploded, and the whole thing came down with a screeching moan. Ancient cupboards split apart on the floor, scattering priceless books in every direction.

'If I can stay behind him, I will live!' Fabian said, and threw himself into an aisle off the reading area. He stopped for a breathless moment, trying to decide the best way to go, then hurriedly picked a direction.

The firing cut out. Was his enemy out of ammunition, or conserving it? He moved as quietly as he could. His men were shouting to each other. He heard the grinding of the Chaos Space Marine's motivators, the sickening, doom-laden clump of its tread. The las-fire had slackened off. Something of an impasse had been reached. The historitors and Guard couldn't breach the battleplate, but they could keep out of the Space Marine's way. The traitor was ignoring them.

He blundered out in front of his foe, skidded to a stop, and ran back the way he had come, but he had been seen. The Terminator moved towards him, its armoured bulk crashing through the shelving. He reminded himself they had sophisticated sensoria, and he held his breath, and jogged away, taking several turns at random. The footsteps of the Traitor Marine slowed, and stopped. Fabian waited.

The Terminator's visual systems were sensitive, so he wondered if the little fires catching in the archive dazzled lowlight modes, confused heat-sight, hiding him. Then again, maybe the Word Bearer was toying with him.

He crouched, moving silently, wincing every time his foot hit the floor.

'Come out, servant of the corpse-god,' said the Space Marine. Its Gothic was archaic, heavily accented, and punishingly raw from the battleplate's voxmitter. 'I will find you, and you will die. You cannot fight me. Give yourself to the gods, and know purpose.'

Servos whined. A suit-light snapped on, the cone clearly defined in the thickening smoke, sweeping the shelves.

Fabian's vox-bead peeped. It was very loud in his ear. He froze, again expecting the Terminator to have heard.

'*Fabian, the crystals are crated, the archive exload is complete. We're ready to go.*' It was Vallia, speaking quietly.

'Then go,' Fabian whispered. 'I'll continue to draw him off.' His response was little more than a modulated breath. He crept forward through the spreading fire. Smoke filled the room, tickling his throat, and making him wish for a rebreather. He stifled a cough. What had been isolated crackles and pops was gathering into a roar. He hoped the noise would hide him.

It did not.

A power fist burst through the wall of shelves to Fabian's left, showering him with burning books and lumps of wood. Lightning arced around cruel fingers. Tiny explosions went off all around the hole. The pages of books whipped up into short blizzards.

'Shit!' Fabian said, and ran.

The Terminator followed through the shelves, the ponderous war suit unstoppable. Wood shattered, books fell down in an avalanche, and the shelf toppled, hitting the one on the opposite side of the aisle, bringing that down too. The Terminator waded through the wood and parchment, smashing it out of its way, inconvenienced not at all by fording this torrent of history.

Fabian tripped, fell and landed badly. The Terminator loomed over him. Fabian's sword, the primarch's gift, so potent in every fight he had been in, felt inconsequential in his hand.

'You ran,' the giant warrior said. 'See how little your corpselord helped you. Open your eyes to the glory of the powers in the warp, and leave this existence free of His tyranny.'

'There is only one god, and He sits upon the Throne of Terra,' Fabian said defiantly.

'Whichever god you choose, you will die anyway,' said the traitor.

The Terminator reached down for him.

A flurry of explosions sparked off the traitor's massive form, distracting it. Chips of ceramite stung Fabian's face and put smoking holes in his uniform. The pain spurred him, and he scrambled backwards. More gunfire was coming at the Word Bearer. It stamped down, and turned about, silhouetted in the yellow fire of dozens of bolt-rounds exploding.

Fabian backed away into cover, and watched as three Sons of Guilliman emerged from the dark and caught the Terminator in a crossfire. Every time the traitor moved towards them, they fell back, never relenting, moving around each other, staying out of reach, until their sustained fire told, the outer layers of the Terminator's armour crumbled, and the rounds worked their way deeper. Subsystems failed, the Terminator's right arm locked, then a bolt found its way into the warrior within, and it toppled forward, dead.

The Word Bearer lay face down, smoke curling from beneath. The Space Marines kept it covered as they came to Fabian's side.

'Historitor Guelphrain,' their leader said. 'I am Sergeant Covarn. We have been ordered by Captain Areios to escort you from this facility. Where are your comrades? Are you alone alive?'

'The others live,' said Fabian. 'I led the traitor away from them. They are down there.' He pointed with his chin, and regretted it. His body was a mass of bruises.

'That was one of the bravest acts I have seen a mortal man perform,' said the Space Marine.

'Thank you,' said Fabian. He bent forward, trying to regain his head and stop his stomach contents spewing out of his mouth.

'It was also suicidal,' said the Space Marine. 'Your death was inevitable.'

'I'm still alive.'

The Space Marine looked at him.

'The Emperor protects, right?' Fabian said. He grimaced. 'Do you have any pain-blockers?'

'My pharmacopoeia is sealed.' Covarn took his elbow. 'Come,' he said.

The archive stacks were burning so voraciously their flames spread across the ceiling, where they bubbled and ran like brilliant, inverted waters.

They found the others on their way to the main exit. Frictionless contra-grav only went so far, and they were struggling with the great mass of boxed storage crystals on the device, pushing it forward a few feet, whereupon it would slide off to one side, they'd stop, return it to its path, then repeat. The Srinagar troops were helping. Rumagoi darted about, forever standing in the way, wringing his hands and giving contradictory orders. Yassilli was getting annoyed with him, and shouting at him.

'Halt!' Covarn called after them. 'We have been ordered by Captain Areios to escort you from this facility.' An exact repetition, Fabian thought. Must be Mars-born.

'Then escort us,' said Yassilli, pointing to the end of the empty cavern. 'We're going out the main entrance. It would help if your men could help us with this grav-sled.'

'You must come away from there,' said Covarn leadenly. 'You cannot go that way. The enemy are scattered all over the facility, and are concentrated in the levels above. The major force occupies the Hall of Utterances. You will not pass.'

'Are they all like that one?' Vallia asked nervously, looking back into the inferno where the Terminator's corpse was burning.

'All adversaries are Terminator armoured. They call themselves the Anointed. They are the Word Bearers' elite.'

'How many are they?' Fabian said.

'Unknown. Twenty, maybe. But they are converging on the relay.'

'The relay!' Rumagoi gasped. His anguish went ignored.

'Only twenty? Areios has eighty of you in here,' said Fabian.

'They outmatch us. Casualty ratio of Primaris Mark Ten power-armoured Space Marines to Indomitus-class Terminator-armoured Traitor legionary elite at close quarters is five point two one to one. They would best us easily. I and my men cannot fight more than two at once, and the probability of defeat is high in those encounters, with a fifty per cent chance of mutual annihilation. We may survive a second fight. We would not survive a third. We must retreat with you. You will follow me. There is an emergency egress tunnel this way.' He pointed through the forest of columns, towards the side wall.

'We can't go out of the front at all?' Vallia said.

'The enemy are scattered all over the facility,' repeated Covarn.

'Then signal Lord Lieutenant Messinius,' said Fabian. 'He has four hundred Space Marines with him on the surface, and the bulk of the Srinagar Fifteenth. That would be enough, surely?'

'The approaching stellar storm has disrupted our communications. He cannot be reached.'

'So, you mean there's an entire army out on the surface, waiting for the enemy to arrive, when they are already here, in the relay?' asked Vallia.

'That is correct,' said Covarn.

'Then what are we going to do?' said Vallia, who was evidently regretting her wish to go out into the field.

'The way you are suggesting leads to the surface,' said Rumagoi. 'We can't go out onto the surface, not for a few hours.'

'When will the full force of the storm hit?' asked Fabian.

'Particle bombardment of Srinagar Primus is estimated to occur within the hour. It is an added complication,' admitted Covarn. 'We have no choice. The enemy will be aware that you are here. They are slow, but relentless. You must leave the mountain.'

'What, right out into a solar storm? In the best case, we'll shorten our lives by decades. We'll probably just die,' said Fabian.

'Lord Messinius says, one problem at a time. For one, I say, cancer is curable, Historitor Majoris Fabian Guelphrain. A bolt-round to the head less so. This discussion is over. You will follow me.'

Making their way up to the great cavern housing the sphere, Cheelche and Lacrante ran right into the aftermath of a fight between the Srinagar XV and one of the Word Bearers. Lacrante wouldn't have called it a battle: the standard humans had no chance against a Space Marine in Terminator plate. Blood running down the stairs warned them, so much of it that it flowed in miniature cataracts over the steps. Cheelche wrinkled her nose at it, but didn't slow, motioning to Lacrante to be quiet. They both unslung their weapons. Cheelche powered up her t'au pulse carbine.

The traitor was a way back from the top of the stairs, stood over the top part of the soldiers' leader. He had been broken in half by a bolt blast to the pelvis. All his lower torso had been destroyed, and his legs were on opposite sides of the corridor. The pulped remains of his men coated the walls, floor and ceiling.

Lacrante stepped back into the cover of the stair top, convinced the sophisticated auguries in the warrior's battleplate would have spotted him already, but Cheelche stepped brazenly out in front of it.

'Oi!' she shouted.

Servo-motors growled loud as caged tigers as he swivelled about to face her.

Cheelche shot four times into the chest of the Terminator, and once through his forehead. Bright points of plasma punched through the ceramite, leaving tiny black holes. The damage appeared inconsequential and Lacrante was certain she was about to be obliterated by return fire, but the traitor did nothing.

'You can come out now, you,' Cheelche shouted over her shoulder. 'He's dead.' She patted her carbine. 'You can thank the t'au for that. For the Greater Good, please! Load of froth, but they make great guns. You people should take note. Lasguns are a waste of time against bastards like this.'

She waddled past the traitor. Were it not for the wisps of smoke curling from the holes in the traitor's chest, he would have seemed alive. His eye-lenses still glowed, the reactor of his armour hummed away deep beneath the plating, but he was dead. The mass of his armour held him upright.

'I wouldn't touch that,' she said, as he squeezed past the Terminator. 'Riddled with the corruption of the warp. Damn shame we can't destroy it. They'll be coming for it. A suit of armour like that is worth more than pure adamantine to them.'

They went on a little further, heading down by a secondary way to the bridge crossing the Spherus Claustrum. Their footsteps echoed through the huge cavern. The relay sphere was ahead. There was a major battle going on somewhere behind them. Lacrante heard many bolters firing. Judging from the noise, not all the traitor force had been scattered.

They reached the main entrance to the sphere – the Final Portal, the locals called it. It was sealed, the guardian of the gate dead with his throat slit within his cage.

'Someone's come this way,' he said, toeing the corpse through the bars.

'I can't get the door open,' Cheelche said.

'Stand back. Leave it to me.' Lacrante waved her away, then burst the outer door with a krak grenade.

'You got your head thing?' Cheelche said as the smoke cleared. 'Past here, we're not shielded.'

'Yeah,' Lacrante said. He fished out a circlet from his pocket.

It was simple, formed from stretchy novoplas elasteen. The important bit was the device at the front, a crystal embedded in a piece of elegant circuitry. It was beautiful xenos work, far lighter and more elegant than the human-made equivalents hanging in a vestibule beside the dead gatekeeper. He settled the crystal in the middle of his temple, where the warp eye was said to hide. With it in place he felt strangely numb. His lips tingled.

They ducked through the hole the grenade had made, into the antechamber.

'Huh,' said Cheelche. She peered through the glass of the inner door, but didn't open it. The bridge ahead was empty. 'There's the relay centre. The Pearl. Leonid wants us to cover it.' She pointed to the side doors. 'There are access tunnels in the skin for the adepts that way.'

The inner door opened to a tumbler cracker. They went into a narrow corridor with a tapering arch for a ceiling, up several flights of coiling stairs. Machines thumped in the walls all around them, filling Lacrante with an emotion like sour regret, though he had no reason to feel that way. Another door greeted them, this one made from warded plasteel.

'Is the thingy working?' Cheelche pointed at her forehead.

'I think so. I can't feel my tongue. Does that mean it is working?'

'Now how am I supposed to know that?' said Cheelche.

'What about you?'

Cheelche made the odd movement of arms that equated to a shrug.

'If you're chikanti, you're either really psychic, or you're not psychic at all.'

'You're in the "not" category?'

She nodded, and rested one of her lower hands against the door. They were smaller and more heavily webbed than the uppers. Lacrante often wondered what her homeworld was like, and how her people lived, but she wouldn't be drawn on it. 'What's going on in here won't be comfortable for me,' she said. 'I've got a soul, like you, but all the magical nonsense won't do to me what it'll do to you. I don't need the amulet.' She hummed and examined the interlocking symbols of the warding runes. 'Now, if I do this, and this...' She passed her hands along dimly glowing lines. 'And then this...'

The door slid suddenly into the wall. A short tunnel awaited. Lacrante expected it to be flooded with light, but it was rather dim. There was a faint chant coming from the other side.

'He is coming, he is coming, he is coming.'

'Aha!' she said. 'Also, ouch. It's like a brick to the head.'

Lacrante couldn't answer. Standing in that corridor was nigh impossible. His nerves fizzed with pain. His perceptions were oddly stretched, like someone was pulling him out of the back of his own head, so that the view out of his eyes was experienced from the end of a long and inconvenient tube. He gripped his head.

'Come on,' said Cheelche. 'It'll pass.'

She took his wrist in a leathery palm, and led him up the corridor out into the sphere. At the end there were five shallow steps that looked bizarrely to go up the wall, until there was an abrupt change of orientation, and he recognised the false tug of grav-plating. What had been the floor was suddenly the wall, and the stairs made sense.

'He is coming, he is coming, he is coming.'

Up the stairs on the inner surface of the sphere, psykers by the thousand stretched away, each bound into a throne. The inner surface of the sphere was all nominally down, so although those that were close were on the same plane of orientation as Cheelche and Lacrante, they climbed up the walls, and arced over, so that those on the far side seemed to be hanging upside down overhead. It didn't help Lacrante's nausea.

They were standing on the beginning of a structure that was

either a tower or a pier, depending on how you chose to see it, that went out between a pair of collection coils for the relay machinery. A giant spark danced between the spheres topping the gathering cones, bridging the pier. Electric faces smirked and howled in the light.

'This way,' she said. There was a ladder. With that reference, the pier seemed to go up.

Tower, then, thought Lacrante. They climbed.

'He is coming, he is coming, he is coming.'

The tower ended in a circular platform enclosed by rails. A console of unknowable purpose occupied part of its circumference, the rest afforded views around.

Cheelche went to the console, and knelt down.

'Ow,' she muttered. 'This is really, really unpleasant.' She rubbed her head.

They had a clear view of the glowing sphere in the centre of the relay, and the bridge that led out to it from the main entryway. From their point of view, the two figures walking along the bridge seemed to be walking directly upwards.

Lacrante took out his magnoculars. He saw a mutant and a woman.

'They're here already. Where's Rostov?'

'He said the enemy would come for the seer, and that he would be there to confront them. Trust him, Lacrante.'

'Don't they know she's dead?'

'It doesn't look like it, does it? We've got our job to do. Cover the Pearl, that's what Leonid wants, so that's what we're doing.' She sucked air through her teeth. 'It's a difficult shot.'

Lacrante continued to watch the figures. 'Why didn't we see them through the door? They must already have been in here when we arrived.'

'The warp, isn't it?' she said. 'It makes no sense, and you shouldn't try to understand it.' Cheelche sighted down her weapon, drawing a bead on the mutant. 'I wish I had my bloody long-las,' she said. 'This is going to be a difficult shot from here, with this gun. Do me a favour and guard me so I can concentrate. Leonid needs us.'

'Alright,' he said, 'But I don't think we have anything to worry about. Those Space Marines will never fit up here. They'll never get through that door.'

Cheelche squinted into the xenos-built scope.

'I'm not worried about Traitor Marines, and they won't be coming through that door.'

Chapter Thirty-Nine

THE SORCERER AND THE INQUISITOR

NEW VERSUS OLD

SHADES

'Interesting,' said Tenebrus. He was looking up, at the astropaths imprisoned around the interior of the sphere, miniature emperors ruling over private empires of pain. Ghostlights wreathed their heads. Corposant shifted in motile mists all through the centre, and every one of them was whispering. They would have been inaudible alone, but together their words hissed around the sphere as soft and sinister as the mist.

'He is coming, he is coming, he is coming.'

'Who is coming, master? Is it the child?' said Yheng. Her hands dripped blood. Tenebrus' sorcery had enabled them to evade the troops stationed in the relay. They had walked past firefights between the Astra Militarum and Kor Phaeron's warriors unseen. Only the guardian at the final gate had to be dealt with by less subtle means, and that fell to Yheng. It had felt good to wield a knife again for something other than sacrifice. She enjoyed murder for its own sake, and the sensation of drying blood tightening on her skin was pleasing.

'*He is coming, he is coming, he is coming.*'

'Who indeed? This child, I would say, whose image pollutes the warp. But who is he?'

'The Emperor?' she said, speaking the forbidden word.

'All things are possible. Kor Phaeron fears that,' said Tenebrus. 'But the Anathema has crafted servants before. Perhaps it is something of that order, one of His so-called saints?'

Tenebrus walked without care for the battle raging outside, discussing the possibilities of godhood as if he were strolling through the cloisters of a librarius.

'Whatever it is, it must be dealt with, and the answer lies in there.' He pointed to the Pearl.

'*He is coming, he is coming, he is coming,*' the astropaths whispered. One let out a loud moan. His soul burned out in a flare of warp-light emitted from his eyes and throat. The machinery bleeding off the excess howled. Pulsing rings of empyrical energy wavered unsteadily up and down collection piles.

'*He is coming, he is coming, he is coming.*'

'This place is dying,' Yheng said.

'Quite,' said Tenebrus calmly. He stopped. He frowned. 'More than that, what we're looking for is not here,' he said.

'What?'

Tenebrus paused, hand up. Yheng felt the prickle of sorcery.

'The focal point for the relay. It is gone.' He frowned. 'I think this is a trap.' Then he smiled. 'Fools.'

'Master!' Yheng called, pointing to a figure stepping out from the sphere. He was baseline human, with blond hair and unusually ruddy skin, armoured in shining carapace, a bolt pistol in one hand, a power sword in the other.

'You are the Hand of Abaddon,' the man said.

Tenebrus bowed his head. 'I am privileged to serve in that capacity.' He turned to his acolyte in the manner of a man making introductions at a social occasion. 'This, my dear Yheng,

is an Imperial inquisitor. Ordo Malleus, I take it?' he enquired.
'They're the ones I usually have to kill.'

'Rostov, of the Ordo Xenos,' said the inquisitor.

'I see,' said Tenebrus in surprise. 'My infamy must have spread if your kind is involved. You will not best me, no matter what little grouping you belong to. Step aside. I may let you live.'

'My duty is all. I go where the Emperor takes me. Surrender.'

'He is coming, he is coming, he is coming.'

'So you can use me? I don't think so.' Tenebrus had something in his hand. 'Besides, your demand supposes you have the advantage, and I am afraid that you do not.'

'He is coming, he is coming, he is coming.'

Several things happened at once. Someone opened fire on them from above. Yheng moved to push Tenebrus aside, but the incoming shots came to a crawling halt behind Tenebrus' head. At the same time, Rostov aimed and fired his bolt pistol, but Tenebrus was a blur, drawing on the warp to deceive. Yheng screeched an incantation, and threw up a shield of energy before them, so that the rounds blew feet away from her master, and Rostov struggled to regain his aim.

Tenebrus came to a sudden stop. 'A poor attempt, my friend,' he said, his voice booming then quiet, never emanating from the same place twice. 'It is my turn now.'

His hand cut down. Reality tore, and out poured swarms of Tenebrus' shades.

The sorcerer rose into the air surrounded by auras of purple lightning, his position forever shifting, his daemonic cyborg servants hurtling around him. Plasma bolts fizzed towards him from high above, but they all missed. Rostov held his hands up against the light, gun wavering uselessly as he tried to track the black shadows pouring into the relay, then their master, and could not draw a bead on either. Yheng was dazzled, awed by her master's warpcraft and afraid all at once. She could do nothing but bear witness.

'You believe this place is safe from me, inquisitor, because the focal mind is gone. I applaud your bravery in facing me, but you are upon a fool's errand. This is a grand choir of minds, all linked. Remove the lead, and the rest will sing on. I hear that song, and will steal it. Now,' said Tenebrus. He closed his eyes. 'Let us see what secrets this place holds.'

He threw out his arms, and the shades scattered like seeds blown from a flower head. Yheng ducked as they hurtled over her head. They disappeared into the shafts and crannies of the relay. Others arrowed out towards the seated astropaths, descending in flocks, skinless jaws distending, techno-arcane probes extending, and plunged teeth and harvesting spikes deep into the flesh of the enthroned psykers.

Their chant ceased. They began to scream.

'Perhaps you should consider surrender, inquisitor,' said Tenebrus from on high. 'I will be as merciful to you as you would have been to me.' He pointed, and the shades raced towards Rostov.

Yheng advanced on him, staff out, keen to earn favour with the inquisitor's capture.

Faced with defeat, Rostov flung himself from the bridge.

'Three traitors in heavy plate are advancing west through the ring.'

'Apothecary needed in sector seven-C. Five brothers down. Gene-seed retrieval requested.'

'This is Lieutenant Banchakay of the Srinagar Fifteenth, platoon three. Requesting immediate Adeptus Astartes support. We cannot hold them. They are breaking through into the security control nexus. Repeat...'

Reports poured into Captain Areios' helm from every quarter. He coldly ordered them according to urgency, conducting a tactical triage, deciding which situations were salvageable with the resources he had to hand, and which were not. Repeated messages to Messinius failed to get through, but he trusted the lord lieutenant would find out that the mountain was compromised. The question was when. The answer dictated how many of his warriors he would lose.

There were seven known intrusions by the foe. Three were of single warriors, and had been dealt with, albeit at great cost. The other four were of multiple Terminators, and they were reaping a terrible toll on the combined Space Marine and Astra Militarum forces. The archives were burning. The main focusing apparatus had been assaulted, the defenders overwhelmed, and the machinery destroyed. A single enemy warrior armed with a heavy flamer wreaked havoc on the upper administrative floors and was still running amok. The adepts had cut the air supply to the quarter to starve the fire, but as soon as circulation was restored, the blazes would begin anew.

There was nothing he could do about that. More than half of Areios' force was fully occupied in the Hall of Utterances, close to the approach to the relay, a place of statues, scribes' desks and thin, elegant buttresses, all insubstantial as cover. The largest group of Terminators, seven in all, had materialised there around their leader, and they were beating everything Areios sent against them.

Calculations raced through his mind, the balance of foe versus friend. He could not win.

His instincts were to keep fighting. He remembered Messinius' words, that he should consider withdrawing. But for the moment the Terminators weren't advancing. They were blocking the Space Marines from getting into the Spherus Claustrum and relay core beyond. Something was happening in there. He vowed not to leave until he knew what.

Their lord was so arrogant, so sure he could not be killed, that he went helmless in that maelstrom of fire, showing a tattooed, coppery face. Eyes shone with forbidden knowledge and terrible power. Areios tasted the burnt-metal spice-smell of sorcery. Ghostly figures whirled around the foe, intercepting his warriors' weapons fire, causing bolts to spin off randomly, or detonate short of their targets.

Areios had no Librarian support. The risk from the relay had been too great. His enemies had no such qualms.

'Continue to press them. Break through to the central sphere,' he ordered into his vox, although he had said it half a dozen times before. Brother Sontis, his Techmarine, was dead in the centre of the hall, armour sparking. Brother-Apothecary Cadeuc worked tirelessly to drag casualties out of the line of fire. Bolt-rounds tore back and forth between the lines, his men in what cover they could find, the enemy standing in full view of their foes, weathering a storm of bolts so thick and relentless it was only due to the dark miracle of warpcraft they did not succumb. They fired with incredible discipline and accuracy, stepping back to reload from ammo bundles mag-locked to their comrades.

The usual support auxiliaries deployed with Terminators were absent, but these most experienced of veterans were not inconvenienced by the lack, and fought on and on. One of them carried an archaic double autocannon that put out a horrendous amount of fire. Its massive shells punched through everything in the hall, shattering furniture into splinters, sending statues crashing down into scattered puzzle pieces. Where they hit Space Marines, they broke armour, rarely killing outright, but leaving the target vulnerable to follow-up shots from bolt weapons. Their effects on the brave but hopelessly outmatched Astra Militarum troops were awful, punching through their carapace armour and blasting them into chunks of meat that flew in all directions.

They were becoming sure of success. One of the Terminators moved out of formation, isolating himself. Areios took a chance.

'Heavy Intercessors, forward. Target epsilon. Concentrated fire, bring him down! Demi-company, cover them!'

His demi-squad of Heavy Intercessors moved forward, their larger weapons standing more of a chance of penetrating the traitor's thick battleplate. Larger-calibre bolt-rounds slammed into the lone Terminator, staggering him, but their efforts attracted return fire, and they were driven back, their double-plated armour not heavy enough to stop the Terminators' combi-bolters ripping one to shreds. Areios sniped with his brothers. They were all clinging to the shallow decorative arches set into the walls. A trio of his bolt shots hit a Terminator right in the face, but ricocheted off the angled planes of his helm and burst in the air, doing no more than knocking the warrior's head to the side. Mortis rune alarms wailed in Areios' ears. One-quarter of his own warriors in the hall had perished. His warriors with heavier weapons were targeted mercilessly by the enemy. The last of the supporting Militarum fell dead.

Not one of the Terminators in the group had fallen.

His strategic displays flashed with microsecond info-bursts, graphics showing compromised armour and dropping bolt stocks. His men carried more ammunition than Terminators did, but they too needed replenishment in battle, and the few times their auxiliaries attempted to enter the hall, they were destroyed. A Space Marine who broke cover to drag in a dropped ammunition box was targeted by the fiend with the Reaper. Six rounds thumped into him, breaking his reactor unit to pieces, and punching into the man beneath.

Areios watched as ammo counts fell inexorably to zero.

The two sides ran dry almost simultaneously, as if some gloating god decided that was the moment for them to face each other, blade to blade. One by one, the guns fell silent. There was a last peal of bolt-rounds from his own men, and the outraged quiet that follows overwhelming noise fell on them all, heavy as midnight.

Their leader looked at Areios directly, the captain was sure, and extended a finger on his massive power fist.

His arrogant, tattooed face twisted into a sneer.

'Finish them,' he said.

The Terminators broke into a lumbering run, boots crashing on the stone floor louder than the death of suns.

It was then that the slaughter truly began.

The historitors fled in a state of controlled panic. The grav-sled had been loaded badly in their haste, and continually veered off to the side and banged into the ferrocrete walls, sending booming echoes down the tunnel. After a few minutes of this, Covarn ordered one of his warriors to help push it. He slung his bolt rifle over his shoulder, and grabbed the sled handle in a wide grip. They made quicker progress after that.

Beside the gleaming blue armour of the Unnumbered Sons, the thin column of historitors were a sorry sight, covered in soot, and wild-eyed. They were more used to books than battle. For some of them it was their first opposed retrieval mission, Logos jargon for combat, and they were shaken.

The tunnel was remarkably level, burned in a dead straight line by melta-cutters out from the hollow mountain's core. A pair of lumens every ten yards provided enough illumination to see by, their perfect alignment running off almost to vanishing point, where the door to the outside, small in the gloom, was situated. Slowly, it grew bigger, and Fabian dared to think they might make it.

Every hundred yards the dark hole of a ventilation shaft opened in the ceiling. As they passed under one of these, the rearguard Space Marine, Brother Meketo, stopped.

Fabian stopped too. 'What is it?'

'A quiet noise emittance, in the twenty thousand cycle range.'

'Can you scan it?'

'It is faint. I cannot get a clear lock.' The historitors were making a lot of noise, despite their efforts at stealth.

'Wait,' called Fabian. He looked up into the darkness. 'Everyone stop moving. Stop!'

The historitors wrestled the grav-sled to an awkward stop three hundred yards away from the egress. Silence fell. The chill air blowing down the shaft made Yassilli shiver. Vallia peered about nervously.

'I can hear nothing,' said Vallia. She was twenty or so feet ahead of Fabian, and her urgent whisper sounded very loud in the quiet. 'What is it?'

'A kind of hissing,' said Fabian.

Meketo panned his helm sensor ridge up. His sensorium must have picked something up, because the Space Marine's body language changed completely, and he became rigid, reminding Fabian of the hunting canids he'd seen on Devolia VI when they sighted prey. His gun came up with mechanical fluidity.

'Move,' said Meketo. He said something into his vox. His brother abandoned the sled straightaway, and came up with Covarn. 'Move now!'

Covarn looked up the shaft. He too brought his gun to bear. 'Enemy probe. Advise abandoning the sled.'

'We can't,' said Yassilli.

'She's right,' said Fabian. 'The archive is burning, this is nearly all that's left. The information in the crystals is vital to Logos efforts, the security of the surrounding sectors and an ongoing Inquisitorial investigation. We have to save it.'

'Then we will cover you while you escape. But be warned, if the probe detects us, the enemy will come, and we may not be able to protect you.'

'I understand. Get the sled moving again,' said Fabian.

'Everyone, speed now!' Yassilli said. The historitors put their shoulders to the push bar of the sled. The surviving Srinagar troopers joined them.

'Ten seconds to contact,' said Covarn.

Fabian squinted up into the dark. There was movement at the edge of the light, becoming clearer as it came closer.

A black shape was crawling head first down the shaft towards them, clad in a shifting mass of black rags. Flexible metal probes tapped over the smooth surface, then withdrew. It appeared humanoid; there was a cowled head, hands at the fore, which padded over the false stone. It could have been some sort of specialised servitor.

'What is that?' Fabian whispered.

'A bioconstruct,' said Covarn. 'A scout.'

Fabian looked closer. 'That's no cyborg. There's something wrong with it,' said Fabian. The rags were floating around like they were in water, and there was a definite sense of wrongness coming off it.

'Unknown risk factor,' said Covarn. 'Depart. We will destroy it when you are nearer to the door to avoid raising the alarm.'

'Too late,' said Meketo.

The creature raised its head, exposing a raw skull with faceted glass eyes.

'We are detected. Signal spike emanation, alarm call.'

For good measure, it shrieked.

Meketo opened fire, a four-shot burst. The aim was good but he did not hit. The construct seemed to shift without moving, appearing on the other side of the shaft as Meketo's bolts sped harmlessly by. Their rocket motors lit the shaft as they sped up, giving Fabian the briefest glimpse of a mass of more of the things creeping down towards them.

'Daemon machines,' said Meketo.

'Auspex reading suggests fifty plus approaching. Go to the others,' said Covarn.

The Space Marines opened fire together, catching the thing when it shifted again. It fell screaming down the shaft, thrashing like a speared serpent, metallic tentacles flailing. Meketo dropped down on it, pinning it to the ground with his knee, and finished it by driving his combat knife through a jewelled eye.

Black smoke roared from its gaping mouth, racing around and around, screaming until it evaporated into nothing.

Fabian was already running.

'Get that sled moving!' he shouted.

The historitors looked behind them. They were straining to keep the sled on course. The door looked further away than ever. A stream of hoots, clicks and screeches howled down the ventilation shaft. Covarn and his men fired upwards.

The things exploded from the shaft in a storm of black.

Bolter fire thundered, catching the daemon-servitors as they poured out of the pipe. They juddered in the air like bad vid-feeds. A couple crashed down and writhed, screaming. The Space Marines backed away, still firing, the three of them putting up a wall of shot even the daemon-servitors could not avoid. The third Space Marine, Sobelius, was engulfed, covered by the things, lifted from his feet as they wrapped themselves around and around his limbs, until he was completely obscured. His bolt rifle continued to flash in the mass, blasting several apart, then they ripped away, and empty armour crashed to the floor.

A few of the historitors were unslinging their weapons.

'Just run!' Fabian screamed, and he pushed.

The door was still two hundred yards away.

Chapter Forty

VRAKON EXULTANT

SHUTTER

CEASE PURSUIT

Terminators ran into battle with the Primaris Space Marines. Power fists contacted with ceramite with the noise of heavy ordnance. A Primaris warrior was lifted from his feet, and hurled upwards, spinning from the impact, limp and lifeless, his chest destroyed completely, body burning with corrosive atomic dissolution. He crashed into a wall, loose organs shaken free, and landed dead, another of the Imperium's great hopes cast down.

Areios barely registered the casualties as he moved in to attack. He threw down his bolt rifle, drawing his pistol and power sword. He dodged a blow from a Terminator, and took his revenge. His sword carved open a trench on the warrior's chest, obliterating the blasphemous sigils he wore, but one blow would not be enough. The warrior lifted his arm to cover the broken plate, and swung again, sweeping his power fist round in a wide slap. Areios dodged it. The duel could not be one of parry and riposte. If the Terminator hit him, he was dead. This was a game of avoidance, and of timing.

Areios turned his back step into a full turn, putting all his enhanced strength and the might of his armour into a blow that shattered the Terminator's elbow, and the legionary's arm swung down uselessly. With his opponent's chest exposed, Areios raised his gun, and fired into the crack in the breastplate. Bolts spanked off the armour, until one penetrated deep, exploding in his chest cavity. The warrior fell – not dead, Areios' sensorium told him, but incapacitated.

He turned to find his next target, his enhanced mind simultaneously processing the dreadful toll the enemy Terminators were taking on his men. He locked on to a Terminator embattled with two of the Sons of Guilliman, and ran at the melee.

Something hit him from the side, smashing him clean off his feet. Energy coursed through him, burning out the systems of his battleplate. The nimbus of energy around his power sword crackled out. When he tried to reignite it, smoke poured from its generatorum unit, and the dispersion nodes buzzed.

His armour alarms wailed, its machine-spirit quickly rerouting power. The strength returned to his legs, and he thrust himself up from the floor. Something had broken inside him. He tasted blood in his mouth.

The hall was on fire. The wooden furniture and tapestries on the walls were burning. Columns of smoke dipped and bowed towards the floor. Through them came the enemy leader.

Areios raised his pistol and fired every bolt it carried directly at his head.

The Dark Apostle twisted his hand. The bolts veered aside from him harmlessly, exploding on the walls and ceiling.

'Are you the best the Corpse-Emperor can do?' the warrior said. 'In all the times I have faced you, I have yet to feel anything but contempt for you vaunted new Space Marines.'

He swiped at Areios with one of his enormous gauntlets. Clawed fingers screeched through the air. Areios dodged back.

He tried to restart his sword, then again. The disruption field flared back into life.

'Ten thousand years of His so-called wisdom picked over, for this?' said the Dark Apostle. 'Warriors that think like machines. Spirit replaced by the vanity of technology. Where is the heart and the fury of the Legions of old? Where are your souls? And they call you an improvement. You should know who ends you, Primaris. I am Pridor Vrakon, Bearer of the Word. Submit yourself to me, and know the salvation of the Four.'

The warrior advanced another step, striking with the butt of his gun, then his right power fist. Areios stood his ground, ducking the swiping gun, so it passed a hair's breadth from his face. He only just caught the power fist. Rival disruption fields roared and crackled as his sword slid between Vrakon's claws, threatening to cut into the gauntlet, but the Dark Apostle twisted his wrist ever so slightly, trapping the blade between his fingers.

He stared into Areios' eye-lenses. 'You are a captain. A hero of your dying god. Never have I seen anything less deserving of the rank.' He twisted his wrist further, breaking Areios' weapon. The blade shattered. The power field burst with a dazzling blast of blue light that temporarily blinded Areios, but did not seem to affect Vrakon.

Areios shoved back, widening the gap between them. It was a desperate and ill-judged move. As the captain staggered, the Dark Apostle raked down. Fingers wreathed in disruptive power tore Areios' arm free, the smoking remnants clashing onto the ground. Areios roared at the pain.

'To think the sons of the Emperor are so weak,' Vrakon said. 'I expect a challenge from you, every time I face you, and every time I am disappointed.' He swiped again, an ursine blow, breaking open Areios' breastplate. Another blow ripped the pauldron from his ruined arm.

Areios fell to his knees. Blood poured from his chest and arm.

His shoulder was broken. Sharp bone splinters pressed into his lungs, and his breath had become a rapid, suffocating hitching. Pridor Vrakon stood over him, peering contemptuously over the rim of his armour.

'Pathetic,' he said. Then he turned about, and left Areios to die.

Fabian felt useless. He couldn't push the sled, he couldn't fight. His brain screamed at him to sprint away, leaving his fellows to the monsters racing at them. Only discipline held him in place.

'Move! Move! Move!' he shouted.

The door was a hundred yards away.

The surviving two Space Marines fired into the mass of things pouring out of the pipe. They could not miss. Daemon constructs dropped, shattered into pieces of machinery and stolen flesh. Their Neverborn essences fled with hideous shrieks. But there was an inexhaustible horde of the servitors. Each time one of the Space Marines had to reload, they got a little closer, and Fabian couldn't stop himself counting the limited number of spare magazines each one carried.

'Get this thing going! Get it going!' Yassilli was shouting. She shoved Rumagoi aside, for he had crumbled into panic and was worse than useless. 'Keep it from hitting the damn wall!'

Three of the Astra Militarum soldiers interposed themselves between the left-hand bumper and the wall, the direction the sled seemed mulishly determined to head. Swearing and shouting, they kept it from turning, though it threatened to crush them against the ferrocrete, and it steadily accelerated, until they were sprinting, and the door finally drew closer.

Meketo's bolt rifle fired its last. He tossed it aside and drew pistol and knife. Sergeant Covarn kept back the daemon things on his own a second longer, then they surged into the two Intercessors. There was shooting and the flash of bolt explosions within the mass, and the death shrieks of banished daemons, then the mass surged on.

Some of the historitors and soldiers turned back. The Srinagar sergeant took command, shoving them into a double firing line. Fabian didn't look behind, eyes only on the door beyond the sled. The crack of lasguns took the place of lost bolters, and they fired for surprisingly long, then ceased. The way the sergeant's clipped orders of 'First rank fire! Second rank fire!' became gurgling screams would haunt Fabian's dreams for months afterwards.

He could hear the daemons behind him, hissing and chittering nonsense sounds, but beneath that was a meaning almost apprehended, of pain and damnation.

He turned back, drew his own pistol and sword, preparing to sell himself dearly.

'Get to the door! Get to the door!' he cried, and fired. The racing mass of shadow swallowed the light of his gun.

He didn't see the door open. Only when his las-shots were joined by the howling glare of plasma streams did he realise they were not alone. Superheated gas blasted into the daemon constructs, tearing them to pieces. They flapped down, aflame. Freed daemons fled wailing into the warp. The raucous blast of boltguns followed.

Fabian turned and ran. Space Marines were flooding into the corridor. Hellblasters and Intercessors pushed past the sled, and were firing past him. He felt the whip of passing bolts disturbing the air. Torrents of plasma singed his skin.

He reached the warriors and, still firing, they parted enough for him to pass through.

Messinius was there at the head of his men.

'You heard,' Fabian said.

'I heard,' said Messinius. 'Our troops are moving in to secure the relay. They took us by surprise, but they will not hold here.'

'Any news from the fleet?' Fabian asked. Space Marines were unloading the sled and carrying the crates out of the corridor. There was an antechamber on the other side, with a wide gate. Through thick glass he saw an unnatural glare.

'None. The flare is reaching its peak. We will know soon enough whether we are victorious, but I do not think the battle in the void goes against us. We would be seeing bombardment by now, or more troops. Besides the force here, there have been no other reported landings.'

Fabian nodded. Messinius hustled him through the door to join the other historitors and soldiers. A trio of Aggressors passed the other way, pilot lights on their flame gauntlets burning. More Space Marines followed them. The door closed just as the Aggressors set to work, burning back the last of the servitors with promethium fires.

'Come,' said Messinius. 'I have a shielded transport waiting for you outside.' Space Marine serfs in heavy radiation gear were draping lead-weave blankets over the historitors. One was handed to Fabian. Fifteen Space Marines waited by the outer door, carrying the crates saved from the sled. Their armour was gold in the savage light from outside.

'When that door opens, you must run,' said Messinius. 'An Overlord is fifty yards from here. Once you are under its void aegis you will be safe, but do not delay. Run as fast as you can. If you fall, one of my men will retrieve you. Do not remove the blanket. Stay out of the light.'

Fabian pulled the blanket over his head. He could see nothing. Messinius guided him into position.

'Are you ready?'

'I am ready.'

The doors opened, and Fabian ran.

He could hear the scream of engines nearby, already running at lift-off power. He could see the light of the particle storm around his feet. It changed the look of the rock, as if an extreme analytical filter had been applied to a pict to bring out its features. The light was harsh, and yellow, and the atmosphere crackled with ionisation. It burned his feet. He could feel the harshness of it stinging his skin through his uniform and his boots, seeding who knew what cancers in his flesh.

He hit someone, they both stumbled, bounced off each other again. He regained his feet, and ran on. The vile touch of an active void shield crawled through his skin, and the burning stopped, though the light remained. Space Marine arms caught him. The blanket was withdrawn.

He had time to see the whole of Srinagar burning under the yellow light. The Overlord rested on a plaza of some sort, and the mountainside dropped away on the far side. Out on the plains, the great grazing beasts were clamped to the ground like limpets, waiting out the fury of their suns. Fabian could only just make them out. The void shield rippled with colourful aurorae that shifted under stellar currents, obscuring nearly everything.

'Get aboard,' the Space Marine said, and pushed him towards the port-side ramp. The starboard ramp gaped wide, and the Space Marines ran the crates carrying all the knowledge of Srinagar into the other hull, while the dazed members of the historitor mission were shoved into their seats. The exercise was done in moments, the ramps closed, and the Overlord lifted, turned, nosed into the sky, then accelerated brutally. Gravitic force pressed Fabian into his seat. He struggled to keep conscious.

He saw the glorious aurorae around Srinagar, but consciousness was hard to maintain. When he found himself in the medicae section of the *Saint Aster*, and alert enough to enquire about the progress of the battle some hours later, it was done.

* * *

Tenebrus floated upwards over the bridge to the centre of the relay. Visions flooded into him from the minds of the astropaths being consumed by his shades.

He saw pleas of help from dying worlds.

He felt the regret and misery of people drained by their toils.

He felt the pride of others that they served their god.

Fragments of messages from a lost fleet.

The rantings of a corrupted astropath on a world fallen to Chaos.

Refugees calling for assistance that would never come.

He saw a child, a man, a golden figure, a seated warlord writhing in pain.

This last was different. This was not a message or a guilty emotion. He zeroed in on it, pushing aside all the thought forms and jumbled feelings of the dying psykers. There were strata to the suffering here, horrors accreted round the grit of existence, the layers in the blackest of pearls, but as he pushed through them, he glimpsed a beach where the sun shone, bright and innocent. He saw it for what it was: true clairvoyance, not allegorical thought or a trick of the warp. As he immersed himself in the echoes of Mistress Sov's great revelation, he could feel the ocean breeze. He could smell the salt. It was a world, untouched by the warp or by the war. But where?

That, he could not discern.

There was a flash, a man, a woman, a village, and wrapped in a blanket, no idea of its importance, the child.

A stab of pain felt at several removes chased the vision away. The astropaths were failing by the dozen. He heard their death screams. He saw the pillars of their soul-light spiking from their bodies. The warp was pressing in. Each fleeing soul had so much power that the fabric of reality was eroding as they passed from one reality to the next. Danger approached.

'Time to go,' he said, and descended to Tharador Yheng's side. 'I have learned all I can here.'

'Did you find the location of the child?'

'Regrettably, I did not,' said Tenebrus. He watched his shades swarming around the sphere. How many there were, even he did not know. 'But I know more than I did. The accumulation of knowledge may seem slow, Tharador Yheng, but morsel by morsel it grows into revelation. Now, our exit.'

From under his robes, Tenebrus took out a dagger and flourished it before Yheng's face. Its form was inconstant, but it mostly seemed to favour the shape of a long, leaf-shaped blade of stone: flint or obsidian.

'A second athame?' she said in disbelief.

'Yes,' he said. 'A chip of the same blade that Kor Phaeron bears. Most of their original wielders are dead, but the knives live on.'

Another psyker died, then another.

'How long have you had that?'

'A very long time,' said Tenebrus. 'Perhaps, when we are safely home, I shall tell you how I came by it. You have seen it before, you know. How do you think we travelled from Gathalamor to the *Paracyte* when the corpse-guard came for us? I hid the knife from you then. Now, I think, it is time we shared our secrets. But first, escape.'

So saying, he cut through the fabric of time and space. He held out his hand. For once, Tharador Yheng took hold of his inhuman fingers willingly.

The shades shrieked, and drained through the rift like oil escaping a ruptured container. The psykers wailed. More and more of them were giving out, small explosions of spiritual power that tore at the materium. Things on the other side of the night were gathering.

Together, Yheng and Tenebrus stepped out of the world.

The rift closed. Moments later, the mountain began to shake.

* * *

Pridor Vrakon gutted another Space Marine. He wrenched out his power fist, watching the warrior's innards twist and blacken on his fingers. The mountain trembled. He frowned, and looked to the relay door. He no longer sensed Tenebrus. That meant either the Hand had failed, or he had gained the knowledge they both sought.

'This place is dead,' he voxed. 'The sorcerer has left. The relay is dying, we are clear for teleport. Prepare to withdraw.'

'My lord,' one of his men voxed, barely audible over the howl of the stars. *'Space Marines are entering the facility in force.'*

'We are done. Fall back!' he commanded. 'Fall back to me. Activate teleport beacons.' Corposant gathered around him. The air chilled. A Space Marine charged at him, power sword raised to strike.

'You must wait for another time, corpse-worshipper,' Pridor Vrakon said. 'You have lost this battle.'

The weapon passed through shimmering light. Thunderclaps of displaced air rippled around the facility as every Terminator, living or dead, was pulled into the warp, and thence to the *Dominant Will.*

Rostov watched the shades racing into the warp rift cut by the sorcerer, and let his shrouding fall.

He was on his back, tangled in cables that had caught him and slowed his fall. He'd miscalculated how much the warring gravity fields in the sphere would slow him. He'd expected a gentle descent with uncomfortable but survivable acceleration at the bottom, but he'd been wrong, and now both his legs were broken, and his forehead was gashed.

The cables had saved his life.

'By the grace of the Emperor,' he said.

He rolled onto his front, pushing himself free with difficulty. There was a door leading into the service tube that supported

the Pearl. Getting onto his elbows, he dragged his useless legs
behind him.

'Cheelche,' he voxed. Static from the particle storm filled his ear, a strangely regular pulse, like the beat for an unfinished song. 'Lacrante,' he tried. He crawled on. The service door beckoned. Psykers were dying all around him. It was only a matter of time before the machinery of the relay was overwhelmed, then it wouldn't matter if he made the door or not. The whole planet would be lost to daemonic incursion, but he had to try.

'Cheelche, Lacrante.' He reached the door. His fingers brushed plasteel. The door was unlocked, its access light green, but it might as well have been buried in rockcrete. The stud to open it was at chest height, an impossible distance in his state.

'Cheelche, Lacrante...'

'Leonid?' Cheelche's response was scratchy. She could have been on the far side of the sun. *'You're alive? We saw you fall. We thought you were dead!'*

'I didn't fall. I jumped,' he said. He looked back up at the stud. It was so far.

'What?'

'Listen to me. Cheelche. Get the shutter open. The psykers are dying. Reality collapse is imminent. The Neverborn are gathering. I can feel them. There will be a full-scale incursion, and we will lose this world.' He kept the pain at bay by dint of will, but he had his limits, and agony was eating through his mental discipline. 'Expose the psykers to the storm. Burn them from the relay. Do you understand?'

Static.

'Cheelche?'

'Yeah, yeah, sorry. I lost you there for a moment. Lacrante's injured. I understand. Open the shutters. Kill the psykers. I'll try. Shooting that sorcerer didn't work though.'

'I don't have any better ideas.'

'Where are you?'

'If I survive, I'm at the base of the sphere, by the supply column. I'm going to try to get inside the service tower. Find me there.'

'Try? Is it locked?'

Rostov rested his forehead on the smooth skin of the sphere. 'It's complicated. I'm injured. Just do what I say. Emperor go with you.'

There was a pause.

'Emperor go with you too, Leonid.'

He cut the feed.

The stud taunted him, just out of reach. Rostov had slain warlords, looked inside the minds of the most evil men in the galaxy, tortured innocents, condemned cities to death, and he had done all of it willingly, for the Emperor, but now it seemed that the most difficult thing he would ever be asked to do in the course of his duties was simply to stand up.

It was either that, or die.

Gritting his teeth against the coming pain, he tugged off his gloves, put his hands upon the metal, and using only the friction of his palms on the door, began to pull himself up off the ground.

Broken bones grated on each other. His left leg was not so bad, only the shin was broken there, meaning he could, with great pain, get onto his knee. His right leg, however, had snapped at the thigh. Putting any weight on that pushed him close to passing out.

His hand slapped against the door. His other hand followed. He pushed on the steel, and pulled. Amazing, how much grip the Terran hand can exert when flat and pressed down. He needed to do this two times, maybe three. It was the kind of act an uninjured man could do in a moment, without thinking; now it seemed impossible.

He lifted again, hauled again. He pulled his left knee up. Each bump on the way sent spikes of agony through him. Then, miraculously, he was upright, leaning on his left knee, his right dangling as a painful liability.

The stud was on the right of the door.

'Oh, Emperor, how you love to test me,' he said. He reached as far as he could, and swiped at the stud. He missed by the depth of a fingernail.

He bit his teeth together hard. He knew what he had to do. It was going to hurt.

He leaned a little to the right, and reached again.

His finger hit the button as his weight transferred to his broken right thigh. It collapsed immediately under him, and he screamed. Rarely had he felt pain like that. But the door opened, and he fell into the service tower as Cheelche opened fire.

He pulled himself inside. Mercifully, the door closed automatically behind him.

The surviving psykers howled like beasts. Witch-light blazed in their faces. Their bodies shook. Every few seconds, one would go off like a flare, their soul pouring out all at once, reducing their body to ash. The machines that gathered up the overflow were glowing far too brightly.

Lacrante could feel the things on the other side pressing through, and he was not psychic; that meant they were close. He leaned against the base of the tower pier. Blood ran down his back. There was a deep wound in his shoulder inflicted by one of the daemon-servitors.

Cheelche knelt next to him. They needed to be close to the door.

'As soon as that shutter opens, we're going to have to run,' she said. She squinted down the carbine at a cable holding up a counterweight that held the shutter closed. 'I really wish I had my damn long-las,' she grumbled. 'Big blocks of iron,' she said. 'We're lucky you people are so primitive.' She fired again. The plasma pulse vanished into the metal of the shutter itself. She cursed.

'If the chikanti are so smart, how come it's us that rule the galaxy?' said Lacrante. He was watching the psyker nearest to them. Her back was arched rigidly, like that was its proper shape.

'The galaxy? That's debatable. One million worlds from billions? You're a mould stain, not the supreme race.' She fired again. The plasma pulse raced away from them. 'Shit!' she said, followed by some probably much worse words in her clicking alien tongue.

'Long-las?'

'Shut up, ape boy,' she said. She breathed.

The woman in the throne nearby was changing. Her screaming mouth distended, like that of a serpent preparing to swallow its prey. Her skin ran horribly, re-forming, gathering itself into spines and whistling orifices.

'Cheelche...'

'Shut up,' she said.

'We're running out of time.' Lacrante took the unilateral decision to put a las-beam through the woman's head. As soon as she was dead he spied another psyker writhing. 'There's another one. I can't shoot them all.'

Lacrante walked painfully around the sphere interior. Even with the psy-block strapped to his head, psychic pressure emanating from the astropaths made him feel weak as jelly. Things scraped around at the back of his skull. His mouth watered uncontrollably. He reached the second psyker. The face of this one was stretched out wide and drumskin-round. Something was pushing through from the other side, all points and spines. He found himself entranced.

When red eyes rolled into being in the astropath's hollow eye
sockets, he squeezed the trigger.

He looked about. More than half the astropaths were dead, slain by psychical overload or the sorcerer's semi-daemonic constructs. The rest were writhing, and more and more were showing the signs of transfiguration.

'Cheelche!'

'I'm trying!' she shouted back.

He went to her again. 'We should leave, maybe find a control station or something, open it that way.'

'We've no time,' she said.

The mountain shook. The psykers screamed. On the far side of the sphere, one exploded in a shower of gore. Through the still-twitching remains, something was emerging.

'This... time...' said Cheelche.

She squeezed the trigger.

The plasma pulse streaked through the air, cutting the cable holding the counterweight. A huge drum wrapped with steel hawser began to turn.

'We're going,' she said.

They ran. The clattering of the shutter rolling back boomed around the chamber, chasing them into the corridor. Over it came the shrieks of astropaths succumbing to possession.

The shutter opened. Lacrante felt the light pouring into the relay as a physical blow. He screwed his eyes tight, fearful he'd go blind.

Cheelche groped behind her, hands over her eyes, until she found the door switch. The portal slammed into place.

Lacrante opened his eyes. He could hardly see.

'In the nick of time?' he said.

'Let's hope so,' said Cheelche.

'Traitor fleet is changing heading,' Second Lieutenant Semain relayed.

'Diomed?' Athagey asked.

'All of them are firing their manoeuvring thrusters. Our augury says their engine output is undiminished. They're not coming back for another pass. They're breaking from combat. We've got them on the run.'

A cheer went up. With an angry shout, Athagey silenced it.

'Quiet!' she said. 'Don't you see? If they're running now, we can't catch them. This is not like the Word Bearers to flee. Who knows what objectives they had, and what they may have achieved.'

'Shall I order pursuit?' Diomed asked.

'Flare status,' Athagey barked.

'Stellar weather front hitting in one hundred and twenty seconds,' reported Basu. 'It has already reached Srinagar Primus.'

'Quartus Delphus One and Two?'

'One is already in the weather front. Two will be hit half an hour after us.'

Athagey half stood from her chair. The twin suns were noticeably brighter. The Chaos fleet was scattered. She could bring some of the enemy to bay, but her ships were stretched out, vulnerable to counter-attack, and with their shields worn down by two hours of battle, vulnerable to the stars.

She didn't know what to do. Her pulse raced under the influence of the stimms. Her thoughts stampeded through her mind, loose and dangerous, presenting her with dozens of contradictory options. Attack, or stand down? Bloodlust warred with reason. She froze, giddy, her stomach in knots. If she had been alone, she would have staggered, intoxicated, to her throne, to let the thundering of her heart and soul calm.

She could not do that. Moments passed.

'Groupmistress?' Diomed asked. Dozens of eyes looked to Athagey for guidance.

Athagey's face contorted. There was only one viable option.

'Emperor's living corpse!' she spat. 'Order all ships to stand down pursuit. Cut power to engines. All vessels to divert full power to void shields and brace for flare impact. Close the shutters. It's over.'

The hubbub on the bridge died.

'Get on with it!' she shouted. The shutters were closing. The suns' light was getting painful. One by one, the tactical hololiths went out. Battle schema on gel screens were replaced by sheets of static. The last she saw was the Chaos vessels vanishing, impossible to see with the naked eye against the stellar glare.

'Eloise,' Diomed said urgently. Her eyes flicked from Athagey's nose to her chin and back again.

Hesitantly, Athagey raised her hand to her face and wiped. Blood stained her hand. Her nose was bleeding freely.

She tugged out a handkerchief. Her temples throbbed. Her skin was tight, her throat swelling, wanting to close up. She'd taken too much vitadandum; she had to excuse herself.

'Diomed, as soon as the storm has passed I want deep augur sweeps of the entire system,' she said, with as much authority as she could muster. 'Get a message to Quartus Delphus Two, tell them to start pursuit as soon as possible, if they can salvage anything from this mess with a couple of ship kills, I'll be grateful.' She strode out of the deck, trying not to stagger, though the deck felt insubstantial beneath her boots. 'If you need anything else, I'll be in my quarters.'

Areios' backup helmplate fizzled. Tiny, less immersive than the deep retinal systems the Mark X armour had as its primary display, it existed for use in the direst of need, and therefore possessed datasplays relating only to physical health and armour integrity.

Sluggish tracers showed a dying heartbeat. Urgent patterns of light spoke of a struggling pharmacopoeia. His armour was no better. Outline picts showed red in every plate, every system. It would not serve again.

Ferren Areios' life slipped away. Deep under his Primaris programming, he remembered a boy, fleet of foot and lively; a short life awaited him, but it might have been joyous, if not stolen for the needs of the Imperium. He had died already, he thought, he would die again, and properly now. No methalon cold awaited him, no endless tests or millennia of hypnomat nightmares.

He greeted it calmly.

Patterns changed, flickered back, changed, locked. Lights blinked green.

A massive jolt of electricity surged through Areios' body. Muscles contracted so hard that they tore. Broken bones ground on one another. Snapped teeth cut into mashed gums. His hearts pulsed quicker, then died.

A sudden dry heat ripped through him, emanating from a place in his chest, but spreading wildfire-quick, until his whole body was aflame. Nothing in his broken battleplate could reduce the pain. Nothing in his altered physiology could dampen it.

There is no agony like life.

As the Belisarian Furnace consumed him, he heard a voice from far away.

'It's the captain. He's badly injured.' The voice came close, then became quieter. 'Serfs! Here now.' A vox-click from a helm. 'Urgent medicae evacuation required, one subject, level zero, Hall of Utterances. Signal ahead and prepare the medicae facility aboard the *Saint Aster* for immediate surgery. Augmetic implants necessary. Prioritise him.' Another vox-click. 'Activate that grav-bier. Gently, now. Get him out of here, quickly.'

Hands grabbed at Areios, so many hands it seemed, until he was covered all over with painful, gripping fingers. His armour was taken from him. The plates came away with hot, angry sensations, like they were part of him torn free.

Someone worked a device into the medical port on his thigh. There was the stab of something into his flesh through the inter-face collar, a hiss that was oddly loud, and coldness spread from the port point throughout his burning body, calming the fires.

Consciousness receded. The voice spoke one last time before blackness took him.

'Inform the lord lieutenant that Ferren Areios lives.'

Chapter Forty-One

REACTOR DEATH

MORTIAN'S TRUTH

BOTHO'S CHOICE

Sonorous bells tolled warnings of imminent destruction. The vessel quaked as its boiling plasma heart went into arrest. Soon the false sun would slip its bonds, and break the Chaos ship.

'This way, it is this way!' shouted Botho, waving Lucerne up a minor corridor. 'The hangar where Mortian was sent is not far.'

The ship rumbled. Power fluctuations were causing integrity fields to fail. Without the effects of their molecular binding, the two-mile ship was becoming unstable. With each violent shudder the floors rippled. Metal rent. Mechanisms failed. A pipe broke, spewing hot gas into their path. Fires licked around displaced wall panels. They saw no more Word Bearers, and the remaining mortal crew scattered when they sighted the Space Marines. The few that held their ground died, cut down by Lucerne and Botho without them breaking their stride.

Lucerne checked the chrono running down in the corner

of his field of view. The reactor would hold another five minutes, no more, possibly less.

The gravity was fluctuating. Lucerne activated his mag-locks, and voxed that Botho should do the same. He was responsible for the boy now.

Alarms wailed. An explosion in a side room ejected a scatter of smoking metal and a burning spear of fire, intense as a blowtorch. They leapt through it, Botho batting out the flames it set on his void armour as they ran.

A crowd of mortal crew was coming towards them down the corridor. A priest led the mob, crimson-robed, a livid octed branded into his scalp. Lucerne levelled his bolt pistol.

'Leave them! They are fated to die anyway,' said Botho. 'Up here.'

Lucerne lowered his gun.

They turned left, running towards the outer hull. Another, bigger explosion shook the vessel. The deck plating squealed apart between Lucerne and Botho, revealing sparking cables beneath. Lucerne vaulted the gap.

They entered the hangar via an upper door leading onto a control gallery. Instruments for the cranes that shared the ceiling with ducts, pipes and cabling lined the side. Thick black smoke was rolling up from below, and Lucerne cycled his vision systems to better see. Botho ran ahead, ducking under a fat pipe. There was a staircase beyond, heading down the inner wall of the hangar, passing over three short landings before leading onto the flight deck. The atmospheric shielding was still operational across the launch aperture, and the hangar retained an atmosphere though its physical gates were open to the void. The stairs were made for standard humans, and bounced on their bolts under the weight of Lucerne and Botho.

There were seven landing pads in the hangar, arranged in

a staggered zigzag. Three were occupied by Thunderhawk
gunships. One of these was ablaze, and it was this that was
pouring out the black smoke. Another was covered in roaring
daemon faces. The targeting lenses of its weapons glimmered
with a fell light. When Botho ran towards it, Lucerne hauled
him back.

'Corrupt machine-spirits,' he said, shaking his head. 'We must
hope the last one is viable.'

There had been hard fighting in the hangar. The bodies of
mortal crew lay everywhere, bearing the horrific wounds of
Adeptus Astartes weapons. Many of them were tatters of meat,
blood and uniforms, unrecognisable as human beings. Botho
ran ahead, calling names. There was no answer.

Six dead Heretic Astartes lay among the dead mortals.
Lucerne ran past two whose battleplate had been shattered by
boltgun fire. A third was locked in an embrace with one of the
Black Templars, the warriors leaning on each other drunkenly.
Both of them were battered, their armour broken and bloody.
A fourth had a chainsword punched through his chestplate, and
was propped up on the length off the floor, arms dangling, his
killer dead from a plasma hit not ten feet away.

'They are dead. My brothers!' said Botho, with a mixture of
anguish and ecstasy. 'They have gone to the Emperor. May they
glory in His light. Soon, I shall join them. Praise be!'

The final gunship was ahead, ramp down. The neutral light
of machines spilled from the hatch. A tractor waited nearby,
towing claw uncoupled, a promethium tank on a trailer
behind it. From this, hoses snaked towards the Thunderhawk. Lucerne took it as a sign that the ship had been recently
refuelled.

'I do not think it is our time yet,' said Lucerne. 'Come on!'
He dragged the neophyte on.

A tremendous detonation shook the Chaos ship. Through

the pale blue glimmer of the atmospheric shielding, Lucerne saw a pillar of fire gush outwards from the hull, speckled black with broken metal. Its edges curled with the colours of venting plasma.

'This vessel will die in moments,' he said. 'We must be away.' They reached the ramp. 'On board, now.'

'Can you fly it?' Botho asked.

'I have had some training,' said Lucerne. 'Let us hope it is enough.'

He had one foot on the ramp when a commanding voice called to him from behind.

'Drop your weapon, Primaris. Do it. I have a gun trained on you. It will end your unholy life.'

'Mortian,' said Lucerne. He turned around slowly.

The Chaplain was sprawled against the side of the tractor. There was a large crater near his left armpit. The bolt had taken out the ceramite outer layer and the underweave. The flesh beneath was exposed, a raw pit. Blood ran down from his open mouth grille.

'I was waiting to see if you had survived,' Mortian said. 'You Primaris are difficult to kill.' In his fist was a plasma pistol, charge coils bright and ready to discharge. 'Put your gun down.'

'No,' said Lucerne. 'You will kill me anyway. The chances of me slaying you are slim, but it is possible. It is not possible if I put my weapon down. Why should I?'

Mortian growled. 'Step aside, Botho. Cover him.'

The neophyte stepped back down off the Thunderhawk ramp, but he did not raise his boltgun, and beneath the visor of his armour, his face was conflicted.

'No,' said Botho. He let his boltgun dangle from his fist.

'Then you damn yourself,' Mortian said.

'He sees your madness, Chaplain,' said Lucerne. 'You would

kill a loyal servant of the Emperor, for what? Why didn't you shoot me in the back?'

'Where is the honour in that?' said Mortian. 'When I die I will look the Master of Mankind in the face, and He shall find no fault in me.'

'After killing me,' said Lucerne. He shook his head. 'No. You want me to know why, that's why. You are self-righteous. You want me to know why you are going to kill me.'

Mortian growled out a laugh. 'I owe you that, at the least.'

The ship shuddered. Another plume of gas erupted from the side, washing the hangar with colourful fires.

'Then be quick. The reactor of this vessel will detonate in one minute. You do not have much time to deliver your sermon.'

Mortian shifted his weight. He was in a great deal of pain.

'Nothing to say?' Lucerne said. 'Then I will tell you. You killed the men who came to help you. You slaughtered them in cold blood, but not before killing your own Marshal Angevin. I saw the blast patterns on his armour. You did it.'

Mortian grunted. 'We all did. We took a vote.'

'Why?' said Lucerne. 'Had you taken the reinforcements as intended, you would still be alive. You could have served the Emperor whom you love and honour for hundreds more years.'

'Because you are impure!' Mortian snarled. 'You do not deserve to fight alongside us. We are the work of the holy God-Emperor of Terra, you are the work of Belisarius Cawl. You are unclean.'

'Our creation was ordered by the Avenging Son himself. Roboute Guilliman asked Cawl to make us. He is the son of the Emperor.'

'He is an apostate, an unbeliever. For the moment he fights for mankind, but how long will it be until the call of the Throne of Terra overwhelms him, and he follows his brother Horus into treachery?'

'There was a Custodian with the torchbearers sent to help you. Did you murder him as well?' said Lucerne.

'He chose his side. He, like Angevin, refused to listen to reason. He paid for his betrayal of the Emperor's vision with his life, though he nearly broke our crusade before he fell.'

'You are insane. You have led this crusade to destruction.'

The ship shook terminally.

'Better to live purely than allow the Emperor's holy work to be polluted,' said Mortian. 'We shall see in a few moments who is right and who is wrong, when we stand before the Emperor Himself. I shall be elevated to His undying legions for all eternity, while you are cast into the seething pits of the warp for the blasphemy of your existence. I tell you this because you fought well, and only that.' Blood dribbled down his front.

Klaxons were screaming from everywhere. The counter in Lucerne's helm was running down to zero. A series of violent expulsions from the reactor culminated in a detonation that tore a wide portion of the ship free. It raced away from the craft in a shimmering cloud. The deck swayed, the weakened Mortian's aim wavered, and the plasma pistol went off, firing wide. Lucerne made his move.

He opened fire at Mortian with his bolt pistol, but the Chaplain rolled aside, and his bolts punched holes into the cowling of the tractor. The hangar deck buckled, pushed up into a pressure ridge that sent Lucerne, Botho and Mortian off balance. Lucerne recovered first, running at the Chaplain with his chainsword whirring. Mortian rose up awkwardly, and met him with his crozius, the field flaring into life around the head as he swung, evading Lucerne's parry to smash him in the chest, breaking his breastplate. The Primaris Marine was hurled back by the impact, into the side of the Thunderhawk. Alarms squalled in his helm. Sealants bubbled out of cavities in the broken underlayers of his battleplate, but the void sealing was compromised.

Mortian staggered towards him, fresh blood leaking from the crater wound in his chest. He dragged his crozius along the floor, drawing the sparks and flashes of dying matter from the metal.

'I will be glad that my last act is ending you, blasphemy.'

With a cry half of triumph and half of pain, Mortian swung his crozius arcanum up from the ground, and raised it over his head.

'In the name of the undying Emperor of Mankind, I end you, abomination of Mars!'

A gun barked. Mortian jerked. The flaring end of a bolt-round burned in his wound.

The crozius fell from his hand with a clatter. He looked up from the hit.

'Botho...' he said. The bolt's mass trigger tripped, the munition exploded, and Mortian collapsed to his knees. Breath wheezing, he looked at Lucerne, hatred blackening his final words.

'You shall never... be one... of us,' he said, and toppled forward.

The neophyte came to Lucerne's side, and took the Primaris Marine's arm.

'You killed him,' said Lucerne.

'Too late,' said Botho. 'For too long I did nothing.' Lucerne got unsteadily up, and leaned upon the neophyte. 'I was a coward. I let them slaughter my brothers. Those that voted against Mortian's course of action were killed.'

'So you voted for this madness?' said Lucerne.

'I am a neophyte. I was not permitted. I did not agree, but said nothing, to my eternal shame.'

The ship leaned. The grav-plating on the flight deck was failing.

'Your shame can be expunged through penance, brother. The

Emperor has a plan for you. Get aboard,' said Lucerne. He limped free of Botho's support, up the ramp.

'Wait.' Botho picked up Mortian's crozius. 'This should be returned to a Chapter holdfast so that a more righteous man might wield it.'

Together, they boarded the traitor gunship. Lucerne hit the closure button as they passed, and the ramp lifted, sealing the hull with a hiss. Botho helped him into the cockpit. Lucerne raced through the activation sequence, bringing the engines up to flight power without pre-firing them, and skipping many other safety protocols. Bits of the hangar's infrastructure were falling from the ceiling, crashing down onto the ships. A length of girder clattered from the Thunderhawk's prow.

The chrono counter in Lucerne's helm was glaring an angry red. Four zeroes in sequence.

'Hold on, neophyte,' said Lucerne. 'This will not be easy.'

Lucerne throttled the engines up. The landing claws released, and the vessel rose. The hangar's atmospheric field flickered out, sucking out all the air into space in one exhalation. The fires burning in the wrecked Thunderhawk went out. Bits of wreckage tumbled into space, bouncing off their vessel.

Shouting prayers to the Emperor, Lucerne turned the Thunderhawk about, and accelerated away from the ship into the fury of the wider battle. Lance beams flashed around him. Explosions sparkled off towards the system's prime world where capital ships exchanged parting shots. If spotted out there they would not last long, but he had a more pressing concern.

The Thunderhawk's augurs read a steep climb in energy emissions from the Word Bearers cruiser. The explosion followed a moment later, the reactor's death obliterating the vessel and leaving a rapidly expanding ball of fire in its place. Lucerne pushed the ship to its maximum speed, but its acceleration could not hope to outpace the superheated gas chasing them, and it caught them, rolling them around. He and Botho were thrown about in their restraints. Machine-spirits wailed, then the wavefront was past, the fury of the explosion dissipating into a glowing nimbus that slowly faded into the black.

Lucerne righted the Thunderhawk, and aimed it away from the battlesphere.

'The Emperor protects,' he said.

THRONE OF LIGHT

Chapter Forty-Two

DINNER AND AN INTERVIEW

STAR CHILD

SECRETS SHARED

Once again, Fabian was roused from his slumber by someone pounding on his door with the subtlety of a siege drill. He rolled over, feeling muzzy from a late night, wincing as he rolled on his bruised ribcage, forgotten until too late, eliciting a stream of blasphemy.

'Emperor alive,' he groaned. 'Why does nobody ever want me urgently late in the afternoon?'

He swung his legs out of bed. There were slippers there.

'For my feet,' he said dully. He was not very good after waking.

The knocking resumed.

'I am coming!' he yelled.

'They can't hear you, you realise that? I thought the returned primarch only recruited the brightest of minds for his Logos.'

Fabian looked over his shoulder. Finnula Diomed lay under the rumpled bedclothes, her hair flopped messily over her face.

'I'm not sure about that. I think we were chosen because of our attitude, rather than our aptitude.'

'You can handle semantics in the morning, but not waking?'

The hammering on the door recommenced.

'Throne!' said Fabian.

Diomed rolled over. 'There's a vox-comm right on the table by the bed. Try that.'

Fabian flailed about so much trying to press it he would have knocked over the lamp if it hadn't been screwed into place. He clicked the button.

'I'm coming!' he shouted. He stood. 'Aren't you rising?'

'No,' she said. 'I'm on mid-watch duty today, so I'm staying here.' She burrowed into the covers.

'But this is my room!' he said.

'Yeah, well,' she said. 'It's my ship.'

Fabian had no reply to that. The banging continued.

He got dressed on the way to the door, but was not looking his best when he opened the slide-portal. When he found who was on the other side his frown turned to a smile.

'Racej!' he said. 'I was beginning to think you were not coming back.'

'The primarch's orders stand. You are my ward. I shall not desert you.' Lucerne sniffed the air and looked over Fabian's head. 'You are not alone in there. Who is with you?'

'Never mind. Diomed. We had dinner. I interviewed her for the record.'

Lucerne raised an eyebrow.

'Is it time to go?' Fabian said.

Lucerne nodded. 'The fleet is moving on to Vhospis. We will leave them here, and tread our own path. Warp conditions are favourable for transit to the galactic north. But we have a few hours left before the *Interlocutor* is ready to sail, and there is an inquisitor that wants to see you.'

'Rostov?'

'That is his name. Groupmistress Athagey wishes to speak with you also.'

'Right. Then I'd better put my uniform on.'

'I would say that is an excellent idea, Fabian.' Lucerne stepped aside, revealing a youth standing behind him. He had been completely hidden by the Primaris, but he was still much bigger than Fabian: a young Space Marine. 'This is Neophyte Botho. He is also accompanying us.'

'To Vigilus?'

'To Athagey,' said Lucerne.

The youth wore a puzzled expression.

'This is Fabian Guelphrain, the historitor I told you about,' said Lucerne.

The youth bowed his head and saluted, arms crossed in a formal aquila. 'It is a pleasure to meet you, my lord.'

'Oh, I think the pleasure was all his,' said Lucerne.

Fabian raised his hands. 'Racej, will you...'

'What?' he said.

'Just,' Fabian clenched his hands. 'Give me fifteen minutes.'

'You can have seven.'

'Fine,' said Fabian. 'Seven.' And he shut the door in Lucerne's face.

Athagey was waiting for them in her ready room. She had a drink beside her, as usual, and was peeling an apple with a paring knife with exaggerated care, for she was once again jittery with stimms. Fabian had expected the woeful Athagey: though the battle was a victory, with several enemy vessels claimed, it was far from her usual dramatic triumphs. But aside from the side effects of the stimulant, she was in good humour, and when she smiled at him in that particular way, Fabian, with sinking heart, easily guessed why.

'What have you done with my first lieutenant, historitor?'

Fabian felt his face go bright red.

'Nothing,' he said too quickly.

'He has interviewed the lieutenant,' said Lucerne. 'For the record.'

'Oh, I see,' said Athagey, giving him the sort of smile that made him want to dissolve.

'Over dinner,' said Lucerne, not very helpfully.

'Yes, alright, Racej, that's enough, thank you.'

Lucerne looked at him. With half his face obscured by the rim of his pauldron, Fabian could not tell if he was smirking or not.

'I am merely furnishing the groupmistress with the information she requested, historitor.'

'Thank you, brother-sergeant, I am asking the questions,' said Athagey. 'Now, Historitor Majoris Guelphrain, did Finnula furnish you with the information you requested?' She cut a slice from the fruit and popped it into her mouth, smiling widely around it.

If the floor had grown teeth and swallowed him whole, Fabian would have been happy.

'Yes, thank you. I have a full history of your campaigns and victories. It will make a fine addition to our histories of the crusade,' he said, hoping in vain to deflect Athagey's attention with flattery.

'I shall quiz her on your interview technique later,' said Athagey. She sniffed. She cut another slice of apple, and thankfully seemed to grow bored with teasing him. 'You are moving on. Brother Lucerne has informed me.' She pushed a flimsy across the table with a finger, leaving a smear of clear juice upon it. 'I note that you have done a remarkable job in spreading the Logos throughout the groups under my command. Roboute Guilliman will be so proud.'

Fabian composed himself before speaking. 'They will not

trouble you. In time, you may find them an asset. We are not
here to judge or to constrain. There are dozens of other Adepta,
departmenta and divisio with that remit. We are here to help, to
find the truth, to attend to strategic objectives that you, while
dealing with the larger problems of the crusade, might not have
time to address.'

She sniffed, flung one booted foot upon her knee and leaned
back in her chair. 'We shall see. At least this woman you're leaving in charge here knows the void. Rogue trader. Proper sort.
Her selection would have been deliberate, yes?'

'It might have been,' said Fabian. 'But not solely for reasons
of flattering you. Yassilli Sulymanya is the most talented and
bravest historitor I have trained.'

'Fine,' said Athagey. 'But if she annoys me, I'll lock the whole
lot of them up in one of the holds. Clear?'

'You and Yassilli will get on famously, I am sure.'

'Right. Now, what about this fellow. Who's he?'

'This is Neophyte Botho,' said Lucerne. 'The last surviving
member of the Angevin Crusade. He will be joining the Primaris
reinforcements we brought with us when the *Cantatum Bellum*
rejoins the fleet. They will then submit themselves to Lord Lieutenant Messinius' direction.'

'That's nice,' said Athagey. 'And do we have a reason why this
has not happened before?'

'A matter of honour,' said Lucerne. 'They fought bravely, and
died well for our Emperor. There is no more to it than that.'

'I see,' said Athagey, who obviously did not believe that was
the whole story. 'You will not join them?'

'I will adopt their colours. I am a Black Templar now, but my
duty lies with Fabian beyond the Nachmund Gauntlet.'

'Well,' said Athagey. 'That is a perilous road, and I wish you
luck.'

The door machine-spirit gave out a clarion.

'Inquisitor Leonid Rostov,' it announced.

'Let him in.' She looked at the neophyte. 'I don't think this is for your ears, my boy,' she said.

Botho took the dismissal well, rose, and bowed. 'The Emperor protects,' he said. 'I look forward to fighting beside you, madame groupmistress.'

The door rolled open. Botho left. Rostov entered the room slowly. He leaned heavily on a black cane topped with an eagle's head, and motorised callipers helped him walk. His red-skinned face bore a thick scar, obvious and white from machine-induced healing. He seemed no weaker for his wounds. The air of authority he carried about him smothered all levity. Fabian once again felt a thrill of fear at his presence. The more detached part of his intellect thought it a strong reaction to someone who was just a man. The rest of him wanted Rostov to go away.

'Please,' Athagey said. 'Sit.'

Rostov took a seat by the groupmistress. It took him time, and he struggled with his legs. He seemed an entirely joyless person, bereft of frivolity, as plain and serious in purpose as the cornerstone of a mortuary, but when Athagey offered him a drink, he accepted, and the way he tasted the spirits on his lips suggested some enjoyment.

'Gentlemen, lady,' he said. 'I apologise for summoning you here. We all have duties to attend to. I promise not to detain you any longer than is strictly necessary, but alas, it is necessary.' He turned the glass precisely one quarter turn, then back again. 'I have two matters to broach with you. The first is the Hand of Abaddon. Tell me, what do you know of him?'

Fabian looked at Lucerne. As was his habit when he thought Fabian should do all the talking, Lucerne was looking at the wall.

'You may answer freely, you need not be afraid.'

'Did you just read my mind?'

Rostov nodded.

'I thought you said that you had only limited ranged ability as a telepath,' said Fabian.

'I did say that. And it was true.' He took in a considered breath, and held it uncommonly long before breathing out. 'I will be honest with you all. This is not my usual line of work. I am of the Ordo Xenos. All my career as an inquisitor, all my time serving my mentor as his interrogator, practically my entire life, has been in the pursuit of malign alien influence. Ancient technologies, malevolent beings hiding in our societies, unwanted interference from other species – these are the matters I was trained to deal with.' He picked up his drink. 'But something is happening, right now. I have felt it. I have seen it. The eternal war against the warp, and a glimpse of how things could be. There is an awakening of sorts underway. So you are right, historitor,' Rostov said, pointing a finger around his glass at Fabian. 'I did say my telepathic ability is limited to contact. I did not lie. And yet I can see what you are thinking now with little difficulty. A few months ago, I could not do this, and that is most troubling.' He drained his glass, and gestured to Athagey with it to be refilled.

'A man after my own heart,' she said, and filled it very full.

Rostov took a large mouthful.

'I am changing. The universe is changing. There are forces moving here that defy mortal comprehension. My abilities are getting stronger. I am not the only one. There are people out there, right now, who have never so much as evinced the merest flash of psychic talent who find themselves sudden witches. The number of recorded psykers is going up across the Imperium, more so in the sectors bordering the Rift. The abilities of psykers like myself are growing. And yet these matters are the remit of the Ordo Malleus and the Ordo Hereticus. Now I ask myself, should I step back, and return to my border wars and my fight in the dark places against the vermin that would usurp our worlds? Or is this more important? Is there something happening that is more important than anything?'

His voice changed, becoming sharper.

'Fabian Guelphrain. I understand that your historitors have made great strides in cataloguing the data-logs of the relay.'

How he knew that, Fabian did not know. He could have guessed, he could have intuited it with his powers, but he said it with such certainty it was obvious he just knew, for a fact. That suggested informants somewhere. Fabian was not surprised.

'We have.'

'And you have noticed a pattern?'

'We have.'

'Will you share with us what that pattern is?'

Fabian cleared his throat. Even he could not deny a direct request from an inquisitor.

'It was as Adept Rumagoi said. A sense of immanence. A sense of overwhelming power. There are multiple references to a winged figure seated on a throne. That figure stands. I'm no expert in the warp but I can take a guess at what that might mean.'

'I have seen this too. At the end there, when the choir began to speak as one. They said, "He is coming."'

'Is it...' said Fabian. His mouth was inexplicably dry. He could not bring himself to voice the thought. 'Is it Him?'

'That is the question, is it not?' Rostov shifted decisively in his chair, leaning in, the action of a man who has taken an important decision. 'I will tell you something few people know. Some time ago, there was a notable action undertaken by a pair of inquisitors named Alexio and Fortez, a successful endeavour. Despite the fact that the pair of them had diametrically opposing views on many matters of philosophy, they deemed this particular threat so great they combined forces.

'The target of this action was a group named the Cult of the Star Child. There was fanciful talk among this cult that the Star Child was some kind of benevolent entity that would lead mankind to salvation, perhaps an expression of the Emperor, god made flesh again. It was all lies, and the cult was rooted out, and destroyed at a gathering on Levilnor IV with the aid of the Salamanders Chapter of the Adeptus Astartes. However, four of their leaders escaped.'

'Why are you telling me this?'

'Because I wonder if this evil is seeping back into the universe.' Rostov turned his glass around in his gloved hands. 'Belief is a very dangerous thing.' He leaned forward a little further, and Fabian thought he seemed old beyond his years. 'Now the other matter. The Hand of Abaddon.'

'I know the name.'

'I am aware, but explain to me what you know. I want to hear it from your lips.'

'While we were on Gathalamor some of the prisoners taken from among the cultists spoke of the Hand of Abaddon,' said Fabian. 'Fellows of yours, other inquisitors, they found all this out. I am sure they would be better able to help you.'

'Maybe,' he said. 'But you are here and I am asking you.'

'The Hand opposed the primarch on Gathalamor. There was some kind of weapon, very powerful, warp-powered. It took out a whole battle group, more or less.'

'A mutant, yes?'

'Yes,' said Fabian. 'A sorcerer. An evil witch. Some said his name was Tenebrus. There was another there, Kar-Gatharr, they said, a Word Bearer. He was slain in combat with the Adeptus Custodes. Some of the prisoners named him as the Hand instead.'

Rostov drank more of his drink.

'It was not the Heretic Astartes who was the Hand, but this

Tenebrus, I think. I saw him in the relay, on Srinagar. There is some connection between this child and he, and the relay. I am certain that is why this system was attacked in the first place. But there is a problem. I have been chasing the Hand of Abaddon since the Battle of Machorta Sound.'

He reached inside his jacket and pulled out a rolled-up pict, and smoothed it out in front of Fabian. It was grainy, and captured at an odd angle, but clearly showed two figures: a mutant of hideous aspect, and a human female.

'Is this Tenebrus? Is this the Hand of Abaddon?'

Fabian examined it closely, then nodded. 'Going from the descriptions I had on Gathalamor, yes, it is.'

'I see.' He sipped his drink. 'I stated his title to him. He admitted it himself. We must therefore assume that he is the Hand.'

'You sound displeased,' said Fabian. 'This is a breakthrough, surely? Forgive me, I am not an inquisitor, but if one of my investigations were progressing as well as that, I would be happy. Even though it has not reached its conclusion, you are closer to the end, and the destruction of this enemy of the Emperor.'

Rostov nodded. 'That would be so,' he said. 'Only, after the Battle of Machorta Sound, I interrogated one of the Word Bearers priests. Delving into his mind was a dark and damaging exercise, but in his memory I was able to see the Hand. The man I saw matched descriptions collated by my master, Inquisitor Dyre, before his death, though we did not have the title then.'

'Then what is the problem?' said Fabian.

Rostov tapped the pict. 'The Hand of Abaddon my master was following, the person I saw in the mind of the priest?' He shook his head. 'It was not this man.'

'Master?' Tharador Yheng spoke quietly. The shades were restive, dangerous. It would take them days to calm down after their excitement. Her words, said so quietly, set them rattling. She gripped the tray she carried more tightly.

'Master?'

Tenebrus sat in meditation, eyes closed, long-fingered hands clasped over his chest. He looked more inhuman than ever, his relaxed face closer to that of a carcharodon than a man. His skin was grey-white, face strangely round; his lips had all but disappeared, leaving his mouth a slit. His nose was receding, she noticed. He was changing, engaged in the race that all sorcerers must complete, outrunning mutation that would strip them of humanity to attain their goal of power. His wound was still raw. Seepage glued his robe to his side, and there was no certainty that when he healed the gift of Tzeentch would not return. She felt a stirring of pity for him.

'Master,' she said a little more loudly. 'I have brought you refreshment.'

She put the tray down. There was a ewer of wine and a goblet, and a thick steak carved from the leg of a slave bred and fattened for the slaughter. Tenebrus' appetite for human flesh had become so acute it required its own logistics to feed.

'Master,' she said again, and dared to reach out to touch his shoulder. The shades did not like that, and they hissed warningly.

Tenebrus' head rolled towards her. His eyes opened a slit, showing starkly black in his pallid face.

'Tharador Yheng,' he said. 'For what reason do you disturb my meditations?'

'You must eat, master, for your wound to heal.'

'Must I?' he said. He looked at the meat and the wine, then unfolded himself, and reached for the goblet. 'You are very solicitous,' he said. 'Yet I feel I have rewarded you many times over for the little loyalty you have shown me.'

'I do not understand, master.'

'I have revealed most of my secrets.' He smiled sharp teeth

at her. 'It is time you repaid the favour. You must choose your path, now.'

He was on his feet serpent-swift, taking her by surprise, arm shooting out, clawed hand held before him. A great force clamped hold of Tharador Yheng's throat and flung her backwards. She squirmed in the invisible grip of sorcery, trying to free herself before she was slammed into the wall crawling with shades behind her, but they hissed, and moved aside.

Tenebrus walked towards her, still limping, his wound bleeding again, but his power was undiminished.

'You were sent to me by Kar-Gatharr to spy,' he said. 'I have known it since the start of our association.' He waved a hand, and in the air an image appeared, wavering as if projected on a wall of boiling smoke: she and Kar-Gatharr in their final communion years ago. 'When Kar-Gatharr first brought you to my chamber upon Gathalamor, I saw potential in you.' His hideous smile widened. 'You truly are blessed by the gods. But the gods can be cruel, and they set us against each other. He tried to induct you into his faith. The question is, how far did he succeed?' He moved his fingers closer together, causing the pressure on Yheng's neck to grow. 'I have told you that the only useful service a person can accomplish in this universe of ours is to themselves. So I ask you, Tharador Yheng, whom do you serve? My plans enter a dangerous phase. I cannot have an acolyte who will whisper every word I say into Kor Phaeron's ear. Answer truthfully. I will know if you lie.' His voice had acquired a fiend's growl.

She struggled to speak, her hands clawing at the unseen fingers around her neck.

'I serve myself!' she croaked. 'None but myself! I always have. I always will. I would kill you if it would make me more powerful. I care nothing for anything, or anyone.'

'Why do you seek power?'

'I...' she choked. 'I... will be... no... man's... slave! I wish to be free!'

'I see,' he said. He opened his fingers wide. She fell down hard to the floor, cutting her knees on the deck plates, where she knelt, heaving for breath.

He hobbled over to her, and got down beside her. He put a finger under her chin and lifted it, until she was looking deep into his black eyes. His breath made the chains on her cheeks swing.

'Poor Kar-Gatharr would be most disappointed. You have strayed far from his path.'

Yheng forced words out of her raw throat. 'I learned what I could from him, but already by the time the primarch's armies came to Gathalamor I could see the limitations of what he taught me. It is the nature of all tutelaries to see their motivations in the hearts of their students, whether they are there or not. I would have discarded him if he had not died.'

'There's a warning for me there, I suppose,' he said.

'I have served you faithfully since then,' she said. 'Why doubt me?'

'Because that is not true. Since I plucked you from the surface of the cardinal world, you have looked both ways,' he said. 'You have been considering betraying me to Kor Phaeron, and following Kar-Gatharr's wishes.'

'But I did not, and I will not.'

'No,' said Tenebrus. He released her face and stood. 'So now you will follow me, until my purpose is outlived, or you find a better teacher?'

She looked up at him. Blood ran from several of her piercings.

'I will do whatever it takes to ensure I remain free,' she said. 'One day I may kill you. I shall not lie. But you have much to teach me.'

He nodded approvingly. 'It is unhealthy to have competition

from those closest to you, but in truth my life has been long, I enjoy your company, and you have such potential. So let us keep our arrangement as before, if you can swear your loyalty to me, until such time as you need me no longer.'

'I swear,' she said, and bowed her head in supplication.

'Well then, until the day we must kill one another,' he said. 'It is time to begin the next stage of your education. Where shall I start?'

'Wherever you wish, master.' Yheng's eyes gleamed.

'What do you want to know, Tharador Yheng? The origins of the knife I carry? The changes that I have undergone? The nature of my power?'

With a tinkle of fine chain, she got to her feet. 'Teach me it all. I want to know everything, master.'

Tenebrus smiled his wide, wide smile.

'Then so you shall, my acolyte, so you shall.'

Appendix: Notes on the Crusade

As the last loyal primarch, Roboute Guilliman, returned to Terra after his rebirth, the traitor Kor Phaeron was already preparing for war, constructing a grand strategy to destroy faith in the Emperor and disrupt the supply of psykers to the Golden Throne. After its beginnings at Talledus, the unfolding War of Faith was to prove one of the most serious threats to the early crusade.

ATTACK ON TALLEDUS

Even before the Cicatrix Maledictum tore across the sky, the missionaries of the Word Bearers were at work within the Segmentum Solar, appealing to the downtrodden masses with promises of individual power and freedom most citizens could only dream of. Slowly, surely, these agents implemented Kor Phaeron's plans against the Imperium. Primarily targeting the shrine and cardinal worlds administered by the Adeptus

Ministorum, the Word Bearers seeded heretic cults throughout the segmentum, their efforts increasing when the Rift opened. Then they waited, watching while Guilliman returned to aggressively reorganise the Imperium's government, then begin to gather the Indomitus Crusade. They bided their time as Guilliman departed Terra, not acting until he was fully invested with the retaking of Gathalamor, until, a little over a year since the Great Rift had opened by local reckoning, Kor Phaeron struck.

The Dark Cardinal launched his war in the Talledus System, Tertius Sector, Segmentum Solar. Talledus was a rich prize, boasting a number of sacred worlds administered from the capital planet of Benediction. Talledus provided an important source of income for the Adeptus Ministorum, with Benediction being one of the most influential Ecclesiarchical worlds in the whole Segmentum Solar. But disruption of the Imperial Church's income was not the Dark Cardinal's goal. He was concerned with the currency of souls, seeking to undermine the Emperor by depriving Him of His worshippers, while increasing the power of his own gods. Capitalising on the brutal repression of divergent Imperial sects within the system, Word Bearers priests founded numerous cults, who erupted into rebellion as soon as the signal was given.

Forces of the Word Bearers, Night Lords and Iron Warriors invaded. Initially they were opposed by the Adepta Sororitas. Talledus played host to several Orders, but many more were summoned by visions to the system's aid. Also present were numerous Astra Militarum regiments both native to Talledus and from elsewhere, while a mixed force of Cadians, Salamanders, Black Templars and White Scars later arrived with Battlefleet Pharas.

On Benediction, the Word Bearers attempted a mass conversion of the populace, but miraculous happenings opposed Kor Phaeron's warp horrors, and strengthened Imperial faith.

Soon after, Captain Mir'san of the Salamanders arrived with a company of his warriors, already blessed with Primaris tech. The warp was thrown into tumult as Word Bearers rituals summoned daemonic hordes, only for them to be cast back by the miraculous rising of the blessed dead from the grave.

Out in the Tears of the Emperor asteroid belt, Night Lords using blasphemous psychic technology to lure Imperial ships to their doom were hunted down by Vanguard Space Marines of the White Scars.

More successfully, the Iron Warriors attacked the world of Ghreddask. The sons of Perturabo deployed the *Scarax Krond*, a Soul Harvester, a gargantuan drop-fortress housing daemon engine manufactoria. As soon as it landed, the *Scarax Krond* began creating armies of daemon engines, which spread out across the world. Knight House Mortan opposed the landing, but the Soul Harvester was protected by the fallen houses of Khomentis and Vrachul, and Mortan suffered badly at their hands. Castellan Dramos of the Black Templars Rutherian Crusade was later to make planetfall on Ghreddask, and attack the *Scarax Krond*; however, he was unsuccessful in his attempt to destroy it, and was slain in the process.

HUNT FOR THE BLACK SHIPS

Kor Phaeron left the ongoing war at Talledus, heading out to orchestrate further uprisings and attacks across the Segmentum Solar, almost always on worlds holy to the Imperium. For the second part of his strategy he unleashed specially assembled hunter fleets of his Legion. Provided with the most capable Navigators, guided by the fell sorceries of the Powers, these small, fast armadas sought out the Black Ships while they were in the warp. Already the Imperial Tithe had been seriously compromised, leading to a disruption of the delivery of psykers to fuel the Golden Throne and a build-up of psychic individuals that certain worlds struggled to contain.

In order to re-establish supply lines, the Adeptus Astra Telepathica had gathered its Black Ships into the 'Flights of Crows' that followed the battle groups of the crusade fleets, descending in carrion flocks to strip reconquered worlds of witches. Elsewhere, the usual smaller groupings were formed into larger fleets to offer protection. However, large parts of the Segmentum Solar were regarded as less dangerous than elsewhere, so the Black Ships often had their escorts reduced to support vessels heading into more deadly territory, leaving them vulnerable to the predations of Kor Phaeron's Word Bearers.

THE PSYCHIC AWAKENING

Wherever they operated, the Black Ships had a daunting task ahead of them. The Great Rift was spilling the stuff of the raw warp into the galaxy at an unprecedented rate, driving the slow evolution of humanity forward. Although the effect was most pronounced in those systems closest to the Rift and other immaterium-materium interfaces, there was a sudden increase in the number of psykers being born right across the Imperium. The true magnitude of their emergence would not be felt for a couple of decades, as newborn humans matured and came into their power, but right from the start, numbers of recorded witches climbed steeply as people with little or no prior psychic ability found themselves developing uncanny powers, while those already possessing these talents began to experience increases in the range and potency of their skills.

The results ranged from the merely disruptive to the catastrophic. Even worlds little affected by the war found themselves struggling to contain their psychic populations. The worst cases led to daemonic incursions, plagues of non-daemonic warp entities such as enslavers, and the subjugation of worlds by psykers whose abilities exceeded all measurements of the Imperial Assignment. The enemies of the Imperium were quick to use these 'Wild Talents' in their armies and insurrections. When faced with persecution and death, most witches had little choice but to throw in their lot with the forces of Chaos.

THE STAR CHILD

The greatest consequence of this psychic tumult was to occur at the heart of the Imperium itself. Certain sects within the Ecclesiarchy began to preach that the Emperor was stirring, and their belief had some evidence to support it. As black as those days were, miracles abounded. On Talledus, the ghosts of the dead rose up. Imperial saints came to the aid of beleaguered armies. Readings of the Imperial Tarot made the difference between disaster and triumph, while reports of the mysterious Legion of the Damned became ever more frequent. Wherever Guilliman went, the warp storms stilled, allowing his armies to make rapid headway.

A number of strange coincidences and odd phenomena reached the primarch's ears. He discounted them at first, but as time went on, he was unable to do so, and became disquieted. All across the Imperium were people who claimed to have been visited or guided by the Emperor. Many of these were burned as heretics, but in other cases their words and presence provided succour to the desperate, and encouraged those who had no hope of salvation from other quarters to fight back against mankind's enemies.

A few years after the crusade began, visions of a golden infant interspersed with those of a blindingly radiant being rising from a throne began to be reported across the astropathic network. Beginning in the Segmentum Solar, and confined at first to background noise, the sort of low-grade psychic interference churned up by the currents of the warp, these visions became clearer, and spread. Though their import was hotly debated, certain seers both loyal and traitor interpreted the visions as a possible sign of direct action by the God-Emperor, leading to a great outpouring of faith on the Imperial side that was matched only by the enemy's dismay.

Among the most heretical interpretations were parallels made with the insidious belief in the 'Star Child', promulgated by a cult which had been destroyed some years before the Great Rift opened. The news of these visions was to cause great upheaval within the Imperium, as many of the mighty suspected them to be a trick of the enemy, while others insisted they were of divine origin. The factional nature of Imperial politics was complicated further as ideological lines were drawn, sometimes to be defended with violence. Still others, more learned than most, and not all of them human, were deeply troubled by these supposed miracles.

As a result, certain esoteric orders on both sides were spurred into action, desperate to learn the truth and exploit it before their enemies could, whatever that truth might be...

ABOUT THE AUTHOR

Guy Haley is the author of the Siege of Terra novel
The Lost and the Damned, as well as the Horus
Heresy novels *Titandeath*, *Wolfsbane* and *Pharos*,
and the Primarchs novels *Konrad Curze: The Night
Haunter*, *Corax: Lord of Shadows* and *Perturabo:
The Hammer of Olympia*. He has also written many
Warhammer 40,000 novels, including the first book
in the Dawn of Fire series, *Avenging Son*, as well as
Belisarius Cawl: The Great Work, the Dark Imperium
trilogy, *The Devastation of Baal, Dante, Darkness in
the Blood* and *Astorath: Angel of Mercy*. He has also
written stories set in the Age of Sigmar, included
in *War Storm*, *Ghal Maraz* and *Call of Archaon*. He
lives in Yorkshire with his wife and son.

YOUR NEXT READ

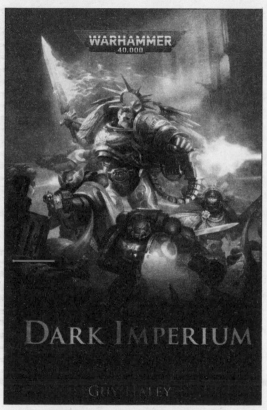

DARK IMPERIUM
by Guy Haley

The first phase of the Indomitus Crusade is over, and the conquering primarch, Roboute Guilliman, sets his sights on home. The hordes of his traitorous brother, Mortarion, march on Ultramar, and only Guilliman can hope to thwart their schemes with his Primaris Space Marine armies.